OUR FEET WALK THE SKY

WOMEN OF THE SOUTH ASIAN DIASPORA

EDITED BY
THE WOMEN OF
SOUTH ASIAN DESCENT COLLECTIVE

aunt lute books
SAN FRANCISCO

First Edition
10-9-8-7-6-5-4-3-2-1

Aunt Lute Books
P.O. Box 410687
San Francisco, CA 94141

This book was funded in part by a grant from the National Endowment for the Arts.
This book would not have been possible without the kind contributions of Rusty Barcelo.

Cover Art: Arpana Caur
Cover Photo: Jean Weisinger
Cover and Text Design: Pamela Wilson Design Studio
Typesetting: Debra DeBondt

Senior Editor: Joan Pinkvoss
Managing Editor: Christine Lymbertos

Production: Cristina Azocar Cathy Nestor
 Vita Iskandar Indigo Som
 Lisa Kahaleole Chang Hall Kathleen Wilkinson

Production Support: Jonna Eagle Melissa Levin
 Jamie Lee Evans Fabienne McPhail

Printed in the U.S.A. on acid-free paper

Graves of Academe first appeared in *The Women's Review of Books* (Feb. 1992).
We would like to thank the following for kind permission to reprint copyrighted material. We apologize for any errors or omissions.
The Garba and **Yuba City School** © 1991 by Chitra Banerjee Divakaruni. From *Black Candle* by C.B. Divakaruni (Corvallis, OR: Calyx). Reprinted with permission from the publisher.
Predicaments of the Hyphen © 1994 by the Regents of the University of Minnesota. From *Fictions of Feminist Ethnographies* by Kamala Visweswaran (Minneapolis: University of Minnesota Press). Reprinted with permission from the publisher. (Different version from original.)
Search For My Tongue © 1988 by Sujata Bhatt. From *Brunizem* by Sujata Bhatt (Manchester: Carcanet Press). Reprinted with permission from the publisher. (Different version from original.)

Library of Congress Cataloging-in-Publication Data

Our feet walk the sky : women of South Asian diaspora / edited by
 Women of South Asian Descent Collective. — 1st ed.
 p. cm.
 Includes bibliographical references.
 ISBN 1-879960-32-X (alk paper) : $12.95
 1. American literature—South Asian authors. 2. American
literature—Women authors. 3. American literature—20th century.
4. Women authors, South Asian—United States—Biography.
5. Feminism in literature—United States. 6. Women's rights in
literature. 7. Ethnicity in literature. 8. Women—South Asia—
Social conditions. I. Women of South Asian Descent Collective
(Organization)
PS153.A84097 1993
810.8'09287'08995—dc20
 93-36354
 CIP

Acknowledgments

Our Families:
Shirley, Harshad, Jay and Sunil Bhatt
Shashi, Inder, Bunny and Neety Kalra
Shashi, Jagdish, Gauri Kohli
Shushila and Moti Malkani
Kirupa, Lakshman, Arun and Prasanna Rasiah

Special Thanks To:
Manuela Albuquerque, Francis Assisi, Vani Bathala, Jonathon Brennan and Jacqueline Gallo,
Nancy Bunty, Miriam Chiang-Louie, Anna Chu, Alfonso Fillon, Kwok-Yue Fong, Ganim's Deli,
Ramesh Goonetilleke, Inderpal Grewal, Nina Kabir, Yamindira Kanagasundaram, Helen Kim,
Diana Kuderna, Yin Ling Leung, Nathan Luna, Shoba Menon-Hiatt, Mark Min, Davis Park,
Avani Patel, Lalita Prasad, Reena Sachdev, Parna Sengupta, Shilpa Restaurant, Young Shin,
Jane Singh, Niru Somasundaram, Jennifer Sprotte, Padmini Srikantiah, Viji Sundaram, Jyoti Talisetti.

Also Thanks To:
Sarita Aggarwal, Rick Albers, Michele Anderson, Nita Bellare, Gian Paolo Biacci, Elizabeth Brown,
Ray Cardoza, Carlos Castellanos, Ashok Chetandani, Lifang Chiang, Serena Choi, Yogesh Chugh,
Christy Chung, Renu Dhinza, Mira Esmile, Lula Fragd, Arnaldo Garcia, Milan Gupta,
Priya Jagannathan, Usha Jain, Sandeep Johar, Shanti Kalathil, Suman and Moti Kashyap, Elaine Kim,
Maxine Hong Kingston, Ila Kriplani, Arvind Kumar, Ashda Lalwani, Mi Yeong Lee, Suzanne Lester,
Lothlorien friends, Maha Malik, Chandra Mohanty, Helene Moler, Jyoti Nanda, Sophia Park,
Sanxe Patel, Steven Poulos, Tara Raman, Nilmini Ratne, Nusrat Retina, Sandeep, Nitya Sethuraman,
Pravina Shukla, Nidhi Singh, friends from smell this, Shabnum Tejani, Mini Timmaraju,
Madhu Vijayan, Rama Vora, Laura Warren, Judy Weninger.

Organizations:
Asians and Pacific Islanders for Reproductive Health
Asian Immigrant Women Advocates (AIWA)
Asian Woman's Shelter
ASUC—University of California, Berkeley
Calyx
Carcunet Press
Center for South Asia Studies—U.C. Berkeley
Department of City and Regional Planning—U.C. Berkeley
Empowering Women of Color Conference (EWOC)
Federation of Indian Americans (FIA)
Graduate Assembly
India Currents
India West
University of Minnesota Press
Narika
Shamakami

Thanks to all of our families and friends
who have lovingly/grudgingly become a part of this book.

To those women whose stories we have not been able to include:
we hope this anthology speaks to your experiences.

Thanks to the Aunt Lute staff for their support and dedication.
To Christine Lymbertos, and Vita Iskandar, who have given so much more than we could have ever
asked for, thank you for making this book happen.
Finally, a special thanks to Joan Pinkvoss for believing in us. Her continual patience, support and
committment to this book were invaluable.

Credits

**FINAL EDITING/FINAL PRODUCTION/
WOMEN OF SOUTH ASIAN DESCENT COLLECTIVE**
Sheela Bhatt
Preety Kalra
Aarti Kohli
Latika Malkani
Dharini Rasiah

EDITING, JANUARY 1993–MAY 1993
Sheela Bhatt
Preety Kalra
Keshini Kashyap
Aarti Kohli
Latika Malkani
Dharini Rasiah

**May 1991–August 1991
Phase 1: Organizational/Outreach**
Sheela Bhatt
Aarti Kohli
Latika Malkani
Bella Mayani
Avani Patel
Dharini Rasiah

**September 1991–December 1991
Phase 2: Organizational/Outreach**
Sheela Bhatt
Anu Anchal Bhatta
Meeta Gawande
Keshini Kashyap
Latika Malkani
Bella Mayani
Avani Patel
Kalpana Pyati
Dharini Rasiah

**January 1992–May 1992
Phase 1: Editing**
Anu Anchal Bhatta
Meeta Gawande
Preety Kalra
Keshini Kashyap
Latika Malkani
Bella Mayani
Kalpana Pyati
Dharini Rasiah

**June 1992–December 1992
Phase 2: Editing**
Sheela Bhatt
Preety Kalra
Keshini Kashyap
Aarti Kohli
Punam Luthra
Latika Malkani
Manisha Modi
Dharini Rasiah

Others Who Have Contributed Their Time and Energy Throughout This Process:
Mirula Furtrero
Salma Jevanjee
Kiran Lall
Ruxana Meer
Jignasa Patel
Kimpreet Puar
Sona Saha
Nisha Sohal

Foreword

This anthology comes at a critical point in South Asian American history. As one of the least-studied ethnic groups in the United States, people of South Asian origin have been overlooked by historians and social scientists as well as by scholars of Ethnic and Women's Studies. Although South Asians formed one of the smaller immigrant groups to the U.S. at the beginning of the twentieth century, in the post-1965 immigration era their numbers have vastly increased. Since the late 1970s South Asian Americans have constituted the fourth largest Asian American community in the U.S.

In spite of their significant numbers and long residency in the United States, South Asian Americans remain peripheral to any discussion of American culture, experience, or history. As with many other marginalized groups, they are absent from the dominant discourse of this country. Early South Asian immigrants to the U.S. challenged the exclusionary immigration and naturalization policies which limited their opportunities and restricted their numbers. Contemporary South Asians, who have made their homes in the U.S. since the 1960s, are contesting their position on the periphery of American life and culture.

This compilation is the first comprehensive work to focus on South Asian American and South Asian immigrant women in the United States. It represents a pioneering effort to collect the creative works, personal histories and critical essays by and about women of South Asian descent—women who trace their origins to India, Pakistan, Sri Lanka, Bangladesh and Nepal. In this collection we find diverse expressions of identity and experience that provide us with a sense of who these women are and how they define themselves in terms of their gender and ethnicity. It is through the voices in this volume that we begin to see how women of South Asian origin locate their positions within their respective communities, within wider interethnic networks, and within national and international social, economic, and political frameworks which impact upon women's lives, both in the United States and in South Asia.

During the first few decades of the twentieth century only a handful of South Asian women entered the United States with their husbands. Restrictive immigration laws kept the community small and the ratio of women to men skewed. By mid-century South Asians in the U.S. numbered approximately six thousand; researchers calculate that of this total, fewer than one hundred were women. The Immigration Act of 1965 created a more equitable system for entry into the U.S. by abolishing the national origins quotas which had severely limited Asian immigration. By 1970 South Asians were arriving in the U.S. in unprecedented numbers. It was not until the mid-1970s, however, nearly ten years after passage of the immigration reforms, that the gender ratio was balanced.

As a second generation South Asian American, I grew up hearing stories from my mother of the earliest immigrant women from South Asia who preceded her arrival in the U.S. Many of these stories eventually inspired me to become a researcher in the field of South Asian American history. My mother would carefully recount details and incidents from these women's lives, narratives that included descriptions of racist encounters and frustrating discriminatory laws which prohibited resident aliens from becoming citizens or owning land. These women's stories frequently centered on the loneliness and isolation that they experienced—their longing to see their families again or to be in the company of other South Asian women. But just as frequently these accounts reflected resolve and fierce determination to make the United States home for themselves and their families.

In this anthology we find some of the same sentiments still echoing among contemporary women of South Asian descent. We have an opportunity to hear these women speaking about their concerns in their own words. They do so with passion and eloquence, with humor and pathos. Through their words they place themselves as ethnic women within an American cultural context. While their articulations reveal global concerns and connections to homelands, these women are grounded in America; it is their home.

The compilation and production of this book is a testimony to their determination. The Women of South Asian Descent Collective has demonstrated that cooperation, collaboration and hard work can be sustained in spite of their outside work. Because several members of the Collective are my former students, I have had the opportunity to follow the anthology's progress from its inception and have seen their incessant labor over the past two years. I am grateful for their efforts and for this book which expands the literature on ethnic women in the United States.

Jane Singh

Table of Contents

THE STRENGTH THAT MENDS HER SOUL

MY FEET FOUND HOME

OUR FEET WALK THE SKY

Introduction

We first came together two years ago, as students at UC Berkeley, to compile writings by South Asian women. When we sat down to begin the project, what emerged from our discussions was a common experience of alienation. Whether in other women of color forums, in South Asian groups or in white liberal organizations, the result was the same: our presence and concerns were largely discounted. We also spoke of our dissatisfaction with the larger South Asian community because it had failed to be supportive of our individual attempts to create social change within and outside of the community.

What kept us together throughout this difficult process was facing issues which had never been addressed. There is a unique type of relationship that has come from working together as a group on what is important to us. Through our interaction with one another, we have reinforced a more positive image of ourselves as South Asian women.

We initially came together in the spring of 1991, through a U.C. Berkeley class, taught by Jane Singh, on the history of South Asians in America. One of the first of its kind, the course discussed South Asian immigration history in the U.S. as well as in the diaspora. It was clear that there was a lack of material on the effects of immigration on the entire community and the little documentation that did surface, focused primarily on men and their experiences. Three women from the class were frustrated by the lack of information on South Asian women and their inability to find a compatible South Asian women's community. Their discussions resulted in initiating the first meetings of our group.

Through word of mouth a handful of us came together to compile writings by women of South Asian descent. We ourselves come from different backgrounds—culturally, socially and economically. We are both 1.5 and second generation South Asian Americans because some of us have spent our childhood in South Asia, while others have spent it in the U.S., England and Canada. We come together from Ethnic Studies, Development Studies and Anthropology—similar fields with different theoretical approaches. We hope our diversity has given each of us a unique perspective on the material we were editing.

Through this process, we realized the importance of creating a personal support network and being able to reach out to other South Asian women. We decided that we would accept submissions from South Asian women who had emigrated from South Asia, even if only temporarily, or were children of immigrant parent(s). Although we hoped to include a discussion of issues such as family, sexuality, and community, we did not limit the content or length of the submissions. We wanted to represent as many experiences as we could, especially those on the margins.

Stretching our limited budget and exploiting any resources, we began our outreach. We placed advertisements in South Asian publications, posted flyers in South Asian businesses and did mailings to community groups and campus departments. Our personal contacts were

also continually harangued and harassed to spread the word. In retrospect, the majority of our contributors seemed to have found us through word of mouth.

Throughout '91 and '92 the composition of the group evolved as a result of the transiency of the university setting. Women came and went. To continue to allow for the diversity of experiences, the group did not create guidelines as to what sort of commitment was required from members until after the fall of '92. At that point we had officially stopped accepting submissions and we felt that some continuity needed to be established with our contributors. It was then that the group solidified into the present collective. Within the two-year editing process, we edited several hundred pieces. Each one of the submissions was delegated to an editor who was responsible for communicating the group's collective edits to the contributor. In an effort to respect the author's work, we explained the reasons behind our comments and then listened to their response, which we then communicated to the rest of the group. An individual editor could not proceed until the group came to a collective decision. This back-and-forth process involved numerous phone calls and faxes (nationally and internationally) through which we came to develop close relationships with many of the women in this book. The final four months included weekly meetings with our publisher, Aunt Lute, who provided us with additional edits on the submissions. At this point the collective was meeting daily, often working twelve-hour stretches at a time. We have come to realize that the nature of a collective is a long and compromising process and we are grateful to those contributors who understood and were sensitive to our difficulties.

We wanted to fully represent the South Asian community through the writing we received. In order to have a balance of viewpoints, we solicited works from writers throughout the South Asian diaspora and from many geographic, class, religious and sexual backgrounds. During the process we discovered that we held differing viewpoints, from each other and from the contributors. Issues were only resolved when a complete dialogue had taken place. We realized that although we thought we were taking more time, our thorough discussion helped fully clarify why we were making certain decisions. We came to respect our process as a balancing tool with which we tried to preserve the integrity of an author's work, while at the same time, allowing ourselves to critically assess the content.

In order to include more voices, we have defined "South Asia" more broadly than most. We define it as including India, Pakistan, Sri Lanka, Bangladesh, Nepal, Burma and Afghanistan. We hoped that people from these backgrounds would recognize the similarities between their experiences. It was also important to us that the reader get a sense of the diversity of the South Asian women's community. Although we realize that many of our contributors currently reside in the U.S., their stories reflect the varying social values and customs from other parts of the diaspora. We have come to understand that South Asian women's solidarity throughout the diaspora is necessary to increase our visibility.

We were encouraged that many of the pieces we received addressed sexuality. Our group wanted this anthology to be a place where South Asian women could feel comfortable in expressing their sexuality because, within our community, this aspect of our identity has been repressed. However, the open discussion of lesbian/bisexual issues was still limited.

Marginal experiences within our book also extended to religion and class. Because there were fewer pieces on minority religions of South Asia, we were sensitive to how they were represented. We made an effort to balance the positive and negative portrayals of them because

we realize there is a wide spectrum of reactions to religion. We know that religion is a divisive force within the community and we did not want to fuel that sentiment.

The larger South Asian community in the U.S. does not acknowledge or is unaware of its class divisions. We wanted submissions on the experiences of women working in such places as canneries, small businesses, the garment industry or in agriculture because we wanted to acknowledge their lives as being part of the experiences of women of the South Asian diaspora . During meetings we had ongoing discussions about why we weren't receiving as many submissions from them. We realized their lifestyles may not permit the time to write and, therefore, wondered whether writing could even be a tool for these women to communicate their experiences. Though oral histories would have been a way to document the stories of these women, we were only able to find one completed history and didn't have the time or the resources to initiate a full oral history project.

We included pieces in which it was evident that English wasn't the contributor's first language or where we foresaw grammatical and structural changes. We recognized some had unique experiences to share and felt that it was important to preserve their way of telling their experiences. In other pieces, we edited with the contributor so that we could help them maintain their voices by making things clearer while still preserving their dialogue and intent. We got submissions from women whose careers didn't revolve around writing as well as those who normally would have been hesitant to write.

We did not attempt to universalize grammar throughout the book because South Asian women come from a variety of cultures, where English may or may not be the first language or if it is, can often vary from country to country. We saw that the pieces evoking a sense of a woman's history and identity through her own language were far more powerful than any polished translation. Aunt Lute was extremely sensitive to this issue as well.

The glossary was a little more complex in that we had to weigh a variety of factors. We debated over the idea of an extensive glossary but decided that it was not necessary because this book is primarily for South Asians. We recognized the diversity of South Asian languages and cultures and selectively chose South Asian words that we felt were important to the context of each piece and created a glossary at the end. We also wanted the non-South Asian reader to make an effort to try to understand the more basic words in order to get a sense of the bi/multilingual vocabulary of many of the writers.

One of our main concerns throughout this process has been to create a balance of viewpoints. It's evident from above that there were very specific ways in which we attempted to do this. However the last piece of the book presented us with a dilemma. We did not want to end the book referring to a particular South Asian language, region or religion. However, Sujata Bhatt's poem, written in Gujarati and English, was a piece which stood out to all of us because it encompassed many of the emotions and conflicts which were reflected in other pieces of the anthology. We hoped that readers would be able to acknowledge one woman's particular experience with her own regional language and then transpose it to their own experiences. We wanted to end showing the inter-connectedness South Asian women have with one another.

Through this anthology, we have gained a great deal of strength, which has allowed us to examine and define our own South Asian identities. We hope that this book, as a resource, will generate an even larger dialogue on South Asian women's issues.

September 1993

*

Lighting The Fire
Beneath Our Homes

Monica

GAURANGI KAMANI

with knotted knees we tunneled
under the zinnias crowded pink hid
the soldiers and golf ball slowly
white in daddy's measured swing
you leaked whinnying giggles and small-girl fret
damp into my picture books

frogged under glasses I danced
to your prodding, my charades round-mouthed
you squealed me into silence
stretching puckered fingers in the humid forays
of glossy 'fillum' stars dislocated
from my wall to your embrace

beauty and her tail—we fought
to be the thief, the reckless monster
growling faster than the whip
as the last joke was lunged
where you were the killer I would have stayed
a horse, a bird, a powder doll stuck
to the mirrors—still six—in the dirt

we are the rigours of those daughters
who lasted the present tense
twice in lifetimes could we cast out again

> I was a thickening woodcut
> You were the window pane
> I was the kiss that waited
> You were the rival game

> I was a truefalse answer
> You were the dusted chalk
> I was the rain of Surat
> You were the Rajput rock

Daddy

ZAINAB ALI

It's two a.m. and Daddy isn't home. He's never home anymore. Not since Amee went to India for Ramadan a month ago. He spends all his time at the whore's house. The whore, Sabana, his "other" wife: tall, big-boned, forty-two and with long, bushy, black hair that always scares me because it reminds me of witches. She flings it back and forth, looking longingly over her shoulder at Daddy, even when we're at Muslim get-togethers. But he's so proud, so proud to have two wives when no one else in the Muslim community does. Daddy thinks that it's because the other men aren't "true men." And if they were, they wouldn't have enough money to keep a whore even part time, much less *all* the time like Daddy. He actually says this while he picks up my two-year-old half-brother Jameel at the Eid Festival at the local mosque.

His long, sparse hair that he combs over to camouflage his balding head, dips down and forms a shape that, because of the irregular hair lengths, resembles a triangle suspended in midair—a triangle that is connected to a bumpy scalp. I can't help but stare at these craters that pepper his delicate scalp. They are the aftereffects of three operations he's had to uproot hair from the back of his head and to plant it on the top, middle area.

The operations failed to accomplish what they promised: a full head of hair. Instead, only small hills, pits and gorges remain. That, and black splotches left by Clairol Nice-and-Easy Color Treatment when Daddy tried to dye his hair Natural Black. Apparently it's not so easy to apply the color treatment because Daddy always misses the few remaining strands of his fine, brownish black hair, and a Natural Black drop falls and settles into a crater or next to a mound on his scalp. From a distance, it appears as though black caterpillars are slowly, haphazardly climbing and diving into small mounds of flesh. But Daddy doesn't seem to mind.

As he straightens up with Jameel in his arms, his eyes wander proudly around the room, like a peacock displaying its colorful feathers. Daddy's feathers are his four sons—my half-brothers—and his younger wife, the whore. Jameel is the youngest of my four other half-brothers. The oldest is only eight years old; Daddy's in his upper-fifties. This has caused a lot of problems between him and Sabana because, she says, Daddy will die before her children are past adolescence, so no one will be left to support her and the "shits"—that's what my brothers and I call our half-brothers. This is the reason she won't get her tubes tied. She says that when my father dies, she'll need to be able to conceive so that she can marry another man and give *him* children. So what will she do with the four children she's had with my mother's husband? I wonder.

Daddy never does, though. I don't think he cares. Daddy's only cares are himself and his business. In his spare time he hits his kids, swears too much, talks on the phone continuously and is always absent. And when he is home, he's on the phone with the whore.

"Put the little one on the phone," he whispers into the phone receiver, actually believing that the others in the room can't hear him. Perhaps he's hoping that the TV will drown out his voice, or even that we'll be naive enough to presume he's talking business with someone. *"Papa,"* he sweetly calls Jameel, who he still refers to as "baby" even though he's already four years old. "What does my *papa* want from the store, does my *papa* want a Ninja Turtle?" There is a pause in which I presume my half-brother is listing his latest desires. I glance at Amee from the corner of my eye to see what her face reveals, if she's in as much pain as I am. But she seems too interested in the movie on Cinemax to care about who Daddy's talking to. But I care. I glare at Daddy—*my* Papa—who seems so stupid…talking 'baby-talk' on the phone at his age.

Your time was long over, Daddy, I think spitefully, so how dare you now sit across a room from your wife and fifteen- year-old daughter and speak with the bastards like we don't know what's going on. What angers me even more is knowing that I can't do anything but watch him disapprovingly, so I do the only thing I can: I scowl.

I suddenly see his eyebrows grow together—skin folding one over the other on his forehead. "I told you you could come, now shut up about it," he quietly orders the listener. I assume it's Sabana because he has no reason to be upset at the shits. I smile. *Give it to her Daddy. Give it to her.* I smirk. I relish the next five minutes, savoring each word—annoying, nagging, dumb, lazy—just as I'd savor each second of her funeral.

He suddenly hangs up. After a moment's silence, a silence in which I feel his anger and tension, he turns to Amee and asks her the time of the poetry party they're having that weekend. So that's what the whore wants to come to, I think bitterly. I already grow tense at the thought of walking around my house, embarrassed because she and the shits are here.

"Why?" Amee asks, turning toward Daddy. Daddy doesn't answer. "Now, you promised that you wouldn't bring her here." Amee's voice grows louder with anxiety.

"I won't," Daddy quietly replies without turning to look at her. Amee isn't satisfied. I'm not either. She presses on. "She has her own community with those Uganda people. Why does she want to make friends with my friends? Why doesn't she have any shame? I never go to her community, even when they invite me. Who wants to go and make a spectacle of themselves—both showing up with the same husband, chi!"

"I said I won't bring her," Daddy's voice is too loud. I can hear my heart beating. My fingers instinctively go for my mouth and I start biting the skin off around my nails. I heard him promise the whore he'd bring her, but who the hell cares anymore. Leave it alone, Amee. It's not that big a deal, just leave it alone. I try to warn her, squeezing my eyes shut and hoping my thoughts will travel to her mind. Amee crosses her legs and begins rapidly, violently swinging one back and forth.

"I've already lost so many friends in the community because they don't approve of your actions. No one invites us to their home anymore. There are no more functions to which I can wear my sarees and jewelry. And the one chance I do get to see them, you want to ruin it by bringing her and the little kids that call you 'Daddy, Daddy' in front of everyone!"

"No one's going to care, they all know," Daddy finally confesses.

"No! I said no. I only have a few friends left. And some of them are even two-faced enough to want *her* friendship when they've known me for twenty years! I don't know what

5

they see in her. She reads *The Enquirer* and is stupid enough to believe the things written there. She actually sits in public and talks about Elizabeth Taylor's latest birth of alien children. And they listen to her so carefully. No, I won't give them that chance. I just won't. I will not allow you to have her here. I will not be humiliated in public, over and over again." Amee will rattle on for hours now about how empty she is and how badly Daddy has treated her.

Stop it, I think harder. I want to reach over and place my hand on her leg to stop the swinging, but instead I tug at the skin on my finger. I wait for him to lose his anger and yell back. Tonight it doesn't take long because he's already had a fight with the whore over the same damn party.

"Shut up! I said shut up! This is my house and I'll do what I want. If you don't like it, you can leave. If you can't handle it anymore, *leave.* You're so jealous of her. I'll just throw you and your kids out on the street and we'll see how you survive then."

"Allah gives and takes, not you!" Amee retorts, her voice wavering with pain and oncoming tears. I slowly get up from the sofa and walk silently up the stairs to my room. My fingers between my teeth, I bite harder and harder, licking the blood between the bites. I think about its cool, bittersweet taste as I shut my door and climb under the covers.

It was useless for Amee to argue with him. Daddy's set in his ways. He does exactly what he wants. The whore will be there, no doubt about it. She'll come after a full day in Macy's beauty salon where she'll get Lancôme makeup, facials, massages, and her nails manicured. And Amee will have spent the day cleaning the home and laboring over the hot stove cooking chicken curry and beef kabobs for the guests to eat. She'll come while Amee has finally set foot into the shower five minutes before the guests are to arrive because she wants everything to be so perfect. Then the whore will greet them while Amee is trapped in her room getting ready. But Amee will suddenly get scared that the whore is befriending her friends and she'll run downstairs without even drying her hair or putting on lipstick. Then the whole party will be consumed with the whore swinging her witch's hair while she glides in and out of conversations with my mother's friends, in my mother's home.

Afterward Amee will wonder why the women who have watched me grow up are suddenly more enticed by the whore. She'll wonder if the whore looked better, younger, prettier than she. Amee doesn't realize that she herself is the most beautiful woman in the world, so she'll cry all night. Heavy sobs will escape through her mouth and I will want to fold her in my arms and rock her all night, caressing her silky, black hair and singing her a lullaby:

"Hhmm hhmm boi,
hhmm hhmm boi,
jingle ala boi,
machi ala boi,
hhmm hhmm boi
hhmm hhmm boi,
Meri ama jaan,
meri peyri jaan,

rona nahi na,
meri acchi jaan.
Hhmm hhmm boi.
Hmmm hmmm boi."

But these are tears that my brothers and I can't wipe away because they are meant for our half-time Daddy. A half-time husband who leaves a cold, empty side of my mother's bed every other night while he sleeps at the whore's house. An emptiness that brings my mother's tears of loneliness.

Instead of retaliating, she does his laundry, cleans his toilet, sometimes even baby-sits the whore's children while husband and younger wife frolic around town. And she always cooks his food. Even when he spends the night at the whore's house, he comes home early the next morning and expects to be fed. No ordinary meal either. He must have hot parathas and fresh curry: authentic food that makes my poor, tired mother's fifty-five-year-old body sweat as she leans over the hot kitchen stove.

Amee worries about us, her children. She wants us to have the best in life, so she's martyred her own for our sake. She says she doesn't care anymore as long as we're happy. But I know she cares. Call it a woman's intuition. Call it a daughter's insight. I know she cares. I think that she visits India so frequently just to escape this hell-hole called a home.

It wouldn't be such a bad thing if Daddy didn't spend all his time with the whore and their shits as soon as Amee left. They actually expect my brothers and me to do all the chores then. Daddy even expects me to do his laundry while he takes the whore out to Lee Ann Chin.

"Nadia," he calls out in his gruff, deep voice. I crawl under my covers and bite the skin around my nails.

Shit, I think. Here it goes again. After a moment's silence, I hear my bedroom phone ring. The first ring, I know it's Daddy. But as it continues ringing, my certainty wanes. It might be a friend with important gossip. I bite harder. Shit, I think in confusion, and grab the receiver before the rings stop.

"Nadia," I hear Daddy's deep, crackling voice. He's calling from his phone downstairs.

"Huh?" I cradle the receiver between my neck and shoulder while creeping back into my warm quilt cocoon.

"I've left some dirty shirts in the hamper. Can you do them tonight?"

"Uh-huh." I answer, my heart suddenly softening when I picture the stained, wrinkled clothes he's worn for the past few days. It's what Amee would have wanted me to do, I tell myself. "No problem, Daddy." He clicks off. That night I do Daddy's clothes, all the time swearing at the whore and wishing I had never picked up that damn phone.

I did Daddy's clothes every summer for three years. This last summer, when Amee returned from India, Daddy told her right at the airport that the only problem he was having with her gone was the lack of fresh clothes.

Amee's face looked tired after the long, two-day journey. The circles under her eyes had grown darker. The wrinkles seemed deeper. I sighed deeply and put my arm around her. Our heads tilted simultaneously toward each other and touched gently. She lifted her weary eyes towards Daddy as he continued talking about his dirty clothes.

7

"Why didn't you give them to the dry cleaners?" my Amee asks, lifting her head from mine, her eyebrows drawn together.

"Why can't your daughter do them?" Daddy retorts. Daddy only comes to the "your daughter"—which can be interchanged with "your son...nephew...father...brother...sister..." part when one of us fails to do what he expects from us. If I had done everything "properly," "obediently," Daddy would have said "Nadia did it." I realize that it's not quite the same as the "my daughter" sentiment, but it's the best Daddy does, so it's what I settle for.

This time, his words cause me to look away. My brothers, Farzard and Elias, are claiming Amee's suitcases. As they do, I watch them laugh and hit each other jokingly. Both my brothers are very tall so it doesn't take much to see them in a crowd. I've always envied the carefree way in which they're able to laugh and play while I've always felt burdened by my mother's pain, by the dark circles under her eyes.

I listen to her tender voice as she asks in disbelief, "Nadia? Why should *she* do your laundry? You have another wife that should do it. Why do you have her? Not just to watch soap operas and go shopping, I hope. She should be made responsible also." My hands immediately found my teeth; Amee usually doesn't speak up for herself like this. I expected Daddy to lash out at her, tell her that he owns the house so I must do what he wants as long as he supports me.

But this time, Daddy only nodded his head in agreement. He made no sign of protest. But a look hovered over his face that said that he had never so much as even thought of Sabana having responsibility.

The following spring, while Amee was in Hyderabad, the witch came over every other week or so to try to clean Daddy's clothes.

"Nadia," she calls my name. I've never hated my name, but I hate it when she uses it. It makes me cringe like I would at some old man saying my name lustfully as his eyes roam over my body.

"Huh?" I ask. I don't like to give her the satisfaction of saying a full "yes." I stand outside the laundry room watching her, satisfied that Amee had given me permission when she told Daddy to get Sabana to do his clothes, and not to feel guilty about taking over her duties to Daddy while Amee's in India.

"Do you know where more of your father's dirty clothes are?" Before I can reply, she goes on. "I have to wash them and my back already aches from climbing these stairs. Boy, I tell you the man has so many clothes, I feel like I wash them over and over again and they still show up. They're like grass, no matter how much you cut it, it grows again." She laughs stupidly at her own attempt at a joke.

I chuckle too, but only because I've learned that if I don't show fake courtesy, she fills Daddy's ears with lies about how insulting I was to her that day. Then Daddy lets me have it. He won't speak to me for days. I hate that because it makes me feel invisible.

"He has so many stains and they just don't leave." Her shrill voice drones on.

The whore comes to my mother's home to do her laundry so that she can search Amee's dressers and closets. I remember one year, by the time Amee returned from India, the whore had cut up all her pants and left them useless for my mother to wear. Another time she stole Amee's driver's license and ID for U.S. Swim and Fitness. Daddy only shook his head when

Amee told him. So now I watch her carefully while she scampers in and out of Amee's room, pretending like she's so busy hanging the clean clothes and getting the dirty ones.

I think she's finally given up, though, because she's stopped lingering in Amee's room. Instead, she brings two three-hour-long Hindi movies to watch while the clothes are busy in the washer and dryer. "Look at this," she says while holding up a light green button-down shirt. "The collar looks terrible. Nothing I do will remove the stain."

"Did you try Clorox Non-Chlorine Bleach?" I ask. "Or even Era Plus?"

"My back aches so much. I just can't stand it." Her voice drones on. I suddenly am overcome with rage and I want to scream, shove her to the ground and pounce on her. Then grab her by her witch's hair and beat her head on the kitchen floor, all the while screaming, "Fuck you, you whore! Get the hell out of my mother's house!" Instead, I tear some fresh skin off my fingers and watch fresh blood seep out.

After a few hours of seclusion in my room, I venture out into my home again. I head downstairs and find that the shits have eaten everything from Milky Ways to Doritos and left crumbs and sticky wrappers all over the carpet and floors. I stare at Daddy who is in his spot on the loveseat, the far right corner next to the glass table that supports his phone, his life.

He sits there in his grey wool sports coat he's worn all week. Stains on a light pink shirt stare boldly back at me from under his jacket. I fight the impulse to help Sabana with the clothes. He had a choice when he married her, and it is not my responsibility to do his cleaning, I remind myself. Besides, Daddy's a messy eater, he'll mess his shirts up even if I do wash them. I imagine him eating: taking huge amounts of food at one time and stuffing it into his mouth. He then chews…loudly, while spit sometimes shoots out of his mouth. Normally I walk away from the table, my mother's smile following me because after twenty-four years of marriage, she's used to his flying spit, his whore. But I don't know if I'll ever be. Perhaps it's because I grew up in America where it's unacceptable. No, I admit, it may be more acceptable for Hyderabadi Muslims, like Amee. But she's still a woman. Whatever holds Amee to him is beyond my comprehension. But so are my sympathies for him.

Now, I stare at him as he sits on the phone. The TV is still on after his kids tuned it in then headed for the basement to play, the answering machine is reading out its messages with the time and date that each person called, and Daddy sits on the phone talking to Ben, his business manager. They're talking about a tenant who won't leave an apartment even after the lease has expired.

"Take him to the goddamn court," Daddy orders Ben. Daddy sits calmly on the sofa, the noise of the TV and answering machine not quite reaching his occupied mind. His eyes are shut, revealing light blue veins that run across the lids; two fingers from his left hand are held slightly inside his nose and are pushing its tip up. Amee teases him by saying that he does it to force his wide nose higher, to give the impression that it's thinner. "Just get plastic surgery," she always quips. "That's never going to work."

I watch Daddy on the phone and am struck by another one of my sympathy bouts for him. I try to dismiss it by saying that it's the stains on his shirt that make him look vulnerable, but I notice that his cheeks are lying low on his face and he looks darker with fatigue. I admit to myself that he works hard, but it's still no reason to treat Amee and us the way he does: always threatening, always insensitive.

He interrupts my thoughts when he finally looks up from the phone. He seems surprised that I'm standing there. He jerks his head up in a quick motion that asks me what I need. I look from him to the carpet, then back up. His eyes follow mine to the carpet, I think he understands me, but he addresses Ben again. "If he wants to stay, he has to give me money. I have twenty people lined up for that apartment. If he can't pay the rent completely now, we'll draw up an agreement. Otherwise, get him out of there." That's one thing I *do* like about Daddy: he's a good-natured businessman even though he has a habit of exaggerating. He'll never force full payment out of anyone who can't do it right away. He'll always give you a chance to come up with money. But again, where is that sympathy and understanding when it comes to his own family—that is, his legitimate family?

I cross the living room and enter the dining area: more of a mess. I shut my eyes, my fingers rise to my mouth, but I refuse to indulge. I march on, my feet crunching on Doritos. Forgetting why I came downstairs, I hear the screams of the kids from the basement, the noise from the TV, answering machine and, of course, Daddy. I run back up to my room to take cover.

On the way, I see the bathroom light on so I walk in to turn it off. To my distress, Sabana is in there ironing Daddy's clothes. Shit, I think.

"Can you believe how many clothes your father owns?" She begins as soon as I enter the room. "All this ironing and washing has really been bad on my back…" I watch her as she continues to rattle off her ailments. I think of Amee and how she does this all year, not just for a month or two. The whore knows it, and she doesn't care if I know it too. The shirt she's ironing still has food and ink stains on it. I think that it's out of wickedness that she doesn't clean his clothes properly. Dad will simply get Amee to do them.

The whore waves goodbye to me while her hair whips in the high wind. She, Daddy and the shits are going to dinner at Rudolf's Bar-B-Que. As she turns away, I am about to make a face at her—or even flip her off—when I shudder at the thought that she might have eyes in the back of her head that are watching me. Her short, dumpy legs propel her to the white Cadillac—a car that she chose for herself even though she's failed the driver's test every single time she's taken it since the first time, sixteen years ago, when she arrived in America—but she proudly settles into the passenger's seat. I notice her lipstick has stained her teeth red, and I smile, thinking of her entering the restaurant with the stain.

Sabana. She's got it made. She married a wealthy, middle-aged sucker looking for youth and she's doing some strong sucking of his money and our happiness. Sabana. Always dreaming about Richard Gere and Kevin Costner, wishing she was Elizabeth Taylor. Some say she truly *was* a whore, selling her body to men while she was in Hyderabad. Rumour goes that she still visits some of her clients when she returns, sometimes even when Daddy accompanies her back. Daddy refuses to believe these rumours even though his personality is such that he'll believe any other rumour that may fall into his ears like a honey drop. But I believe these rumours. Women who marry other women's husbands can only be whores.

Daddy was always sleeping around. It's what I remind myself of every time my eyes soften for him. Amee has told me stories that make my skin crawl, swim, jump and high-dive. Like the time I saw a photo of him with a naked hooker sitting on his lap. The Polaroid was just lying there on the fireplace mantle. As though he wanted us to see it. As though he felt

he accomplished so much by having a ghastly pale, blonde-haired woman sitting shamelessly, erect on his lap. If not one whore, there will always be another.

I never understood why Daddy needs a whore. Amee's so beautiful, and she's always been more than understanding of his ways. I have a feeling this is one of the reasons he strayed: I've learned from her that women can't allow a man to dominate or he'll take advantage of his position. And I mean any man, not just Indian.

I think this is one of the reasons why Daddy lets Sabana talk of her plans for after his death: she doesn't let him get the upper hand. Maybe it's just because he knows that after he dies, she won't be far behind, so what's the use in bickering. Or, maybe it's just because she's a younger woman, not by much, but still younger, so Daddy worships her.

Some say Daddy sees no fault in Sabana because she practices black magic. She puts some herbs that she gets from Hyderabad into his food and cooks it. When he eats it, he becomes completely intoxicated by her. Her food is strange. Daddy sometimes brings it over for my brothers and me when Amee's in India. There's an odor that comes from it. When the curry is hot, I can't smell it much. But I remember times when I put her curry into the refrigerator, the next morning it comes out as solid as frozen meat. Amee's never does that. And even though it's frozen, her curry smells like rotten meat that's been lying in the afternoon sun. The smell is so strong that even though the Tupperware is always covered, I can smell it as soon as I open the refrigerator door. I usually shove it in the garbage disposal because I'm scared to even put it in the garbage can.

Others have said Sabana practices stronger black magic while she's in our home in India. While renovating the home once, the carpenters found a doll plastered inside one of Daddy's bedroom walls. It was a black magic doll. No one wanted to touch it, so they brought a beggar from off the street, gave *him* money, and had *him* remove it. Sabana swears that she had no idea who could have put it there. But no one else has the keys to our home and it was at a time when *she* was in India.

And even if Amee had been there at the time, no one would have even suggested *she* would do something like that. Everyone, including Daddy, knows that Amee doesn't believe in that stuff. Sometimes I do though. How else could a man be so unjust with his first wife and kids, and me?

Ramadan a month of fasting in commemoration of the forty days and nights that Mohammed spent in the desert; the fast lasts from dusk to dawn every day

Eid Festival the day that the Ramadan fast is broken, celebrated with feasting and festivities

Summer at Home

MADHURI SANGHVI

It was the summer of the abortion I spent
 at home.
It was the summer of our mistake I spent alone at home
 with my parents.
It was the summer after our enchanted careless spring together
 no siblings were home.

It was the summer of the abortion I felt panicked in the
 presence of my parents.
It was the summer of the abortion I had to grow up and
 take care of myself because Mom and Dad couldn't.

It was the summer I had morning sickness I couldn't
 look my parents in their eyes.
It was the summer I regretted ever having sex I had to begin
 living in two worlds—one at home and one my own.

It was the summer of my abortion
It is the summer of my abortion that never leaves me.

In Search of Daughters

NEERA KUCKREJA SOHONI

Daughters grow
And the mother in you
weeps
for the baby you once knew,
clasped
close to your breast.
Teen years
arise now
like powerful barricades,
hilltops that block
and shade the memory of
sunfilled days.

Where did it go
that childhood trust
the velvet grip
of playful, little fingers? Now my outstretched arms
fold away empty,
like garden chairs
on misty mornings.

Feet of time like clay.
They leave no
footprints on our
beaches.
In my children's albums
are new faces, stickers,
certificates
but no photo of me, or my
motherhood.

A Period

ANU MURGAI

My stomach is my brain's garbage can, thought Charu as she lowered herself onto the cool surface of the toilet seat. A snapshot of Sunsweet Prunes flashed in front of her eyes. She sighed as her stomach responded to the pressures flooding her body.

Her eyes had grown accustomed to being open. They roamed over the sharp lines of the tiles on the floor, the random scratches, lewd poems and declarations of love etched on the walls.

If I had been studying last night, this wouldn't have happened.

Her stomach looked brown and bloated. It felt big. Her period was about to begin. There was a gallon of Liquid Drain-O bubbling and boiling inside her.

Maybe I'm pregnant. I deserve to be pregnant.

Come on now. Be sensible. You just kissed him and...

Even the words were ashamed to form in her brain.

You cannot be pregnant.

She held her stomach. Every inch of her body felt heavy. She bent over her stomach, all the way to her knees, beyond them.

Just now it was dusk in Delhi. The sky blushed as the sun winked at it from behind the trees. Ma was waiting for the particular click when Papa would push the gate, his briefcase clutched in one hand, files stuffed under one arm.

She sucked in a lungful of air. Still her stomach stuck out, like a round shiny stone.

Papa was sitting on the bed. His briefcase was open, and files and papers were littered around it. His glasses were perched on the tip of his nose. Papa was sitting, Buddha-like, with his arms folded, gazing into the air; he was searching the ceiling for solace. "Charu," he said, "you should remember this when you are all alone there." His forehead was wrinkled with lines. He tilted his head to see her through his glasses. "Don't do anything with boys. Others around you will be doing it. But they are wrong. When I was there, I didn't do any mischief. Don't even start anything. God will be very angry with you."

Of course she didn't believe the words.

She believed the earnestness with which he forced them out of his heart, in the love that filled the pools of his eyes, that intoxicated him so that he followed her from room to room, muttering about her flight there, the books, her clothes, the food, her room, the college...and every hour of the life she would live there.

Look at what you did, Charu. Look at what you've done, you idiot!

Ma is thinking of me right now. She is writing a letter to me in her head while I sit here on the toilet, sniffing the air for blood.

The bathroom door swung open with a creak. A pair of feet stood in front of the sink. Charu could hear the sound of a toothbrush against teeth.

It was time to wake up.

When she shut the door to her room, everything fell in shadow again. Only a sliver of light drew a yellow line under her door.

Parts of her life lay in heaps around the room. Her economics book occupied center stage, accusing her of indifference. The sheets were half off the bed; one end of the mattress was naked. The closet was still open. Her jeans lay on the floor.

She looked at herself in the mirror and thought, if you saw me right now, Mark, you would never look at me again.

Two dry and flaky arms protruded out of a pink nightdress. A line of drool was thickly drawn on one side of her lip; her chin was shaded white. A tuft of hair waved six inches above her head. Her eyelids were so tightly squished together that her pupils were bulging out. Her stomach was pushing against the nightdress.

There was a knock on the door. Debbie walked in before Charu could say anything.

"I knew you were awake, I heard you rip those blinds off the wall," she said. "Lunch? Why haven't you taken a shower yet? And where were you last night? I thought you were studying, but you weren't in when I came back last night."

"Let's go to lunch," said Charu.

As they walked toward the cafeteria, Charu said, "I saw Mark yesterday."

"At the library?"

"At the party."

"The party? What was he doing there? What were *you* doing there?"

Debbie flicked her hair back; there were two rugby players walking towards them.

Charu looked at her feet. The minutes of last night seemed to be ticking on the path. She was afraid to look up; she knew the hands of the clock were reflected in her eyes.

The music had been really loud. Charu had shut the door and bolted the windows. Still, the music had seeped in, vibrating her chair, distracting her mind, till she'd shut her book and gone to the party, thinking that she could relax for a few minutes before she returned to economics.

"The music was really loud," she said. "I went downstairs to see where all the noise was coming from." Debbie was looking behind her at the rugby players.

"He kissed me."

"He what?" Debbie stopped in the middle of the path. "Who? Mark? Mark! Mark kissed you? When? Why? How did it happen?" Her eyes were large circles of shock.

Pride oozed out of Charu.

She felt happy, a woman, one of those to whom something had happened.

It had been dark. She leaned against the wall, close to the door, and still, she felt it...the music crackling the bodies of Melanie and Alex dancing close together.

"Hey Charu." Mark was standing next to her. His hair flopped over the edge of his pudgy face, his cheeks were red, and his eyes had a glint in them. "I knew I would find you here."

Debbie was waiting for Charu to say something.

"He saw me at the party."

15

Charu had said something to him. He'd replied. When he turned, she could see the little curls of hair at the bottom of his neck, peeping out of the green sweater. He was close to her, his palm was on the wall behind her. He brushed her hair away from her face once. His face was unlocked, he was looking at her...nobody had looked at her like this before.

"Let's go outside," she heard her own voice say.

Outside, it was cool and dark and silent. The grass yielded under her feet; minute dewdrops splattered on her ankles. The wind was ruffling the tips of the grumbling trees. Moonbeams danced between the trees in silver shoes, stamping out the darkness.

Everything rushed by slowly. She felt the cold stone wall against her back.

He kissed her.

He was still holding her hand.

"I've never done this before," she said. A bead of anxiety formed in her brain.

"That's all right," he whispered close to her ear. "I haven't done this too often myself. And I'm American."

Dull circles of light fell from the lamp posts watching over his dorm. As the door swung open, there were people everywhere.

Footsteps thumped towards them in the corridor.

"What if somebody sees us together like this?" she blinked. In the flash between light and darkness, there were a pair of bare round feet. They pressed down upon bald patches of carpet. A pair of feet, with baby ginger toes and pink oyster-shell nails. Weed-like hair dug into the big toes.

The feet were coming closer. A shadow quivered upon the tips of her shoes.

They were Papas's feet.

She snatched her hand away and hid it in her pocket. It was red-hot and crackled against the soft lining.

He switched on the light in his room and locked the door. They were alone. There was a rich, pure feeling radiating from him.

"Charu, I'm so happy," he said, and laid his head down on her shoulder.

She could see the pimples of his face and smell the day's sweat on his body.

He put his arms around her waist and kissed her nose.

Her stomach gurgled.

"You're not going to tell me anymore, are you?" Debbie was standing in front of her, hands on hips.

Tears welled up in Charu's eyes.

"You can tell me later," said Debbie.

They walked on.

"Do you like him a lot?"

"I don't know."

"Do you like him a little?"

"That's not important. My parents are more important. I came here to study, you know!"

"You can't study twenty-four hours a day, Charu. Besides, there's a lot to learn from sex." She peered into Charu's face. "Are you going to tell your parents?"

"Are you crazy?"

"He is rather good-looking. I would never have thought…He must have liked you for a while. I wonder…We'll have to investigate this. How much time did you spend with him?"

"A few hours, I guess."

"Before or after the kiss?"

She walked back alone to her room after lunch. The afternoon sun was stretching itself, ready for dusk. Its fingers spread themselves beyond the roof, cutting sharp shadows in front of the dorm.

Today she felt full. Her body was stuffed with emotion and pride and womanhood. Things were happening to her. She was in it, in that life she had been watching from the sidelines for two years. She remembered the admiration on Mark's face.

There was a rose lying outside her door. Deep red, with silken petals knit together.

Love, Mark.

The phone rang. Some freshman picked it up immediately.

"Charu, it's for you!"

"Hey Mark." A smile touched her eyes. "Thanks for the…"

"You're welcome. What time did you wake up?"

"Twelve-thirty. I barely made it to lunch."

They laughed together.

"Can I see you sometime today?"

"Not today, Mark." She bit a large chunk of fingernail. "I have to write a paper for International. I didn't do any work all week. I'll probably have to stay up tonight."

"Don't worry too much. Just do it. Good luck."

"Thanks, Mark."

There was silence on the other side. Then,

"Thanks for last night. Uh…See you tomorrow, Charu."

"Bye."

She locked the door behind her. Her lips felt dry and swollen.

The thoughts began to bubble up again, from her stomach, and she swallowed.

"Charu!" Debbie was knocking on her door.

Go away, please, thought Charu. The doorknob turned and then stayed still.

Now her thoughts were frothing over, touching her skull. They would burst out of her at any moment.

She rushed to the bathroom.

She traced the lines in the tiles on the cold floor with her toes. Her head felt heavy. She pressed it with her palms.

Debbie came into the bathroom. She was singing. "You make me feel like a natural woman." She stood in front of the mirror, tugging her hair this way and that, patting down one tuft, raising another.

Any moment now, she would turn around and say, "That must be you, Charu. I recognize your feet."

Debbie went into the shower. Soon the smell of Dove reached Charu's nostrils. She crept out of the bathroom.

Her cheek caressed her pillow. Her last thought was of Mark walking towards her, staring down at the cobblestones, his books in one hand. The afternoon sun was pouring gently over him.

When she woke up, it was seven-thirty and raindrops were rolling down the windowpane. She had missed dinner.

Oh my back aches. She poked her stomach; it dipped in and then, pushed out again.

My period will start tomorrow, she thought.

She put on her coat and left the room.

Outside, the wet street gleamed in the darkness. There were puddles of all shapes and sizes. She jumped over the Indian Ocean and began walking on Asia. Rainbow circles floated on top of the Arabian Sea.

Her brain was floating above her skull. Her thoughts were crowded above her eyelids, struggling to get out. She turned her head upwards until all she could see was a patch of sky.

A few branches crisscrossed her vision. The moon glowed like a neon bulb behind grey clouds.

Do I like him?

Well, I think he's good-looking and nice and intelligent and funny and I think about him all the time.

I hate liking him. I'm Indian.

Maybe I am two persons in one, and neither of them knows about the other.

In the mist she imagined Mark, hunched over with his shoulders scrunched together, scrawling tiny letters on a yellow legal pad with his yellow pencil.

He didn't know about her parents.

She was on the path leading to the train station. The mist hung over the ground and the yellow sulfur lights of the station glowed like oil lamps. A figure lay huddled on the bench.

Ma had told her this when she was home last year. Ma was standing in the kitchen, staring at the onions and garlic, coughing and gasping in the frying pan.

It was so dark that night you couldn't see the heap of files on Papa's bedside table. Ma woke up when the bed creaked. Thinking it was the mouse again, she turned over, but the mattress moved and Papa's figure rose up in the darkness. He was stretching the skin on his forehead, pushing his hair back, kneading his forehead as if the skin were too tight. Ma switched on the light. His eyes were opaque; he said, "Charu. We have to bring her back. How can she live there alone? She is so small. What if something happens to her?" So Ma ran to fetch him a glass of cool water and stroked his head as he gulped it down, tears and all. Then he lay down again. But the mattress shifted all night; the sheets slithered off the bed. When the sun was up, the crow clan was meeting on the telephone wires, and the dog was scraping the front door eagerly. Papa was still asleep, his small feet tangled up in the sheet.

The ground trembled. There were faint vibrations on the train tracks. She felt the air rushing towards her. Then the train was there. The great wheels pushed the air onto the wet ground; it escaped with a hiss. Only the gold line on the side of the carriage glinted. It snaked through the trees, curving around corners. It thundered past, shadows changed shape on the ground, the windows shook slightly.

She went back to the dorm.

The phone was ringing.

Even before she woke up, Charu knew it was for her. She tumbled out of bed and raced down the hall.

Three goddamn a.m., said the clock above the door.

"Phone call fraam India faar Charu Mehta," said the Indian operator. The phone wheezed and crackled. "Will you accept?"

"Yes."

"Please hold."

"Charu!" Papa's voice echoed from thousands of miles away. "Charu! How are you? Hold on, hold on, your mother wants to talk to you."

"Charu! We were worried, we haven't received a letter from you in two months—are you all right?"

"I just mailed a letter yesterday," Charu lied. "You'll get it soon. Don't worry, I'm fine. I've just been very busy."

"Wait, your father wants to talk to you."

"Charu! How are you?"

"Don't worry, Papa."

"And your studies?"

"I got an A on my last paper."

"Well done! If you need any money, just borrow it from your uncle. We'll pay him. Don't scrimp and save more than necessary."

The voice disappeared, and her brother came on the phone.

"Charu," he shouted, and suddenly she was smiling. "Did you get my drawing?"

"When did you mail it?"

"Today."

"I'll get it in ten days then. How is school?"

Ma was saying something about an expensive call in the background.

"Call Mummy," screamed Charu.

"Six minutes," intoned the operator.

Charu was pacing up and down, up and down.

"Give us two more minutes," said her mother.

"Ma, how are things going there? What's the gossip?"

"If I start gossiping now, this phone call will cost us a thousand rupees," Ma laughed. "I'll tell you everything in my next letter."

"How's Papa? Has he seen a doctor yet?"

"No, he hasn't. You will have to take him when you come here in the summer."

"Tell him to go today. It's an order!"

"Okay. Write soon. We miss you. We are all looking forward to seeing you. Your brother is saving all his pocket money because he wants to buy a plane ticket for you."

"Tell him to write to me!"

The phone spluttered.

Then the dial tone appeared again.

19

The cafeteria was almost empty when she walked in. A man in a white cap was singing, and mopping the floor with every beat.

It wasn't empty enough. At one table, Debbie and several other friends were in the middle of a fierce discussion.

Oh no.

Look straight ahead, she told herself. Keep your eyes on Debbie's face. Debbie waved, and Charu's legs walked to her table. She was greeted with a chorus of affection.

"Hey Charu! Where have you been!...Are you on a diet? I thought you didn't like cereal!...I think she's been avoiding us," said Debbie.

"Too good for us, eh?"

"Mark's been looking for you, Charu," said Debbie loudly. She pointed with her knife. "He's sitting over there."

Charu crushed a floating Cheerio with her thumb.

"Are you going to eat that now?" asked Debbie's friend.

Another Cheerio appeared on the surface of the milk.

"I hate cereal," said Charu.

A dot of heat touched her back and grew. She knew he was looking at her. I wonder if Debbie is staring at him, she thought.

Debbie leaned sideways and placed her elbow in Charu's tray.

"He's ogling you," she said.

Charu looked up.

His eyes were loving her. His hand was frozen to his fork.

Why is he doing this? How can he care so much when he doesn't know how I feel? Does he care about me? He's probably more interested in his feelings than in me. He doesn't know me at all.

She popped a soggy Cheerio into her mouth, pushed her chair back and marched over to his table. Debbie's voice followed her. "She's been very busy lately. She hasn't gotten any sleep."

"Mark..."

He looked up, his arms stretched out towards her and then, withdrew.

"Can I see you sometime today?" she said.

"Sure. I'll come by this afternoon."

"Thanks."

Charu went back to her room and locked her door.

Her brain was empty, but today, the walls were speaking to her.

Maybe pre-menstrual syndrome caused Friday night. It was all a result of excessive horniness.

I couldn't love him. I love my parents, and love is like an elephant, squishing and squeezing and blocking out everything else.

Her stomach muscles were expanding and fighting each other for space. She swallowed two Midols.

Colorful pictures, thick and heavy, flowed out of her brain. Mark kissing her with his eyes closed, his hand on the nape of her neck. Mark smiling at her. Mark, slumped in his chair, hands in the air, talking about Africa.

The awful guilt! If only it were in one part of her body, in an arm or a leg or an ear. She could cut it out and throw it away.

She felt unwashed and dirty. Her nostrils could smell blood. She went to the bathroom and washed her hands with soap.

She sat down on her bed and crossed her legs. She straightened her back until all the air in her stomach hissed angrily, and placed her hands on her knees.

What should I say to him? First, I should ask him to sit down. Then…

Perhaps, to begin with, I should talk about normal things like my paper and his classes. Then…

Maybe he will forget to come. He might have a lot of work to do.

I should be frank and clear. I should tell him everything in exactly the sequence I thought about it the past two days.

He will never understand. He will hate me and he will laugh about it with his friends.

There was a knock on the door.

I forgot to comb my hair.

She had been lying down on her bed since God knows when. She pushed her hair down as far as it would go.

"Come in."

He stood at the door, hiding his hands in his pockets, pulling them out, then sliding them back in again. His feet didn't move, but the rest of his body was shifting, his eyes were flitting from her face to the dusty table to the books on the floor and back again to her face. His sweater fell loosely over his khaki pants; he had forgotten to iron them again.

"I have been thinking about this," said her voice so suddenly that she jumped.

He was walking towards her with a little yellow piece of paper in his hand. He held it out to her, and then laid it on the bed. "Read this first," he said.

Charu pointed to her chair. "Do you want to sit down?" she asked, but he was already sitting down, on her bed, next to her.

"Go ahead," he said. "Read it."

A little yellow piece of paper with tiny writing.

"Anything you say is okay."

The words began to blur, and she looked past them to the patterns on the bedcover, staring at the lines crisscross and merge and separate until she could see no more. She buried her face in her hands.

I understand, Charu, he said. No matter how you feel, I understand. Don't worry about me.

I can't do it anymore, she said to the darkness of her palms. I can't go out…I can't.

I understand, he said.

Her throat had dried up.

Please go away, she said.

The first tear slipped past her fingers, down to her thigh, as the door clicked behind him.

Child

PARIJAT DESAI

Let me go to my freedom.
Let my joyous feet pound in thoughtless rhythm.
Let my hips swing and stop to a clangin cowbell.
Let my flattened hands push upward on an imaginary ceiling.
Let my arms crash through it with sudden energy.
Let laughter ricochet through my ribs
Until it reaches my lips
And I can hold it no longer.

To My Beloved Teenager

LALITA GANDBHIR

I noticed signs at the age of twelve.
By fourteen the situation had surely changed.
I realized that you think your mother
Has no manners whatsoever.
From your point of view I am
'Hopelessly out of it,'
My values and culture are 'ancient,'
My taste in clothes 'old-fashioned,'
My choice of color 'lousy,'
And my knowledge of any subject 'worthless.'
At times I hear you openly wonder
How your 'clueless' mother
Has managed to survive all these years.
You hate to go out with me and your father
Because we might run into one of your friends,
And to be seen in public with your parents
Would surely ruin your reputation.
Once I visited your schoolteacher,
For you that was an ultimate disaster.

When you're at home you seem to think you're the only one
 that lives here.
You cannot understand why I consider your room a fire hazard
Though your bed, desk, bureau, floor
Are cluttered with books, clothes, CD's and junk.
You don't comprehend why I want you to turn down
Loud music that blares from your room
Though normal conversation is impossible.
Do you know your showers that last forever
Since you became a teenager
Have doubled our bill for hot water?
You are always on a diet
And you wonder why I am upset
When you claim home-cooked Indian food is fattening

And then go out for french fries, hot fudge sundaes and double
 cheeseburgers.
You think our phone is your very own personal possession
And it exists so you can endlessly chatter.
You don't seem to understand why I interfere
With your life though I am your mother.

My childhood was so different. I could have never put on
 an act like yours.
My family would have never tolerated such disrespectful behavior.
If our move to a different culture was an error,
I would gladly return home now,
But I realize the move will not help you.
For I know despite trips to India, cultural school,
association with other Indians
you have imbibed a heavy dose of Western culture.
Moving will not erase the Western influence.
Whether your father and mother like it or not
You are American and want to be part of the Melting Pot.
For now we can only keep on loving you
And hope for the best.
The situation is out of our hands.

Requiem

SUNITA VATUK

Jacket pockets filled
with kleenex, kajal, quarters—
fully equipped. We stamped the gravel
with our heels, waited for a sign.

Clinging to my arms Gramps entered
the room Grammy's daughters can't.
I heard someone say sayonara
on an answering machine.
I controlled myself and didn't cry.

Our faces reflect in black lacquer.
I couldn't just leave her
there, I kissed the box goodbye.

Grammy wouldn't just go up to her underarms;
she floated, her head out.
Looked onto the ocean.
She watched the sail.
Held her breath when it went down;
our adventure made it frightening.
She couldn't follow us listing
way over to go fast
until the sail floated dreamlike
to the water, spilling
Edith, too, her glasses sliding
beyond sight into the ocean.
Edith swam back to shore.
Then, the sand washed off the sheet,
the orange life preservers reflected
on the clean white deck.
Running before the wind, we could
no longer hear it. Daggerboard
pulled up to run over lobster lines

left a hollow gurgle in the slot.

Sanj made a boat that rigs
just like the real one.
He'd thought he'd be an architect.
Melissa's the wild one.
Aruna has a temper.
Sunita sulks.

Chinese silk flowers in
the parlor. Not enough chairs.

You must be Sylvia.
She must be Brian's wife.
He's Gary's sister's husband.
Sign the book, so
they'll know who came.

Jai's the baby.
Arna has a baby.
Kristen sat at the grownups' table
even when she was seven.

Grammy sinks. We hold our breath
and turn up the drive.
The sign reads
Dead
End

The priest rushes in
shakes Sylvia's hand,
"Sorry I'm late."
He talks of wheat
stumbles on his metaphor in the dark
lost his way in his light & hope & death & glory.

We stare at him blankly
waiting for him to stop
politely crossing ourselves murmuring *and to you.*

When do we wail?

Toshi

PREM PRASAD

> The drums, the ignorant men, the untouchables, the
> animals, and the women deserve regular beating.
>> *Valmiky, writer of the great*
>> *Indian epic Ramayana*

Toshi is a name abbreviated from the full name Santosh. The meaning of Santosh is patience.

I will tell you a story. It is a story of one girl or three into one...like the packaged container of ice cream...vanilla, chocolate and strawberry...no, it is not a joke. We all know we package people; we stereotype them, wanting to forget the hidden inhumanities underneath the laughter we do not want to acknowledge or we are afraid to confront.

My name is Toshi.
I died at the age of forty.
I was married when I was thirty years old.
But my bridegroom was told I was twenty.

After I was twelve my mother started telling lies about my age. Whenever someone asked "How old is Toshi?" my mother replied, "she is twelve years old."

I was ignorant. I did not know there was something like time and age.

To tell you the truth I froze at the age of twelve. I did not know each month when you tear off a page from a calendar it means something...it means an added month to a person's life. Nothing special happened to me after I was twelve. I was removed from my school. I was in the fourth grade. I stayed the same size in my body.

I liked my school. It was a small school in a small town with trees of mangoes and guava fruit. I cried when told I was through with education. "You have learned enough to write the number of garments you may give to the washerman every week for laundry," my grandfather yelled when he saw my tear-soaked face.

I had nothing much to do at home. I followed the same routine: feeding parrots, running behind my mother and doing needlework with red, blue, green, gold and yellow threads. Their

27

elastic subservience to my whims excited me and, like their loops turning into paintings plotted on a white piece of cloth, they were my real world, moving in circles…wait, I know one story also…you want to hear it…it is about a prince on a horse…I know a story about a prince on a horse.

A prince will come on a horse, my mother said, and then you will be a mother like me. You will have a princess, one like yourself.

I was married at the age of thirty. The prince took such a long time to come because I was struck with fever which paralyzed the right side of my face. I recovered slowly, with a residual bend—a tilt in my neck.

The women friends of my mother clucked their tongues. "What a shame!" My mother stopped telling me the prince on the horse story.

One day to everyone's surprise a prince came along. He was sixty-four years old. I was thirty years old but for the public I was twenty only. My mother whispered, "Girls are girls, their age has no significance."

I was too dainty for my prince…too much spoiled by my parents. The new household was full of people…boys and girls and relatives, a sign of good fortune and good luck. My prince told me to take care of them. I was his fourth wife.

I worked hard. I worked as much as my hands could do. I was not left any more time for red, blue, green, gold and yellow yarn to plot the beautiful flowers and stems on a piece of cloth. I had pots and pans. There were boys and there were girls…girls as vulnerable as I was.

The youngest in the house was my Toshi, my child…I gave her the clean cloth and the red, blue, green, gold and yellow thread I brought from my mother's house and taught her the story of the prince on the horse.

Do you know my mother's name was also Toshi?

Mother

KOSAR SAIRA

I am so excited to see you
I love you
Mother, no matter what, I know I will always love you
You mean so much to me
I can't wait to see you and hug you
I just want to see you before you die
I don't want to regret not seeing you
I've cried for you
I've wanted you my dearest mother.

I wish you didn't have anything to do with that evil son of yours
The one that is full of evil, hate for women
The one I long to kill
The one I hate with all my heart
The one that took my self-respect, dignity
That invaded my body and mind
The one that is pure evil
Full of evil
The woman beater
The one that beats women
Physically and mentally.
The one that fucks women
Just by looking at us
The one that fucks women
By beating us up.

I hate him
I want to kill him and
always will

The son of a fucker like himself
My father.

Blues, etc.

SUNITA VATUK

driving home let's do this different
we make up a crazy route
down a maze of dark alleys twisted around
so I lose my sense of direction
(as always up by Armitage and Kenmore)
his face frozen in the light of passing street lamps
then dark
would he hurt me
if I've hurt him
you were the one who told me how
you can always tell where you're going
in Chicago if you know the numbers
of the main streets
keep the grid in
mind
there's numbers on the street lamps
(you're driving too fast for me to read them)

we crash through an industrial non-neighborhood
the street shows through in the snow
railroad tracks thrust us up

This poem is dedicated to my five-and-a-half year old daughter: NATASHA,
and does not have a name because I could not put a name to it.

HUMA DAR

My dearest darling Natasha,
Tashi Rani, I salute your courage!
You had the strength to change your name
before I got to change my own.
Without telling me, at school one day, December,
when you asked your teacher to erase 'Farooq' from your name
with liquid paper,
were you trying to erase the pain as well?
Were you trying to block the hurting, prying fingers?
Were you trying to tell me what your father was doing to you?

You believed him when he said
he'll cut your tongue off, if you tell Mama.
You believed him when he said
he'll take you so far away from Mama,
you'll never be able to see me again.
19th January, you told me:
"See, isn't that what he's done to Zavain?"
I did not have any answer;
I had never thought
my children's father could be so very cruel.
Please forgive me, Natasha
for trusting him with you
thrice a week
half-an-hour each time.

I promise you today, as God is my witness:
Never again will you suffer that pain.
I promise you today:
you'll have your brother back,
your Zavain.
I promise you today:
we'll be together again
soon, one day.

With all my love
Mama

31

Gender, Class and Cultural Conflict:
Indu Krishnan's Knowing Her Place*

LATA MANI

It takes a long time to figure out where you belong. That's the pain of being, sort of, a second generation immigrant child.

<div align="right">Vasu, protagonist, Knowing Her Place.</div>

You see conflicts...see a conflict is often perceived to be more serious than it really is, you know, sort of, the mind, so to speak, exaggerates it...often. I'm not saying it's not real for the person who's experiencing the conflict, because it's very difficult for that person to, sort of, step out, you know, and, sort of, look at the conflict from a distance and see, okay, here is a conflict and you have to decide one way or the other how much is this decision going to affect, what is the effect of this decision going to be...you know, if you made the wrong choice how much damage is there going to be, right, I mean, probably not much in most situations...probably does not matter that much which way you go...It does matter somewhat, but I'm saying in terms of degree it probably is not that important...Well, if, if...if it's not that important which way you decide, then what is the conflict? A conflict is important only if the decision is going to seriously mess up something one way or the other, otherwise it's just your mind that's playing games on you, making you believe that something is terribly important...very often they're not.

<div align="right">Raghu, Vasu's husband.</div>

What's the conflict? I won't decide what I want to be, I just am how I am, like Popeye.

<div align="right">Gopal, Vasu's elder son, late teens.</div>

I feel you're experiencing conflict because of what you went through as a child...As far as I'm concerned you have no conflict now.

<div align="right">Ashok, Vasu's younger son, early teens.</div>

Growing up in two cultures, or coming from one to live in another, is like moving in two directions at once, or like being in two places at once. For those who haven't experienced it, it seems a simple matter of picking and choosing the best of both worlds, but for some of us, it's more painful than that.

<div align="right">Voice over, Indu Krishnan,
director of Knowing Her Place.</div>

Indu Krishnan's film, *Knowing Her Place* (1990), documents Vasu's struggle to confront and work through the anguish and alienation that has been tearing her apart. Vasu's immigration history is an unusual one. Unlike most women of her generation, Vasu grew up in the U.S. and was sent to her grandparents in Madras, on the eve of puberty at age twelve. She returned to the U.S. upon her arranged marriage to Raghu four years later and has lived there ever since. Vasu speaks of being aware, right from childhood, of a duality within her. She describes this duality in terms of a conflict between America and India and of not knowing her place in either location. The documentary charts Vasu's painful journey coming to terms with this conflict, a process that includes her attempted suicide and subsequent healing through therapy. According to Vasu, counselling enabled her recovery, in large part, by empowering her to realign familial relations and set limits upon those social expectations she had found intolerable but had been unable to resist. Her compliance had thus been secured at a cost. The dutiful daughter, wife and mother was left feeling embittered, trapped and terribly alone, faced with the collective incomprehension of a mother apparently untroubled by the social prescriptions that had shaped her life, and a family that construed Vasu's problem as one of her own making.

Knowing Her Place is a beautifully crafted and moving film, disarming in its simplicity. Both visually and aurally, the intercutting between India and the U.S. works well to suggest the complex internal geographies inhabited by immigrants. What is especially welcome is that the film refuses the tropes of an aestheticized nostalgic representation of India—stock scenes of cows, tribes, traffic and the United Colors of Reds, Greens and Yellows—for the particulars of the houses and streets that form the contours of Vasu's middle-class experience of South India. The camera never denies its presence. For instance, in its documentation of the micro-politics of family dynamics, the camera frequently lingers on Vasu's face long enough to register the corrosive effect of others' words upon her. These haunting moments capture the depth of her sense of betrayal. Their intensity is unsettling, reminding viewers of their complicity with the camera in eavesdropping on what is a private though not uncommon family drama.

Indu Krishnan follows Vasu in framing her conflict as a cultural one: of how to find a balance between America and India. The binaries America and India form the organizing axis of the narrative. When the gum-chewing, comic-reading, rock-and-roll-loving Vasu is dispatched to South India to be under the supervision of her grandparents and is subjected to isolation during menstruation, she says, "The American part of me wanted to ask questions." The bit role assigned her in the preparations for her marriage is described as "typical Indian culture." The narrator adopts a similar analysis. In noting a contrast between Vasu at home and at work, for example, she states, "At home she was traditionally Indian, but at work she could sound and act quite American."

Despite the 'torn between two cultures' rhetoric, the film's material consistently exceeds this description. As the incidents accumulate and the plot gathers force, it becomes patently clear that Vasu's troubles are specifically female ones. Indeed, the film's greatest potential contribution might be to initiate discussion of the gendered nature of cultural conflict in the South Asian diaspora. For given that there is no rupture in patriarchal power with migration, merely its reconfiguration, the consequences of diaspora are specifiably

different for women and men. This is partly what accounts for the incomprehension, by Vasu's husband and sons, of the depth and nature of her internal conflict. Gopal can claim kinship with Popeye in his desire to be what he wants to be. And of course, his devoted middle-class family obliges him by paying rent on a separate apartment for him so he can live the lifestyle of his choice. Would a daughter of the Varadhan family have received a similar response? Probably not. As for Vasu's husband: the equivocations, hesitations and facile generalities that constitute his reading of Vasu's conflict are a paradigmatic instance of an apparently enlightened Indian liberalism which is all the more devastating for its pretensions. It proposes a free-market model of human action which effaces the 'invisible' structuring hand of patriarchy and renders women's anguish into self-generated confusion and psychosis. His interpretation of Vasu's conflict is quoted in full above, since it is a particularly good instance of this kind of discourse. Raghu feels no conflict, but then why should he? His passage to the U.S. has been relatively smooth, thanks to class and male privilege. Vasu's benefits from her class position, on the other hand, are tempered by her femaleness.

Indu Krishnan and Vasu are not unmindful of the place of gender in Vasu's turmoil. Vasu is quite explicit about her anger at having been denied an education and at being married to Raghu at age sixteen. She speaks eloquently of feeling trapped, unable to be other than the all-providing mother and wife, yet resentful of such impulses within herself, and of her being taken for granted by the family. The Thanksgiving scene is most poignant in its representation of the casual arrogance and sense of entitlement of Raghu, Gopal and Ashok and their effect on Vasu. Such dynamics are very powerfully captured by the film. What is unfortunate, however, is that they are written into a narrative of cultural displacement which evades the specificity of gender and depends on stereotypic propositions about America and India alike.

For instance, if we were to take the film's analysis of Vasu's situation at face value, we would have to accept its conflation of modernity with America and the accompanying equation of tradition with India. The film attributes all of Vasu's self-questioning to her 'Americanness' and her acute sense of familial responsibilities to her 'Indianness.' Ergo, her 'Indianness' acts as a break on the potentialities for individual self-fulfillment implicit in her 'Americanness.' If this were the case, how would we account for the fact that Vasu's struggles in relation to her family are shared by many U.S. women? And what of Indian women who, since the nineteenth century, have challenged the social and cultural prescriptions constraining their lives?

The discourse framing the documentary— America vs. India, West vs. East, Modernity vs. Tradition—has a long and complex history for Third World women. Its consequences for South Asian women in the diaspora bear thinking through. Briefly, questions of tradition and modernity have, since the nineteenth century, been debated on the literal and figurative bodies of women. It thus comes as no surprise that the burden of negotiating the new world is borne disproportionately by women, whose behaviour and desires, real or imagined, become the litmus test for the South Asian community's anxieties or sense of well-being. For instance, the fear of dating that consumes many South Asian families is primarily a fear of women dating. Although many parents may worry about interracial marriage for what it might imply for them in old age, there is little attempt to control men's sexuality. Women meanwhile are quite frequently policed with the stick of tradition: it is women who are called on to preserve

the ways of the old country. Needless to say, both parents are complicit in this. And the vision of India brandished before the second generation is often of a socio-cultural space free of gender and generational conflict, one in which everyone knows and loves their place in society. (Caste and religious divisions, on the other hand, are readily acknowledged, even nourished, in the diaspora, but that's another story.) This is a peculiarly distorted view of contemporary social relations among the Indian urban middle classes who form the most appropriate point of comparison for most immigrants to the U.S.

It is this view that produces such apparent contradictions, as in second generation women college students in the U.S. enjoying far less freedom than their counterparts in India. More tragically, it leads to a naturalization of Indian 'tradition' and to the assumption of its generalised, uncritical acceptance in the subcontinent. Critical questioning thus becomes aligned with a negation of Indianness. As a strategy for managing dissent it is especially chilling, since challenging parental authority and aspirations leads to a troubling sense of inauthenticity. Women, made responsible within this discourse for upholding tradition, are particularly vulnerable. Caught between parental desire for conformity with cultural norms that are at odds with their peers' and their own often uneasy integration into U.S. society, many second generation women find themselves literally struggling to know their place and identity. This then is the broader context in which Vasu may be found to identify her unhappiness over her role in the family as a conflict between India and America.

What of the director, Indu Krishnan? Is her framing of the film as a conflict between cultures also to be located within the context just described? Perhaps. But there is another possibility. The ways in which the terms of Krishnan's commentary are consistently called into question by the film's material may point to a problem at the heart of feminist representational practice: the relation between the critic and the subject/object of her analysis. On the one hand, an empathic relationship was surely necessary for the kinds of conversations and scenarios Indu Krishnan was able to film. In the ultimate analysis Vasu's pain may have been socially produced, but revealing her vulnerabilities and those of her family is an exceptional act of courage. The strength of the relationship between the director and the subject of the film would have been vital to enabling such a project. But on the other hand, empathy and identification may also have produced their own constraints, making it difficult, for example, to challenge the terms of Vasu's analysis of her own experience. After all it is Vasu's relationship with her family that is at stake. One possible reading of Krishnan's commentary is that given these constraints, she persisted in adopting Vasu's analysis even though the documentary itself underscores the inadequacy of its terms for grasping her situation.

By contrast to its reductive binary framing of the problem of cultural identity, the film is refreshingly complex in its representation of women's agency. *Knowing Her Place* documents the multiple ways in which Vasu is both inscribed within, and also manipulates, the dynamics of gender and culture. Even in the Thanksgiving scene, in which her alienation from her family appears total, thanks to their disrespect and derision, Vasu can be found challenging—almost baiting—Gopal to admit to his Americanization. She asks him if he would have been satisfied with a typical South Indian meal instead of the roast that she has so painstakingly prepared. This is no innocent question, but a familiar scenario in which many things are simultaneously at stake. The mother seeks recognition and approval for her efforts

in pleasing her son, in particular her attempt to bridge the gap between the Indian home and the American world outside. At the same time she is registering both satisfaction and displeasure at her son's assimilation into this world. It is a barely coded exchange about allegiance and betrayal, shot through with maternal ambivalence. Gopal sidesteps this minefield, first by proclaiming indifference, and then by claiming that if she had served him Indian food, he would simply have gone home and cooked himself spaghetti. His response, which acknowledges neither her labor—physical or cultural—nor her fears and/or desires, wins him this round in the dinner table war of words between mother and son. It is a classic instance of the limited tactical position conferred on mothers within a patriarchal economy which valorizes them for having borne sons, but then makes them vulnerable to the latter's whims and fancies, a problem that begins early and only intensifies with age.

Later in the film in a conversation Vasu has with uncles in India, Gopal becomes a resource for her in enacting her own difference vis-a-vis her family there. Here she can recount the details of Gopal's lifestyle, with relish, to uncles puzzled at a notion of 'independence' that refers not to Gopal's capacity to earn his own living, but to a situation in which he is supported by his parents while living 'his' life in 'his' own apartment. Vasu's mobilisation of cultural difference in this instance is marked by neither ambivalence nor anguish. Unlike with her mother, husband or sons, she is not seeking her uncles' approval or acceptance, only to enjoy the effect of her words on them. Americanness in this context is simply an unambivalent index of cultural difference, even superiority.

By representing Vasu in a range of situations in this manner, *Knowing Her Place* is able to document the intricate workings of class, culture and patriarchy in Vasu's life. The contours of her struggles are fundamentally shaped by her class position. Hers is a war against feelings of worthlessness and devaluation, a search for her own voice. The resolution of Vasu's problems through therapy and employment must be seen in this context. Therapy offers women a way to individuate, to learn to separate their own desires from those legislated for them by family and society alike. The capacity to imagine oneself apart from one's family is a hard-won achievement. But the ability to transform the conditions of one's life with the help of this new wisdom is also enormously aided by class privilege. It may be tempting to some to interpret *Knowing Her Place* as a caricature: life imitating modernization theory—"Encounter with America leads Indian woman to challenge Indian traditions. Ensuing internal conflict resolved through therapy and a career of her own." The 'India vs. America' metanarrative might prompt such a reading. To conclude thus, however, would be to advance reductive tabloid interpretation that ignores the wealth and complexity of the material contained in the film—a complexity which consistently and compellingly exceeds any simplistic reading.

Home

PREETY

I stand pounding at the door. Staring at the door. Will you come out? I hear the water running and picture your tears sliding down the drain. Each time you go into the bathroom I don't think you'll ever come out. I fear the water is taking you away, allowing you that chance to be free. I hear the water and think that is the only place left you can go. I picture your blood running with the water, moving slowly down the drain. People in despair never come out of the bathroom; they die in there. I don't think you will come out. I don't think you want to come out.

Mumi, hold me and tell me you are okay behind that closed door; that door that separates us.

The screams fill my ears. No silence, no peace. Glass breaks. You are the one he blames. He burns a twenty dollar bill because we do not have money to pay the bills. He is drunk. I think he will fall and the house will burn. We all could burn.

He is the man. We must all see his power. See that he can hurt us. See that he can kill us. He wants us to live in fear. He hits you and you fall on the ground. Those hands do not caress, they only strike. Blood stains the walls. What can I do? I want to hide the knives. There's a pair of scissors on the table.

He hears my screams. He works in a factory all day and cannot come into a house that is screaming. He hates my screams. They mean I love you. His eyes look at me in disgust. His smells suffocate me and I want to vomit. Get away from your mother. He curses at me in Hindi; he wants to kill me. He shoves me onto the floor. I lay there dissolving. I cannot leave you Mumi. I will not leave you.

I feel as though I am still in you. I am your pain, exist as your sorrows. What you do to yourself, you do to me. What he does to you, he does to me. Tied up, in-between. I'll save you Mumi. I'll save you.

Leaving Yuba City

CHITRA BANERJEE DIVAKARUNI

She has been packing all night. It's taking a long time because she knows she must be very quiet, mustn't wake up the family. Father and mother in the big bedroom downstairs, he sharp and angular in his crisp ironed night-pajamas, on the bed-lamp side because he reads the Punjabi newspaper before he sleeps, her body like a corrugation, a dark apologetic crease on her side of the big white bed, face turned away from the light, or is it from her husband, salwar-kameez smelling faintly of sweat and dinner spices. Brother and his new wife next door, so close that all week bits of noise have been flying through the thin wall at her like sparks, murmurs, laughter, bed-creaks, small cut-off cries, and once a sound like a slap, followed by a sharp in-drawn breath like the startled start of a sob that never found its completion. And directly underneath her bedroom, grandfather, propped up on betel-juice stained pillows to help him breathe, slipping in and out of dreams, nightmares where he calls out in his asthmatic voice hoarse threats in a dialect she does not understand.

She moves on tiptoe like she imagines, from pictures seen in magazine advertisements, a ballerina would move. Actually she is more like a stork, with that same awkward grace as she balances stiff-legged on the balls of her feet, her for-the-first-time painted toes curling in, then out, splaying fuschia pink with just a hint of glitter through the crowded half-dark of her bedroom. She moves back and forth between suitcase and dresser, maneuvers her way around the heavy teak furniture that father chose for her. Armchair. Dressing table. Narrow single bed. They loom up in the sad seep of light from her closet like black icebergs. Outside, wind moves through the pepper trees, whispering her name through the humid night. *Sushma, Sushma, Sushma.* She has been holding her breath, not realizing it, until her chest begins to feel like there are hands inside, hot hands with fuschia-pink nails pushing outwards, scraping the lining of her lungs. Now she lets it out in a rush, shaking her head with a small, embarrassed laugh.

Two weeks back, wandering through the meager cosmetics section of the India House drugstore, killing time as she waited for grandfather's asthma prescription to be filled, she had seen the fuschia nail polish. She hadn't been looking for anything, what was the use when mother and especially father believed that nice girls shouldn't wear makeup? But the bottle leaped out at her, so bright and unbelonging in that store with its dusty plastic flowers in fake crystal vases on the counter. *Take me, take me,* it called, a bottle from a book she had read in grade school, what was it, a girl falling through a hole in her garden into magic. But this voice was her own, the voice that cried into her pillow at night. *Take me, take me.* There in the store she had looked up at the faded Christmas streamers wrapped like garlands around the pictures of the gods hanging above the cash register, Ganesha with his inscrutable

elephant head, Krishna with his calm flute, his eyes like opaque water. *My life*. Her fingers had closed around the fuschia bottle. That's when she knew she was leaving.

So when at brother's wedding all the relatives said, now it's Sushma's turn, and Aunt Lakshmi told her mother she knew just the right boy back in Ludhiana, college graduate, good family, how about sending them Sushma's photo, that one in the pink salwar-kameez with her hair double-braided, it was not hard to sit quietly, a smile on her face, tracing the gold-embroidery on the border of her sari, letting the voices flow around her, *Sushma, Sushma, Sushma*, like the wind in the pepper trees. Because she had already withdrawn her savings, two years' salary from working at Bharat Spices grocery, money her mother thought she was keeping for her wedding jewelry. The twenty-dollar bills lay folded under her mattress, waiting like wings. Below the bed was the old suitcase she had taken down from the attic one afternoon when no one was home, taken down and dusted and torn off the old Pan Am tag from a forgotten long-ago trip to India. Even her second-hand VW Bug was filled with gas and ready.

Now she pauses with her arms full of satiny churidars, kurtas with tiny mirrors stitched into them, transparent gauzy dupattas in sunset colors. What is she going to do with them in her new life in some rooming house in some downtown she hasn't even decided on, where she warms a can of soup over a hot plate? But she packs them anyway, because she can't think of what else to do with them. Besides, she has only two pairs of jeans, a few sweaters, and one dress from when she was in high school that she's not sure she can still fit into. Three nightgowns, long-sleeved, modest-necked. From old habit she folds them in neat, flat, gift-boxed rectangles. Comb, toothbrush, paste, vitamin pills. She puts in the bottle of hair oil and lifts it out again. *Nice girls never cut their hair. They let it grow long, soft as silk, braided tightly down their backs*. That's what father and mother had looked for when they arranged brother's marriage. She stands in the shadow in front of the mirror with its thick bulging frame. She pouts her lips like the models on TV, narrows her eyes, imagines something wild and wicked and impossible, short hair swinging against the bare nape of her neck, a frizzy permed mass pinned up on her head. She throws in the bottle of nail polish.

It's time for the letter now, the one she has been writing in her mind all week. *I'm leaving*, it says. *I hate you, hate the old ways you're always pushing onto me. Don't look for me. I'm never coming back*. Or, *I'm sorry, I had to go. I was suffocating here. Please understand*. Or perhaps, *Don't worry about me. I'll be fine. I just want to live on my own for a while. Will contact you when I'm ready*. She pauses, pen poised over the paper. No. None of it is right. The words, the language. How can she write in English to her parents who have never spoken to her in anything but Punjabi, who will have to have someone translate the lines and curves, the bewildering black slashes she has left behind?

She walks down the steps in the dark, counting them. *Nineteen, twenty*. The years of her life. She steps lightly on them, as though they have not been cut into her heart, as though she can so easily leave them behind. She puts her hand on the front door, steeling herself for the inevitable creak, for someone to wake and shout, *kaun hai?* For the pepper trees to betray her, *Sushma, Sushma, Sushma*. The suitcase bumps against her knee, bulky, bruising. She bites off a cry and waits. But there is only the sound of the neighbor dog barking. And she knows, suddenly, with the doorknob live and cold under her palm, that it's going to happen,

that the car will start like a dream, the engine turning over smooth, smooth, the wind rushing through her open hair, the empty night streets taking her wherever she wants to go. No one to catch her and drag her back to her room and keep her under lock and key like they did with Prema last year until they married her off. No one to slap her around or scream curses at her or accuse her of having thrown mud on the family name. And sometime tomorrow, or maybe next week, when she's far far away where no one can ever find her, Las Vegas, Los Angeles, she'll pick up a phone and call them. Maybe the words will come to her then, halting but clear, in the language of her parents, the language that she carries with her, for it is hers, too, no matter where she goes. Maybe she'll be able to say what they've never said to each other all their lives because you don't say those things even when they are true. Maybe she'll say, *I love you.*

Yuba City town in Northern California settled by Indian immigrants from Punjab

*

Surrounded By The Walls
Of Our Community

False Realities

MAYA DEVI

They hold assumptions
 About my chastity
 About the reasons behind my emotional outbursts
 About my whereabouts.

Meanwhile, I continue to pretend I'm someone I'm not.
 I continue to wish I could go far away; knowing that even if
 and when I do, my problems won't.
 I continue to push away the day that I and They have to
Face the reality tucked away behind the illusion we've created to live in.

Shards

KAMAL KAPUR

I returned to India for a vacation—India, my demon lover, whom I could neither accept nor reject. I got off the plane in faded blue jeans and realized at once that though my rebellion in dress had some relevance to my own family where the women wore chiffons, silks, starched cottons, how ridiculous a gesture this symbol of elected poverty was in India, where the majority of the population could afford nothing but faded, ragged or no clothes at all.

My real gesture of rebellion (or was it vanity?) at a time in America when the young were growing their hair as a symbol of reversion to wilder, more primitive, less civilized states of existence was to cut my hair—not, I must admit, as a protest against conformity to nonconformism (as much as I would like the distinction). I came from a very traditional Sikh family, and Sikhs, male or female, are not supposed to cut their hair.

It isn't that I didn't feel pangs of guilt at cutting my hair. But my initiation into the horrors of revolt had taken place long ago. In boarding school, where we had to wear shorts for our early morning PT, I wore the usual school uniform of flannel trousers—even in summertime—because I didn't want to show up in front of our PT instructor, whom I had a crush on, with furry legs. I was reprimanded again and again for this. Finally, I had no choice but to wear shorts or be exposed to the wrath of the instructor in front of the entire school. That morning I faked a pain on the right side of my lower abdomen, where I knew the appendix was supposed to be. I was rushed to the school infirmary. The doctor diagnosed an extreme and urgent case of appendicitis.

I was operated upon within days, and in order to come be with me my father had to take emergency leave. It was during the Indo-Pak war of '64 and he was commanding a brigade on the border. As he sat by my bedside holding my hand, worrying about me, worrying about the front, I itched to tell him that if only our religion had allowed me to shave my legs with impunity, all this would not have happened.

But the battle of the hair wasn't over yet. I only had one appendix and after about a one-month period where I was excused from PT because I was recuperating, I had to face the issue all over again. Bravely I decided one morning to face the ridicule of my classmates and went to the field in shorts. The hair on my legs became darker, longer, more curly, more bristly in the reflection of others' eyes. Standing in line I imagined the girls aside me stood further away than the usual arm's length, and when the instructor inspected my line he lingered longer than with the others and would have had, I supposed, if I had looked up to see it, a look of utter disgust in his eyes.

That very day I borrowed a little blue plastic razor from a friend and locked myself in a bathroom to do the dreaded deed. Even the angle of the light in the bathroom was foreboding.

The dripping of the tap in the bucket as I lathered my legs seemed to foretell of impending disaster. The blood that rushed from the first nick I made in my shin was—I was sure—my father's blood as he lay dying on the battlefield.

But nothing happened, except smooth shiny legs that I was proud to display in my shorts. God evidently had better things to do than concern himself with whether I shaved my legs. This was my first lesson in youthful freedom from the shackles of religion and god. Through my subsequent transgressions I wasn't so much rebelling against god as recognizing how much larger he is than all our religions and ideas put together and how he tests and tempts us when we have chosen paths too narrow for our destinies. Whenever humans put themselves and their gods into forms too confining to contain them in all their chaosmic entirety, it is he—lover of their reducible and undefinable, defiant of the authority of men's procrustean institutions, defiant of the molds of their minds and of comforting but confining patterns—who breaks them.

From here onwards I took whatever freedom I needed—to experience myself, to discover and know the truth of the bare, forked animal that I see every time I look in the mirror.

Is this why I have gone so very wrong? Is this why I find myself cooped up in this basement on Ash Street at the age of thirty-nine, shedding, shedding everything I've been, my breasts, my pudendum, alone, terribly alone, as in a cocoon suspended in infinity, orbiting a black hole from whose gravity there is no escape? Was she right, was Amrita, my sister-in-law, right that day, three years ago, when George had left to pursue semi-virginal, sweet, fat-assed Fanny, and I had returned shamefaced to the bosom of my family whose every value I had rejected?

We are sitting at the breakfast table—yes, that's the rule. The entire family must sit together for all three meals. The talk turns to my mother's nephew, Darshan, who has rejected yet another prospective wife, who his parents had arranged for him to "see," on the grounds that she talked when he went to see her.

"Why?" I ask. "Shouldn't girls have tongues? Listen girls," I say to my two nieces, "when someone comes to 'see' you, make sure you don't eat anything on the table—Darshan rejected the last one because she ate a pastry while he was 'seeing' her; and not only that but she even lifted up her eyes to check him out! Keep your eyes lowered, dutifully open your mouths when they want to check out your teeth and remember, leave your tongues behind in the bedroom under your pillows..."

The girls giggle, but Amrita pounces on me with a vigor I didn't know she had. She had always been soft-spoken and polite. "Enough! Enough! No more! I don't want their heads filled with any feminist ideas. This is our system, this is the way things are done in this country, and soon, very soon—they are already thirteen and eleven—they will have to be 'seen' and I want them to behave the way girls are supposed to in these situations if they are to get good matches."

She says this with a conviction and a force that shuts me up. These are her girls— though how I wish they were mine! For years George and I had fornicated on cue, dutifully,

forcibly, charts and thermometers and such, but without result. And she has a right to bring them up the way she thinks she ought to, the way she was brought up herself. I don't have the energy for confrontation this morning.

I go upstairs to my bedroom to stare again out of the window at the storm-tossed barren almond tree that beat intermittently upon the panes of my window all night long. It survived the storm, but my mother has already told the maali to cut it down: it bears no fruit.

There is a knock on my door, and Amrita enters in a huff.

"Did you let them see *Little Darlings* on the video?"

"Only about ten minutes of it. You told me to shut it off then, remember? And I did."

I speak in a voice that sounds strained and tired and unable to lash out. Though she is a few years younger than I, she is my older brother's wife, and therefore senior to me in the family hierarchy.

"But they say they have seen it."

"Well, I didn't show it to them. You can ask them if you like. You seem to think I'm corrupting your girls."

"No, no, nothing like that … they had said to me when I turned the movie on by accident that they had seen it, so I thought…"

"Well, I didn't."

I clam up. She leaves the room. In sheer defiance I take a cigarette out of the coat pocket in which I hide them, go into the bathroom and smoke it. Sikhs are not meant to smoke, so I'm going to smoke. I don't give a damn if they smell it on me. I wish they would smell it on me, yell at me, so I would be compelled to leave their house, to which I am told again and again I do not belong. A daughter's place is with her husband, her in-laws are her parents now. This house belongs to your brother, Virinder, and his wife, Amrita. They inherit everything. That's the way it is in our society. Stay with us as long as you need, we are here for you, we love you, but remember, you do not belong here.

It's unfair! It's unfair! I've said it over and over to my parents, and all I get in reply is: this is the way of our society. This is the way it has been, this is the way it is, this is the way it will be.

I feel like a fiend. I am supposed to simply accept. I am supposed to be meek and passive but I feel enraged. My blood turns to gall. I say to myself, I will sue the lot of them. But the thought brings no peace. I cannot accept the way things are and I cannot fight them. I cannot stay, and have no place to run away to.

I feel stifled in the clean, neat house. Take your ideas, your fine clothes, your velvet furniture, your polished surfaces and shove them. Yes, I dress grubbily. Is that why you left me, George…say, is that why? You are grubby yourself, but you can be, you are a man, after all. Yes, I think girls ought to be allowed to do everything men do. Have I been abandoned because I am not "feminine" enough? I talk when I feel the need, I do not cross my legs when I sit. Yes, I think you are a wimp, Amrita, bringing up your girls in such a niminy-piminy way. It all comes from leading such a protected life yourself. Bring up your daughters exactly as you were brought up, even though the way you were brought up has not in any way taught you how to live or feel or think deeply. Oh, you went to college because it improved your market value, but only for a year, because getting a degree would have made you too old for

a good match. You learned how to cook, to serve food aesthetically, to dress in a modest and pleasing manner, to react politely in indelicate situations. Whenever your father farted at the breakfast table as he read his newspaper, you and your sisters were not to let on in any way that you had heard the sound. You were to pretend as if nothing had happened.

I break into a rage, perseverating on my revenge: Wax up the orifices of your daughters, Miss Niminy-Piminy! Mold them how you please. I shall never have anything to do with them and you again. I shall cut myself off from the lot of you who have lived such narrow, stifling existences, fly in the face of all oppression, cut off all ties with clan, society, husband, turn into a suppurating sore on their faces, plunge headlong into the tumultuous sea of suffering and delight, clamp my mouth on the hairy phallus of existence and suck all its sweet bitterness.

But the rage brings no relief. I feel caged in it. And afraid. I have allowed myself too much freedom. I'm like a little girl who has lived in a doll's house, and now all of a sudden she has grown up. Her arms stick way out of the windows, her head has shattered the ceiling and emerged, unhoused and roofless. The shards of the house stick to her like flakes of eggshell stick to an eagle's fledgling. Perhaps for her now there is no return.

In the eye of my fear I come face to face with what I might become. I see myself behind bars in a loony bin, sitting on a cold stone floor, slobbering on my chin, picking on my sores with vacant eyes. I see the caretaker stop near my cage and explain to the visitors of this human zoo:

"She was a writer once. The cable of her anchor was too short to reach bottom in the depths in which she had allowed herself to wander in her lust for experience, her hunger for the truth of her existence. Lost. Gone over to the other shore. She stepped out of the charmed circle in which society contains her brood. She overstepped the boundaries of her strength; she miscalculated her power; she forgot the fragility of her femininity. Tragic, isn't she? And the irony of it is that, deluded into invulnerability, she had scoffed at failure and its expression in the tragic vision of life."

Visions of terror are dispelled by a knock on the door. Amrita enters, and I return to myself and see that I have, unawares, stripped myself of all my clothes. I stand there stark naked as she enters. She's terribly embarrassed. She apologizes profusely, then shuts the door again. Yes, yes, I have tits. Look. I cup them in my hands before the mirror. And I have legs, and things between them. Cunt, asshole, taint, as George had called it once. T'ain't pussy, t'ain't asshole. The first bleeds, pisses, gets wet and swollen due to chemical reactions produced by lust and desire. The second shits, farts and itches. How about that, lady? Does it shock you, you who are so clean, your cracks all polished, waxed and plastered over by your upbringing?

I prance about, put on my usual, crumpled clothes and open the door. She floats into the room in her french chiffon, in her best smile, being her usual, conciliatory self.

"I hope you don't mind what I said."

"No. No I don't mind. They are your girls. Keep them. I just don't want anything to do with them. I'm interfering with their upbringing, I'm corrupting them, so it's best for me to stay away."

Her face quivers. Her eyes are puffy and pink. She's been weeping beneath her makeup.

"You're taking it all too seriously," she says, calmly. "Corruption...what a strong word. I only mean that these girls have to live a particular way. They have to have arranged marriages. They have to live in this society, so what's the point of telling them things that will only cause confusion in their minds?"

"You don't want them to think?"

"No. I don't. It makes you unhappy. Thinking produced my nervous breakdown two years ago. Acceptance, resignation...these are the things that produce peace."

"Peace! You think you have peace? You think your parents have peace? You think my parents have peace?"

"As much as is possible, given the human condition. But the point is I don't want my daughters to live the way you have lived. There is too much suffering..."

"Suffering! But that's part of life, don't you see? Part of knowledge, part of peace, I mean the real peace, not the peace that comes from wearing blinkers and living in the shallows..."

"Listen. I'm not saying your way of life is wrong. I may secretly even envy you your freedom. But this is not what I want for my daughters. If you were a mother you'd understand my protective feelings towards them."

Okay, I say to myself, I'm not a mother and may never be one. That's the worst, isn't it? No man, no home, no child. I can live with it. Maybe.

I look out at the almond tree as she keeps talking about how she doesn't want to give her daughters the freedom I was given by my parents—to get lost in. She's implying that. I have no answers, only a tight constriction in my chest.

The barren almond tree bears birds. They sit, plump, like ripe fruit, dotting its twig-like branches, and preen themselves when they're not singing. Or they just sit in contentment, their little eyes half-shut by a white membrane, and sway on the branch.

"Nobody gave me freedom, I took it. And I'm paying the price for it."

"It's too high. I don't want my daughters to be alone like you."

Though her hands are outstretched in supplication there is a new aggressiveness about her stance. Lioness and cubs, bitch and pups.

She wants for them a life of blessed innocence, peace and comfort in the shallows and I would drag them over the coals of experience and knowledge, deprive them of home, hearth, husbands and the sounds of children. The milk of kindness flows in her teats, poison in mine.

I begin to feel like the wicked witch in all the fairy tales, who curses little girls to sleep and death, isolation and lovelessness.

After much rage a calm comes. After much struggle, surrender. The hands tire of clenching and sheer weariness releases their hold on things. I open my clenched hands and release her daughters to her.

But no peace comes from letting go, just a freezing up of the heart in the endless winter of hopelessness. Bloodtight scabs grow on the mouths of wounds, boulders are rolled into the mouths of springs. Look, look here at this breast, it has turned to stone, and there, a little pebble-sized patch of stone on the belly. Whatever can, falls off, the rest turns hard. Soon all of this perishable, palpitating plasma, this quickening corpuscle will harden and jell into stone. I will endure as rocks endure, as mummies in their tombs endure time, waiting for the sound of a hammer and a chisel. Waiting for the sound of freedom.

To: Sri Lanka

ZAVEENI KHAN

You
are a distant light
beyond my reach,
a repelling attraction.

I unclasp myself
from your grasp, unaware
of your mocking strings
reaching across the vast ocean,
forgotten bars, discarded memories
of pain, poverty, despair.

Your urgent pulse like
the beat of a drum
reminds me of your disenchanting self
through letters,
rationed income, rationed peace
kindling a hopelessness
that kills day after day.
Yes, I breathe like you,
voluptuous tormentor.

You're wearing a blood-soaked
garment; souls of your children
nurtured with your own soil and
massacred by your religions.

I love you, I hate you
my land, my people
loosen your gentle fingers
will you?

The Garba

CHITRA BANERJEE DIVAKARUNI

The nine sacred nights of Navaratri
we dance the Garba. Light glances
off the smooth wood floor of the gym
festooned with mango leaves
flown in from Florida. The drummers
have begun, and the old women,
singing of Krishna and the milkmaids.
Their high keening is an electric net
pulling us in, girls who have never seen

the old land. This October night
we have shed our jeans
for long red skirts, pulled back
permed hair in plaits, stripped off
nail polish and mascara, and pressed
henna onto hands, kohl
under the eyes. Our hips
move like water to the drums.
Thin as hibiscus petals, our skirts
swirl up as we swing and turn.
We ignore the men

creaseless in bonewhite kurtas.
In the bleachers, they smile behind their hands.
Whisper. Our anklets shine
in the black light from their eyes.
Soon they will join us in the Dandia dance.
The curve and incline, the slow arc
of the painted sticks meeting red on black
above our upraised arms. But for now

the women dance alone,
a string of red anemones
flung forward and back

by an unseen tide. The old ones sing
of the ten-armed goddess.
The drums pound faster
in our belly. Our feet glide
on smooth wood, our arms
are darts of light. Hair, silver-braided,
lashes the air like lightning.
The whirling is a red wind
around our thighs. Dance sweat
burns sweet on our lips.
We clap hot palms like thunder. And

the mango branches grow into trees.
Under the flashing feet,
the floor is packed black soil.
Damp faces gleam and flicker in torchlight.
The smell of harvest hay
is thick and narcotic
in our throats. We spin and spin
back to the villages of our mothers' mothers.
We leave behind

the men, a white blur,
like moonlight on empty bajra fields
seen from a speeding train.

Navaratri Hindu festival celebrating goddess Durga or Amba lasting nine days

Garba traditional Gujarati women's folk dance performed during the Navratri festival

Dandia ras a traditional Gujarati dance in which both men and women dance in a circle; each participant uses two colorful sticks

Conformists Trip

LALITA GANDBHIR

It's a party.
Amar and Neena arrive with their kids and promptly separate.
Amar joins other men in the living room.
With their drinks they talk
stocks, real estate and jobs.
The kids head toward the basement,
Neena joins other women in the kitchen.
She does not forget to offer help to the hurried hostess.
Most women are dressed in salwar kamiz or sarees
and talk of children, jewelry, sarees and recipes.
Neena overhears men's discussion
and has an urge to comment.
Though she has the knowledge,
she supresses the urge
and avoids temptation to discuss the topic
with another woman at the party,
in deference to traditional roles.

Dinner is served.
Women feed the young children.
Some fix plates for their husbands,
engrossed in lively arguments.
Dinner's finished.
Women scramble to help the hostess.
After many "Please don't bothers" and "Thank yous,"
the kitchen is cleaned and dishes put away.
Party is over.
Couples with their kids start to trickle out.

Neena and Amar say "Good-Bye, Thank You" and leave with their kids.

Yes, it was a short trip into the era gone by,
as we recreate the India as it was
complete with male and female roles.

52

Though we are so unlike our mothers
and hypocrisy torments us,
we feel obligated to hold onto a piece of our culture
in this new world.

On my back

LATIKA MALKANI

Lying
on my back
I watch
the glass of juice on the windowsill
fall
staining the sheets.
Thinking about
moving again
feeling weak
rootless
making me crazy.
Thinking about
the craziness of all the world
about
wanting approval
but fearing the blueness
accepting my sentence
an easy acquittal.

Thinking about
a solid element
not gas or liquid
a kitchen
of cousins
(where aunties argue
and talk-story).

Thinking that
we need to plant our feet on grass
even though it's gonna move
and send us marching again.

And thinking that
with a paintbrush

we'd color this world clearer than it's ever been
and then
we'd reach a place
where tangerine sheets don't bother anyone.

Feminist Consciousness In Woman-Centered Hindi Films

SHAMITA DAS DASGUPTA

Movies are considered to be the most popular medium of mass communication in India. Although the impact of movies on the Indian populace has not yet been studied systematically, scholars focusing on films as popular culture speculate that its influence is quite strong. This influence may be estimated crudely by the fact that in the last two decades several film stars have been achieving resounding victories over veteran politicians in major elections. Not only have film stars been gaining footholds in politics, but they have been steadily coming to the forefront in many other arenas of social activity. Bombay film actors have lately been leading environmental, communal harmony, anti-dislocation, social change movements, as well as heading organizations in India.

Interestingly, the far reaching influence of Hindi films does not stop at the geographic borders of the country of their origin. When Indian immigrants reached the shores of the U.S., they brought with them their love for the familiar world of Hindi movies. In a new and unfamiliar country, the immigrants sought collective symbols that would represent continuity through their dislocation. As Indian immigrants started arriving in the United States en masse, specialty shops carrying Indian groceries and films on videotape mushroomed all over the country. These ethnic stores have served the unique purpose of re-establishing connections between immigrant Indians and Hindi films in the new world.

The Asian-Indian Immigrant Community and Hindi Films

The Indian immigrants who came to this country after 1965 have aspired to be economically successful in America while preserving their cultural uniqueness. As a way of successfully retaining their traditional culture, many have adopted a pattern of renewing their cultural commitments on a regular basis. The community continues to develop vast networks of temples, associations and festivities. Hindi films have become a common way for immigrants to keep in touch with their natal culture.

The significance of Hindi films in the lives of immigrants may be partially assessed by the popularity that film personalities seem to enjoy in the expatriate community. Almost invariably, Hindi film stars perform to huge crowds of Asian-Indians at entertainment mega-events in major U.S. cities. Film stars from Bombay are often chief speakers at Indian political, social and cultural functions that take place in the U.S. The role of "Grand Marshal" of parades held to celebrate auspicious occasions in the immigrant community, such as India's

Independence Day, are generally reserved for Hindi film stars. To showcase their talent at Indian-American beauty contests and other community festivities, daughters of immigrants dress according to the latest fashions of Bombay cinema and dance to songs from Hindi films.

We must recognize that the urgency with which the Asian-Indian community is determined to preserve and continue its cultural identity goes far beyond the lives of the original immigrants. Indian parents expose their children to values, attitudes and behaviors congruent with the traditional Indian culture. Thus, along with religious ceremonies, cultural events, language classes and regular visits to India, they use Hindi films as subtle teaching tools. Since Hindi films serve as a cultural link in the lives of immigrants, it is imperative that we examine the messages imparted by these films.

Commercial versus New Wave Hindi Films

The bulk of Hindi films produced each year are a mixture of family-drama, romance and action-violence, with a generous sprinkling of song and dance. These films are popularly referred to as "masala" or formula films. The treatment of women in Hindi "masala" films has been a concern of feminists and social scientists in both India and the U.S. Generally, the presentation of "good" women in commercial Hindi films has been without variety. They are portrayed as long-suffering and submissive. The ideal woman in Hindi films has traditionally been a controlled, chaste, surrendering individual, not afraid of sacrifices for the good of her family. The "bad" woman, on the other hand, has been depicted as westernized, individualistic and sexually aggressive, ready to lead men to their ruin. Ignoring the actual variability in the lives and responses of women, the Hindi film industry has repeatedly reinforced the notion that the glory of ideal Indian womanhood lies in the tolerance she shows toward society and men, even when she is brutalized and victimized.

This routine depiction of women in commercial films was challenged by a small number of directors who came to be known as the "new wave" group. The beginning of this trend is generally traced to the end of the 1960s. The films made by these directors started a parallel movement to provide an alternative to the stereotypical Hindi "masala" melodramas. The new wave films avoided formula themes and focused on portraying social realities. More than any other topic, exploration of women's status and social roles became pet themes for new wave directors. Women's subordinate position in society and the conditions that generate it were featured repeatedly in these films. Unfortunately, the movement did not last long. It started to fade within a decade of its beginning.

Despite its short life, new wave cinema has affected formula films and the film industry significantly. The popularity and financial success of new wave films affected various aspects of commercial movies, including the portrayal and treatment of women on screen. During the late 1980s, dozens of Hindi films, in which women retaliate for atrocities meted out to them, were produced in the commercial line. Films such as *Sherni* (Tigress), *Zakhmi Aurat* (An Injured Woman), *Mera Shikar* (My Prey) and *Bhrashtachar* (Foul Behavior) present women as avengers who punish miscreants on behalf of their families and themselves. Even the character of the "mother" in Hindi cinema has undergone a drastic change. Mothers are now being portrayed as vital, attractive and assertive, fighting against injustices even if they have to oppose their husbands.

There has been an increase in the number of films with women as main characters. In addition, the representation of women on the Hindi filmscreen has undergone shifts that many have claimed to be feminist. However, these films have yet to be analyzed for their underpinnings of feminist consciousness. Here I evaluate a select group of Hindi films to assess the extent to which a feminist consciousness is present. Feminist consciousness is defined here as an awareness of women as victims of social oppression and the patriarchal world order. I also examine the extent to which Hindi films articulate the issues and concerns of women as a group whose legitimate rights are being infringed upon by an unfair social system. The intention of this paper is not to critique the cinematographic merits of the films but to assess the images of women they portray and the feminist issues they voice.

Analysis of Woman-Centered Hindi Films

The sample for this study was drawn from a random selection of fifty full-length feature films, produced between 1975 and 1990. Out of the pool of fifty, only sixteen were retained for this analysis. The films were available on videotapes in Indian stores in a midwestern city and an east coast town. All sixteen films selected for this study had overt feminist themes and articulated issues concerning women. Eleven of these sixteen films are considered to be new wave, whereas the other five cannot be categorized as such. All the films in the sample were produced during the heyday of the new wave movement, in the 1980s. The high percentage of woman-centered films in this sample does not necessarily reflect the realities of the Hindi cinema market. The sample may have been affected by the idiosyncrasies of individual store owners who select the inventory of videos each shop carries.

Among the sixteen films included in the analysis, there is a definite class bias in the selection of protagonists. The central figures of only two films are tribal or lower-class poor women, living in urban slums or villages. One other film, *Kamla,* portrays a poor tribal woman whose character is overshadowed by a rich and sophisticated urban heroine. In total then, only three films in this sample provide glimpses of the lifestyles of poor classes in modern India. Three other movies, *Mandi, Umraojaan* and *Mirch Masala* are period pieces. The rest of the films deal with women of the upper classes.

This study divides the films, by their dominant themes, into two broad categories: (1) description of women's status in society and (2) protest against women's subservient role. Three subcategories, victimization of women, women's right to make decisions and the development of women's identity and autonomy, were also identifiable in the films. None of the categories were set a priori, but emerged after the films were viewed. Nonetheless, the categories could hardly be labeled mutually exclusive, since most of the films combine the two thematic categories. For the analysis, therefore, the films were grouped according to the dominant themes.

Description of women's status in society. The focus of this category of films is the depiction of the existing state of affairs of women. The majority of these movies deal with victimization of women in various spheres of life. However, they are limited to mainly descriptive presentations, and protests or impetus toward change are left implicit.

Victimization of women. The issue that seemed to provoke the filmmakers most is that of victimization of women in society. Either directly or indirectly, twelve out of sixteen films deal with this topic. Women are presented in these films as helpless prey in the hands of powerful men and of an even more powerful social system. Women's existence as individual beings is shown to have negligible value in society. In many cases, even women's survival is threatened without the support of men. They are easily brutalized by their husbands—or by powerful men in society as an indirect way of punishing their protectors—cruelly sold in the marriage market to the highest bidder, and unfeelingly discarded when men have no further use for them. For instance in *Kamla,* an urban journalist purchases a woman in a village market as proof of the continuing flesh trade in India. He abuses her further by displaying her as an object to his colleagues in the city. While he glorifies himself as a liberator of poor women, he is unable to recognize his own complicity in his own wife's oppression.

Three movies specifically focus on the traditional system of arranged marriage as a tool of social oppression and a means of denying women their individual wishes. In all three films, women are married off without consent and against their active opposition. In one case, where a woman dares to exert her wishes she suffers the breach of her fiance's promises and the ensuing social humiliation.

Nine films deal with the overt sexual exploitation of women. These films show that prostitution, rape, traffic in women, abduction and other sexual violence against women have become institutionalized in society. A clear difference emerges in the types of brutality women of differing classes suffer in these films. In five films lower-class poor women were shown as victims of the most blatant indignities and the severest physical abuses. In *Aakrosh,* two tribal women are shown as the victims of horrifying rape and murder. In the beginning of the film, the wife of an activist who rises against the rich and powerful men in the village is brutally raped and murdered. In collusion with the village chiefs, the law enforcement officials arrest the activist for this murder. Later, the activist himself publicly murders his unmarried younger sister, as the life of a woman would not be worth living without any male protection. In contrast to these overt brutalizations, the victimization of upper-class women in this category of films seems to be more indirect, subtle and psychological.

Protest against women's subservient role in society. This category of films distinctly claims social rights for women and articulates egalitarian values.

Women's right to make decisions. A woman's right to make decisions is a theme that recurs in nine movies. These films present the female role in Indian society as highly restrictive. Since a woman's status is defined by her male protector, the female role is marked by a complete dependency on him and his decisions. The films in this category critique the validity of this oppressive system and champion women's self-determination. The exploration of choice is definitely not limited to finding partners of the opposite sex, but extends to lifestyles as well. Women protagonists in five films revolt against the patriarchal system by boldly choosing a lifestyle they desire. These women rebel against the ideology of unquestioningly obeying their husbands and leave home rather than accept a situation they cannot abide. In four films women opt for a life of work outside their homes, and in two cases they even forsake the traditional security of a husband. The protagonists in the three films reject the traditional system of marriage and the spouses picked for them by their elders.

Except for those in *Mirch Masala* and *Umraojaan,* the female protagonists in this category belong to the upper classes of society and are educated as well as affluent. In *Mirch Masala,* a story set in the end of the last century, two women of different classes dismiss the dictates of the powerful men in their village, risking violence in order to follow their conscience. In *Umraojaan,* a story of a nineteenth-century courtesan, we witness an outcast woman's fight to assert the right to choose her own lifestyle.

Women's identity and autonomy. The development of women's identity, as separate individuals, with hopes, desires and ambitions of their own, is the theme of only four films. However, these four films depict the gradual awakening of consciousness in upper-class women. Enjoying privileges that their class affords them, they suddenly come face to face with situations that shake the foundations of their euphoric existence. As a result, they become aware of the psychological conditions that keep them and all women subjugated in society. The films then concentrate on the process of development of their individual identities. In *Arth,* the affluent and sophisticated heroine is suddenly left to fend for herself when her hitherto loving husband gets involved with another woman. His betrayal pushes her to independence, both emotionally and financially. Through the process of acquiring the tools for survival, she discovers her own autonomous identity and develops an awareness of women's plight in society.

Through their process of awakening, the protagonists of these films not only understand the need for women to have distinct identities, they come to recognize economic self-sufficiency as an essential component of emancipation. This particular wisdom seems to propel them toward a struggle to gain financial independence from their spouses. The upper-class heroines of these films definitely do not represent the average Indian woman, but her highly educated and westernized counterpart.

Discussion

The films in this study manifest a strong class bias regarding the types of subjugation and victimization that women suffer in society. All sixteen movies analyzed in this study clearly recognize that economic independence is critical to a woman's struggle for independence. However, for the lower-class woman, the fight for autonomy remains limited to gaining financial stability and physical security. The issue of gaining psychological freedom and individual identity seems to be reserved for her upper-class sister. Lower-class women, portrayed in only four movies, are meted out more blatantly brutal physical and sexual abuses—such as rape, murder, abduction and trafficking. In these films, while lower-class women suffer public brutalization, upper-class women are victimized subtly within the private sphere. They meet with psychological oppression within the family. However, the films' depictions of upper-class women living lives without violence is a distortion of reality. Women's everyday experience of domestic violence and sexual abuse among all classes is evidence to the fact that class is hardly a protector against gender-based violence.

Although all sixteen movies in this sample deal with the unconventional topic of women's emancipation, only two, *Subah* and *Mirch Masala,* show the courage of being truly optimistic. In all the other films, when women revolt against the patriarchal system, their victories are ultimately rendered Pyrrhic as they are forced to give in to the anguish of a lonely

and discontented life: poverty-stricken women in the films *Chakra* and *Aakrosh* are defeated by social forces that are too powerful for them; the sex-worker protagonists of *Umraojaan,* "*Mandi,* and *Bhavna* either die or succumb to a life of despair while the exploitation continues; the middle-class heroines of *Khandhar* and *Yeh Nazdikiyaan* are doomed to lead desolate lives.

In most other films where women revolt against their spouses, they are either forced to accept their husbands' terms for reconciliation or are relentlessly destroyed by the social juggernaut. In *Kamla,* a movie touted for its pro-feminist stance, the heroine, through a crisis, awakens to the inequities inherent in a woman's role, only to compromise in the end by agreeing to stand by her man in his time of need. In *Arth,* another film centered on women's psychological emancipation, the heroine takes a bold step by refusing to reconcile with her contrite husband, but then she reinforces her femininity by embracing motherhood. That women can be alone and happy is still an unacceptable concept on the Indian screen. In *Ek Baar Phir,* a film about women's right to choose her partner, the educated upper-class heroine leaves her husband's home only after she finds a boyfriend to support her. In *Log Kya Kahenge,* the heroine takes the ultimate step in asserting her right to choose her spouse: she murders the husband forced on her. Consequently, she is punished not only by the law of the land but by divine justice—she becomes insane. In almost none of the movies do we see women winning the battle of equality. They seem to be doomed from the beginning.

The two definite exceptions in this bleak and pessimistic parade of films are *Subah* and *Mirch Masala.* The upper-class heroine of *Subah* not only establishes her right to work for a career, she ultimately chooses a lifestyle that has no place for her somewhat insensitive husband. In her search to find independence and individual identity, she leaves behind her child. A contrast to this individualized feminism is *Mirch Masala,* a story set in the late nineteenth century in an Indian village. The working-class heroine rejects the sexual advances of a powerful colonial official, thereby incurring the wrath of the men of her village. While the men decide to hand her over to the official, the women of the village unite across class lines to execute resistance. This resistance occurs at several levels: at home, at work and in the community—against official oppressions, individual men, the whole community and traditions. Finally, the women win by utilizing indigenous tools of resistance. They defeat the official by throwing ground chili powder in his eyes; the powder they themselves produce in the village factory. *Mirch Masala* is also the only film in this sample where collective action by women is shown as a powerful method of resistance and of bringing about change.

Notwithstanding the tendency to glamorize and romanticize, a consciousness regarding women's rights seems to be emerging in this set of films. Indisputably, the Hindi film industry has produced some films that are dealing with certain issues and concerns of women. However, the films remain limited in the scope of their exploration of gender inequalities. The majority of films restrict their vision to direct violence perpetrated on women. Inequities in occupational opportunities and wages, lack of maternity leave, barriers to upward mobility, and women's resistance and agency are generally ignored in these films. Furthermore, although the films in this sample purport to stand in defense of women, they still do not portray them as completely autonomous individuals. For example, women are invisible as workers. Also, we hardly ever get a glimpse of other aspects of a woman's life, such as her

friendships with other women, interactions with different social institutions, or her ambitions. All the films are preoccupied with women's relationships to men. Such simplistic representations of women tend to ignore complexities in their lives and reduce them to one-dimensional beings.

Although these films portray women's lack of rights in society, there is a general reluctance to draw the analysis to its final conclusion: equality. The films have curtailed their visions to representations of women only as victims in an androcentric world. In these films, women who dare to resist patriarchal mandates are invariably forced to compromise or be destroyed. They rarely emerge as victors in the struggle for equality. In fact, the films seem to be torn between contradictory messages. On the one hand, they purport that women should be treated justly in society, and on the other, they fall short in letting women deviate from the traditional role prescriptions. If not overtly, at least covertly, sacrifice and surrender are still women's crowning virtues.

The messages transmitted by these films to their viewers are not very encouraging; neither can they be labeled as feminist. Although there is acknowledgment that a woman's lot is unfair, little hope is offered regarding changing that situation. The inherent message in these films seems to be that women who resist patriarchal domination cannot expect to be rewarded for their actions.

As diasporic Asian-Indians continue to view Hindi films, it is vital that we critically study the messages inherent in this mode of cultural reproduction. To dismiss cinema only as a source of entertainment is to overlook the significance it has in influencing human behavior. A medium as powerful as Hindi films may be harnessed to carry messages congruent with the principles of gender equality in realistic terms. Otherwise, we may be condemning our daughters and sons to participate in the traditional power imbalances that have plagued our films and our society.

Table 1. List of Films Viewed

Names of Films	Year Released	Director
1. Aakrosh * ✦	1980	G. Nihalani
2. Agni Pariksha	1981	K. Mazumdar
3. Ahista Ahista	1981	I. Shroff
4. Ardh Satya	1983	G. Nihalani
5. Arth * ✦	1983	M. Bhatt
6. Bato Bato Mein	1979	B. Chatterjee
7. Bazaar *	1982	S. Sarhadi
8. Bemisaal	1979	H. Mukherjee
9. Bhavna * ✦	1984	P. Bhatt
10. Chakra * ✦	1981	R. Dharmaraj
11. Chupke Chupke	1975	H. Mukherjee
12. Dillagi	1979	B. Chatterjee

Names of Films	Year Released	Director
13. Disco Dancer	1982	B. Subhash
14. Do Aur Do Panch	1980	R. Kumar
15. Don	1980	C. Barot
16. Ek Baar Phir * ✦	1982	V. Pande
17. Ek Din Achanak	1990	M. Sen
18. Ek Hi Bhool *	1981	T. Rama Rao
19. Grihapravesh	1980	B. Bhattacharya
20. Jadugar	1989	P. Mehra
21. Jeewan Dhara	1982	T. Rama Rao
22. Jung Baaz	1989	M. Kumar
23. Kaamchor	1983	B. Chatterjee
24. Kabhi Kabhi	1976	Y. Chopra
25. Kamla * ✦	1984	S. Mundra
26. Katha	1984	S. Paranjape
27. Khandhar * ✦	1983	M. Sen
28. Kissese Na Kahana	1983	H. Mukherjee
29. Lakshmi	1982	B. S. Thapa
30. Lamhe	1990	Y. Chopra
31. Log Kya Kahenge *	1979	B. R. Ishara
32. Mandi * ✦	1983	S. Benegal
33. Mehendi Rang Layegi *	1982	D. N. Rao
34. Mein Intequam Loonga	1982	T. Rama Rao
35. Mirch Masala * ✦	1987	K. Mehta
36. Mohan Joshi Hazir Ho	1982	S. A. Mirza
37. Panchwin Manzil	1982	J. Sidana
38. Paar	1987	G. Ghosh
39. Rocky	1981	S. Dutt
40. Shakti	1982	R. Sippy
41. Silsila	1981	Y. Chopra
42. Sindoor Bane Jwala	1981	D. N. Rao
43. Shradhanjali	1981	A. Gangooly
44. Spandan	1984	B. RoyChoudhury
45. Subah * ✦	1984	J. Patel
46. Umraojaan *	1981	M. Ali
47. Vijeta	1982	G. Nihalani
48. Yeh Nazdikiyaan ✦	1982	V. Pandey
49. Yeh to Kamal Ho Gaya	1976	T. Rama Rao
50. Zanjeer	1973	P. Mehra

* Films retained for study
✦ New wave films

To My Grandmother

AMITA VASUDEVA

I want to speak with you Mathaji
To let the rhythm of the
Punjabi words roll off my tongue
To tell you who I am
To tell you
How I think
To tell you…

I want to hear
Our family's history
To hear
Stories of your childhood
To hear you tell
Your memories of the British rule and India's partition.

I long to know how you think
I long to exchange ideas with you.

But I am trapped by my English Only
Tongue that keeps me from explaining.
I am shut off from you by my English Only
Ears that don't always understand.

Purification

gracepoore

It was there one afternoon—a stain on my panties, the color of dried plantain juice. "Amma, I have a brown patch on my pants," I said at the lunch table.

Mother dropped the ball of curried rice she was about to pop in her mouth, and stared at me. "What patch? Where?" she rapped.

"I dunno. It just came. On my knickers." I noticed a strange look on her face. In silence she kept her eyes on me, then tossed the ball of rice into her mouth and chewed.

I bit into a piece of chicken. Of all the chicken curries I had tasted at other people's homes on Deepavali, Mother's was the best. She made it so her chicken was tender without falling apart in shreds inside the gravy. Her spices blended just right so the hotness didn't stick in your throat. I picked another piece of chicken off my plate, curry collecting in the creases of my palm and soaking into my finger tips. Long after I had eaten, the scent would remain as it always did with the curries that my mother made.

"Ma, can I ride Peter's bike after I finish my homework?" Jeevan's voice crashed through the silence. He was my nine-year-old brother. Dad did not like him riding bicycles since the time he fell and grazed his knee so badly, he had a purple scab for two months.

Mother ignored Jeevan. She went on shaping another ball of rice in her plate while he sat licking his fingers. Jeevan tried again, "Ma, can I…"

"How many times have I told you not to lick your fingers. If you've finished eating, go and wash your hands," Mother scolded even before he could complete his sentence.

"But I haven't finished eating," Jeevan complained.

"Then hurry up and finish," Mother snapped and poured a glass of water.

Jeevan was not ready to give up on the bicycle and went on pestering her. "So, can I ride Peter's…"

"Take your food into the hall, Jeevan," Mother jerked her head sideways and turned to him. I looked at her.

"But you're the one who told us not to eat in the hall," Jeevan argued.

"Take your food and eat it in the hall. I want to talk to Geeta."

"But why?" Jeevan whined.

"Will you stop asking bloody questions and just do what I tell you? Take your plate and get out there!" Mother yelled, her hands furiously mixing curry and rice.

Jeevan knew he was in for trouble if he stayed one minute longer. He picked up his plate and walked out of the kitchen. Mother thrust back her chair, went to the sink, washed her hands and disappeared into the bedroom. I followed her, my lunch and hers half-eaten on the table.

65

Behind closed doors, she thrust a soft white object at me and said in a cold voice, "Put this between your legs." I stared at what she held out to me, a large slice of bread with a loop on each end. "Put it in your panties," she ordered.

I took the bread from her. One side felt smooth like one of Mother's saris, the other side a little rough, with a fine net-like surface and a blue line running up and down the middle.

"Go on. What are you waiting for? Adjust that between your thighs," Mother broke into my thoughts.

I had no idea what to do. "How, Amma?" I asked.

"Can't you do a simple thing?" she bristled and snatched the pad from me. Then she picked up her sari, lifted it halfway up, and held the pad between her thighs. I had never seen anything above mother's knees, so the sight of her thighs made me forget the pad. There she stood, exposed, green lines snaking under her light brown skin. Instantly, Mother noticed and pulled her sari down. In her eyes I saw what I felt in my heart, and I wished I had never seen my mother's thighs. Then it was my turn.

I kept trying to hold my skirt down while fumbling with the pad inside my panties, unable to see what I was doing, yet unwilling to expose myself like she had. Then I heard her say, "This evening, when Dad comes home, he'll get a belt for the pad." I wondered where the belt would go. Mother went on. "You put the loops into the belt hooks so the pad won't move."

"How long do I wear this?"

"Till your period is over. Every time it gets dirty, you change it. There's newspaper under the sink. Wrap the pads in that and throw them in the front dustbin, not the one in the kitchen. Take it to the front, understand?" I pulled the panties up over the pad. "Tomorrow, you stay home. I'll write a note to your teacher."

But I had a netball game. I had to go. "Ma, Mrs. Koh told us not to be absent. I'm playing netball."

"I'll write a note," she silenced me.

"But Mrs. Koh said not to be absent."

"I'm telling you, you can't go."

"But I'm not sick, why can't I go?"

"When did you get such a big mouth? You aren't going and that's final."

"But Mrs. Koh…"

"Who the hell is Mrs. Koh? Is she feeding you or am I? If Dad hears you talking like this, you'll get a bloody lashing." I felt the pad lodged between my thighs. I remembered Dad's terrible temper; I thought about the brown stain, and held my breath.

Mother opened the door and walked out. I sat on the bed and cried quietly. How would I explain to my teammates? What would Mrs. Koh think? Through the open door, I watched Mother clearing away the lunch dishes and felt tears roll down the bridge of my nose.

The next five days were a mystery. Mother gave rules she had never given me before. "Don't take the dog out, don't let Jeevan sit on your bed, don't you dare wash your hair today, you'll get black circles under your eyes. Wait another three days."

Then she screamed, "How many times have I got to tell you, throw the pads in the front dustbin!"

When I yelled back, "I forgot, Ma," she got angry and screamed even louder, "I've told you before, that's girls' stuff and you have to be careful not to let Jeevan see it."

Jeevan never knew why I stayed home from school. Dad told him to mind his own business when he asked about me. I never said a word because Mother said not to. So Jeevan told the neighborhood boys that I had chicken pox.

Twice a day, Mother made me eat a stiff sweet paste of crushed green peas mixed with brown sugar. In the mornings, she forced me to swallow raw egg yolks and drink ginger oil to strengthen my womb. Meanwhile, a tight pink elastic belt girdled my waist and cut into my flesh. My brown stain became a sticky red liquid which Mother called "menses." My stomach ached right below my belly button and all through my lower back.

For a week I missed school. I thought about the netball games and wondered if I would ever play again. Once or twice, I asked Dad if I could go to school. At first, he just said no. The second time, he threatened to smack me so I stopped asking. Most of the week I stayed in bed and read Enid Blyton's mystery books. This part was fun, the only part that was fun.

Soon the pain in my stomach stopped and the blood started to go away. Mother told me I could soak my clothes with the others' again, and I did not have to hang my panties at the far end of the clothes line where spiders built cobwebs to catch beetles.

Just when my sickness was nearly gone, Mother gave me something I had only seen in Tamil movies, a costume that women wore when they danced before a king or some rich man who turned out to be a villain. She gave me a satin, yellow midriff blouse and a sweeping, yellow sequinned skirt made from one of her new georgette saris. The skirt came down to the ankles and the blouse had press studs down the front and little eared sleeves.

"Tomorrow you wear this," she said. "Uncles and aunts are coming here and pastor is doing a prayer service for you."

"Why are they praying?" I asked.

"It's our custom. Every girl must go through it," she answered, ending the conversation.

All day that day, Mother stood over the kerosene stove, cooking Indian sweets. She grumbled about the price of cardamom and worried about not having enough food to feed the guests. When I asked her again why people were coming to our house, she said it was a celebration. When I asked what we were celebrating, she scolded me for wasting her time and told me to leave the kitchen.

At three o'clock the next afternoon relatives poured into our small terrace house, invading every room except mine. Mother said I had to stay in the room till she called. I lay in bed, listening to the laughter and chatter around me. Two aunts came in to ask how I felt. My cousins peeked through open window louvres. Uncles stood at the door, glancing at me occasionally, but never venturing close.

After awhile, they all left me alone. I tried to read *The Mystery of The Missing Red Coat*, but my mind kept wandering outside. Soon, only my eyes were in the book. My ears pulled my head outside, to the stories floating around behind the closed door. Uncle Arthur was having a cataract operation. Aunt Esther was going to marry an engineer. Mrs. Dorai's daughter failed Oxford. Cousin Joshua's son was coming back with a Jaffna bride.

From the kitchen, smells of mother's cooking wafted through the house. I had watched her pile our special rose-colored plates with gulab jamuns glistening with thick sugar syrup.

She had unwrapped fish-shaped steel trays from tissue paper and arranged golden ladhus next to creamy white burfi. This morning, she filled Pyrex bowls with chicken curry and yellow rice spiked with cloves and cinnamon sticks. I lay on the bed and tasted her food on the back of my tongue, wondering when we would eat.

As the sun turned a bright orange outside, Mother came into my room. "Grandcousin Ivy is going to bathe you now," she said and left. I sat on the edge of the bed, terrified. I didn't know grandcousin Ivy.

"Geeta, come. Your bath is waiting." I heard Mother call. I waited by the door. Someone knocked and said, "Geeta, your amma is calling," but I did not move. Maybe if I stayed in the room, Mother would come in again and I'd ask her about grandcousin Ivy. But Mother did not come in. Instead Dad tapped on the louvres. "Oi! Geeta, Amma is calling you. Are you deaf?"

I turned the door knob and stepped out. The uncles stopped talking. The aunts smiled. I suddenly felt trapped and ashamed. Why were they looking at me? What had I done?

The hallway leading to the bathroom seemed to go on forever. I kept walking, my eyes to the floor. Something gripped the middle of my stomach and I felt my legs grow weak.

When I reached the bathroom, grandcousin Ivy was waiting. I had never seen her before. I looked down at her feet and saw a covered pot. I entered the bathroom.

"Come, take off your clothes," she said. I had never undressed before another human being. Not since I was seven and knew the meaning of shame, knew that Jeevan was no longer my brother but a boy, that uncles were no longer uncles but men, and girls were girls who must hide their bodies.

I looked shyly at grandcousin and tried to catch her eye, but she fussed with the towels and pretended not to see me. I shifted from one foot to the other, all the time looking at her face.

Suddenly, she snapped, "Tcheh! Come on, come on. Hurry up. I haven't got all day." I tried to unfasten the buttons on my dress but my fingers were frozen.

"I say, what's this nonsense? Don't stand there like a statue, child. I've seen dozens of crotches before." I winced at her vulgarity. Who was this woman with a hard, proud face? Why did Mother invite her?

Grandcousin bent down and took the cover off the pot. A powerful smell of warm milk rose up and filled the air. Then she straightened up and looked at me, hands on her hips, waiting.

My hands shook as they passed over each button. Finally, the last one was undone. I stood naked against the cool tiles of the bathroom wall. Grandcousin signalled for me to come forward. I moved towards her and squatted on the floor. Mumbling a prayer in Tamil, she picked up the pot and tipped it over my head. Warm milk streamed lazily down my eyes, soaked into my hair and clung to my eyelashes.

"Okay, everything is done!" she announced. I saw the whiteness of the milk against my skin and remembered the time when we had moved into this house. Dad had boiled milk on a charcoal stove in the middle of the living room floor so that our house would be protected from evil spirits. Mother said the milk would purify the air.

I remembered that time, six years ago, and suddenly I understood everything. The milk was purifying me. It was taking away the pollution of my blood.

Grandcousin left the bathroom. I stayed to wash up, to scrub away the sickening liquid, drying quickly on my body. I soaped and scratched at the milk, hating it, hating her, hating them...most of all, hating my blood.

When the bath was over, I dressed in the sequinned skirt and shiny blouse. Mother led me out in front of the relatives and made me sit next to her. The Reverend Thangaraj read a prayer and offered a blessing. A hymn was sung, the benediction received. Then, all eyes fell on me. They studied my face, my hair, the color of my skin. They looked carefully to see if I would make a suitable daughter-in-law someday. Finally, done with their scrutiny, they came over and shook my hand.

At the other end of the room, Dad stood up and invited the guests to begin eating. Soon, one by one, they swarmed over the feast Mother had laid out for them and forgot my presence. I sat in my chair and watched them. Amidst the smells of ladhus and gulab jamuns, chicken curry and spiced rice, I became invisible again.

Epilogue:

The Tamil custom of observing a girl's first menstruation through ritual and ceremony is an acknowledgement of her rite of passage to womanhood. While this custom can serve as a powerful and positive affirmation of her femaleness, in practice it evolved as a means for the girl's family to publicize their daughter's availability for marriage. Hence, the ceremony is more for the family than for the girl herself.

In time, as more and more middle-class urban Tamil families like mine encouraged education first, marriage later, women put off marriage until their mid or late twenties, even early thirties. With this development, it seemed as if the custom of celebrating a girl's first period would become an actual honoring of her rite of passage rather than a mechanism for placing her on the marriage market. Yet it hasn't. For while a Tamil girl may no longer need to marry when she is an adolescent or young teenager, her puberty marks the point at which she is ready to produce children via the institution of marriage. Hence, everything, from her dietary changes during her period to her ceremonial clothes, inform her and others around her that she has inherited the role and responsibility of being a potential wife-mother.

In my family, the menstruation ritual took on an added dimension due to their Christian belief that menstrual blood is impure. Not only was the girl to be "celebrated" for coming of age but she was also to be "cleansed."

The use of milk to purify is a Tamil and Hindu custom. However, as with many immigrants living in the South Asian diaspora, cultural practices persist in co-opted forms irrespective of religious affiliation or belief systems. Hence, cleansing with milk became simply a Tamil, no longer a Hindu, custom while serving a Tamil Christian function.

No doubt, exposing one's culture to a foreign audience is like sharing a family secret that discredits family honor. Yet there are practices in all cultures that need to be revised, re-interpreted, and/or eventually discarded because they disempower individuals. There was great hesitation in writing this story, an even greater hesitation in submitting it for publication, but it was a necessary act—to give voice to anger and to transform experience into narrative.

"Purification" is written for several reasons: to expose a custom that is meant to celebrate but in fact humiliates girls and women; to defy the silence that all cultures impose on those who question and challenge repressive customs; to protest forced participation of children in rituals that have no meaning to them, that frighten and strip them of their dignity as people; and to confront those who practice the very customs that disempowered them at some time in their lives, but who perpetuate them in exchange for social status, who pass on these traditions to the generations after them in the name of preserving a cultural heritage.

I write this story for my nieces so they will not have to go through what Geeta went through for growing up female in a christianized Tamil family.

Deepavali the Hindu Festival of Lights, to celebrate the return of the mythical hero Rama to Ayodha

The Little Yellow Jacket:
The One I Made Before You
Were Taken Away

HUMA DAR

What time was it when I switched the lights off?
What time was it when I stitched the last button on?
…on that little yellow jacket.
It was 5:00 a.m., 1st of January
I was up the whole night.
Stitching each stitch
with the threads of my love
for the flesh of my flesh
and the bones of my bones
for the fruit of my womb
and the light of my eyes.

Zavain!
Where are you now?
for eight months I carried you inside me
—yes, eight not nine!
because the man who claims you in court today
kicked me and hit me
pushed me and slapped me
till I bled…
The pain I suffered did not worry me
but the thought that I might lose you
before you were born
stole my sleep.
Did you feel my love then?
Do you feel my love now?

When you nursed at my breast
and looked deep into my eyes
the world dissolved around us.
The bedtime tale, the little prayer,
your head on my arm till you fell asleep

When will I have that peace again?
Eyes half-closed, calling me, hugging me,
when will you crawl into my early morning bed?
Zavu, do you really believe your father
when he says you'll die if you are with me?
The mother who fought death
to give birth to you
The mother who spent nights on the TV room chairs
because your crying disturbed your father
The mother who sleeps on your pillow to hug your fragrance
The mother who stitched that yellow jacket for you.

Obstacles of Abha Sharma Tyagi:
An Oral History

Interviewed by FRANCIS ASSISI
Transcribed by KIRAN LALL

It is time that somebody should listen to me.

I was married on 18th June '67. I came from India in '68, May 23rd. From '68 to '71 I was here when my husband was going to school. He has a Ph.D. from UC Berkeley in civil engineering. Now he is a professor. My son was born in Oakland.

My mother educated herself and she supported a family. She took care of the worldly side. My father, in India he is a saint! His name is Ramesh Chand Sharma. He used to be a teacher, a high school teacher. Whatever poor teachers make, half of that went to the charity. My father is a devotee of Ramakrishna and Vivekananda and ever since I was five years old, he has Jayanti every year and I talk about the life of Ramakrishna and Vivekananda. So this is the secret of my strength. God.

My earlier education was through Hindi and Sanskrit, so it took me a while. You know, English I learned as a second language and it was quite stressful. But once I went to graduate schools, it was okay. '79 was a monumental year for me. That time I was a linguistics Ph.D. candidate and my classmates were the United Nations. Students from Turkey, Czechoslovakia, France, Germany, Israel and of course America. I went to Austin, Texas for summer school and there was a mingling of some of the best minds. My own professor was Dr. Ingerman, Francis Ingerman, who has been in Hall of Fame.

And my husband, Avdesh, just wanted to control me—with money, with everything. He would beat me up because I wasn't getting good grades, he would beat me up because I wasn't cooking, he would beat me up because I was late coming home...things like that. I telegrammed Kennedy. That is my fatal attraction—Kennedy. Edward Kennedy. So I said I will join his campaign if he could feed me. That was the only thing, I was hungry. And that was the major episode when my husband really bruised me. I went to India and it took my father two months to heal me.

I came back and I was just very angry. Very angry. And then he beat me up again. Then he put me in the hospital. The memory is hazy. I don't want to recall that black hole in Oklahoma. But, during 1980 I stayed in the State Hospital for less than a week. And there also, there was nothing wrong. I was not tearing my clothes. I was not threatening to kill anybody or myself. It was all political. Just a system. He was the professor and I was nothing. By the time I hired an attorney and set in to divorce, he took me out of the hospital. He didn't

want the divorce; he wanted me under his control. He didn't know that I'm not a person to be controlled.

Ever since that, I'm after the system. After Mr. Watson and Freud...and all that professional psychiatry and psychology...I'd banish it if I could. The problem is that Dr. Watson and Mr. Freud have done a lot of damage to the human psyche. And Skinner. Those three were the worst psychologists and they influenced the whole thinking here in the West. You know, one year I spent in clinical psychology and I was just totally appalled by their thinking. I began to understand why these psychiatrists and psychologists have been reading meaning into my words and actions, which is not there, because of their thinking. I was impressed by Maslow's thinking. I could relate to the terms of self-realization and basic needs.

There are many psychologists and psychiatrists who I am going to sue ultimately for misdiagnosis, for increasing my misery instead of helping me out. There was a child psychologist who became our marriage counselor. He decided that I was manic-depressive, and that diagnosis was so ingrained that even my son thinks that he might have a tendency to it. And still there is no basis. Eventually I got the inside story. That man was a wife-abuser himself. It was my misfortune that I kept running into these people.

In Kansas I miscarried twice. You know, I was diagnosed to be psychologically pregnant. So I'm really a self-sufficient woman. I can produce my own children from my mind, my body. I don't need a man for that too. Truly a self-sufficient woman. With my first child, for four months I didn't know I was pregnant. I had no sign, like morning sickness or anything. And my period didn't stop. So of course I didn't know. And the same thing happened with my second child. My husband said, "Here you go again." Then the urine test was negative. And I just kept quiet for six weeks and then went for a blood test. And lo and behold I was pregnant. Then I was accused of not being pregnant with him. I said, then, whoever I am pregnant with, go ahead and kill it if I care. So I have been pregnant with God, then, if not him. I don't think that I am capable of self-producing, but if Mary produced Christ, maybe I can produce too. I don't know. You decide. I have become a modern mystery for modern medicine. My body here has been checked from toe to head, every single pore of it the government knows. Every pore of my body, there is record of it. And the only thing wrong with me is I get headaches which my mother gets too.

In '80 we went to an Indian conference in Toronto. I wanted to talk to FIA counsel in New York, on women—the status of women in Indian society. I wanted to cover from Rig Veda to current state. And by that time, I was going through a lot of inner thinking, sort of rebelling to the control he was putting me through. At that point, he was the faculty advisor for the International Student Association. The Indian Association. I drove from Toronto to New York against Avdesh's wishes. He tried everything to prevent me but I wouldn't hear of it. And there was an Indian Association there. A representative said that I can't represent Kansas. I said, "I'm not representing Kansas, I'm representing myself." Then I was told that since I am an American citizen, I cannot still participate there. And I was just totally...I was really upset. Two doctors from New Jersey came to help me and said that she is Indian, too, and she can be part of it.

I used to write poetry. I had a diary. And at the conference, I recall, many people talked to me. I was in the audience and I started asking those petty questions, so somebody included

me in the panel, and then they ultimately asked me to say something. But after, I was totally angry and upset. What I was originally planning to say, by that time, I wasn't ready to say it. So I read my poem. There was a reporter from *India Today* there and he said he wanted me to publish it. So I tore that page and gave it to him. After that my diary disappeared.

In '80 we moved from Kansas to Oklahoma. When my daughter was I think a couple of months old, I participated in ERA rally, that was a big rally in Oklahoma City. I was also member of NOW. So in Oklahoma I really started getting involved with women's organizations. Expressing my views and things. And I was penalized for that. I was put in the jail for causing disturbance at home, and for fighting with my son. Avdesh was still beating me up. I have all the police reports with me. I am sitting on it. And our son used to be mediator when he hit me. At one point he was totally confused. He was talking loud to me and I was talking loud to him. So mother could be put in the jail for talking loud to her son. And then, I was again. It was a sort of crisis. I couldn't understand these laws, these worldly laws, Oklahoma laws.

And worse, I was also jailed for two nights for a twenty-two dollar overdrawn check, while I was wearing a two hundred dollar business suit. I had jewelry that was more than two thousand dollars. I was jailed for two nights for twenty-two dollars. You know he was with them. And the system helped him. During that time I also tried to run a business. A gift business. And the Stillwater, Oklahoma merchant community did not treat me right. They would not do business with me and things like that. Also I bought a restaurant against his wishes.

In '84, there was the court hearing and Oklahoma gave him the children. I think somebody has been watching me and, behind the scenes, has been involved in my crucification. My three-year-old daughter was taken away from me. I lost the custody. Nobody could understand why. Then within six months, I went back to living with him. Very depressed. I couldn't bear her hurt. So when he asked me to come back, I went. So from '84 to '88 I lived there again and then I got a job here in California. The final decree was not filed.

In '88 I decided to move to California and my daughter decided to come with me and he let her come. And then for a year I worked with Burnwall Clinic in Simi Valley. Working with the stroke patients and they had start kits and all that. During that period I just burned out. So in April of '89 I had a very severe headache. I became disabled for six months and I went for workers compensations which is still in process. Nothing has come out of it. There was another girl they hired who was less experienced. They promoted her, gave her raise but they wouldn't give me medical aid. And when I was disabled they put me on medical hold. They fired me without any insurance. So they are also on my blacklist.

The decree was finalized on 18th June of '88, without my knowledge that he had done so. And on 21st June he was back here in California sleeping with me. And I'm amazed and scared of my own self. That over the years, the disparity that became. You know Avdesh started in the beginning encouraging me and crossing my "t's" and dotting my "i's" and then once I took off, I just left him behind so much that he could not relate to me. I had been always a first-class student and Sanskrit master, so my mind was already developed and it just was a matter of time. I just took off and left him behind. He was very jealous. One thing was that he was very, very jealous. I was teaching at the University of Arizona. At the time, I must have

75

been about twenty-two maybe. So these men I was teaching were mostly my age. Graduate students. They would stop after the class for some explanations like that, and we used to go for lunch there, and we would naturally walk outside the classroom and I'd be still explaining and he would ask me what I was talking about. I had to tell what I was talking about. So that was the main problem, over the years he just became very, very insecure and jealous, and yet I didn't see why.

So we are into '89. I interviewed with Cannerview State Hospital. They had a full-time position and I got the position. But they wanted my twenty years of medical history. Sacramento put a hold on it. So I was not hired there. Then I tried for a substitute position with Simi Valley school district. But they told me that because of my accent, they couldn't hire me. I should have taken that in writing. It was clear discrimination. And then I interviewed also with the Adventists Hospital there. They interviewed me and they didn't give me the job. As if somebody was pulling their strings and wanted me out of Simi Valley. So it came to that. I was with all this experience and all these degrees and I was standing in the welfare line. Totally demoralized and out of money. So Swami Swahananda of Vedanta temple loaned me thousand dollars. And in December of '89 I got this job here in Torrance.

My friends asked me who was next in line after I divorced. And I said there are only three eligible men: Prince Charles, Edward Kennedy and Governor Jerry Brown. And ever since, I have been carrying on this joke. I don't have delusions of grandeur. This is my way of protecting myself. I am fully aware that they will not marry me or will not be interested in me so just to keep men away from me.

Now I have, I think I have, realized myself. I have been alone now for two months. I have a lot of time to meditate on my guru mantra from Swami Swahananda and I am rather doing well. This is a point when I'm employed. I would not be labeled as a mentally deranged person, as people have tried to do to me. I have sort of integrated the paranormal and the normal and I am doing all the things a normal person does and yet I am doing some paranormal things. I feel very, very energetic. And I feel, when I close my eyes and meditate, a sort of blinding light. And some of these experiences my father has had and he has conveyed that to me.

Recently I was listening to Brian O'Leary, one of the astronauts. He has written a book on exploring the inner space and outer space. He was talking about the same things! And I said, "Hey! These people, all these so called sane people, are talking about it." I felt empowered. So I called the Senate and left a message there that let Bush know that I know that his boys have been after me for the last ten years and just lay off. And one of these days I'm going to sue the State of Kansas and the State of Oklahoma who put me in the hospitals and have really tortured me.

Now the time has come when people will not take me to be an abnormal person or sick. You take whatever angle you want, this is my story. I think it should be told. It is sensational. It has all the qualities of fiction but it is fact. I don't pretend to be a teacher or preacher, I am just a human being and I have rights to every pleasure a man has or more.

*

The Laborers Of
This War

Parvati

NATASHA PRATAP

It was study time again. Every evening after dinner, Parvati schooled her eight-year-old son. Together they had written out the English alphabet on a piece of cardboard discarded by a clerk in their neighborhood. Parvati was too poor to send Anand to a real school and she had long since given up expecting any help from her husband. He would lie in the darkest corner of their small but cozy, improvised hut and drink. When he was not drinking, he was hung over. He spoke only to ask Parvati for more money, but was still very much a part of the house—like an old piece of furniture that had outgrown its use, but hard to part with simply because it had been around so long.

Anand and Parvati sat by the single lantern in the room and talked. She did most of the talking. Parvati didn't discuss Maths, Science and Economics, but spoke instead of values, of honesty, respect and sometimes love. Anand listened attentively as always. He used to wish that he was in a proper school like some of the other kids. But Parvati made him realize that they didn't get to spend as much time with their mother as he did, and so he was happy.

The flame in the lantern flickered off. The kerosene was over. It was time to go to bed. Parvati straightened the mat they were sitting on, and spread an old sari over her son. As she kissed him goodnight, she whispered in his ear, "Keep these lessons in mind, son. You may be tested, but in the long run you won't be the loser."

Parvati moved the lantern back near the choolah, where she would need the light to cook the next day. She was as efficient in the dark as in the light. She took off her sari and began to pull her hairpins out. Her dark skin swept past the circular mirror taken from an old broken compact case. Bending her knees, she moved lower to see the bold line of red running through her middle parting. Appearing first on the day of her marriage, it had been with her ever since. She nurtured it as she did her son—a fresh layer each day building on the previous one. She stood silently for a minute or two and then moved towards her husband. Sitting next to him, she folded her hands and said a prayer. Then, hugging her legs in under her torn petticoat, she huddled close to him. He was already asleep.

Parvati's voice chimed through the Bhatt's flat as she sang popular Hindi film songs while washing the vessels. She chose either upbeat love songs from recent movies or classic numbers that contemplated life. She sang them both with equal vigor, often deliberately striking her copper bangles against the metal vessels to join her on a particular note. This was the last house she had to work at. It was always the last house because she had arranged her routine that way. The washroom in this house was the most comfortable. It was located in the back corner of the terrace flat and provided a view that made her job as pleasant as it

could possibly be. Every now and then Parvati would raise her head and take a deep look at the surrounding plants as if she were breathing them in. She knew green was good for the eyes. The dai had told her so when she was delivering Anand.

"Arré Parbati bai!" the woman in the house called out.

She never said Parvati's name correctly, assuming perhaps that Parvati would not care about finer points, or maybe even that she would not notice them. Parvati had noticed but she had decided it was no issue to argue about. "Coming Asha bhabhi!" she replied, washed her hands and went in.

Asha bhabhi was arranging some flowers in a vase in the bedroom. She turned towards Parvati when she felt her presence in the room. "Can you stay a little late tomorrow? It's Pinku's birthday and we're having a dinner. You know how it gets when there are so many people coming." She sounded almost apologetic. "I'll have to take out the new crockery. It's foreign and really delicate so it must be cleaned immediately after." Why did she always try to make things sound so out of her hands? "I don't think it will take very long but you definitely won't finish in one hour."

"I wouldn't mind at all, bhabhi, but my son Anand may get hungry if I stay too late." She could see Anand waiting at his usual spot outside the hut. He always got impatient after the sun had set and it was too dark to walk around.

"Oh, that's not a problem. You can take some food home from the dinner."

Parvati said that would make it easier. Asha bhabhi returned to her flowers. Parvati remained in the room and spoke again with slight hesitation, "Bhabhiji, I needed to ask you something."

"What? You want an advance payment again?" She continued to play with flowers.

"Yes, bhabhi. It's just that…I mean you know…my husband…"

Asha bhabhi turned around abruptly and blurted, "But your husband's going to be with you for the rest of your life! Why don't you just kick him out of the house? How long does he plan to live off you?"

Parvati looked straight at Asha bhabhi, shocked. She began to twiddle the corner of her sari. Asha bhabhi had turned back even more abruptly to her flowers. But she was now fussing with them absent-mindedly. She switched around the tube roses and gladioli, and then again, and then jerked them all out of the vase. A light spray of water flew from the stems as they breezed through the air.

Still holding onto the flowers, Asha bhabhi spoke. "I'm sorry, Parvati. I've already given you two months advance." She turned around to confront Parvati. "What will Sahib say if he knows I'm paying the servants so much? Unnecessarily, because of you we'll have a fight."

Parvati flinched. "No, no! You please don't fight with Sahib because of me. I'll manage. It's okay."

As Parvati headed towards the terrace Asha bhabhi stopped her, "Wait, one second." She stretched her hand to reach her purse behind the vase. Flicking through various papers in it, she took out a five-rupee note and held it out to Parvati. "Here, keep this."

"Thank you, bhabhi," Parvati said, "But it's all right. I have enough money to buy some bread for tonight." And she walked back to her vessels.

On her way home, Parvati headed towards the baniya's shop. He was the closest baniya to her house, so she would go to his shop often. Even if she didn't, he would have heard of

her because she was one of the most talked about persons in the neighborhood. Most people who knew that she ran the house herself, thought highly of her. She was famous for the evening lessons that she gave Anand. With the question of her husband, however, reactions were divided. The women seemed to bear a sympathetic shoulder, while most men believed that she was powerless against him. "But she deserves it," they would say, "God knows, in her previous life, she must have been cruel to her husband."

The baniya greeted Parvati as she approached, "Good evening Parvati behn! How are you? I hope you are very well!"

By now she was quite familiar with his ingratiating ways. Leaning on the counter, Parvati answered, "What to say, Ramlal? How different could I be from yesterday? Is everyone at home fine?"

"Oh, yes, everyone is in very good health! You know Somnath, my eldest son? He was studying in school—that new English high school."

Parvati had heard this several times. At first she had just accepted it as a piece of information, a matter of fact. When he repeated it, though, she became angry at his boastfulness, then envious of his position, even insecure about herself. But now his comments were so much a part of their every encounter that any reaction seemed redundant. So she would look up, wonder-eyed and smile. Ramlal went on. "I remember the first day we took him to school. Such a small boy, he couldn't even say his name properly. But I tell you, how boys grow up! Now he has passed his SSC exam also! In fact, we just got the result yesterday! Second Class! If he had worked little bit harder he would have passed with First Class. But, anyhow we are all very happy!"

Parvati congratulated him and conveyed her best wishes for Somnath. She told Ramlal she needed three buns. No, she didn't want any butter. Yes, she knew she could always pay later, but she really didn't want the butter. She had some dal left over from the previous evening. The baniya called out to one of his workers telling him to bring three buns quickly. No butter. Parvati behn had come.

Parvati stood at the counter waiting and the baniya continued. "I'm sure one day your Anand will also go to school. Never lose hope. All the holy books talk of miracles. How can they all be wrong! I tell you, it is a good thing that you are preparing him in advance!"

Parvati stood up straight and moved a step back from the counter. She began to say that the lessons she had taught had nothing to do with school but stopped herself. Taking a deep breath she said simply, "With the good wishes of his elders, I'm sure he'll be okay."

"Oh, of course! Our wishes are always with him. What are we here for? After all, earning money is not the only thing in the world." He was about to continue when the bread was brought in, neatly wrapped in an old newspaper.

"Four rupees, twenty-five paise, Parvati behn," he said as he rolled some thread off the ball behind him and held it between his teeth to break off. His hand was stretched to measure out the amount needed to tie the package.

Parvati untied the knot on one end of her sari and took out the money it held—a pink two-rupee note and several coins. She separated them across the counter, adding aloud the value of each one to the previous. It totaled four rupees, ten paise. She looked up at Ramlal. He pretended to be deeply engrossed in knotting the thread. She concentrated on him but he focused on the thread, refusing to face her.

"I'll take only two buns, Ramlal," she said, giving up. It was so like him to offer butter that she wouldn't want and then ignore this need for bread. Disgusted, she stared down at the mosaic tiles. Some big chips, some small, compacted together in one design.

"Changed your mind already?" asked Ramlal looking up. He faked a chuckle. She ignored it. "Uh…three, seventy-five," he said, taking out one of the buns and pulling the newspaper over the other two.

She pulled some of the coins back towards her, and piled them up in her left hand. She took the packet that Ramlal handed her and made sure she said thank you before leaving.

Home was only a dozen huts away. She walked peacefully but briskly. Anand would be waiting for her. She loved to hear his little stories about the things he'd done all day. Sometimes he'd pick up torn pages from magazines and build a story around them to tell her. Lakhan, the man who sold peanuts, had a whole collection of paper he used to sell the peanuts in. He would save for Anand those that he thought would make interesting stories. In return, Anand would share the story with him.

As her own house came into view, Parvati saw a crowd of children. They seemed to be pulling maliciously at someone in the center. Anand rarely played with the kids so he wasn't involved in their squabbles. Nevertheless, Parvati found her pace quickening. There were two kids in the center. She recognized the dark brown hair skimming a gray collar. She panicked and her walk turned to a light sprint. She hoped Anand was not hurt badly. Then just a few feet away, she suddenly stopped. It was Anand that was hitting the other child, Ravi, the taxi-driver's son. Ravi's lip was bleeding and the other boys were trying to tear Anand away. They made way for Parvati who headed straight for Anand. She firmly pulled him apart from Ravi, and slapped him across his face, right in front of the gaping kids.

Parvati apologized to Ravi and wiped his lip with her sari. She led him into her hut. He was hurt but too shocked to cry. Anand followed slowly but stopped at the entrance.

"What's this bad smell here, aunty?" asked Ravi. Parvati saw him cringe and hold his breath. She glanced at Anand who was looking straight at Ravi. Ravi was staring at the man sprawled in the corner of the hut where the smell was strongest.

"We'll finish fast and take you out, okay?" Parvati gave Ravi a smile he didn't return. She dipped her sari into a glass of cold water and rubbed it gently against Ravi's lip once again. Then she turned towards the makeshift shelf made by her trunk standing on end against the wall. Opening a small wooden box that stored a variety of things, she pulled out a tube. It was almost entirely flat except for a small portion near the cap. She noticed Ravi flinch as she squeezed out some white cream. "Don't worry," she said with a smile and rubbed it around Ravi's upper lip until it disappeared into his skin. She lifted him up to her compact-case mirror, so that he could be sure the cream didn't show. He seemed pleased. Parvati invited him to dinner but he said he wasn't hungry. She noticed him swerve himself away from Anand as he walked out of the hut.

"Who was that?" a coarse voice called out from the corner. It was accompanied by a stream of Johnny Walker breath. Parvati said it was the taxi-driver's son. She offered no explanation and he didn't inquire further.

"Give me some money," he said.

Parvati said she didn't have any.

"You're lying," he growled back.

Parvati said, well she had little over one rupee but she needed it to buy food the next day.

"Why don't you just take some money from one of the houses you work in? They're so fat and rich, they won't even notice."

She didn't reply.

"You're going to die poor, huh, you poor woman."

Parvati remained silent.

"Go to heaven in rags," he said in a half-muted voice. "No clothes to wear in heaven. Ha, ha, huh poor, poor…" He continued to mumble and eventually turned on his side, faced the wall and fell asleep.

Anand came in and sat by the trunk. Parvati lit the choolah and placed the aluminum container of dal on it. He waited a while and said, "It wasn't my fault, Mama. I only wanted to play seven pins with them." Parvati was listening but she continued with her cooking. "They had only six plastic bottles and said I could play if I got a seventh one. I told them I didn't have one but that I didn't think it would make much of a difference." Parvati stirred the dal with a wooden ladle. "And then Ravi started laughing. He said obviously I didn't have one because I didn't have anything. My father never worked and my mother only washed other people's dirty vessels. I told him nicely to shut up. I said he was insulting me but he wouldn't stop. He said he was sorry but he was only telling me the truth. The other boys started laughing too. Mama, they said he was only being honest. I didn't know what to do. I was confused. You said one should always tell the truth but I was still getting very angry. And they wouldn't stop laughing. So I had to hit him. To make him stop."

Parvati took the dal off the choolah and put a tava on it. She placed the bread she had bought and pressed it down with the same ladle. She used the time it took for the bread to roast to collect her thoughts. Maybe her lessons in values were pointless, after all.

Anand was looking at Parvati. There was a faint sadness in his eyes. Parvati turned to him and said, "I'm sorry I hit you." She opened her arms and Anand gave her a hug. She held him tightly for a few silent minutes and then said cheerfully, "Come, have dinner." She placed a bun and a bowl of dal on each of two plates and gave one to Anand. "Let me give Papa his dinner," she said and walked over towards her husband. She shook his back which was still turned to her. He grunted and said he didn't want dinner, he wanted money. "Dinner will probably do you more good," Parvati said, "C'mon, wake up." He shoved her hand off his shoulder and said, "Sell my dinner and give me the money." She left the plate by his side and went back to Anand.

After eating, they sat by the lantern. Their daily lesson ended early. It had been a long day for both of them and Anand fell asleep soon. It was quite cold and Parvati kept her sari on. She moved the dinner plate aside and crawled close to her husband. He started a little as he felt her touch and then put his arm around her waist. She slept well.

Parvati could tell that it was going to be a beautiful day. She awoke surprised by the sunbeams hitting her face. How had they penetrated the thick, black curtain that hung as a door? Realizing that she had overslept, she dressed herself in a hurry.

The neighborhood seemed particularly lively that day. The children were out playing in larger groups than usual. The women at the water pump were singing folk songs. Their colorful pails lay full beside them. When Parvati noticed that some of the men too had not gone to work, she was sure there was something about. Just as she stood thinking, a coconut that the boys were using as a ball rolled over to her feet. One of them ran up to her and she asked him whether there was anything special going on. "How can you forget, Paru tai," he said, "Today is the town fair! It only comes once in a year. Aren't you coming?"

"Yes, beta. I'll come on my way back from work. You have fun when you go." He said he would and ran back to his game. Parvati thought of the previous year's fair. Anand had been sick and was upset that he could not go. She had gone, hoping to find something cheap to buy him. But it was the annual fair and most things tended to be overpriced. She had really liked one paper windmill, but it had cost more than she could afford and so she had bought a balloon instead. Anand had loved it but he had not known about the windmill. Parvati tried to remember how much money she had. Thirty-five paise left over from buying the bread. If she didn't spend it all, she could probably buy the windmill this year. But then she would have to take some money out of her trunk; money she had saved for her husband's birthday. It was still two months away, though, so she decided she would take Anand to the fair when she got home from work.

Parvati was surprised at the energy she had when she got to Asha bhabhi's flat. Climbing the stairs, she could hear people laughing and talking loudly in the flat. She listened but only caught phrases: "...no, no she's over forty...son needs braces..." None of the voices sounded familiar and she recalled that they were having a dinner party for Pinku baba's birthday. She was suddenly excited herself. She rang the doorbell three times before someone heard it and let her in.

There were more people inside than she had imagined. Adults. Probably friends—they weren't discussing family gossip as relatives did. Why did all these big people invite mostly their friends when it was their children's birthdays? But it was a trivial matter.

The house was enchantingly decorated. There were multicolored streamers and balloons all around the living room. Silver and gold mobiles hung at the windows, and every time the wind blew in a melody of tinkling sounds breezed through the room. The cake was in the center of the room. It had been cut already, and its shoe shape was still recognizable. Parvati smiled to herself as she realized the reason. Pinku baba had a fascination for shoes. Even though he was only four years old, he was extremely self-conscious about the shoes he wore. He had more shoes than anyone in Parvati's family would ever own. He was the first son in Asha bhabhi's family after three girls. Parvati knew that his parents really doted on him. No wonder his birthday cake had been placed on the brand new glass table with carved marble legs. Right beside it, a small sofa was covered with hundreds of boxes. Wrapped in shiny paper with ribbons and bows they made the living room even more colorful. For a brief second Parvati wished she had a birthday gift for Pinku, but her thoughts were interrupted by a tug at her sari. Three well-glazed white teeth were sparkling at her through Pinku's smile. He was wearing an outfit she hadn't seen before. Pants with a top attached to it. The top had straps and wasn't really a whole top. He had new shoes on to match. In some houses

even the children were quite fashionable. Pinku was waving his hands in front of her. Holding him under his arms, Parvati swept him up and swirled him in the air. He giggled and the momentary breeze made the mobiles tinkle again. She sang him the same song she sang Anand on his birthday each year. It was full of good wishes and blessings and advice to be humble always.

There was a tap on her shoulder and Parvati turned around to find Asha bhabhi. "I hope you remember I told you to stay for longer today."

Parvati had forgotten that bhabhiji had told her she could take some food home. Now she need not remove any money from her savings to buy dinner. Not wanting to mention the food, she only said that she would stay. She was holding Pinku and pulling his cheeks playfully.

"Don't waste time, Parvati. Too many vessels have piled up already. Otherwise, you'll only be late." Asha bhabhi held out her arms to Pinku and said, "Come beta, Radha aunty wants to meet you. She has a surprise for you!" Pinku slipped into Asha bhabhi's arms and Parvati headed for the kitchen.

She took off her glass bangles, but left the metal ones on. Then she collected the two different detergents she was supposed to use. The steel gray powder was to be used with a plastic gauze on metal cooking vessels. The glasses and serving vessels were more delicate and had to be washed with the liquid soap and wiped off with a sponge. Parvati believed that liquid soap couldn't possibly be as efficient and she often used the powder on non-metals as well. Once, Asha bhabhi had angrily shown her some scratches on a plate. Parvati had apologized but did what she wanted to anyway.

While scrubbing the plates crusty with pilaf, samosas and chocolate cake, Parvati thought of the party. It was so lively. Even though they weren't talking of interesting things, they seemed to be having fun. Whenever enough people get together, it's fun, she thought. Like at the town fair. She was supposed to go to the fair after work, but had forgotten she was staying late. If she went home first she wouldn't be able to make it on time. Anand would be upset but it would be better if she went directly. At least that way she could get something for him.

Work lasted an hour-and-a-half longer than usual and Parvati was exhausted. The guests had left already and Pinku had gone to bed. Parvati made polite conversation with some of the other servants while she put on her bangles and got ready to leave. She knew there was a lot of food left over and was wondering how to bring it up when Asha bhabhi walked into the kitchen. She had not forgotten. Dressed in a cotton kaftan, hair hanging loose and face bare without makeup, she looked very different from the woman who had hosted the dinner. The way she switched in and out of roles was intriguing. Asha bhabhi wrapped enough food for Parvati and her family in aluminum foil and thanked Parvati for staying late. She said Parvati was a great help and she was glad that she had been working for them for the past five years.

By the time Parvati got to the town fair there were hardly any people or stalls left. Many hawkers were packing up their goods. One of the lit stalls had small leftover balloons stuck to a white bed sheet. That was the rifle-shooting stall. Tiny pieces of rubber now hung from where the other balloons had been attached to the sheet. They helped complete what must

have been a circular rainbow. Parvati had watched many win prizes at that stall and the accuracy of their aim frightened her.

There were paper plates and cups strewn all over the brown grass. Parvati noticed short sticks bent at one end. They were used to hold cotton candy. She glanced around for the stall of windmills. It didn't seem to be there. At least it wasn't open. Parvati slowly traced the circular arrangement of the stalls and stopped at one. There were no windmills up but she recognized the owner's face.

"Excuse me bhaiyah. Aren't you the one who sells windmills?"

The man smiled instantly. "Yes, yes," he said.

"I remember from last year," Parvati said.

"Oh, thank you very much, Mehdem." He held his hands together, folded up front in appreciation. He stood smiling like that and when the silence lasted too long he became suddenly embarrassed. Releasing his own clasp he pointed to a suitcase standing by the tent and asked, "Do you want to look at some now?"

"Please," said Parvati, "if you're not in a hurry."

"How can I be in hurry when you are coming for second time, Mehdem? But you made it just in time. I was about to close shop."

He opened an old suitcase and Parvati was taken aback by the splash of colors that hit her eye. This year the windmills had two layers of paper. Almost like having two windmills! Heaped together, they created a sea of colors. The hawker picked a few up and held them out for selection. Parvati was amazed at how different each one looked. After some time she picked one that had the most purple and the least orange. That would have been Anand's choice. "Forty-five paise," he said.

She flinched. "Last year they cost only thirty paise."

"I know Mehdem. But what can I say? You are a lady, you know how much the prices are rising everyday. We have to adjust."

She stood still, looking at him, not wanting to leave without a windmill. He sensed her problem and asked, "Do you have less money, Mehdem?"

"Yes, bhaiyah. I have thirty-five paise."

"Achha, never mind. It is nighttime. I am closing shop. You can take it for thirty-five." He tore a sheet of newspaper in half and wrapped the windmill in it. Parvati thanked him and helped him pack up the rest of his stall.

"Don't want any food today?" called out Ramlal from his store as Parvati neared home.

"No thank you, Ramlalji. There was a party in one of the houses so I have enough food for tonight."

"Now that your husband has gone it will probably be enough for tomorrow also."

"What do you mean?" asked Parvati. She felt her body stiffen and her pulse rate increase.

"Don't you know that the police came and took him?" he said, trying to sound surprised.

Parvati gritted her teeth, frustrated with his pretences at a time like this. "No, no," she said. "I haven't yet been home. Tell me what happened." She was speaking faster and had started fidgeting with the packet she was holding.

"Same thing as before," Ramlal continued. "He tried to run away with two bottles from Raghu's shop but he fell before he could escape."

Parvati's mind flashed back to the previous day. Anand had wanted a bottle for seven pins. She frowned and shook her head, snapping back to Ramlal's words.

"Raghu phoned the police and they took him away. Poor fellow was bleeding. I tell you Parvati behn, why do you bother with these everyday problems? Just..."

But Parvati was already running home.

Anand stood at the door. He was staring at Parvati running towards him. "Where's Papa?" she asked but ran into the house before he could answer. She stared blankly at the empty spot where her husband usually lay, then looked back at Anand. He stood unnerved, watching her intently. She looked around the rest of the hut and then again, as if some dark corner would unexpectedly reveal his presence. But only the stench of alcohol remained. The small hut suddenly seemed to have too much space. Parvati turned back to Anand, her face contorted close to tears. His cheeks were puffed up and he narrowed his eyes to focus on his mother. She couldn't decide whether he was furious or pouting. Probably both, she decided and slumped to the floor. The paper and foil packets dropped by her side.

"It's all your fault, Mama," Anand began, his voice raised. "Everyone thinks you should kick Papa out of the house. Why do you keep him? He only causes trouble."

Parvati slowly turned her head upwards to look at her son. Normally, she would have hit him for such audacity but she felt drained. She sat silently.

"You didn't even come back early to take me to the fair. All you do is teach me. And I listen for your sake. To keep you company. I want to go out and play seven pins. I don't even believe in your lessons."

Parvati shuddered at this mention of lessons. She had always feared he would react this way sometime. That would be a sign that he'd grown up. But he's only eight, she thought.

"They're just words Mama, just words. Useless like Papa is."

Parvati hugged her knees in, folded her arms on them and rested her chin. She listened to Anand as if she had heard everything he was saying. God knows she had run through it in her mind several times before. She thought she could predict almost every sentence he would say. But she was wrong. There was more than she had expected.

A cold breeze pushed through the black curtain and Parvati felt a chill creep into her toes.

"I don't think there is anything wrong with stealing. Last week you said that Papa was wrong for stealing but at least he gets what he wants. They'll keep him in jail for some time and then he'll come home again. Just like he always does. It's the same thing, again and again. And if you don't give Papa money, he'll steal again. But he's happy, Mama. At least more than you are. I'm going to run away and be happy too." Anand was shouting. "And you know what else? No one laughs at Papa. They laugh at you." He turned his back to Parvati and suddenly ran off into the courtyard.

Parvati buried her head in her knees. Anand's voice echoed in her ears. They laugh at you. They laugh at you. They laugh at you. They laugh at you. Parvati's head throbbed with the echo. The words closed in on her and she couldn't think. She shut her eyes and saw colored lines zipping past her. They were comets, they were ribbons, they were whips, they were windmills. Her head was spinning and she had no idea when she fainted.

When she came to, it was because Anand's soft voice was nudging its way into her terror. "I'm sorry, Mama. Wake up. Please, wake up." As her mind cleared, Parvati saw the windmills flash again and she groped in the darkness for the newspaper package. Finding it, she clasped it tight and took a deep breath. She then opened her eyes and handed Anand the packet. He tore open the newspaper and sat entranced by the windmill. Then he smiled and hugged Parvati. She embraced him gently and helped him to hook up the windmill near the black curtain. Then she insisted he go out and wash up before dinner.

Left alone, Parvati busied herself with heating the food she had brought home. She served three plates, realized her mistake, and began to empty the contents of one back into the vessel. But she lost her grip. An unexpected clanking of metal destroyed the silence as the dinner plate slipped out, scattering the food about the floor. Parvati looked up to the black curtain as it moved forward. She waited. Only the wind entered. The jewelled vanes of the windmill spun against the dark background.

Of Course Kumbhakaran Was Not a Woman

RUPAL SANGHVI

"Of course Kumbhakaran Was Not a Woman…"

me thuk gae
me thuk gae
kya karun
me kya karun
koy nahi
mere lie koy nahi hai

mera naam kis ke kan pe hai
mera naam kon puchega
mera rona
meri hasi
khyal he?
aj me puchungi

Hr roz we see, hamari mothers, our masis, our kakis, our sisters, ourselves…hr roz
 we know
we live the double standards of our culture.
we see women married off.
deprived of making their own decisions,
deprived of education
they are the property of their parents and then their husbands. from her father's house
to her husband's house, her life travels.
when does she get to her house?
everyone closes their eyes to this

it is said: these young women don't need education, they will find their happiness
through other paths (bhakti to their family, for example).
no one told her of the pot-holes that gray foggy day her verghordo
took to those roads, that "path." no one tells her anything, except: jeeti raho, beti.
which they really hope she does

89

for all their sakes.
everyone closes their eyes to this

kya karun?
me kya karun?
Kumbhakaran stri tho nahi tha.

Kumbhakaran the brother of Ravana who, among other things, was known for sleeping half the
year and eating the other half

Maria

GAURANGI KAMANI

Maria watched me sitting on the toilet, my seven-year-old body half-sunken into the porcelain bowl. She left the bathroom door open and went about her chores. She knew it would be a while before I was done. She had to wash my behind with a tumbler of water, as I couldn't reach around to rinse myself without tipping into the commode.

I sat on the toilet for hours, playing teacher to a classroom of imaginary children. I taught them how to silently explore the bodies of sleeping servants, how to lift up hems and unbutton blouses. I supervised their awkward attempts, making them repeat the actions till they got them right. Finally Maria would show up to wash me, and I squealed as she hurriedly jabbed her fingers into my bum and splashed me with water halfway up my back.

The servants had their own squat toilet in the back of the house, but Maria preferred our "Western-style" commodes. When she had to go, she pulled me into the bathroom with her and I loudly announced to anyone listening that I was going to do Number Two and slammed the door shut. Maria sat on the toilet, giggling and grunting. I swung back and forth on the sagging curtain rod, my legs dangling in Maria's face. We sat with the door unlocked, excited by the idea of being discovered, but nobody ever found us out.

Maria slept on the floor next to my bed every night. She slept on a thin mattress without a sheet to cover her body. By morning, the buttons on the front of her dress were often undone, and the hem was hiked up around her hips.

Many nights I would cautiously reach in past her dress to her chest, folding the material back, exposing her cheap nylon bra. The bra covered her loosely, so I could reach under the cup to stroke her breast. But before taking her whole breast into my palm, my movements invariably jostled her and she pushed my hand away.

"Let me," I commanded her, "I'm not going to do anything."

"It tickles," she mumbled, rolling over. I returned to my bed, frustrated by my clumsiness. I shut my eyes and relived the exact sensation of exploring Maria's body, mentally steadying my nervous hands and gracefully covering both her breasts with my adoring fingers.

I heard the front door slam and the key turn in the lock, and I knew that my mother had left. Saturdays were my mother's shopping days. I knew Maria would sneak into the shower. Normally, she bathed out of a bucket in the servants' quarters, squatting down fully clothed, sloshing water over her head with a tumbler, just as she had always done in her village. But slowly she was getting used to the pleasures of our home.

Maria slipped into the bathroom and locked the door. She knew I was aware of her showering every week, but she also knew that I wouldn't tell my mother. Maria was afraid of

me, even though she was a grown woman and I was a child. There was never any doubt in my mind about who was in charge.

I heard the shower come on, and the water beating against the tile. I had removed two panes of glass from the bathroom vent which let out onto the balcony. Standing on my chair I could see exactly what I wanted without being seen myself. I stepped up to the gap between the slats of glass and looked down.

Maria was washing her hair, sudsing vigorously. Her eyes were closed. She was humming, and her long nipples were tipped up as she reached around to soap her back.

She rinsed the soap out of her hair, lathered her armpits, and then bent at the knees to rub between her legs. With every motion backwards, her hand disappeared from view.

I was stunned to be looking at her. My legs shook and my head swam so I had to lean forward and rest against the frosted glass. Maria spread her buttocks to let the water in, arching her back, then bending forward. I felt her fingers moving as though they were my own and I suddenly wanted to share with Maria how excited I was.

I giggled, and Maria looked up. She saw my face and screamed. She covered her body with her hands and crouched down until she was bent over on the tiled floor and her breasts and thighs and belly were hidden within the tight embrace of her arms.

She cried and begged, but the water ran into her mouth so her pleas came out as gurgles. One breast swung free as she reached up to turn off the shower tap. She moaned to me to leave her alone, she hadn't done anything, it wasn't fair, she just wanted to finish bathing.

She slipped and lost her balance. She fell back onto her elbows, legs spread wide and breasts bouncing. She scrambled to cover herself back up. I told her she could stay in the shower as long as she wanted, I wasn't going to do anything to her. Maria whimpered and cradled her head on her drawn-up knees. She just sat there. It was over. I stepped down and dragged the chair back into the room. I sank down onto the bed, exhausted.

My mother didn't like Maria very much, because Maria answered back. My mother was irritated by Maria's playfulness, and grumbled that she and I were always up to something. Servants were meant to do work.

Maria came to live in our house when I was born. She was a dark, thin woman with a few gray hairs, a wraith who moved around like she were invisible. She was sometimes in the room for many minutes before I noticed her, at which point she stiffened, dodged, cleared her face of any expression, then surrendered herself to being visible.

Maria had children of her own in a village far from Bombay, but since the children were grown up, she claimed that they didn't need to see her anymore.

In the evenings she and I went for a walk along the sea wall across from our apartment building. There we met other women named Anna and Sylvia and Rosie who worked as maids and who also wore dresses. They spoke to each other in Konkani for hours, tightly holding down their dresses which ballooned in the strong sea breeze.

We also had two men working in the house, a cook and a housecleaner. The cook was a dark, puffy-faced, moustachioed man who resembled a bandit. He prepared exquisite food, and was the envy of all my mother's friends. He had never tasted most of what he cooked for

us, because he was a strict vegetarian. His face revealed only boredom. We didn't know what his real name was. My mother had always christened our cooks 'Babu,' so that's what we called him.

Ram, the housecleaner, had worked in my father's office for forty years before being transferred to "houseduty." He was a fixture in our house and everyone ignored him but me. He was an older man with long legs that were tight with ropy muscles. He wore very baggy shorts, and I could lie down on the floor while he was cleaning the house and look up his legs. It was all darkness in there, except for his rounded buttocks. The two men slept in the servants' quarters attached to the kitchen.

Every night my mother locked the door of the servants' quarters, so that Babu and Ram couldn't enter the house at night. Every morning at dawn, my mother unlocked the door to let them out. She never entered their room.

The cook fixed the lock so it wasn't really locking. Every few nights, Maria went into the servants' room. She would return before dawn and quickly fall asleep on her mattress. I always heard her come in. She knew that I knew, but also that I wouldn't tell. When I asked her what she did there, she said she helped the servants to fall asleep. I imagined that like little children, Babu and Ram lay down on her outstretched legs and she dandled them on her knees until they drifted into slumber.

Maria didn't say anything about the shower incident. But on Monday morning when it was time to braid my hair for school, she sank the comb into my scalp and jerked it through my knotted hair until I screamed. She shushed me, smiling maliciously. "Sit still," she whispered, "or I'll pull your bloody hair right out."

Every night that week I dreamt of a woman running down the street, tearing off one article of clothing after another—shoes, socks, coat, skirt, blouse, scarf—until she was down to her panties. She could not remove that last bit of cloth. She started again, fully clothed, tears streaming down her face in anger. She ran toward me, removing the clothing bit by bit, looking straight at me with pleading eyes. She came closer and closer, until she finally ran over me. It was terrifying.

I woke up one night with my heart hammering in my chest and I cried out in fear. There was no response, only the whirring of the ceiling fan. I was sick to my stomach. I had to find Maria.

The cockroaches scurried out of sight as I turned on the kitchen light. I walked to the back and pushed on the door to the servants' room. It was unlocked and swung back silently. Behind the door was a small passage that zigzagged around into the dank, still chamber where the men slept.

I stood a moment in fear, forgetting why I was there. The air was thick with a pungent odor, an odd mixture of hair oil and urine and sweat. It was the smell of Maria. It was the smell of the cook.

There were two string cots in the room, and as my eyes adjusted to the darkness, I saw the forms of Babu and Ram on the two beds. Maria was nowhere to be seen.

The room was stifling. The men were snoring, deep in sleep. I checked under the beds, then checked behind the door of the squat toilet. Where was she? I would have to wake up

the cook to ask him and then he would know that I knew and he would get scared and run away from the job. And then Ram would be suspected as an accomplice, and my mother would have to let him go as well.

Suddenly I heard Maria's long sigh and the cook rolled over onto his back and there was Maria, her thin body coming up for air. Her dress was unbuttoned, the hem dragged up to her waist. Between her legs I saw a dark patch, and the nightmare came rushing back into my head, about the hole between Maria's legs where the men's heads disappeared when she lay them out on her legs right up against her crotch and dandled them. Inside her hips the heads nestled, and when I poked at her bum the way she poked at mine on the toilet, out came the eyelashes, tongues, ears of Ram and Babu.

The next day I decided. I told Maria I would have her fired unless she did what I wanted. "Baby, don't tell okay, don't tell, baby, okay?" she begged and pleaded. She let me push aside her blouse, unsnap the bra, and push the nylon fabric out of the way, up against her neck, framing her breasts with the twisted, absurdly pointing cups. She bit on her lips and sucked in her breath as I pushed and pulled on her nipples. She tried not to giggle, but no matter how rough I was, she felt ticklish.

When I tried to reach beyond her stomach, Maria writhed and twisted and crossed her thighs tightly. I asked her what she was hiding in there and she gasped, "Same as you, baby, only same as you."

I was unhappy. Maria's nipples told me nothing. The woman in my dreams wouldn't leave me alone. I tried to block her out of my dreams by not sleeping. But she entered my daydreams and leapt around, running down the street helplessly, losing her clothes endlessly. I threatened Maria again. I said I had to see what she was doing with the cook. Maria stuck out her jaw and dared me to tell my mother. She said matter-of-factly that now I was caught, that if I told my mother anything, she could tell my mother something too. Maria would only lose her job, but I had to live with my mother forever.

The sleepless nights exhausted me. I cried and cried at night, but the woman ran down my mind, her footsteps louder and heavier, her clothes clinging to her, suffocating her. She tore them off herself in a hopping-skipping rage, eyes wild with fear.

I had to get into the servants' quarters.

I lay down on Babu's sagging cot, clutching my stomach and groaning. Maria and my mother came running. "Oooohhhh…" I moaned. "My stomach, I can't get up!" I drew my knees into my chest and clung to the edges of the cot.

"What, baba, what is it?" My mother knelt on the floor and tried to feel my stomach. "Don't touch me, don't touch me!" I screamed. "I can't move. Please just let me sleep here."

My mother stiffened with disgust and stood up. "You can't sleep on this filthy mattress. You have your own bed. We'll carry you there and you can sleep till morning. Maria, grab her knees and I'll take her arms."

"Why can't I just sleep here!" I screamed as they picked me up. I thrashed and twisted but couldn't get free. Maria murmured "left, right, left, right" in time to my scissor-kicks, all the way to the room.

"Where do you get these ideas," my mother fumed. "We give you a nice clean house to live in and you want to sleep in the pig-sty!"

Three flying cockroaches on the wall, all waiting for Maria. She entered the room and I slammed my fist against the wall. One cockroach flew down and then right up Maria's dress. Maria screamed, threw down the clean laundry and danced around the room in terror. She pulled off her dress and squirmed out of her bra and panties. Out jumped the brown whirly-top, fluttering like a butterfly around Maria's bouncing breasts. She picked up a shoe and swung at the cockroaches, one-two-three, missed them and watched them fly up to the ceiling. She stood with her legs apart, following the cockroaches with her eyes, shoe raised to strike.

There she was, naked and shaking. I walked behind her. The cockroaches paused on the ceiling. Maria concentrated on them with her neck craned back. I lay down on the floor right behind her, and looked up the crack of her legs. The cockroaches didn't move. Maria wasn't aware of me underneath her. Between her legs there was a lot of hair...could have been moustaches or long nose hairs or even somebody's head.

I sat on the floor of the bathroom, my back against the door. Maria sat on the toilet, her dress pulled down around her knees, eyes shut in concentration. "Oh baba," she grunted. "Save me, Mother Mary!" she gasped. I could see it was tough for her, what with all the heads inside. Would she take my help....

"Can I poke you a little bit?" I offered eagerly. Maria swayed back and forth on the toilet. She opened one eye and stared at me. "If you can't clean yourself, how can you clean me?" she asked slowly. "You'll put your finger in the wrong place and my bum will stay shitty."

"What wrong place," I asked.

Maria squealed with delight. "You think children are born all shitty or what, baba. You think I would touch your bum if that's where babies came from?" Maria hawked up a gob of mucus and spat contemptuously into the basin. "You people grow up in these big-big houses and you don't know which hole is what!"

"Don't shout at me," I cried, utterly confused. "I don't have any other hole. It's not my fault," I said stubbornly. "Only married girls have that other hole."

"You bloody basket," Maria said bitterly, "you can't fool me with your tricks. One is not enough for you, and that's why you're after my hole! You go take your mother's if she doesn't want it. You just leave my thing alone."

I sat naked against the long mirror in my room and looked at what was between my legs. Thin, purple skin, folding this way and that. What hole? I touched my navel. I dug into the opening and winced at the pain. The hole was closed. Bloody woman telling me lies, I fumed. I'll fix her once and for all.

I lay in bed listening to the first screams from the servants' quarters. It was still dark outside. The woman running down the center of my mind was slowing down. She could rest

95

for a while, now that Maria would be leaving. I got up, made my bed, put on my school uniform and went into the kitchen.

The cook squatted dejectedly outside the kitchen door, head in his hands. Inside, my mother was at the door to the servants' room, dragging Maria forward with all her strength. My mother's hair was still uncombed from sleeping, falling to her waist. Maria's hair was stiff and matted around her head. They were screaming at each other.

"You get out now, you get out of my house!" my mother shouted, over and over.

"Don't touch me!" Maria screamed, trying to free herself. She saw me and called to me helplessly. "Save me, baba," she cried, "or your mother will kill me."

"Get out, get out, get out," my mother shouted. "You shameless woman, I have a young daughter in the house!"

Maria slammed my mother against the refrigerator and freed her arms. My mother stumbled, holding the back of her head in pain. I ran up to her. Maria fixed me with eyes of hate.

"Mummy, mummy," I said, holding onto my mother's waist.

"It's okay, I'm okay," she groaned. "Your father's still asleep; we mustn't disturb him. Call the watchman at the gate. Tell him to come up with the janitor right now. This woman has lost her mind."

"But mummy, what's happening?" I asked innocently.

"Don't ask questions!" she snapped. "You want this woman to kill us all?" I ran to the intercom, called the watchman and ran back to the kitchen. Maria and my mother stood facing each other, breathing hard.

"All these years, I knew there was something wrong with you. How stupid I was to let you stay!" My mother's voice trembled with anger. "I'm sending you back to your village. You have spoilt my household. Ungrateful woman. You pack your things and get out. And take that son-of-a-bitch cook with you!"

"I don't want him," Maria spat. "He's nothing to me. You keep him to make your mutton fry, cheese toast and what all. He stinks of your food."

My mother covered her face. "You people just won't learn," she cried helplessly. "Such shameless behavior when there's a simple child in the house. Thank god she told me that something was wrong or you would have really twisted her mind."

Maria raised an eyebrow and looked at me sardonically. My heart jumped into my mouth. For a minute she was back to being naughty, old Maria, and I smiled hesitantly. But then her lip curled and she snorted in contempt.

"Simple my foot," she sneered, looking me up and down. "Bloody basket, this girl is more shameless than dogs."

"Just listen to her," my mother murmured in disbelief, "who could tell she is a mother of children herself!"

The doorbell rang. My mother motioned for me to watch Maria and ran to answer the door. "It won't be the same after you're gone," I whispered to Maria. "We always had so much fun." Maria stared at the wall, ignoring me.

The watchman and the janitor, two bent old men in khaki shirts and shorts, entered the kitchen, saluted me limply and walked hesitantly toward Maria. She stepped back, curled her fists and growled. The men looked around helplessly for my mother.

96

My mother firmly took Maria by the hair, and the two men twisted Maria's arms behind her back and marched her out of the front door. Maria grimaced with the pain of being pushed and pulled, but said nothing. At the lift, the men pushed Maria in and my mother let go her hair. My mother pulled out some money from inside her sari blouse and told the watchman to go with Maria in a taxi to the train station, buy her a one-way ticket to her village and make sure that she was on the train when it pulled out of the station.

"Don't worry," my mother said firmly to Maria, "I'll send every last thing of yours by parcel post." My mother pulled shut the lift door and Maria started crying. "I don't want anything, memsaab," she whimpered, "I just want to stay here with you and baby."

The lift descended, and my mother pulled me to her. She shivered involuntarily. "You just can't trust servants any more. Just can't trust any of them to take proper care of children."

"But I'm so small," I cried. "Who will take care of me?"

"I know, I know," my mother soothed, stroking my hair. "I'll check in the building and see if anyone knows of another ayah."

"But mummy, I need somebody today, another Christian girl!" I pleaded.

"Of course, sweetie, I'll find a girl today itself, and this time younger, okay? So you have someone closer to your age to play with."

I smiled at her and jumped up in excitement. "Can I call her Maria?" I asked happily.

"Of course, my darling," said my mother, hugging me and leading me into the house. "You can call her anything you want."

Konkani a derivative (dialect) of the Marathi language.

Viewpoint From A Female

SAJANI PATEL

Just the other day, my parents, my sister, my younger brother and I were working in the backyard under the hot burning sun. We were pulling weeds and fixing up the yard. We all wanted to go back inside and chill, but we had work to do. My brother got up and went over to my mom.

"Mommy, the weeds are making me itchy. Can I go inside?"

"Okay. Go inside and answer any phone calls that come," she replied. I don't believe this, I thought to myself. Why does he get to go inside and relax while we're practically breaking our backs pulling weeds.

"Mother, may I please go inside? I don't feel so well," I said.

"No, you can't. There's a lot of work to do." Oh my god…why does my lazy brother get to go inside again? It's not fair. We all should have to do the same amount of work. Every time we pull the weeds he always finds an excuse not to do it. Later, when I confront my parents and ask them why he always gets the advantages, they say that they treat us all equally. But anytime he wants to go out, even on a school night, he gets to go…while we stay at home and beg. Why does the male sibling always have so many privileges and advantages? I have compared this to other Indian families and they are all like this too.

It totally seems like men always get what they want, leaving their sisters empty-handed and exhausted. We women have to learn how to cook and clean, and get an education. I know my friends and I will all go to college and have good careers and we will have to take care of the house and the kids. Why do people, mainly parents and men, assume that men are the hard-working ones in this world and deserve to be treated like kings or something? Women work just as hard or harder than men. We're always second to them. Ever since the beginning, people have been treating us like this. Sometimes I feel as if women are imprisoned in this world for men.

Sexual Lynching

NEERA KUCKREJA SOHONI

Judge
You sit there
in your armoured chair
soon to be an imperial
seat of justice
Don't lynch me
you say, just think of all
the Blacks you have maimed
 killed for their
 penis size
My penis,
is mine, and the bedroom
too;
what pictures I hang on
its walls,
 my pleasure
Am here to defend
my honor, you say
 but I won't
be queried on honorable
 speech
 or conduct
I have no views nor words
I will not be lynched,
 electronically.

Hill, she is another
 matter
take her
rape her if you will—women are
attuned to hard words,
harsh penises,
they are Sabine and supple
large breasted, with tight

vaginas;
their ears like their bodies
 accustomed to being
invaded;
no
 fifth
 sixth or
 seventh
amendment,
guards
their safety
or sensibility.

Ye senators,
vote me in, to
revoke the prime
conqueror; vote
for her yet, and
you deny
manhood and its
right to
unilateral
 pleasure.

Alone and Exploited

LALITA GANDBHIR

Nargis walked out of Jamuna's Indian grocery store. The door shut behind her with a bang and locked itself. Jamuna, a short stocky woman in her mid-thirties, sat still on her little stool behind the counter that held the cash register. Her untidy hair rolled in a single skinny braid, salwar kameez smelling of spices, heavyset legs wide apart, she stared at Nargis from the time she had walked out until she disappeared.

Sabeena, standing near the counter, her face tear-stained, also watched as Nargis walked away. Sabeena stood there a few more minutes after Nargis had disappeared, trying to control her emotions. Except for an occasional shrill, piercing sound of children's laughter from Jamuna's adjoining apartment, total silence filled the store.

Sabeena dried her face with a handkerchief and looked at herself in the small stained mirror on the wall. She pulled a compact out of her pocketbook and powdered her face, hoping to cover up the redness caused by crying. She went into the apartment to pick up her five-year-old son Naz, who slept in the midst of Jamuna's playful children. She carried him out to the shop and picked up her pocketbook, leaving all of her sewing where it was. On her way out she glanced at Jamuna, who still had not moved and was just staring at the dark road outside the door.

After fastening the seat belt around Naz, Sabeena, six months pregnant, slowly got into the front seat. As she drove, the appalled look on Nargis's face kept flashing before her. And Nargis's troubling words hammered over and over in her brain. "You are exploited, you fools!"

That's impossible. Sabeena, daughter of a rich businessman, pampered since birth, expected to marry into a wealthy family and to live in splendor, surrounded by comfort and servants waiting on her all the time—what had happened to her?

Sabeena thought of her ancestral childhood home in India. She had played in this home, secure in the knowledge she imbibed at a tender young age. Some man will always care for you, provide for you, look after you; you must be submissive and obey him for man is supreme; a woman cares for the children, cooks and sews because she is the weaker sex and can't deal with the difficult, hostile world; that is a man's job.

At times Sabeena had her doubts. For instance, their maidservant Bijibai, from the lower class of society, was quite a woman. She had kicked out one husband who beat her and remarried another man with whom she fought if he upset her. She washed other people's clothes for a living and was economically independent; she feared no one, male or female. At times Sabeena envied the woman's two daughters because they could freely wander around by themselves and go to all the shops and festivals in town. Sabeena, on the other hand, went nowhere without a chaperone. Despite her admiration of the independence enjoyed by Bijibai

and her daughters, Sabeena never rebelled; she accepted her situation without question. Though Sabeena graduated from high school with honors, a major argument ensued about her continuing her education. Her grandmother and mother opposed college education on the grounds that a girl does not need it, and that, because attending college was considered improper, it could hurt her chances of marrying into a good family.

But Grandfather supported Sabeena. Men nowadays want an educated wife, he said. She should speak English, host parties, dress properly and travel with her husband. Women sometimes are left alone and have to care for themselves and their children. I want Sabeena prepared for that, just in case. He then went on to tell a story of his own grandmother. All her relatives were killed in a war, and her village was wiped out. She hid in the jungle for two days with her two small boys until the enemy left. Born into a wealthy Muslim family, she had never worked with her hands, but she was a strong woman. She traveled to another village, worked hard at menial jobs and managed to feed and raise two sons. She even started her own business and ultimately bought back her ancestral home. A fierce woman, she survived catastrophic losses. I remember her. Everyone scoffed at his story. But though Sabeena's father insisted she would never face anything like that, her grandfather prevailed. Her mother, however, insisted on an all-girls college. So Sabeena attended home science college for girls and learned languages and humanities, and, of course, more of what she already knew: cooking and sewing.

In her third year of college her parents started to look earnestly for a proper match for Sabeena. Because she was tall, slender, graceful with curly black hair and large brown eyes, Sabeena's match was easy to arrange. And, just as Grandfather had predicted, Sabeena's college education, fluent English and modern way of dressing proved very helpful. Though Hussen's mother did not want a college educated daughter-in-law, he went ahead and married Sabeena.

During discussions of arrangements and at several parties that preceded the wedding, Hussen's parents proudly mentioned his younger brother Jaleel. A medical doctor who went to America for further training, Jaleel could not attend, but he sent a telegram on the day of the wedding.

Hussen, an architect, worked for the family firm. After they were married, Sabeena, of course, went to live with Hussen's family. They were well off and his mother supervised several servants who looked after all the household chores. With very little to keep her occupied, Sabeena spent her time reading, sewing and cooking fancy meals that everyone appreciated.

One night Hussen casually informed Sabeena of his future plans to migrate to America. He did not see the need to consult her. Sabeena had some reservations, but she did not oppose his plans. She had learned that a man decides what he does with his life and a woman follows.

Her father, though, was not so conditioned, and her mother's conditioning apparently fell apart when she heard of Hussen's plans. "You did not tell us of your plans before the marriage," they objected. "In America women have to do all the housework; Sabeena is not used to that. She will be alone in the house when you go to work. What about the cold, snow and ice? Why do you want to migrate anyway?"

Hussen's parents also opposed his plans. "Please, wait until Jaleel returns," they pleaded. "We are old now and would like one of our sons with us."

"I want to go while I am still young," Hussen argued. "I just want to see America, spend a year or two and return home. Besides, you are not old, and if you have any problems, Shama is just down the street." Shama, Hussen's older married sister, lived nearby and had promised to look after her parents until Hussen returned. She also had older sons who could help with Grandfather's business.

Jaleel waited for the arrival of Hussen and Sabeena's Air India flight at the New York airport. He had driven for three hours to get there and seemed very happy to see his older brother. The brothers chattered continuously during the long drive to his apartment. Sabeena listened and looked at America through her rolled up car window. Then, totally exhausted, she fell asleep in the back seat of the car. Hussen and Sabeena looked at Jaleel's small studio apartment and realized they could not live there for more than a few days. The entire apartment consisted of a large room, closet-like kitchen and bathroom. A few days later Hussen informed Sabeena of his decision to move. "We can't stay here. We have to move to a larger city where I can find work. Jaleel says we can stay with his friend in New York until I find work, and we can afford to rent an apartment." He paused for a moment and added, "Perhaps I made a mistake in bringing you along. I should have come alone, found a job and an apartment, and then sent for you."

"No," Sabeena answered. "I did not want to be left alone in India. I want to be with you, always." As she looked up at her husband, she saw insecurity lurking in his usually confident, smiling eyes. That and the prospect of staying with strangers made Sabeena uneasy. When they said good-bye to Jaleel, she cried for the first time.

Jaleel's friends, a couple, welcomed them, and Sabeena and Mina got along well in the beginning. Hussen spent his days wandering around with his resume, visiting different companies.

After a month, he still had not found a job in his field. When Jaleel's friend casually suggested that Hussen should take any available job, Sabeena sensed that they had overstayed their welcome. No longer comfortable at Mina's house, Sabeena wanted to move out. "Please, take any job," she pleaded to Hussen. "I will look for a job too if you will let me. We can't go on living here."

"Don't pester me. I will do as I please," Hussen exploded. "And no, you can't work outside the home."

"But don't you see? They no longer want us to live here," Sabeena said, trying to hold back her tears. "You are out all day; I am here. Or let's go back home," she timidly suggested.

"You can go back," Hussen snarled at her. "I intend to live here. This is a rich country with many opportunities and luxuries. I don't want to go back to the dull life we had at home."

Dull life! A home where everyone loved them and pampered them, where the weather was always reasonably warm, and everyone spoke their language. Though Sabeena failed to understand, she once again accepted his decision. After all, what choice did she have? If she were to return home against Hussen's wishes, he might divorce her; thus causing her status and that of her family to plummet. Besides, no one, not even her parents, would support her decision. Hussen did not mistreat or beat her, run around with other women or drink. So on what grounds could she leave him?

The next day Hussen found a job at a copying place. With money borrowed from Jaleel, they rented a one-room apartment in Queens. While not as nice as anywhere else Sabeena had lived, she was happy because at least she had a home to call her own.

Hussen worked long odd hours, so Sabeena was often alone at night in their apartment. She watched television, read and listened to music, but at times she longed for her home in India and was very lonely.

Around the corner from Sabeena's apartment an Indian woman, Jamuna, operated a business for her husband. She and her husband lived on the top floor of a three-family row house. On the first floor she had an Indian grocery store in the front, its shelves packed with Indian herbs, spices, grains and cereals. In the back room she had saris, 22-volt appliances for export to India and assorted Hindi movie cassettes.

Sabeena visited the store to buy groceries, but she could only look at saris and other items because, for the first time in her life, she could not afford to buy such things.

Gradually Sabeena and Jamuna came to know each other, and one day Jamuna asked Sabeena to babysit her children for $1.50 an hour because she had to run errands. "I can't," Sabeena answered. "My husband won't let me work for money."

"Oh! That type! Old-fashioned man!" Jamuna muttered. "Do it anyway," she suggested. "He'll never find out." When Sabeena still seemed reluctant, Jamuna suggested, "I will give you a sari or groceries instead of money." This barter proved more acceptable to Sabeena, so she started to babysit for Jamuna's kids, who called her Auntie. Sabeena enjoyed contact with the children, and wanted the experience because very soon she would have one of her own. Hussen never found out about the indirect babysitting income.

After Jamuna discovered that Sabeena was a good cook and an expert tailor, she came up with another business idea in which she tried to interest Sabeena. "Why don't I start to take cooking contracts for parties? You can help me cook, and also you can sew salwar kameezes and blouses. I'll bring in customers, and we can share the profits."

Sabeena liked the proposition, but was concerned about Hussen's reaction. "We can't do this secretly. I will have to ask Hussen."

Sabeena knew with a baby coming soon they had to have more money. Hussen had found a temporary part-time job as an architect and still worked at a part-time job at the copy shop, but resented the whole situation. He wanted a decent apartment, furniture and a luxury car; and eventually to go into business and make it big. He tried hard but couldn't get anywhere. He could not even find steady employment. Whenever he was home, his moods varied widely: from kind and considerate to rude and angry. He did not understand his pregnant wife's emotional needs. While he had a vague memory of all the love and attention his sister received when she was pregnant in India, he recalled such support as being given only by women. So, he neither knew what to do nor saw any need to learn. Even though his mother's letters contained pleas for him to take care of Sabeena, he was too busy with his quest for success to be bothered with such trivia.

Worried about the shortage of funds and her inexperience in caring for a newborn, Sabeena felt helpless and lonely; she turned more and more to Jamuna for emotional support and company. Jamuna was also alone most of the time. Her husband Shankar worked very hard to establish the glove manufacturing company he had just bought. Shankar had first started the Indian grocery store, which, with Jamuna's help, he had expanded to include other

items, like the saris. The business eventually began to generate enough money to support their family of four, and they even managed to accumulate some cash. Jamuna had hoped to use the extra money for a visit to India, but Shankar, who saw the limitations of a business that had only an Indian clientele, used the savings as a down payment to buy a small glove manufacturing company. The losing glove manufacturing venture required all the cash he and Jamuna could manage to save and Shankar subsidised it with extra income from the grocery business. Gradually his participation in the grocery business decreased and Jamuna, without complaints, carried alone the burden of running the business, caring for the children and managing the house.

"Only a few more years of this hard work," Shankar promised again and again, "then we'll hire someone to run this shop and you can go home for a visit with gifts for all your relatives. I will buy you the large house you always dreamed of and a nice car." Jamuna listened and hoped.

Constantly seeking ways to generate more cash for her husband's business, Jamuna's latest scheme was having Sabeena cook and sew for a fee, from which she took a cut as the agent who brought in the customers.

Jamuna knew of Hussen's strong objections to Sabeena's working outside the home, but since they needed extra income, she hoped he would not mind her working in the home.

After a dinner shared by the two couples, Jamuna introduced the scheme. Angered, Hussen stood up, stamped his foot and asserted, "My wife cooking and sewing for other people? No way!"

"In India, sewing and cooking for other people is considered demeaning, but the situation has changed," Shankar countered. "A lot of tailors are from the upper class now and make a lot of money; the job of chef in a hotel is now prestigious."

"Please, let me…only until you are settled," Sabeena begged.

"I won't let the customers know who cooks and sews," Jamuna offered. "We'll keep Sabeena's identity a secret. I can talk to customers and, if necessary, take measurements. I'll take orders for food."

Hussen wavered; their financial needs were pressing. He made Jamuna repeat her promise of keeping Sabeena's identity a total secret so that Sabeena would never be in direct contact with customers. She would just do the work. After Jamuna repeated the promise several times and Shankar reinforced it, Hussen consented. Neither husband took the proposed venture seriously; they looked at it as the women's small, side business.

With the combination of Jamuna's contacts and Sabeena's skills, the venture succeeded beyond their expectations. For the next five years Sabeena spent most of her time cooking and sewing for others. Together the two women hired help to cook and sew, and with her own income, Sabeena rented a large apartment and bought a car.

Meanwhile, Shankar's glove manufacturing company continued to limp along, barely paying for its own expenses. Shankar was trying to sell it now. Jamuna's visit to India and her dream house had not yet materialised.

Hussen continued to hold a part-time job as an architect and formed a partnership with another architect. They had rented an office and were trying to land a contract. Most of his paychecks went to pay for his business expenses.

At one of the parties Sabeena attended, she ran into a woman wearing a green blouse and sari. Sabeena had made the blouse. She remembered sewing it.

"How do you like your blouse? Does it fit all right?" she inquired out of curiosity.

"Perfect. All clothes Jamuna makes are perfect, but she charges a lot."

"Really? How much?"

"Twenty dollars for a blouse and forty for salwar kameez."

"What!"

"Yes. That is a lot of money, but a lot of people go to her. They like quality work."

The woman went on talking. Sabeena did not hear. Jamuna paid her only ten dollars for a blouse. All these years Jamuna had cheated her. They had agreed on a commission of twenty percent, but Jamuna had been taking fifty percent and lying to Sabeena about the amount. Sabeena thought of the late nights she stayed awake sewing, her aching back, her once soft hands now rough and worn from cutting vegetables.

After Sabeena recovered from the shock, she walked around the room making discreet inquiries to verify the newly acquired information. During her inquiries she learned of a four dollar surcharge for rush orders. Sabeena often worked very hard to finish rush orders, yet she never received a share of the extra charge. Angry, Sabeena returned home. Once she was back home she could feel the full force of her anger—betrayal from a woman she had considered a very close friend.

Sabeena lay awake all night and finally decided to confront Jamuna the next day after the shop closed. Since Hussen had gone away on an overnight business trip, she did not have a chance to talk the situation over with him. Yet somehow she did not particularly want to this time.

Though Sabeena went to see Jamuna after the shop closed, for the next hour a few late customers kept knocking on the door. Each time Jamuna let them in and Sabeena had to keep quiet. Finally, after they managed to move the children into a back room, Sabeena confronted Jamuna with her questions. A fight started, and just as Sabeena started to cry, they heard Nargis knocking on the door. Nargis, their wholesale fabric supplier, had come by to check for orders. Both Sabeena and Jamuna had known Nargis for a long time, and they trusted her as a businesswoman and a friend. Jamuna let her in. Looking at Sabeena, Nargis asked, "What's the matter Sabeena? Why are you crying? Can I help?"

"Sure you can. I want to go into business by myself. Bring me customers," Sabeena half sobbed.

"Doesn't Jamuna serve as your agent?" Nargis asked in surprise.

"She did until yesterday when I found out she's been cheating me, taking a fifty percent commission instead of the twenty percent we agreed to."

"What? Fifty percent commission?" exclaimed Nargis in shock.

Jamuna turned to Sabeena and began yelling at her again.

"I helped you because you needed money and your husband won't let you work outside the home. He is proud and does not want others to know that you cook and sew for other people, so I brought you customers. I have helped you, and now you are so ungrateful. Because of my help, you have a car and a nice apartment." Jamuna paused for a moment lowering her voice. "Besides, I need the money to help my husband."

"Why do you have to hide your identity?" Nargis, even more surprised, asked Sabeena.

"Because that would shame my family. In our community it is considered improper for a woman to support a man, and to work as a cook and to sew other people's clothes," Sabeena answered miserably.

"What does your husband do? Why doesn't he support you?" Nargis asked.

"He is trying to establish a business."

"For the last several years, while you kill yourself cooking, sewing and running a family?" Turning to Jamuna, Nargis asked, "And why does your husband need help?"

"For the glove manufacturing business he bought. It's not doing very well."

"My God!" Nargis sat down on a stool. "You are exploited, you fools. Your husbands are running around after their dreams, trying to be millionaires, trying to fulfill their ambitions, while you kill yourselves trying to earn money, keep house and bring up a family. Don't you see what's happening? Your husbands are not the breadwinners of the family; you are."

Sabeena thought of back-breaking late nights in the company of her sewing machine and weekends spent cooking. Jamuna thought of her dream house and a trip to India.

"And on top of the whole situation, you take orders from them. You keep your identity a secret and hand over your hard-earned money to dump into sinking ventures. You are exploited! And you, Sabeena, are doubly exploited."

On the way home Sabeena realized the truth behind Nargis's words; indeed both she and Jamuna were being exploited. Each a firm believer in traditional Indian values, had accepted her husband as superior, obeyed his orders without question, and carried the triple burden of providing financially for the family, caring for the children and running a house. Each husband claimed the situation happened to be temporary, but the temporary period had dragged on and on. For too long she and Jamuna had lived a life of drudgery, their youth slipping away, while they helped their husbands try to fulfill their farfetched ambitions. Both husbands had taken their help for granted and were not even aware of sacrifices the wives had made for them. And Hussen had made it possible for Jamuna to cheat her. Yes, Jamuna and Hussen had both wronged her.

Suddenly something else struck Sabeena, something else Nargis had said. "Your husbands are not breadwinners of the family, you are."

"That means I can, by myself, manage to support myself and my kids," she thought to herself. Suddenly a strange joy, a feeling of total elation she had never experienced before transcended Sabeena's whole being. Like her great-great-grandmother, she had always had the potential and the strength. Sabeena decided to think of the next step tomorrow. She could rent a small shop next door, or she could work out her problems with Jamuna. For tonight, though, this elation, this discovery of her own new image was as much as she could cope with.

Kothi bungalow, mansion

We are drifting, aren't we?

RINI DAS

First time here, I saw maple leaves.
"Tell me a story," I ask.
Today, the edges of war
Sliced the fantasies of your
Obstinate ripe breasts.
Ruins were lost for re-building.
Bananas, Oranges, Lemons,
Peaches; all were served
With casualties and all were Black.
The focus is now on the unreason.
Cool, bleak tongue, aimlessly
Tasting the flesh of summer;
While rooms close around us.
But we wait—when we talk
In silence and move among
The still.

"Just tell me a story. Will you?
Among the maple leaves, tomatoes
And brown clay softened with fire."

Tales for a Desert Storm

TEHMINA KHAN

My fountain pen…is my sword…
 it is sharp
 it cuts into the blankness of the white page
 even as Sheherezad's tales
 cut into the dark silence of a Baghdad night
 1001 Baghdad nights
 awakened with colors, dance
 laughter, tears
 wakened to life…through the voice of Sheherezad

My ink…is fluid and warm
 like blood…it is thick…and dark
 it drops onto the page
 pumped from my heart—causing me pain
 like the blood of Sheherezad's daughters
 buried in the rubble of Baghdad
 blood brings forth a scream
 before death

Baghdad…Dar-as-Salam we called you
 City of Peace
 our cradle…The stem of our flowering civilization
 a center where great minds set themselves free
 to weave…
 poetry, physics, philosophy, medicine…
 and tales
 to expand our minds as far as they could go…
 into the sky…the ocean…
 into our bodies…and our dreams
 what libraries we built…and mosques
 beautiful mosques…for worship and learning
Baghdad…so close to the homeland of our parents
 Hajira, Sara, and Abraham
 so close to Karbala

where Hussain gave his life to oppose tyranny
Baghdad...burns to the ground...devastated
CNN calls it "collateral damage"

Oh Sheherezad
 here...far away...in America
 I too heard your tales
 1001 nights...
 and I dreamed myself
 flying on a carpet
 through palaces in a starlit sky
 rubbing a magic lamp
 to find a genie emerge as my friend
 shouting iftah ya simsim! (Open sesame)
 to a rock—amazed
 to find it open into a cave
 full of riches to explore
Oh Sheherezad
 my sister Sheherezad
 you brought light to the dark Baghdad night
 with your tales
 you wove music into the silence

Now...
 the only lights over Baghdad
 bring death to your daughters and sons
 deafening explosions pierce the
 silence of the Baghdad night
 exploding the voices of your tales
 into millions of pieces
 drowning your tales
 in the blood of your daughters and sons
proudly, they carry your wounded tales
 decorated with the blood of your children
they dance...and wave them like a flag of victory
 silenced...raped...humiliated

Oh Sheherezad
 more than 1001 bombs per night
 pound on your city
proclaiming New World Order
 they raze your 5000-year-old civilization
 to dust...and blood...

in the morning
> after hearing your tale
> the brightness woven into the night
>> returns to us
> in that space between dream and wake...
>> our minds go spinning
>> and we begin to weave our own tales...

in the morning
> after the first bombing raid
>> a sleepless nightmare of ceaseless explosions
>>> the smell of burning flesh
>>> endless screams
>>> buildings collapsing like houses of cards
>> we look around...frantically
>>> to see if our mothers...
>>> sisters...brothers...children
>> are buried...alive or dead
>> under the ruins of our homes
>> or burning in a fire
>>> which will not stop...

and on TV...
> the American soldier says
>> "it was like the Fourth of July"
>> "we lit Bag-dad up like a Christmas tree"

so they celebrate your death

Oh Sheherezad
> my sister from Baghdad
>> Dar-as-Salam
>> City of Peace
> What is left of you now?
> Why did they beat you...
>> rape you...silence you?

Oh Sheherezad
> here, half a world away
> they cheer
> as they dance in pools of your blood

waving flags and yellow ribbons
they proclaim New World Order
> over your raped, mutilated body...

And the children of America
 play death on a video screen
 the tales fall short and whither away...
 as they explode cities
 with their hands on mock
 death machines
 watch 1001 blood baths
 with their eyes open wide
Children of America
 play at killing your tales
 instead of listening
And I wonder...
 has the war game actually defeated the tale?

the bombs stop
 the smoke begins to clear
 the smells of blood and burning flesh
 permeate the air
 the screams of grief and pain are so clear now—
 no longer muffled by the bombs
I peer into the rubble
 which was once Baghdad
 brick by brick...I pull them away
 searching...frantically...for you
 Sheherezad...my sister...
 hoping...praying...
 Oh that your heart may still beat and
 from the rubble you will emerge...
 to tell a new tale

Oh but Sheherezad—
 I live here in America
 my eyes do not know you
 they have never seen the land of Hajira, Sara, and Abraham
 my fingers have never touched
 the walls of the mosques, the libraries, the schools
 And the rich language of your poetic tale
 sounds foreign to my straining ears
 and I stand silenced
 bewildered
 lost
I do not know Dar-as-Salam
I only know that it has been taken from me

And my eyes have never seen such a war
 as that which massacres your children
my nose does not know the smell of
 burning flesh
I hear screams of death
 only in my mind

I live…in a quiet apartment
 with safe drinking water
 running through the pipes
and at night I too turn on the TV
 and watch the theater of war
 from my living room
I do not lie awake
 fearing that the soldiers may come
 demolish my home and strip me
 of my womanhood
I have never cowered in fear
 that morning may bring me
 searching for my children
 in the rubble
I do not know the war which kills your children
I only know disgust, anger and sorrow…
 and the feeling of my voice being ripped
 from my throat

Oh Sheherezad
 my fountain pen is a sword…
 it is sharp
 it draws forth blood from my heart…
 and brings forth my pain onto paper
 but tears…rain hard on my dreams

as the sun melts into the sands
 the new crescent shows itself
 and the words "God is Most Great"
 welcome the blanket of darkness…
And the children continue to die…

And we struggle…
 to bring forth a new tale
 to rise…

113

from the dust
and blood
which remains of Baghdad
Dar-as-Salam
City of Peace

India

MINAL HAJRATWALA

I see your remnants scattered
throughout the white man's land

he has melted your wealth
 into his
 and claimed it as his own creation
he has left your nations
 colonized chaotic
 impoverished
he is the richer
 for your existence
 you are weaker for his
he has stained your rivers
 with the blood of your children
 and washed away their souls
he has raped your worshippers
 made heathens of your pious
 made chutney of your goddesses
he has proclaimed you undeveloped
 neglecting your civilization
 ages more ancient than his

and mother India
still
do you forgive?

*

The Fear That Comes From Their Eyes

Can You Talk Mexican?

AMITA VASUDEVA

"**C**an you talk Mexican?"
> They used to ask me.
"No, I'm not Mexican I'm Indian, and besides they speak Spanish,"
> I used to reply, waiting listlessly for their best
> attempt at doing a "raindance."
"Owwow ooh ow ow." Smacking outstretched palms to their little mouths and hopping around.
"Not THAT kind of Indian—Indian from India,"
> I would correct, as soon as they finished whooping.
"Oh…Can you talk Indian?"

Yuba City School

CHITRA BANERJEE DIVAKARUNI

From the black trunk I shake out
my one American skirt, blue serge
that smells of mothballs. Again today
Neeraj came crying from school. All week
the teacher has made him sit
in the last row, next to the fat boy
who drools and mumbles,
picks at the spotted milk-blue
skin of his face, but knows
to pinch him sudden-sharp,
when she is not looking.

The books are full of black curves,
dots like the eggs the boll weevil lays
each monsoon in furniture cracks
in Ludhiana. Far up in front
the teacher makes word-sounds
Neeraj does not know. They float
from her mouth-cave, he says,
in discs, each a different color.

Candy pink for the girls
in their lace dresses, matching
shiny shoes. Silk yellow
for the boys beside them,
crisp blond hair, hands raised
in all the right answers. Behind them
the Mexicans, whose older brothers,
he tells me, carry knives,
whose catcalls and whizzing rubber bands
clash, midair, with the teacher's
voice, its sharp purple edge.
For him, the words are
a muddy red, flying low and heavy,

and always the one he has learned to understand:
idiot, idiot, idiot.

I heat the iron over the stove. Outside
evening blurs the shivering
in the eucalyptus. Neeraj's shadow
disappears into the hole
he is hollowing all afternoon.
The earth he knows is round, and if
one can tunnel all the way through,
he will end up in Punjab,
in his grandfather's mango orchard,
his grandmother's songs lighting
on his head, the old words
glowing like summer fireflies.

In the playground, Neeraj says, invisible
hands snatch at his hair,
unseen feet trip him from behind,
and when he turns, ghost laughter
all around his bleeding knees.
He bites down on his lip
to keep in the crying. They are
waiting for him to open his mouth,
so they can steal his voice.

I test the iron with little drops of water
that sizzle and die. Press down
on the wrinkled cloth. The room fills
with a smell like singed flesh.
Tomorrow in my blue skirt I will go
to see the teacher, my tongue
stiff and swollen
in my unwilling mouth, my few
English phrases. She will pluck them
from me, nail shut my lips. My son
will keep sitting in the last row
among the red words that drink his voice.

Colonization

MINAL HAJRATWALA

You
 native
 steadfast in the tropical forest
 of an island paradise
Inhabit a postcard
 sent by
 white american male
 to white american male
Proudly dressed
 in your
 woven sarong
 green yellow brown
Brown
 bare-chested
 dark-nippled
Oiled and shiny
 with your own
 labor's sweat
Hand-strung
 beaded tied
 necklaces geometrically
 bind your torso
On your head
 a water-filled
 black clay pot balanced
 by strong braceleted arms
You with your
 childbearing stomach
 womanly curves
 native exotic erotic appeal
You on a postcard
 pinned
 to a bulletin board
I look again
 and see
 you are not smiling.

Journeys:
Reclaiming South Asian Feminism

SAYANTANI DASGUPTA and SHAMITA DAS DASGUPTA

This article was born out of the discussions of two South Asian feminist-activists from different generations: a mother and daughter. As diasporic South Asian feminists living in the U.S. we have been fortunate to have each other to help crystallize our political thinking. By sharing and analyzing our experiences, we have been able to critically delineate the content and methodology of our politics. Although our life experiences, identities and activist paths differ, our visions of social change converge and complement each other.

There were times when, as a mother, I despaired about my ability to raise a feminist daughter. Bringing up a Third World child in an immigrant community within the First World was a constant struggle. I wanted to forge a balance between adaptation and marginalization, between progressive politics and cultural preservation, between global and local feminist consciousness. However, the mainstream feminist movement in which I was involved at the time was not synchronized with my identity and could not offer a harmony between these oppositions.

There were times when, as a daughter, I despaired about my mother's double marginalization. While her status as a South Asian immigrant differentiated her from the predominantly white mothers of my friends, her feminist politics set her apart from the predominantly conservative 'aunties' of our Indian community. It was a complicated childhood where I was encouraged to read both Rabindranath Tagore and Mary Wollstonecraft, where I went to both ERA rallies and Durga Puja celebrations, where my cultural identity grew simultaneously with a mainstream feminist cognizance.

Such schizophrenia between mainstream feminist politics and our realities as women of color in the U.S. eventually led to the emergence of our unique South Asian feminist perspectives. Our gender politics as a mother and daughter grew to encompass our status as Third World women. This article describes our separate journeys.

Growing up as a girl-child is not easy. My experience of growing up in India confirms this universal reality. Coming from an educated middle-class family and being my father's pet, I had my privileges. Yet, as a child I noticed the daily lives of my mother, aunts and cousins and could not get rid of the feeling that something was not quite right. The women around me were decidedly taken advantage of, bullied, shamelessly controlled, neglected and abused, and were generally quite unhappy. My mother calmly told me that it was a woman's lot. Women were more tolerant, patient, loving, giving, sacrificing, etc. and there was no getting

around it. Men had to be pampered, taken care of and, from time to time, forgiven. That was just the way it was.

None of these teachings were easily ingested by me. I fought incessant silent battles with my brother, father and other men. These struggles were waged on an emotional level, inside myself. I did not have the clarity of analysis to question any of the individual males in my life, nor was I given the privacy of time to articulate the issues that were tearing me apart. Then, when I reached the age of sixteen, my life became a whirlwind of activities. I got married. By nineteen I had moved to the U.S., which at that time was in the throes of various movements for self-determination and civil rights. Soon I was putting labels to my feelings and was articulating thoughts about women's disenfranchisement in society, in the new language coined especially to express it.

In my seventies-style consciousness raising group I was the only Indian; for that matter, the only woman of color. As the token nonwhite, I was invited to address various feminist groups, join several committees, speak at innumerable panels and attend endless workshops. I kept hearing how wonderful it was that I had decided to participate in the feminist movement, how awful it was that my Indian sisters were so oblivious to their oppression, how women of color were so completely dominated by their men that they forsook the movement that worked to empower all women. I apologized for my sisters and decided to investigate the reasons for their truancy.

Secure in my feminist conviction of a global sisterhood, I decided to introduce issues in my feminist circles that were important to immigrant Indian women. I talked about imperialism, Third World poverty, job market discrimination and a host of other invisible issues. My efforts were summarily dismissed. I was categorically told that since I was in the U.S., I must act like other AMERICANS. My place within the feminist movement was to uphold the agenda that had already been set by the majority. That was my wake-up call. I lost strong relationships with my mainstream feminist colleagues for calling them on their internalized racism.

Since those early years, I have come a long way. Although I have given up paying my yearly dues to the National Organization for Women, I am able to put the betrayal of mainstream feminism in proper perspective. During the development of my feminist consciousness, my work with mainstream organizations was perhaps a necessary step in my own growth; it is no longer. The insidious racism, classism and imperialism ingrained in the mainstream women's movement renders it ineffectual in bringing about all-encompassing social change.

Although I have distanced myself from mainstream feminism, I have enough contact with such groups to realize that not much has changed since the 1970s. I was in a mainstream feminist group whose proposed policy to facilitate the inclusion of women of color brought forth tirades from veteran activists. These activists argued that such policies were unnecessary, since diversity of ideas could successfully replace inclusion of women from diverse backgrounds. I have listened to raging debates among white feminists as to the reason for nonparticipation of women of color in the movement—the conclusion is almost always that these women excluded themselves by personal choice. I have been in feminist academic circles where white women strategized about the best method of attracting women of color to a

particular program: a beginning-of-semester party or personal recruitment. Rather than considering the possibility of restructuring the program to address women of color issues, the focus was on subsuming these women into a preset agenda.

My vision of a unified global movement has been replaced by the practicalities of decentralized movements and the prospects of temporary coalition building. Gender no longer defines a friend or foe to me. My battle lines are drawn against the institutions that support hegemonic structures and individuals who consciously maintain them.

One of my earliest memories is of a Take Back the Night march. I remember holding my mother's hand as we marched among hundreds of other women on the streets of Columbus, Ohio. The darkness was illuminated by rows and rows of flickering candles, held by women whose voices rose in songs of both protest and unity. This childhood incident was permanently etched into my memory, and for years afterward I marked that occasion as the birth of my feminist activist consciousness.

On the wall above my desk where I sit to write this essay are pictures of the traditional feminist foremothers, including Susan B. Anthony, Elizabeth Cady Stanton, Alice Paul, Margaret Sanger. Although these women's eyes have peered down upon me throughout most of my conscious life, it was not until recently that I realized only one of the women looks anything like me. She is, of course, the much-touted mainstream feminist favorite: Sojourner Truth. This display of mostly Great White Foremothers on my wall represents the path my feminist consciousness has taken. As a young woman growing up in 1970s and 1980s America, I was a devoted believer in what I then thought of as 'The Women's Movement.' While still in high school, I cut my political eyeteeth on Gloria Steinem, Betty Friedan and Simone de Beauvoir. In keeping with the mainstream feminist philosophies of the time, I firmly believed in a 'womanspace,' 'womanstrength' and 'womanenergy' that somehow united all female human beings in a universal sisterhood.

While Steinem, Friedan and de Beauvoir gave me my first language about gender oppression, my self-concept as a woman was under a vicious and insidious attack. As a small brown-skinned girl growing up in the American midwest, I internalized the white, blue-eyed, blond-haired beauty standard that was all around me. I was convinced I was some sort of a mutant, an ugly spot on the creamy contours of womanly beauty. My own family, with their 'weird' language and customs, was another constant source of humiliation. Even when I moved to the more cosmopolitan east coast, the myth of the Asian model-minority haunted me, and I was labeled as a 'brain,' a particularly de-sexualizing label. Unfortunately, the white feminist analysis I was ingesting did nothing to explain this reality.

In college, I initially became involved in campus feminist activism. I regularly attended speak-outs, rallies, and yes, Take Back the Night marches. I dressed in the fashion of liberal activism, complete with ankle-bells and Indian-print skirts. These trappings, along with my very brown skin, made me an instant campus political figure. It was wonderful recognition after the denigrations of childhood. Soon, however, I began to recognize the similarities between the experiences. Although my childhood peers were disgusted by my Indian heritage and my college friends were fascinated by it, both defined me as strictly 'other.' For instance, I was once speaking at a women's center meeting about the need to attract more women of

color students, and the only response I got afterward from my seemingly supportive white feminist colleagues was a compliment on how attractive my long black hair looked as I spoke.

Although my white feminist peers were fascinated by Indian clothing, nose rings and religion, they were convinced that I was the feminist exception to South Asian womanhood. I soon grew tired of defending the politics of my supposedly ultra-oppressed South Asian sisters. I found that I had to defend even the objectionable parts of my culture because of the constant vilification. I realized that when I was not being exoticized or tokenized, I was being brainwashed to reject my ethnic heritage in the name of feminism. Furthermore, I was expected to participate in the culture of white feminism, where experiential testimonials, sisterly hand-holding and constant self-indulgent rallies were de rigueur. I realized then that the white feminist movement had become a mini-institution that defined and limited the parameters of acceptable feminism and punished those who transgressed race, class, ethnicity or culture. I quickly rejected my comfortable notion of universal sisterhood, and began to avoid Take Back the Night rallies.

I soon made my alliances with other women of color, and with South Asian women in particular. I realized that the complexity of my reality could not be addressed by a simplistic and exclusionary movement. For instance, an academician recently asked me if I considered myself a South Asian woman or a feminist. This woman, who is white American and a self-proclaimed feminist, continued her categorizing by asking whether I considered myself a South Asian woman or a woman of color. These questions perhaps demonstrate the mentality of the mainstream feminist movement. Clearly, the assumption of the first question was that my ethnic identity was separate from my feminist politics; I could not claim to be both South Asian and a feminist. The assumption of the second question perhaps reflects the grudging and many times tokenistic inclusion of women of color into mainstream feminist consciousness. Interestingly enough, my questioner could not fathom that I could be 'of color' and yet be South Asian. Perhaps she expected me to somehow magically become African American for her conceptual convenience. Thus, despite my initial introduction to feminist consciousness through mainstream avenues, it becomes painfully clear that The Great White Foremothers on my wall never expected to look over a young woman of South Asian descent. They would probably roll over in their graves if they knew that their presence has instigated my critique of mainstream feminism in general.

Discarding the security of the mainstream feminist movement was not easy. Neither was my conscious decision to wed my feminist agenda with my ethnic identity. Until then my relationship with my Indian community had been based only on my birth; now my relationship became an act of choice. As a symbol, I gave up wearing all western clothing. However, this was not enough. I had to develop a feminist agenda in the context of the South Asian community.

I realized that I was not alone in my efforts. Serendipitously, I came together with five other Indian women, all runaways from mainstream feminism. Reclaiming our community was an intricate task. We had to dig through its surface crust of conservatism, absolutism and androcentrism. In turn, the community had to receive us in our many-faceted roles: mothers, activists, professionals, students, wives, feminists, single women. For a while it was touch and go.

Through this turmoil, Manavi was born, the first women's organization in the U.S. to focus on issues of victimization of South Asian immigrant women. Our first concern was whether we knew anything about working with South Asian immigrant women. None of us had any practical training in counseling this particular group, and there were no experts to turn to. We knew our knowledge had to be decanted from hands-on experiences.

My first experience came when I was called by the local shelter to work with an Indian woman who had been brought there after being severely beaten by her spouse. The shelter workers had contacted me because she had not eaten in the three days she had been there, and had refused to change her clothes. I went in and met a middle-aged Indian woman who spoke limited English and wore a long-sleeved floor-length nightdress. As we talked in Hindi, I found out the reason for her self-imposed starvation. She was a strict vegetarian. Although the shelter had provided her with plenty of vegetables to cook with, they had given her pots and pans in which non-vegetarian food had been cooked. Being a guest in someone else's house, she felt that she could not inconvenience her hosts any further by demanding fresh pots for cooking. To survive, she had compromised her principles already by drinking milk from a refrigerator where meat and eggs were stored. She did not feel comfortable in the clothes that the shelter offered her: western dresses. The closest she could get to the modesty a sari provided was the long nightdress. After the victimization experience at home, a shelter should provide women with security of mind and body. However, this particular incident is evidence to the cultural disorientation a woman may feel in a surrounding that is insensitive to her background.

Since then, I have learnt well to work with my sisters. I feel inclined to establish kinship with the women I meet during their hours of crisis. In the last eight years with Manavi, I have progressed from bahen to didi and even to aunty. Many a woman has become my 'little sister.' I became long-term friends with many, share information about my daughter and commiserate in their difficulties with in-laws. Through my work I have learned that in most cases of spousal abuse, a temporary restraining order, much touted by the mainstream domestic violence movement, is not a viable alternative for South Asian women. Without the skills to live alone in a foreign country and the assurance of acceptance within the South Asian community, legal alternatives are ineffective tools.

There are no textbook counseling techniques for the South Asian community. My work with Manavi has taught me to be an activist and a feminist not by dismissing the immigrant community but working within it. I suppose the community has also learned that we will not go away. To a certain degree, our tenacious existence has proved to the community that much of the model minority image is a myth. The reality of domestic violence within the community testifies against the facade of an immigrant utopia. Concurrently, it has been our task to demonstrate to the community that our womanism does not only target individual gender oppositions. Rather, its scope is the institutions, attitudes and actions that subjugate women in society.

Instead of looking at the mainstream movement for direction, Manavi has had to forge new paths that suit our methods of traveling. We have had to redefine terms such as 'empowerment' for our South Asian context. The accepted modes of empowering women as elaborated by the mainstream feminists—speaking out, marches and rallies, living alone,

finding your 'identity'—do not necessarily apply to us. Forcing individuals to make decisions without informational, financial, practical and emotional resources corresponds to virtual abuse. So do various mainstream forums for women's actual and symbolic testimonies of victimization. For many South Asian women, symbols such as Take Back the Night marches mean little. The majority of these marches and their concluding rallies are organized and directed by white feminist groups with no or little input from any women of color. Even though safety is an important issue to all women, not all can relate to the form, chants and the invariable candlelight vigils for victims of violence. In the recitation of the names of fallen comrades at these rallies I have never encountered one that remotely resembles mine.

The speak-outs pose another dilemma for me. I have been invited by many organizers to have South Asian women victims of violence tell their stories at rallies. Although South Asian women have historically used silence as a tool of protest, there is no doubt that the strategy of voicing women's stories is a powerful one. In this patriarchal world, to be heard is to be counted. However, the request to reveal painful and intimate experiences to women who are sisters of convenience only, is an unjust one that does not stand to be honored. The women in the audience at these rallies are the same women who snicker at our arranged marriages, derogate our decision to remain with the husband for the sake of children and feel no compunction at touching the sari or long hair of the 'exotic' foreigners. Thus, the raising of the voices that is considered vital to the fight for justice for one group, becomes a method of disempowering another.

Through the experiences of Manavi, I continuously define and refine my concepts of feminism in the context of my community. No longer is this community limited to the immigrant one that I clearly belong to, but the one that is spread all across the globe. Activists who envision a future world of compassion and equality for all, and have identified their field of action as the South Asian diaspora, are my comrades. The second generation of South Asian activists emerging in this country in recent years is proof to the energy of our community. There is much to learn from this group and much we can teach them. As a South Asian activist my path in reclaiming my community has been a meandering one. I rejoice at the newer generation's clarity of purpose and ability to zero in so quickly. I believe the best we can do for them is to strengthen our own shoulders for them to stand on and hope that they will do the same for the next generation.

What does it mean to be a South Asian American feminist? It's a question I have been asking since I began to conceive of myself in that ambiguous term. The mere phrase 'South Asian' is problematic enough for most people. Far too many Ph.D.-toting college professors have thought that I was from Thailand or Vietnam—a lesson for me to not underestimate the obscurity that comes with claiming South Asian identity. Even among South Asians, the term is too often used interchangeably with 'Indian' for my comfort. Clearly, claiming to be 'South Asian American' invokes even greater problems. I use the term to distinguish myself from immigrants from the subcontinent, since I find the term 'ABCD' (American born confused Desi) far too derogatory of my mental state. Finally, in the backlash era of the 1990s, claiming to be a 'feminist' is dangerous enough; identifying as a South Asian American feminist therefore necessitates explanation.

It was my disgruntlement with the institutionalized nature of mainstream feminism, along with its culture, language and vision, that led me to search for a more complex feminist

politics that incorporated the multiple oppressions of race, language, class, sexuality, immigrant status, etc. As a daughter of Indian immigrants, I looked first and foremost to my family and cultural identity for such politics.

I am very lucky in that I was brought up with a strong South Asian feminist role model: my mother. As a young woman struggling with issues of identity, I drew strength from both her and the many strong women in my extended family. I grew up hearing stories about my great-aunts, who struggled and died in the Indian Independence Movement. In Santiniketan, I often chatted with my grandmother's friends, elderly white-sari-clad women who turned out to have Ph.D.s or at least black belts in Judo. I saw a tradition of Indian women's strength in the Durga Puja festivals I attended, the stories of Chitrangada and other epic heroines, the Rani of Jhansi who leapt bravely through my Amar Chitra Katha comic book.

Nonetheless, mainstream American feminism taught me that being an Indian woman was antithetical to being a political activist. Even among women of color groups, Asian American women seemed to be summarily dismissed as inherently passive and submissive. The conservative diasporic Indian community, which desperately clutches all traditionality in resistance to cultural assimilation, confirmed the idea that being Indian was antithetical to working for social change. I had to unlearn these corrosive teachings and ground my feminist politics in a long history of Indian women's strength.

I began to think of myself as a South Asian feminist, both because the term was inclusive of women from other countries in the subcontinent and because the term 'Indian' was too often confused with 'Native American.' I looked to Manavi, a South Asian women's organization formed by my mother and five other women, for guidance and political direction. By doing feminist work within the South Asian diaspora, I learned firsthand the issues faced by women in my community. However, I grew dissatisfied. As the daughter of a founder member and one of the youngest members in Manavi, I began to wonder how my issues differed from those of my mother and other immigrant women. I realized that as a 'second generation' member of a South Asian immigrant community, my feminism had to be grounded in my own reality rather than that of my mother's.

It was initially very difficult to structure my identity as a South Asian American feminist. In the face of racism and cultural assault, I had always distanced myself from my 'American' experience. Yet, I had to acknowledge the fact that I was a diasporic Indian woman, born and raised in the West. As such, my childhood experiences were determined by the racist and anti-immigrant culture in which I lived. As opposed to South Asian immigrants who spent their childhoods as members of the 'majority' group in their more racially homogeneous homelands, I was always the 'other.' I never felt included in the 'majority' group. Throughout my life, my entire self-concept was based upon being an 'other.' Like all children of immigrants, I have had to juggle with multiple cultures and grapple with my ethnic identity. Simultaneously, I have access of language, education, custom and clothing into the mainstream culture. These experiences differentiate me from most South Asian feminists who immigrated to the U.S. as adults. Although it is vital for me to work with and learn from my immigrant mothers, I must also determine my own feminist politics as a South Asian American woman.

Whether deliberately or inadvertently, today's visible South Asian immigrant community in the U.S. has propagated the idea that South Asian cultural heritage is antithetical to

social change activism. By presenting itself as apolitical, the immigrant community is ignoring our rich political heritage both in the diaspora and South Asia. The 'first wave' Indian immigrants to this country, the majority of whom came as farm workers, were greatly involved in the labor, race and immigrant politics of early twentieth century America. As modern South Asian feminists, we can look to this early community for strong female role models. Such activism can be traced throughout the South Asian diaspora: England, South Africa, Fiji, the Caribbean and South America. Women's participation in social change movements is a rich South Asian tradition.

As progressive South Asian activism gathers strength within the U.S., a rift between the mainstream South Asian and the South Asian activist communities becomes more and more apparent. It is vital for both groups to recognize the destructiveness of such an ideological chasm. While the mainstream South Asian community needs to make space for diverse political perspectives within itself and recognize the historic relationship between South Asian culture and political activism, progressive South Asian activists must also recognize their integral connection to the mainstream community. We cannot hope to be successful feminist activists while ignoring the racism in the mainstream feminist movement, nor can we claim to be South Asian feminists while adopting the Western model of social change. Rather, we must find strength in our heritage of activism and each other.

This article describes the stories of two women only. Our experiences as feminist activists have strongly embedded in us a belief that there is no one monolithic 'Women's Movement.' Similarly, there can be no one vision of South Asian feminist activism. We can only speak for ourselves. As a mother and daughter who have gained valuable insight from sharing our experiences with each other, we hope that our analyses will continue to grow from connections with other South Asian feminists.

Different Small Towns

RADHIKA SITA CHARI

She and I met in a women's bar, "You're from where?" we asked in amazement. So, we had both lived in that same small town. "Do you know…? Did I remember…?" We laughed as we reflected on our coincidental meeting. She told me about her memories at our school—favorite teachers, old friends, running track. As she talked, I recalled my own memories, ones I hadn't thought about in years.

I had been the only Brown kid in this town. My parents had immigrated from India and I was born here, halfway around the world.

I remembered my first recess in that town. The White kids had planned that I would replace the class geek in the game 'the girls chase the boys.' But when she saw me she didn't worry. They didn't mind if she played. She had worn glasses since she was four, but apparently I had the worse handicap. I remembered the history teacher asking me about India. "Why do the women wear the red dot? Why is the cow sacred?" If he had asked me about my grandfather maybe I could have answered him.

Later on, when the Black kid showed up, I was momentarily happy to have found a comrade. But he knew about the Black/White game and danced and joked around the room while the White kids smiled and laughed. He knew not to associate with me.

One year on Valentine's Day, my mother suggested that we make our own cards. It was so much fun, cutting and pasting, thinking of funny sayings. Because the cards were not so small, we put them in long office envelopes to take to school. The next day, as I dropped mine in other kids' bags, I saw that mine were the only handmade ones. I felt stupid and ashamed. The next time, when at my mother's suggestion, I stitched a yellow giraffe for my teacher, I knew better than to give it to him next to all those fancy bought gifts. So I lied to my mother and threw it in the trash.

Remembering that giraffe, I shuddered. I looked at the White woman sitting across from me. What of my reality did she understand? "What do you remember?" she asked. I told her, "I remember you running. I have this vision of your hair flying behind you as you raced around the track, ahead of almost everybody." I had also run track. I had always started out strong, in front even. But with three quarter's of the track to go I would break and fall farther and farther behind, coming in almost last. The gym teacher cheerily would ask me what happened, but then she would turn to the White girl who won to give her a hug.

The woman grinned at me. "It's great to have run into you. I can't believe we're from the same town."

I smiled back, watching her leave, confronted with the horrors of relived memories that I thought I had left behind.

Journal Entry

AMITA VASUDEVA

Passing. I guess I've always pretty much passed as white. Not white in the color; white in culture—outwardly only. Why was it so easy to pass? Because I made an effort not to deny or refute any assumptions people had about me. I never really talked about my heritage when I was younger; there is always that ever-present fear in children of not being accepted, or even harsher, of being cast out, ignored, ridiculed. So I tried to avoid the issue of being different. When my teachers asked me how my "turkey day" was, I was too ashamed to tell them that I ate cholay/bhatura—not cranberry sauce and mashed potatoes. I pretended I got tons of Christmas gifts even though my parents only gave us each a few token presents. When my mom spoke Hindi to me in the grocery store, I hated it; I froze, tense with embarassment and pretended not to hear. I would always look around nervously and then, down because I knew people were looking and I was afraid of their gaze.

Looking. Avoiding the gaze of other people. People looking at me because of my color—that is the scariest thing to me. I feel like they are looking at my insides, at my heart and hating it. I've made so many efforts in my life to stay out of the gaze of other people. Out of the gaze of white people surrounding me. In my high school there were very few people of color and in my class there was only one other Indian girl. I was friends with her—but mostly outside of school. At school I felt that if we walked together or sat next to each other we would be seen as a brown blemish in the otherwise homogeneous white hallways and classrooms. I didn't want to risk my individuality for her in-school companionship. People always assumed that we were best friends or cousins anyway. (Funny, I've never assumed that all those white folks in my high school were related to one another.) When you're different, "the other," they strip you of your individuality. "This Indian girl in my class…" already an image is conjured up about some homely dark-skinned girl with long straight hair. A girl at the amusement park asked me out of the blue why I didn't wear a dot on my forehead.

As a child I hated being thought of as different, because I was alone in my difference. The only other Indian kids I met were children of my parents' friends. Now that I have developed my own strong relationships with other South Asian Americans, I prefer to be recognized as distinct from the white bland mass of non-color and homogeneity that surrounds me. I hate it when people, especially recent Indian immigrants, think of me as a totally assimilated American because I'm not—and I don't make any claims to be. There are certain situations where I am "completely American" and feel natural and comfortable and good about it—because after all I was born and raised in the U.S. And there are of course times at home with my family, or with Indian friends, when I can dress Indian, be around Indian people and feel just as comfortable. But being Indian or American is not a choice I can make according

to different situations, because there is no denying the fact that I am both. Now when I am in a situation where I do feel very American, I don't think of it as passing or hiding but just that I'm being what I am.

La Soledad

ROSHNI RUSTOMJI-KERNS

Katy Cooper was in awe of those few who saw her as wise, beautiful, perfect. She realized that they had been able to see the unbroken, complete angel who stood behind her. The insubstantial being whom she had no talent or craft to see. But these few had somehow, through chance or an oblique vision or an inability to see her solid material form standing before them, recognized the angel.

She knew her substantial self. Her tongue was torn into shreds on the sounds of her Indian grandmother's words, her mother's language, the conqueror's speech. Her eyes had grown cataracts, greys and whites, in an attempt to mute down diverse sights; visions dissolved into revisions. Her brain coiled around the bits and pieces of facts and wisdom offered to it by zealous teachers as she continued to trudge through various parts of the world. Katy Cooper had been known to call herself "the fragmented woman."

Two things had haunted her as long as she could remember: her bruised and aching knees—and angels. Angels and archangels, and even a scattering of the more western cherubim and seraphim, had dropped into her life when she was six years old and had awakened at dawn to see a guardian angel looking down upon her favorite doll. She recognized this angel, and the ones who came after, because they appeared out of nowhere, disappeared into nowhere, and even in their luminous, bleary forms they seemed to her much more sensible than any historical being. She believed in angels. After all she was a Zoroastrian.

The pain in her knees went unexplained by medical doctors and psychiatrists until her final visit to Oaxaca at the age of sixty-two. But this is the much earlier story of her first visit to Oaxaca. Via Berkeley.

She knew that she had been invited to this party in Berkeley not because the hostess, Tracy Robertson, had seen the ever-present angel behind her or even the more substantial her. She knew that she was invited as one more exotic catch in Tracy's net. When they had first met four months earlier at the reception after a Bharata Natyam performance at the Brundage Asian Art Musuem, Tracy had insisted that Katy tell her her real name. As far as Tracy was concerned, Katy Cooper was neither a real Indian name, nor did it suit Katy's physical form or color. Katy assured Tracy that Katy was her real name, given in honor of her English mother. She had consoled Tracy by telling her that she was certainly born in India, in a town called Devinagar, and that Cooper was not an uncommon name among the Zoroastrians, the Parsis, in India. Tracy had never heard of Devinagar and knew nothing about Parsis. But she was delighted by the idea of including Katy in her next party.

Katy accepted the invitation because she wanted to test the strength of her tranquility in the midst of a Berkeley party. She felt a certain affinity with Tracy's main dish. She could

134

smell the Safeway spices which had barely been cooked before being mixed into the casserole of beans, tortilla chips, non-beef-85%-less-fat-sausages and melted cheese. It put forward a brave front, masking the ineptness of Tracy-as-cook and the fragmentation of ingredients.

The Chinese lady was complete. She was supposedly seventy-eight years old. Tracy Robertson had announced it to each guest as she made the introductions. "And this is my dear friend, Mrs. Chou. She is seventy-eight years old. Can you believe it?! Look at that porcelain skin! And that hair! I would kill for such hair and skin! Poor dear. Lives alone. Next block. I keep an eye on her." And as the guests bowed or smirked or shuffled restlessly and put out a hand, she would say, "Oh dear! Don't bother. She doesn't really speak English. I make do with sign language with her." She would smile and bow at the lady and the lady would smile and bow to her. As the evening progressed Tracy Robertson's smile became a bit blurred, her bow became deeper and sometimes she even patted Mrs. Chou on her head. The depth of Mrs. Chou's bow and the tilt of her smile remained the same. She sat in the seat of honor bestowed upon her by Tracy. Back straight. Legs neatly crossed at the ankles. Katy was sure she wore silk stockings. No nylon pantyhose for Mrs. Chou.

Katy's friend Rita was also at the party. Her sari was extravagantly praised by many of the guests. Rita had confided to her friends that it was a synthetic wash-and-wear sari. In the end, Fatima, who had arrived in a kaftan bought at Cost Plus, had to escort Rita home. She had found Rita in the corner of the kitchen, stuck to the wall in silent hysteria. One of the male guests had decided to test the silkiness of her skin rather than that of the sari and her new apartment mates, Carmelita and Annie, had neglected to warn her of the possibility of such incidents—even in Berkeley.

Carmelita Guiterez's huipil was authentic. She had bought it in Oaxaca. Her name was not authentic. She had been named Dolly Conception by her parents in their awkward attempts to shield her from her teachers and gringo schoolmates in Texas. In her frustrated search to find a home for her anger she had changed her name. She was Carmelita and she had seen her own angel. It was herself. She insisted that it was split right down the middle. One side Zapotec in color and form, the other a mixture of the conquering races. Mostly pink and mostly taller. One breast was stamped with eagles and snakes and butterflies and an owl. The other bore a neon crucifix and a plump, bleeding heart.

Annie, who answered to her true name only in her dreams, wore the jeans and cowboy shirt of the race that had visited genocide on her people. Her earrings were true to her grandmothers, her dignity unbroken. Her silence was seen as an invitation to discuss her people openly. One woman approached her and asked, "Are you real?" Even Annie looked baffled. "I mean, are you a real Indian? I mean how much of you is Indian?" Annie answered, "I don't know."

Katy was tired of maneuvering around her fragmented self and, as usual, her knees and ankles had begun to hurt from the effort of talking while standing up. She had discovered that Tracy's casserole had uncooked turmeric generously sprinkled on top of it. After the party, she had told Rita who was acknowledged as the cook in their apartment, to please explain the necessity of cooking turmeric to Tracy. She left it up to Rita to decide if Tracy should be told about the proven medicinal and the believed magical powers of turmeric.

But it was Mrs. Chou who held Katy's interest. Katy pulled her quilted Tibetan jacket closer around her and sat down to contemplate Mrs. Chou. She pointed at the table and asked

if she could bring her something to eat. Mrs. Chou bowed her head in assent. But just as it seemed as if she were about to speak, Tracy brought over a late arrival. "Mrs. Chou this is my dear and wonderful friend, Sam Brentano." Bow. "Sam, this is my dear neighbor, Mrs. Chou." Bow. Sam, who seemed to be a friendly sort said, "Hello Mrs. Chou! You know I had a chance to go to China last…" Tracy broke in, "No Sam. Don't worry. She doesn't speak English. Do you think maybe she was one of those picture brides, Sam? Isn't she quite lovely? So delicate…and look at her tiny feet! Wonder how it feels to wear those expensive pumps on feet which must have been bound…"

At this point Mrs. Chou leaned over, picked up the napkin from Katy's lap, wiped her mouth and said, "I was born in San Francisco. So were my parents. And I have been known as Dr. Ellen Chou ever since I got my medical degree as a young woman. I have practiced medicine in China and in the United States. I am now retired. My feet were never bound. Nor were my mother's, nor my grandmother's. My feet are naturally small and I am rather proud of them. I wear only Italian shoes. I do not dye my hair but I do use a special cream for my complexion." She grinned. "A Chinese secret lotion. Thank you for the party." She got up, bowed and left.

If you were told that Tracy Robertson has never been the same since that party, it was a lie. But the party was memorable. Not only because of the Ellen Chou incident but also because of what followed.

Katy and Annie decided to leave with Carmelita soon after Mrs. Chou's exit. Annie opened the passenger door to Carmelita's car and let it go suddenly. Katy bent over to look in and also pulled back abruptly. A woman sat stiffly in the back seat. She was a strange figure, shrouded in what looked suspiciously like one-half of Tracy's bedroom curtains. Carmelita urged them into the car.

"It's all right. It's all right. No one will hurt you. Get into the car. Just get in!"

Annie and Katy got into the back seat, next to the woman. As Carmelita pulled away from the curb, Annie began to laugh.

"She is…It is…She's not a person. She's not a woman."

Carmelita announced, "I've found her at last."

"Not a person. Not even half a person!" Annie continued to laugh.

Carmelita was serious, "Don't touch her. Just let's go home and I'll show you."

Carmelita carried the covered figure into their apartment. Fatima and Rita came out of their rooms as Carmelita silently set the figure on the floor and unwrapped it. Rita wondered aloud about the presence of the bottom half of a female mannequin in their living room. Carmelita explained that this was not the bottom half of a female mannequin. This was the bottom half of the statue of the Virgin of Soledad. La Soledad herself. Mary, the reigning queen of Oaxaca.

The women waited.

"All my life I have been looking for this bottom half of the Virgin. Since I was eleven. Since I first visited the Soledad Church in Oaxaca with my madrina Glafira, and was shown the courtyard with the ceramic donkeys and told that this was the very spot where the donkeytrain men had discovered the unattended, unclaimed extra donkey with the wooden chest which contained the bust of a middle-aged dark woman. It was promptly hailed as a

miracle by the priests and the bust was claimed as that of the Virgin—especially sent to protect the city and valley of Oaxaca. She was clothed and pedestalled…"

"Pedestalled?" Fatima had already begun a close inspection of the wooden diaphragm, belly, buttocks and legs of the figure. No one thought it strange when she bent down to touch and count the toes; or when she looked up the legs, with odd reverence, to check out if the torso were anatomically correct.

Fatima's unsolicited statement after her examination was, "Pretty real—well, as far as possible. After all, she is wood. Nice paint job. Pedestalled?"

"Since there was no bottom half to the figure carried by the donkey, they built her a solid block of wood and set her up on it. Incredible gown. Instead of the Christ child she holds a lily. She is the Virgin after the crucifixion. No baby, no corpse, no son. An enormous crown on her head."

Rita had long been concerned about the inaccessibility of public icons. "Only you, Carmelita, would have climbed onto a Catholic altar and looked under the skirt of a holy image."

"Didn't. Just guessed that's how it was. I knew that the other part existed somewhere."

Annie had joined Fatima in the close scrutiny of the figure. "How did you find her?" she asked.

"I was laughing so hard at Mrs. Chou's announcement and Tracy's calm acceptance of it that I began to cough and wheeze. Tracy took me to her bedroom in search of some Kleenex. I saw the figure. If you will please notice, the feet on these wooden legs are quite large. No Italian shoes for her. Tracy was quite proud of how she had bought the 'half statue' as she called it, at the flea market in Sebastopol. The guy who sold it to her said that it was part of a column. He had found it in Nepal. Tracy said that she was entranced by the color of the figure. When she left the room, I carried it out through the back door. I'll return the curtain to Tracy."

Katy was not ready to believe Carmelita. "How do you know that this is the bottom half of the statue in Oaxaca?"

"Right color, right size, right shape, right aura." She looked at Katy for at least a full minute and said, "You are the one, Katy. You have to take this part to Oaxaca and join it to the top half."

"I barely speak Spanish."

"That's why. When you get to Oaxaca, you can dress up as a nun—a foreign one, since Mexican nuns are not allowed to wear holy clothes. You can tell the bishop or priest or even another nun—someone in charge there—that you had a vision and found this part which belongs to the Virgin."

Carmelita, with the help of Annie and Rita, dressed up what was by now being referred to as "the Lady's trunk." Fatima made the travel arrangements. Rita wondered if all this was sacrilegious but offered to go with Katy. But Carmelita was adamant: Katy had to do this alone. Katy could not find the right words to express her dismay and fears. Especially since Carmelita continued to assure her that if she were ever to see her own unbroken, complete angel, Oaxaca was the most likely place for the event. Katy agreed to go but refused to impersonate a nun.

Katy's first visit to Oaxaca was brief. Oaxaca did seem like a place where she probably would encounter her own angel. She wasn't ready for it. And she felt rather bitter at barely being able to stand up without the aid of extra-strength Tylenol, while carrying a perfectly strong pair of legs in her suitcase. Wood, she was sure, could not hurt as much as bones and muscles and ligaments.

She was able to enter Mexico by assuring the officer at the airport that the partial body, appropriately dressed, which filled her entire suitcase was no, not a statue. It was a mannequin. Actually a tailor's dummy. Her friend in Oaxaca, a seamstress, had asked for this particular half-mannequin because she was going to specialize in skirts—mini, midi, long— for the tourists. And again no, Katy did not know why she had asked for a mannequin made of wood, but she did know that her friend's sister was going to embroider the skirts. The customs officer's words were, "Señora, I am sure there are half-bodies made of wood to be found all over Mexico." He shrugged and let her go.

Once in Oaxaca, Katy panicked. To approach Catholic priests, trying to explain half a wooden body without the aid of a genuine, acceptable miracle seemed ludicrous. And when she did visit the Church of La Soledad to confront the Virgin, she was so distressed by the poverty at the doors of the church that she left without entering the church. But she saw enough pictures of La Soledad all over Oaxaca to assure herself that this particular Virgin, Mother of God, seemed content to be resting on whatever legs she had been allocated by her devotees.

Katy returned to San Francisco within a week, the "Lady's trunk" never having left the suitcase. Neither she nor the Lady were as fortunate with the San Francisco airport officials as they had been with the Mexico customs official. Katy's explanations of having found the torso in an antique store and her offer to pay the correct amount of duty for bringing in an antique did not raise any shrugs. She and the suitcase were taken into a private room. A dog was brought in to sniff at the suitcase. Katy's comment on the dog being brought in to view the corpse at Zoroastrian funerals went unacknowledged by the two officials as they proceeded to break open the diaphragm and the belly and to slice through the legs of the wooden half-woman. When they found nothing legal or illegal hidden within her, they politely confiscated the pieces of wood and escorted Katy to the exit of the customs room, handing her the suitcase that now contained only a pair of slacks, two blouses, enough underwear for a week's visit away from San Francisco and the Mixtec shawl she had bought in the hotel boutique.

Carmelita and Fatima tried to get back the broken pieces but quickly gave up the idea when faced with the paperwork. No one blamed Katy. When Carmelita took back the curtain to Tracy, she explained the situation. Tracy found the whole episode wonderful, refused to be financially compensated for the abrupt abduction of the column, and was suitably furious at the San Francisco customs officials. She found yet another dark wooden lower body of a woman at the flea market in Sebastopol and presented it to Carmelita. Annie speculated about the condition of porches and columns in Nepal. Rita found an extraordinarily beautiful bust of a dark woman, a prow ornament, at an antique store in Moss Landing. The two pieces were put together and any discrepancies were covered up by a maroon velvet caftan. Katy donated the Oaxaqueña shawl to the Lady who was now a permanent fixture in their crowded apartment. She wore no shoes. She was referred to as La Soledad and sometimes as The Good Doctor in honor of Dr. Chou.

Indian Cookhouse, Castro Street

PARIJAT DESAI

"Keep it moving," ordered the tall, dark-as-an-African East Indian man.
He spoke under his breath, but kept his consonants sharp.
The almond eyes of the Chicana waitress looked embarrassed as she rushed back to refill
　　her water jug.
I looked through the menu, which spoke enticingly to "eat-out" American society.
Paneers, Biryanis, and of course, curries…
What's Indian food without curry?
Unable to break from the rotli-daal-bhaat-shaak pattern of my mother's meals,
I ordered a Vegetarian Thali which offered a little of all the essential components.

As he went into the kitchen with my order, the other light-as-an-Italian-with-a-tan man in
　　charge
whispered instructions and pointed at Table Number 7—
without looking into the chocolate marble-shaped eyes of the other Chicana waitress.
Pondering our facial similarities—hers and mine
I wondered how I knew she wasn't an Indian from India.
Perhaps it was her styled bangs cascading over her straight-as-silk hair.
She looked at me looking at her
as I sat waiting for my Indian cuisine-to-go.

I turned my attention to four men of many shades of white, suited in steel gray.
They discussed, smiled lightly, and chewed.
The meal was incidental.
A couple to their right took in the native ambiance
hoped that the unbearable spices weren't tinging the exhalations that passed between them.
Meanwhile a sequined, embroidered Radha-Krishna flirted on the wall.

My eyes floated over plastic flowers jutting out of an oblong planter that divided the room,
toward an out-of-grad-school Indian man and woman
enjoying deshi food without being pressured to eat just one more paratha,
by an auntie whose cooking bulges from under her sari's palu.
Like young Indians in both lands.
I turned away soon, not wanting to inhibit their interactions with my stares.
So I pretended to stare off into space and waited.

Train

GAURANGI KAMANI

the suitcase swings me up the ladder
a hawker screams to my back—missy!

from one bed of four the old woman stares
from two beds the Americans are flushed
as they pass money out of facing windows
one beggar child scrapes his sores
scrapes the door that shuts behind me

Bombay to Poona on tepid tea and cardamom
the porter tears tickets
waits in salaam for coins dropping

the evening is a soft land
rushing past the cities of light
the night squeezes through whirring shutters

we face each other, old woman and I
we two lie rolling with the carriage the clang of rails
softened by the moaning of Americans

slowing around the curve we scatter
their mingled press a reflection fractured
in the windows of a passing express

the old woman under her veil
shows brows suddenly pinched and hot
the Americans move under me
re-forming on the sweated bed

in the morning the Americans look east and are gone
at the stops the old woman and I
face each other unasleep in slick sheets
when I leave she says what we only hope,
'they didn't take their clothes off once.'

*

She Will Not Be Shamed

Twenty Years After
I Grew into Your Lives

MINAL HAJRATWALA

I tell you who I am
or rather, you discover
secrets hidden in mislabeled boxes,
papers published in other worlds

Twenty years it took me to grow into my own
courage to speak as myself
or rather, to whisper
half-sentences and mostly-truths,
but somewhat better than uttered silences

You grew up in simpler times and foreign nations
such distances have always gaped between generations
yet those places live in me still—
my tongue that savours fish you fried at Sunday barbeque
on the Fiji Islands,
my body whose form India's clothes
still flatter

And it is my body, after all,
that is the site of your confusion—
sexual, bisexual, feminist
but still brown-skinned, black-haired
red-blooded

Alive with the pure blood of our warrior caste
untainted by out-marriage
descended from the Kshaitryas—
men who died for duty
and killed for gods-know-what

I, too, am militant
in my battles for human rights,

for health over hunger, not Pandava over Kaurava,
for freedom to be
other than mother of 100 sons

And the hushed battlefield of our epic
is my brown, bisexual body,
which even you, who made it, cannot accept.

Pandava and *Kaurava* the Pandavas, five brothers, defeated their hundred cousins, the Kauravas, in the Hindu epic *Mahabharata*

Your Raw Menstrual Blood

KOSAR SAIRA

It's like a volcano erupting
It's like a hot melting pot overflowing
It's like being inside a warm cave
It's like the Red Sea
I want to dive in
When your pussy bleeds I want
My fingers
My whole hand to be drenched
In your
Red
Sticky
Thick
Runny
Rich
Clotty blood

Waxing the Thing

GAURANGI KAMANI

When I first came to Bombay to work in a beauty salon, I didn't understand anything. They told me to wax, so I waxed: legs, arms, underarms, stomachs, foreheads, fingers, toes. It's like a game for me. I cover the skin of the ladies with hot wax, then quickly-quickly take it all off with a cloth, almost before they notice that it's there. It reminds me of my village school, where I used to draw on the wall with chalk, then quickly wipe it off before the teacher found out. For me it's all very strange, what goes on with these rich-rich city ladies, but I mind my own business. I'm just a simple village girl. Everything about the city is strange to me, so what's one thing more?

There I was, minding my own business, when one day this Mrs. Yusuf, whose legs I was waxing in the private room, asked me if I would come to her house to wax her *thing*. I was so stupid, I asked her to her face, 'What is this *thing*?'

Now, she was already lying there with her sari pulled up to her stomach, and her legs bent at the knees, and I was trying not to look at her big white panties that she was shamelessly showing me through her wide-open legs, when suddenly she stuck one finger inside of her panties and pulled the material down and showed me all her hair *there*. I felt so ashamed! All this time, I didn't know that the ladies wax down there.

This Mrs. Yusuf said, very sweetly, that only young girls like me are pure enough in the heart to wax it down there. Naturally she wanted me to go to her house to do this delicate job. In a salon, anyone can walk into the private room, even when the curtain is pulled. Some of the other waxing girls told me that they don't do such type of work. Why shouldn't I? If they want to pay me better than at the salon, and on top of that, pay for my taxi here and there, then what do I care.

So I did the work for Mrs. Yusuf, and she told her friends, and before I knew it I had more work waxing things than arms and legs and all. All the ladies like me better because I'm not married. They tell me that marriage will make me rough, like a man, and then I won't be able to do the delicate job.

All our Indians, you know, are so rough and hairy. The shameless Indian men are always scratching themselves between the legs because of the Bombay heat, but the ladies don't have to, because their skin down there is cool and clean. And definitely the smell is also a little less.

I never knew how many kinds of smells could come out of these city ladies' things! Even though they wash night and day and remove every single hair from their bodies, I tell you, some of them smell down there like an armpit. I tell them to put a little baby powder, or maybe even some eau de cologne on the day that I'm coming, otherwise I have to breathe through my mouth so the smell won't drive me crazy. I never used to notice such smells

before, but day in and day out putting wax between their legs, I can't help it, my nose has become very nosey.

I'm not so nosey that I ask them questions or anything, but these ladies tell me anyway about why they like to be waxed down there. These thin-thin ladies like Mrs. Nariman and Mrs. Dastur say that it makes them feel clean, because there's no hair for anything to get stuck to down there. Then the gray hair ladies like Mrs. Patel and Mrs. Loelka say it makes them feel like innocent little girls again, and they even talk with giggly, high voices. But worst of all are the lazy, fat ones like Mrs. Singh and Mrs. Vaswani, who tell me it's so much better than getting a massage, giving so much more energy to the body, keeping the blood going all day and all night.

Mostly I don't listen to what they say, but one lady, Mrs. D'Souza, told me a very sad story. She said that she was married so many years and her husband never liked to do the man's work in her and so they had no children. Finally she got angry and asked him what was wrong with him and he said that it was all her fault, that the hair on her thing was so rough that it poked like pins right into his skin so he couldn't come near her. Poor man! Since then this lady makes me wax her thing every week, even when I can't find one single hair. The whole time, she lies there saying prayers to Mother Mary. At least, these days someone like Mrs. D'Souza can wax. In olden days what must have happened to these poor ladies?

My mother in the village still lives like in olden times. I tried to explain to her that I do waxing to make money, but she just can't understand. She stays in the house all day, covered from head to toe in her cotton sari, so how will she understand? These city ladies are not like that. They understand everything, or how else would they all get rich-rich husbands?

My poor mother—it's so shameful—doesn't even wear panties. And she sits with her legs wide open. All the old women are like that. They're so shameless, they don't even *want* to wear anything down there. Without panties, how can a modern girl control her monthly mess? When my mother was young and she got her monthly bleeding, she just sat in one corner and spread this mud between her legs until it mixed with the blood and became hard, a lid made of clay to close her upside-down, bleeding 'pot.' When she stood up, the hard clay cut into her skin like a knife. For five days she was like that, sitting in one corner with a pile of mud, playing with herself like a mad girl. After the five days, when she tried to break the mud, the hair from down there would be stuck in it and she would pull the hair right off. How she would scream! My god, you would think it was the end of the world. Why such a big fuss over a few hairs? That's the difference, I tell my mother, between her and the big ladies. If she knew what was good for her, she would have pulled *all* the hair out.

The ladies definitely want all their hair out. They make me check again and again for even one single hair that I missed. It's not so easy, you know, unless I shine a torch on it, and anyway, who says I want to look down there? In the beauty salon they told us, if you're plucking a lady's eyebrows, don't look into her eyes; if you're threading her upper lip, don't look into her mouth; so if I'm waxing the thing I don't look inside there!

Of course it's my job to get all the hair out, but I can't help it, sometimes the hair just won't come out. I try once or twice, but these fussy ladies are never satisfied. For half an hour I have to feel around bit by bit for any leftover hair, and then even if I find it, how can I wax

147

just one hair? So I have to try to pull it out with my fingers, but even that is impossible because by then the skin has become all sensitive and slippery and sliding.

That Mrs. Yusuf, my god, the way she shouts! 'I can feel it, I can feel one hair, not there, other side, in the front, no, no, feel properly, grab the skin with one hand and pull with the other, try again, just wipe your fingers if they're sliding, don't think you can rush away without finishing your job,' and on and on. What to do? I don't like digging around in there because I know it's where babies and all come from. But I don't grumble because the fussy ladies always give a good tip. Thank god they are not all like that or I would have to spend the whole day waxing and cleaning the thing of just one of them!

Not that they are in any hurry. They can just lie there all day, I tell you. At least I don't have to work at night, because the ladies only like me to wax during the day. I have to finish before the husband comes home, because the man doesn't like his wife to be locked in a room with some outsider.

Sometimes when there is a new lady who wants me to go over to do her waxing, she will ask, 'How do I know that you will do a good job? It requires such talent and if you do anything wrong, I'll have to go straight to the hospital.' So first I give the new lady the names of some other ladies that I work for, so they can call and find out. And then I tell her that I wax my own thing, not just others', so there's no need to worry. All of them, when they hear this, are so shocked! I'm just a poor village girl, so what do I need to wax for? As though you have to be rich to do it! Am I not a woman like them? Can't I be beautiful like them? If my own sister's husband likes it, then won't mine also want it?

I went back to my village for my oldest sister's marriage, and just to teach her how ignorant she is, I took some wax and clean cloths, and I waxed her. What a fuss that stupid girl made! I had to sit on top of her so she wouldn't run away. But then after the wedding, her husband wrote to me that I should come back to the village and wax his wife again, because everyone in the village tells him he's lucky to have such a clean, high-class woman. Until I return, my sister is pulling the hair out from down there one by one with her fingers.

Everyone has something that they can wax, so why not me? I only wax myself once in a while. It's not so easy for me. To wax down there, since I can't bend down to see properly, I have to sit on a mirror. Who would think I would ever look at my own thing? Even all those big-big ladies never look at their thing…and me, I've seen so many dozens by now.

'Don't wax it yet, you're not married!' the ladies keep saying. 'You're still thin and pure and innocent, and you're not *prepared* like a married woman for what happens down there. You'll start feeling wrong feelings between your legs and then no man will take a chance with you. That's why we don't let our unmarried daughters wax down there.' I tell you these ladies think they know everything. I am going to have a love marriage, and I have enough money saved so that I can give a good dowry. What husband will say no to that?

The real reason these ladies don't allow their young daughters to wax down there is because then the daughters will want to have love marriages! And then all the life's work for these rich-rich ladies will go to waste, because if Indian girls are allowed to marry whichever man they want, then who will marry the ladies' good-for-nothing sons? They're very clever, these rich ladies. But very stupid also. They force their daughters to be beautiful so they can arrange a match with a rich boy, but in the end they are marrying off their girls to boys who

are exactly the same as their fathers, who make this and that excuse and don't touch one finger to their wives who are waxed clean and ready from head to toe.

So every day, there is plenty of business for the beauty salon, giving these ladies manicures, pedicures, facials, waxing, hair cut, massage...And then some simple village girl like me will come along who doesn't know anything and they will cunningly find some way to get her to wax their thing. And when they feel something down there which makes them feel like human beings, then they're happy.

But who wants to listen to what I have to say? So I keep my mouth shut and do my work. When the time comes to get married, I will have saved enough money so my husband can treat me well. Until then, I am living without worries, so what do I care?

Average in the long run

RINI DAS

Amita discovers that the NEC military-green computer terminal has been removed from the table. The cords are gone and the blinking gold c:> is not there. Instead she finds a big tumbler stained with the salts of bureaucracy, filled with water to its brim, standing defiantly on the fuzzy matting of her table.

Her adequate forehead with irrelevant strands of tar-black silky hair is sweating. Mildly, the perspiring globules sink into her hairy eyebrows, partitioned by the velvet black bindi. She glances around with her glutinous dark brown pupils. Her gold-framed glasses remain firmly poised over what her thamma called a perfect nose. She wrinkles her thin veriest lips, as if to suck the sounds of the fan rotating next to her. While the aachal of her white with black kolka bordered Tangail sari dryly crosses onto her cleavage, she slings back her wet plaited hair to expose the powder along the creases of her acned neckline. She is prepared. Unlike, when she came back from the school, two decades ago, and turned instinctively to the right to find her thamma's bed empty and seeking remorse from her.

This time she is already informed about this particular exit. Still when she comes in today she looks ahead, and finds this bosomful of space to gloss over the betrayal. Now that the terminal is gone, she begins to realize how the arrangement of the tables and chairs of the rest of the office had changed over the last one year.

Turning her head to the side, she stares with contempt at the groaning ledgers with vermillion binding. These monsters bear names of consolidated holdings, shafted with a royal-blue dripping ballpoint. So, finally the 1048 KB and all the intermittent kha-khatash…khut khut…kruck…tung tung…tung—the breath of her computer—has gone.

Shibuda's camp of union-tactics had won. People over machines. Yesterday the news reached Amita, through Ram, the peon. He bluntly told her, "Your ledgers will be back again, didimoni, and you have to grow up and play no more."

Kunalbabu across the table had sighed, "Well! so that beast will finally leave us. These new management policies with all this rubbish will go to the garbage dumps, and the civic corporation will carry them to Dhapa. Of course, Amita will miss them," he said to Ram, "but you do understand that I am fifty-four? How can I ever adjust to these machines? Since the days of Nehru, my father worked with the saabs, and now I keep the family tradition and we have increased our business without these machines. All this technology is for the next generation. I am retiring in a few years, I leave it to my nati-natnis to bring the technology, house to house." He muttered on, with a condescending look at Amita, "Shibu did the right thing."

Amita listened demurely. She is thirty-four, and Kunalbabu had walked her to the tram stop after work so many times, even tried to speak to her uncles about getting her married through his gamut of "connections and sambandas."

This morning, she had squabbled with Meena, her household help. "Why have you taken out my high heels? I have told you I wanted my black Bata shoes."

Meena without looking at her, said, "But, didimoni, you haven't worn those shoes in the last one year. Really, I will never understand you. So, many times I have told you, get married, have children, No! Now again you want to wear those shoes."

Amita said mockingly, "I told you idiot, a shoe is a shoe. It is not slippers. Are you my jethima, Haan Meenarani? You think all my life is dependent on that rajputtar. I am not Cinderella. But, I just want my black Bata Ballerinas. Do you know who Cinderella was, you stupid girl?"

Meena ignored her and went away, saying to herself, "Shoes, shoes…will never learn how to dress properly…how can her age woman dress up like a teenager of an ishkool."

So, Amita is with her black shoes, conservatively strapped over her feet. She did feel kind of odd wearing a sari and a pair of shoes. Shoes or brinjals. Which came before? Which came after? Who gets to decide? The wise men say that shoes are for men. It's a sign of success. Brinjals and women—that purple passion—is a dangerous combination. Now that her shoes are back again, will she grow back her brinjals, her lady's fingers, tomatoes, gourd on her balcony? Balcony which is closer to the sky than her shoes to the road. Then again, brinjals are a lavendar habit.

For the whole of last year, she had come home very late. She hadn't been to Chandrika's place at all. In fact, Chandrika's husband came by her bank one day, took her out for tea and inquired whether or not she was having a prem. Seeing she didn't understand he corrected himself. "You are english-medium educated, so you'll call it an affair…what we call prem. So are you having an affair?" She coyly had told him, "Not the way you think, and tell Chandrika that I'll come by some Sunday."

All through the strikes, posters, festoons, spits, manager dholai, she had worked quietly at her terminal.

"Save jobs not computers."
"These devils will take over our history like the British. Fight for your freedom."
"Do you want to eat machines instead of rice?"
"This is a conspiracy to pollute our minds. Inform and refuse."

So, did Shibuda shout. Everyone, including the sweet little boy with the thin little moustache, Sukanta, harmonised in the choral shouting. Except Amita.

Amita watched as they trampled her territory in unison. She fought back with intense typing, as they spray painted. Police injunctions and all the travesty continued until they regaled in victory with aabeer and mihidana.

Amita used to come back late in the evening to the bank. She had started to keep her diary on her floppies. In fact, she regularly had to bribe Srinath the guard with milk, mangoes, guavas, batteries, pens, cherry blossom shoeshines to let her into the premises. Till somebody

squealed. But this time Shibuda's opposite camp came and warned her. Yet nothing much happened. For most of them, she remained an enigmatic, stubborn wench.

Except, she had metamorphosed into a jocular gypsy moth. A big moth fluttering into their imaginations and their chins: double, single, warped, thick, hairy, bald, dented, protuding, chocolate, paan-red, loose, fleshy, bony. The light of the organza screen, which had brought it as a 'heavy bodied, weak flying'[1] tourist into the yellow washed room, made it fly in chiffon desire. It flew faster and faster with independence. Sometimes, then, it would hear Debojyoti say, "Oh! she is merely trying to save her father from giving dowry."

The gypsy moth squirmed, "But I don't have a father."

On another day, it heard someone say, "She is merely trying to sleep with the management. Those men in suits tickle her."

Sukanta, in response had timidly gargled, "How can she be Management's cat, the only candidate for that is my mashi from Durgapur. She is such a cat, she can seduce all men in one night."

The gypsy felt warm in the security of the Light and had pestered the Esc key and Shift F5 and typed on. The moth recalled how the salesmen had finally come and set out the keyboard for her, one Kaalbashaki afternoon. Amita had refused to look straight onto the screen—it might remember that Amita had first dealt with the alien scrap with the usual contempt and repulsion. Excited, Amita had left her table and taken the rest of the day off.

Next day, the chrysalis came out of its hibernation. She wore a maroon Sambalpuri silk, with belphul on her plait, and high heels. Debojyoti had sharked in, "What's the matter? Are you out to destroy a man's heart?"

She sent her weapon of queer look straight through his heart. Later, Kunalbabu told in the carom-board room, "Most probably her lover from England has come back. She had met this boy long ago. He promised to marry her. Then he went off to get a degree in Law and now he has come back."

They implored him for more details. Sukanta asked him how he came to know. Kunalbabu heartily slapped his chest and said, "Her brother is my personal friend."

But she, overhearing this, just bristled and then laughed it off. Her brother has never met Kunalbabu. She let the need for clarification die, as she was busy with Lotus2. A menu of retrieve, save, quit, global, macro, file, delete, insert refuged the nascent, indigo clouds. Then the lessons in BASIC and fixing the troubles created by others came as Amita's predisposed, sulky fate.

Purifying an expression for each of her fingers, she found the ribs responding to her soft caresses. When she asked the right bird, "What is love?" It replied, "syntax error." When she lizarded, "What do you eat?" It giggled, "bad command." When she anteloped, "File a Kiss." It merely said, "File not found."

If the moth could hang by the tail of the comets and journey across the infinite sentences; If the nadir had the equinox; If she were 6 ft. 2 inches; If the tiger sprang into compassion of the dusk; If the water-lilies flew; If peaks had no nipples to suck...

But now she's a widow and she knows a widow leads a vegetarian life.
 'Now I am silent, hate

152

Up to my neck,
Thick, thick.
I do not speak.'[2]

Boomeranging like a hilsha in its course up the river to copulate on the dried mud, Amita jumped to her feet, picked up her bag and ran out of the bank. On her way home, she bought four dozens of bananas. Meena was surprised to see her home so early, and even more when Amita gave her money and asked her to go see a movie. Then, when Meena left, Amita took a bath, dressed herself in red and lit sandalwood incense. She aligned the 48 bananas across her dressing table, picked up the ash-sparkled da, she pronounced on the mantra.

> "chop, chop, chop, chop, chop, chop, chop, chop,
>
> chop, chop, chop, chop, chop, chop,
>
> chop, chop, chop . CHOP,
>
> CHOP. .
>
> CHOP, CHHHHHHHHOOOOOOPPPP.

Tomorrow, Amita will be cremated.

peon name of a job position. Usually is the person who carries messages from/to workers in an office

Dhapa the dump site of Calcutta

dholai bashing

belphur a flower blooming in the summer months, white in colour and has distinct sweet odour

hilsha a species of fish

da sickle-shaped knife, found in the hands of Kali

1. Quoted from Encyclopedia Brittanica.

2. Quoted from Sylvia Plath, "Lesbos," *The Collected Poems*, ed. Ted Hughes (New York: Harper and Row, 1981), 229.

Dry Spell

GAURANGI KAMANI

Grass pluckers stiff in tap-drip pools
Water running four-square in mother's gardens
Toy boats sail the shipping straits
Faint as shingled rosebuds the gardener bakes
In the furnace of tender lawns

By day the peacocks hop shade to shade
Carrying bees and dust on shrill plumes
Fanning out against the desert
By night the women chew wet seeds of guavas
Sweating under a glow worm moon

A gaping sun trickles past tree tops
Past camels sullen with full bellies
The staggering gardener bends into soft mud
Orchard dams crush cool water
Wetting like mouths the dry heels of skin

In a week of fevered desert
The roses bulge their neon madness
Peacocks scream on shining lawns
Plucking plucking
At the misted oceans of green

Madras On Rainy Days

ZAINAB ALI

Mohsin mumbled as he rolled off my stomach and onto the hard bed. I waited until he untangled his legs from mine before I grabbed the covers and folded my body beneath them. There we lay in silence. The lines on his forehead had already formed and his eyes held a blank look as he stared at the ceiling. I didn't dare disturb him. I was thankful he didn't turn my way and begin blaming me; after all, I was still convinced it was my fault, even though my body had surrendered weeks ago.

"What are you looking at?" he drawled in his heavy South Indian accent. The familiar agitated look in his eyes was intensified by his long lashes. I quickly looked away. "Do you think this is my fault, huh? Is that what you think, huh? You cold little..." His hand reached toward my buttocks, pinching fingers ready to take over the talking.

"There it is!" I yelled as I sat up in bed, clutching the covers to my bare chest. "There's that thing I told you about that's always watching me!"

"Where?" Mohsin sat up. His eyes were now calm, indifferent, yet searching the area by the bathroom. I knew he thought I was lying, that he was simply amused by my screams, which had begun three weeks ago, two nights after our wedding night. His grin was so broad and mocking that I couldn't understand why I had not seen it before.

"There! There! In the doorway to the bathroom!" I pointed again, my eyes returning to the doorway to hold the creature's gaze. I didn't want to lose sight of it, but it always disappeared when I tried to convince Mohsin of its reality. "Do you see it?" He had to see it. "Oh God, it's opening its mouth to laugh!" I quickly covered my ears with the palms of my hands and shut my eyes tightly.

"Where did you see it last?" the Alim asked in Urdu as he stepped into our hotel room. I led him to the bathroom and pointed to the space between the door and the wall.

"Here." The striking of rain against the room's window was almost submerging my voice. The Alim's eyes grazed over my body and I lowered mine. I knew, like Mohsin, he was thinking I was imagining this; but I had been seeing it for almost three weeks, ever since the day I discovered my brush missing. That's when I remembered overhearing the servants gossiping about black magic.

"Once they get a possession—any possession, even a strand of hair—they can find a money-hungry Alim to do jadu on that person—chi chi chi." I heard the cook Hamid's disapproval; as a pious Muslim, he condemned both the takers and the givers of money for jadu. I shook my head at their foolishness. I'll have to write Sara about his one, I thought as I stood just outside the kitchen, ready to put an end to their chatter.

"It could be the reason Mohsin Baba has not yet claimed Samena Bebe," Fiza Nanny continued. I stopped. Voices mumbled in agreement, not shock. I realized my problem had become the servant's idle chit-chat even though I had confided only in Fiza Nanny. But then, I became enraged, picturing them inside the kitchen, huddled together in a corner, crouching on the floor, one hand cupping their aluminum plates while the other mixed rice with curry, making mounds to shove into their mouths, all the while, between gulps, whispering about my life. I frowned, burning with shame.

"Has she missed anything?" a woman asked, concerned.

"I will check," Fiza Nanny answered. My eyebrows drew close. They're on my side, I thought, feeling lighter as I continued listening.

I had blamed our wedding night and the next two nights on my exasperating uncertainty; part of me demanded to unite with Mohsin in order to surrender to him, yet I recoiled from this stranger, with whom I was forced by arranged marriage to become intimate. In the years I had dreamed about the wedding night, I had never envisioned my unyielding self would be so strong. I had thought I would be like the bride in the Hindi movie *Khabi Khabi*: In love with a stranger the morning after our wedding night simply because he was now my husband. The dream was supported by my parents who encouraged the love-at-first-sight marriages. So I was convinced that my return to India for marriage would unite me with a Muslim husband and my Indo-Muslim heritage.

But I was repulsed by him, and my repulsion was so strong I was unable to surrender to Allah's will for our union, even though I repeated *La il la ha illa la, Mohammedan Rasoul il la* in my thoughts. Over and over again, *There is No God but Allah, and Mohammed is His Prophet*. It didn't help. That night, I could not submit to Allah's will, nor to my husband. But even now, three weeks later, exhausted by my physical surrender, Mohsin could not possess me. And I felt guilty.

I told Mohsin about the missing brush, and we lay one night, tracing names in our minds of those who would do jadu to steal our happiness. Our suspicions inevitably took us back to one name. It was her name we evoked when we invited the Alim to come to our hotel.

Now I watched him with hope as he entered the bathroom and rubbed the cement walls. "How long have you two been married?" His voice echoed from inside.

"About three weeks," Mohsin answered. I watched him stare at his shoes.

The Alim appeared at the doorway, "And how long has this…um…*problem* been occurring?"

"Since we got married," Mohsin answered again. I kept quiet. I was taught that as a Muslim woman—even one raised in America—it was improper to converse with Muslim religious leaders about such matters.

"Yes, it *is* a serious problem," the Alim replied. His eyes locked on my face, then traveled over my breasts. I crossed my arms, walked to the bed and sat down. "And very sad, too," he continued, his eyes still on me, "especially since this is your honeymoon, right? Is that why you're in Madras?"

Mohsin sighed, his eyes now watching the rain wet the carpet by the window. He was no longer grinning. I nodded, but the Alim turned to Mohsin.

"Don't worry, young man," he said, patting Mohsin's back. "I don't see this as your problem, but as your wife's."

"Mine?" I straightened, crumpling inside at this blatant confirmation of my own fears. The realization that my body no longer resisted Mohsin, that it had relented, even though my mind had not, simply because my bodily battle had become a contest of wills, a strain on me, retreated in face of this new danger. I now believed I had given the jadu power over me when I failed to submit to Mohsin on the first night. The fact that he still could not possess me even after my nightly surrender seemed unimportant, even petty finger-pointing, after the Alim pronounced his statement. Yes, it was the jadu that had worked its way between us, then, pryed us apart, just like Fiza Nanny had told me it would do. Her warning seemed stronger now than when she first uttered it in the hospital, after her own experience with jadu. "What do you mean?" My voice was shaky; my innocence sounded unconvincing even to myself.

He continued to speak with Mohsin, as though I hadn't said a word. "If you don't mind, I would like to begin exorcising her. Now don't be alarmed," he added quickly when Mohsin's mouth opened and I stood in protest. "What she sees is an apparition, and we must get rid of it before it becomes too strong."

"I don't know about this," I interjected.

"Now, don't you want to have a healthy, normal married life with your husband?" He turned to me. I nodded. He continued in a soothing voice. "Well, don't doubt me, then. You can mistrust others in life, but not me; I'm an Alim and I cannot betray the followers of Islam." I lowered my head; his words made sense. Besides, I needed Mohsin to know I would do anything to solve this problem, especially since the doctors had told us there was nothing physically wrong with him. "Now then," he exclaimed, rubbing his palms together, as though warming them. "Mohsin, if you could leave the room, I would like to begin. Oh, and if I could have your permission to touch your wife in the process—I can't touch her without your permission, you know." He laughed piously, his head bouncing up and down. "I'm a Muslim, not one of those Amerecans."

"Oh, sure, sure," Mohsin said awkwardly as he backed toward the hotel door. I wanted to stop him, but the Alim's stern gaze held my tongue. I watched as the 202 on the door disappeared from sight, along with Mohsin's reassuring smile.

The Alim walked toward me, his long, white kurta swaying in the breeze that came through the window; the rain had stopped. I had never been alone with an Alim before, and I felt nervous. For some reason, my mind allowed me to feel comfortable in a crowd of drunken men at the First Avenue bar in Chicago, but not while alone with one Muslim holy man. I reasoned it to be my childhood: I was forbidden to be alone with men, and the Indo-Muslim community in which I was raised separated women from single men. "So," I began, too loudly, "you think this is an apparition I see?" The word made me uncomfortable; it evoked an image stronger than the one I actually saw. But, then, I didn't even know what that was.

"Ah-huh. Do you know of anyone who would do black magic on you to prevent your happiness?" He sat down next to me on the bed.

"Just Mohsin's aunt, the one who lives in Pakistan and came for our wedding. Remember, we told you about her? She's the one who's jealous of Mohsin's success because

157

her son's the same age but got into drugs." I squirmed in my seat as I spoke. I still felt foolish believing in jadu and apparitions, much less confessing my belief while staring into an Alim's face. My brothers and I used to laugh about the Hyderabadi fear of jadu when we visited India. Jadu was certainly not something we feared or let control our lives.

I cringed at the thought of my brothers seeing me now. But it was partly their fault I was in this position. They left, along with Amee and Babbah, immediately after my wedding, leaving me alone for the first time in my life, and in a foreign country with a stranger. Then came Fiza Nanny's sudden and unexpected death. I was unable to cry or visit her grave because Mohsin's mother thought it was foolish to mourn a servant's loss. She began her attacks then, which left me defenseless because I was raised to respect elders. She woke me at six in the morning to cook breakfast, after her son hopelessly panted over me until three in the morning, rolling off my stomach; she would hand me a stick broom to clean the dark bathrooms with Turkish toilets—no running water, no windows, the dirty cement floor where I stood alongside black cockroaches to both bathe and wash clothes with rocks and brittle soap. I remembered how Amee said when she first left India and saw the American bathrooms, she thought they were clean enough to pray in. Yet I was stuck here, and the dark shadows in the bathroom came alive and laughed at me.

"*La-hol-billah-quwat*," the Mullah spat in Arabic on hearing that someone was using drugs. Then, after a brief pause: "Let's get started. Can you come and lie here on the bed?" I moved up and lay on my back on top of the covers. He moved away and began digging in his bag. He removed three candles and three sticks of incense. "Three is an Islamic number," he commented matter-of-factly, "so is five, seven and eleven." I nodded. He went around the room placing one candle on a dresser and one on the window sill as he closed the window to keep out the heavy breeze. He strolled back to me, bent down, lit the third candle and placed it on the night stand next to my head. As he sat down, he reached inside the lamp shade and clicked off the light.

"Can you lift your kurta please?" he asked while lighting one stick of incense. His lips were thin and dark; I suddenly remembered Amee always telling me that my own lips were dark because I smoked. I always lied, fearing to confess "yes" because she would be disappointed in me, calling me a hijra: she knew no decent Muslim woman would smoke. I reached down and pulled my kurta up a little. "I need to have you lift it up higher," he said. I hesitated and remembered a year back when Fiza Nanny got exorcised because her eyes became yellow; the neighbors said it was because some demon housed in her body and was peering out from inside her. Yet, the Alim merely told her to put gold in the bath lagan and take a shower with that bath water while reciting a Quranic verse. She never said that the Alim touched her. Perhaps that's why she died, I thought, because the Alim didn't treat her correctly, like mine was doing. And, he didn't seem to be watching me closely. He's just as uncomfortable as I am, I thought, and I lifted my kurta to my ribs.

"I need you to get it up higher," he said. "If this makes you feel awkward, I can stop now and bring your husband in." His brown eyes looked innocent.

"No, I'm fine," I said.

"Good. May I?" he asked before touching me. "I need your permission as well, otherwise Allah considers it a sin." I nodded in consent, and almost smiled: He was talking to me like a

little girl, the way my uncle did. He reached over and pulled my kurta up to the bottom of my breasts. "Now," he began, his knuckles pressed against my right breast, "this may smart a little." I nodded and swallowed. He pushed my breast up and burned me directly below it with the incense. I watched his dark lips move as he simultaneously chanted a Surah from the Quran.

"How old are you?" he asked as he relit the incense.

"Nineteen." I could still feel the pressure of his hand against my breast.

His lips curled as he blew out the flame. "Such a shame about your husband. You're so young and beautiful." I didn't tell him I knew I wasn't beautiful; after all, it was my ugliness that prevented Mohsin from possessing me. That was the reason he always grabbed the skin on my buttocks and twisted it, leaving marks.

I felt the pressure of the back of his hand as he slid it to my left breast, pushed up and burned me again. "Ouch," I cried, pushing his hand; I knew the feel of his skin would linger in my mind.

"It's only the demon being scared away," he reassured me. I sighed, thankful that I wouldn't hear it laugh anymore. Still, I couldn't bring myself to look in the direction of the bathroom…not yet. I wanted to wait until the Alim completed his task; after all, the Quranic words he muttered, then blew in my face, already made me feel stronger. The pressure subsided. "You can cover up now." I quickly pulled down my kurta.

I watched as he relit the incense. "Can you undo your pants?" he asked gently. I bit my lip. "It will only take a second and we might as well finish it while we're at it." I untied my pajamas and slid them down a little, visions of the past few weeks of self-forced undressings, draining me of my strength. "Spread your legs a little, please." He sounded business-like; for some reason, Hamid's face appeared before my eyes, then quickly left. I moved my legs an inch. I felt his cold hand as he lifted the side of my panty and burned me again, reciting from the Quran. As he reached toward the nightstand, I felt his hand lightly caress my vagina; I squeezed shut my eyes. "Just once again on the other side," I heard him whisper close to my face.

His hand closed on the soft flesh on the inside of my thigh. "You speak Urdu well for growing up in Amereca." He loosened his grip, slid his hand to the right side of my hip and pulled my panty up. I smelled the incense burn out. "Do you want to do the rest tomorrow?" he asked. I nodded again without opening my eyes. "All right, then. You can pull up your pajamas now." I waited until I felt the lamplight on my eyelids; then I pulled up my pajamas and sat up. He set his candles and incense in his bag. His back was toward me and I saw that his kurta was wet with sweat. He turned. I felt I had become intimate with him. I turned away. I stared out the window. The rain had given way to the sun. A blue spider dashed across the glass, its strong legs appearing black against the incoming rays. Then it disappeared behind the gray drape. The room smelled of jasmine. I realized I didn't even know his name. "I think this apparition will go away," he said. "Do you see it now?"

I looked toward the bathroom. There was the head, its eyes peeking out from around the corner of the door, laughing at me, its long white teeth bared. "No," I lied, trying to drown out its laughter. I was angry with myself for hoping the Alim would make it leave. I had to know that the sight of this man squeezing my thigh would only make it laugh louder; the

way it did each time Mohsin rolled off my stomach and twisted my skin; the way it did each time someone left me.

"I didn't think so," he said. "But it could simply be playing a trick. It's best that I return tomorrow to finish." He walked to me, set his arms on my shoulders and smiled. "What a shame about your husband. You're such a young, pretty girl." He bent down, and kissed the side of my mouth as his hand cupped my right breast. "I'll see you tomorrow to finish this session. But you never know how long it will take; it depends on the strength of the demon." He walked toward the door and opened it. Mohsin walked in, smiling.

"All done?" he asked, his eyes full of hope.

"I need to come again tomorrow; we want to make sure it's all gone."

"Sure, sure. Let me walk you down to the lobby." And the two left, my husband's arm around the Alim's wet back.

The Questions of Fear

GAURANGI KAMANI

mother's shadow cuts the doorway
the time, she says, has come

I am silent while her step falls heavy at my side
and the bedsprings moan and wheeze with her weight
her fingers are mine as we trace together
the outline of a husband's face
your man will seem splendid, she dreams
he walks under an auspicious star

I am silent while her breath moves on my hair
and I smell the sweat and rosewater
her thoughts are mine as we see together
plans for the morning, and the evening
the fire will seem lasting, she wonders
is it blessed by the priest

her kiss, kiss of life moves on my lips
she turns my face from the questions of fear
I breathe the silence and the weight cracks between us
our fingers drum a dissonance
the kiss unmet releases her

I am silent while her head rolls back
and rosewater sweat gathers on her lip
the guests will seem happy, she hopes
they will be well feasted

I am silent while the bedsprings sing and groan
and her foot falls heavily away
my sari will seem beautiful, she sighs—

mother's shadow cuts the doorway
the time, she says, has come

Nadia

ROSHANI NASH

"**O**kay, now the other arm." Banoo was sitting up but Nadia sprawled beside her, one leg across her lap, one arm flung carelessly across Banoo's ample bosom. She switched so that Banoo could now stroke her right arm as she spoke.

"The garden was filled with all sorts of fruit trees. We had two guava trees, a mango tree, two chicu, some love apples, a Bengali pear tree, bananas and coconuts. The rose apple tree was diminutive—only four feet tall. The bulbuls attacked that tree. They loved the thin-skinned apples. When you bit into one, it would smell of roses. We would sit up on a branch and eat as much fruit as we wanted. It was just like paradise. It was the happiest time of my life." Her eyes shone when she spoke of this garden, and she looked off into the distance when she spoke, as though trying to see into the garden from where she sat.

"We had mountain crabs walking around in the garden, especially in the monsoon season. The servants would catch them and roast them on the fire for us. One of our greatest delights was to see a mother crab open up her belly and release lots of little baby crabs around her. If one of us prodded her with a stick the little babies would scramble back in and she would close her shell up again." Banoo laughed. "One day your mother and Sheroo were playing on the trellised veranda. They had a crab tied to a string and they were walking back and forth with it when a snake appeared. They ran screaming into the house, leaving the poor crab to fend for himself."

"How old were you when Grandpa died?"

"I was the oldest. I was twelve. Your mama was only three years old then."

"Did Grandpa die of a snakebite?" Nadia saw a half-darkened room, a high four-poster bed polished to a deep mahogany, grey flagstone floors over which slid a large silent cobra, the skin of its neck expanded to form the hood.

"No. He shot a few snakes in his time, but none ever got him. Grandpa died of pneumonia. Grandma and us kids were all in Lonavla at home. Grandpa had gone to Bombay to visit his family. He caught a cold. In those days they did not have a bathroom inside the house. They had a well in the courtyard. He bathed outside and had to climb three flights of stairs to his apartment. He caught cold and he died three days later. It was very sudden and a great shock to Grandma. Your Grandpa was only thirty-six years old and Grandma was left with us five children to take care of." Nadia nodded solemnly, thinking to herself that Grandpa's death had something to do with why Banoo never married and had stayed so close to Grandma. She had become Grandma's youthful companion, never leaving her side, refusing to be married.

"Well. I'm not marrying either," said Nadia to her aunt, removing both her arm and leg from Banoo. She rotated and then lay down on her back with her head on Banoo's lap. Banoo looked down at the beautiful small face.

"No darling. I had a reason. I had a good reason. I did not like men. I never have. Not in that way," she said with a slight emphasis on the word 'that.'

At age nine, Nadia did not really understand what 'that way' meant but she understood that it had something to do with the differences between men and women. She knew Dad looked different because one day she had walked by his open door. He was standing with his starched white shirt already buttoned; he was unhooking his pants from the back of the door and he had nothing else on. It was the only time in her life she remembered her father so exposed, his penis hanging long, limp, between large balls. In the second before she had turned away, she'd sucked in this image of him like a kid inhaling a coke on a hot day, and it had seared itself onto her brain.

"I never wanted to get so close to a man," Banoo said, shaking her head and beginning to stroke the sweet face that lay upturned on her lap. She traced concentric circles lightly with the tips of her fingers on Nadia's cheeks. Then lightly smoothed the beautiful dark brows, back to concentric circles around the mouth and then around the eyes. Nadia gave herself up to the sensation of her skin tingling alive underneath her aunt's fingertips. It felt as though the blood was describing exactly the same circles just beneath her skin that the fingertips were making. Like iron shavings being dragged around by a magnet.

Nadia's mind darted to a British film that she had seen last week. The handsome hero had kissed the heroine at the end of the picture. She would like to be kissed like that. It would be rather pleasant, in fact, she thought, keeping her eyes closed, placing herself in the arms of the hero.

The afternoon was melting away rapidly. The heat of the afternoon was lifting. The curtains billowed in at intervals, blown by the sea breeze. The sitting room faced the west, and the ocean was only eight blocks away. Mother was fond of pointing out that the way the house was situated and cross-ventilated kept it warm during the winter and cool in the summer. The ocean breeze picked up around one in the afternoon as the tides changed. By the time it abated, the sun was losing its strength and the day was beginning to cool. It made the afternoons inside the house very pleasant.

Nadia could hear the cook stirring in the kitchen. He usually fell asleep sitting up on the patla, a low stool, after his chores were all done. Mother was instructing him to make bhajias for tea this afternoon since Grandma and Aunt were visiting. She heard him padding back and forth from kitchen to dining room, with the tea things, clattering the tea cups on the saucers, rattling the silver spoons.

"When will I get my period?" asked Nadia.

"Perhaps two or three years. They say that girls are getting their periods earlier now."

"When did you get yours?"

"I was thirteen years old. We had a separate room in the house. It was on the first floor of the building. It had three or four iron beds and some chairs in it. Nothing else. Sometimes several of the women in our clan got their periods at the same time. That was fun. You were out of luck if you were the only one. Because then there was nothing to do. Sometimes there

163

would be four or five of us, we'd stay up half the night talking. No one bothered with us. At mealtimes our food was left on tin plates by the door. They wouldn't even hand the food to us. It was put on the floor."

"Well, when I get my period I don't want to sit separate," Nadia said firmly, opening her eyes and staring fixedly at her aunt's face. The year was 1959. Nadia felt it was time things changed. No one was going to keep her in a separate room from the rest of the family when it was her "unclean" time of the month.

"Don't be silly, my love," her aunt replied. "Of course you will."

"No, I will not!"

"Chee. Chee," Banoo said. "I won't touch you."

"Yes, you will," said Nadia hugging her aunt as though seeking to wipe away her orthodox views with the strength of her affection. It seemed unbelievable to her that Aunt meant what she was saying. How could she not want to touch her?

"You are mad," said Banoo, giggling. "My prayers would all be spoiled. And it would be a sin for you to come into the prayer room or near the oil lamps."

"God will not think I am unclean, so why do you think that?" Nadia said with the certain knowledge of one who regularly conversed with him and already knew his opinion on such matters.

"Why do you think the body sloughs off the blood? Because it is impure. Every month the body cleans itself of this impure blood. Do you know that when women have their periods they cannot do any pickling or bottling or preserving? It always spoils. Gets a mold on it. That is a well-known fact," she said with an air of finality.

Nadia was somewhat impressed with this fact. Mother had once complained that her pickles had spoiled because she had thought she could get away with pickling the mangoes on the last day of her cycle, but she had lost all eight jars for ignoring that simple rule. Nadia shrugged her shoulders and thought, if the tides could move because of the moon perhaps a jar could spoil.

Nadia's mind darted to the time that Mother had scolded her for getting close to the beggars. They were on their way to a wedding reception in Bombay. They had driven up in their gleaming black Ford Anglia. Chauffeur let them out smartly at the wrought iron gates of the compound and went off to park the car in a quiet gully behind the fire-temple. Sitting against the high compound wall were a row of lepers. Some with a missing arm, or leg, or both. One of them had a flattened face; the nose had withered away completely. All of them had dirty bandaged hands with several or all of the fingers missing from each hand. The bandages were unravelling from the hands that they held out, supplicating for alms.

Nadia had begged her father for a handful of coins for them. As Nadia approached the line, Mother shouted at her to toss the coins, not to get so close. Nadia bent her head, ashamed for Mother and for herself. She did not wish to offend the lepers with the slightest hint of revulsion, so she concentrated on carefully putting the coins in each hand whilst keeping her face serene.

Mother had scolded Father for indulging the child's every whim, and then dragged her off to thoroughly soap and scrub her hands before she touched anything else. But throwing the money at the beggars would have been as unacceptable to Nadia as having food shoved at her and being made to sit separate.

Banoo seemed accepting of this treatment but Nadia recalled something in her mother's voice when she had described what it was like to sit separate. Nadia wanted to cry when she thought of poor Mummy missing all that school. Mother had attended an all Zoroastrian school, and the girls had to stay home during their periods. Mother had especially long and heavy menses and she hated missing that many days of school. There was no way to wash the books and make them clean again if she touched them, so she was not allowed to read. After much pleading they arrived at a compromise. Mother could sit in the doorway on the patla and someone would come by and turn the pages for her if she called out. But sometimes they forgot she was there, or they could not hear her as they busied themselves with the running of the big house, and she would wait for what seemed like hours before she could study the next page of her lessons. I'm not going to let anyone do that to me, Nadia vowed to herself.

An angry hiss came from the kitchen. Cook had just put in the first batch of bhajias to fry in the hot oil. Nadia could smell the chickpea flour and banana mixture. She could see in her mind's eye the little balls rolling themselves over in the hot oil. She got up from the couch and walked into the kitchen. Cook was just taking the first batch out with a slotted spoon.

Nadia reached for the bhajias. "Be careful! They are very hot, don't take any," Mother said. After hesitating a moment, Nadia picked one up.

When I Was Twelve Years Old

PREM PRASAD

I hear the faint twist of voices,
Echoes of silent rooms where the evenings descended
With the swirl of smoke in a small coalmine town.

I used to sit in between two floors,
In the stairs connecting two domains, two worlds.
The first floor where my mother was queen,
And the ground floor where my grandpa reigned.
The lines were drawn between male and female worlds.

I remember hushed voices, broken laughters, dried tears.
The double fold of darkness in the stairs.
I took a flight, many flights, still I am bound,
Crouched. I remember when I was twelve years old.

I remember the screams of women,
Their lives, their destinies confined in chaddars,
In the Burkhas, in gunghats,
Among the boiling pots of dal and rice,
Their minds regulated between washings and cleanings,
Their bodies bursting with the unwanted pregnancies.

I remember Shakuntala, she got married at the age of
Fourteen and she was widowed when fifteen.
I remember Shabi, she was tall and big.
No one chose her, she waited and waited,
One night, in front of my school in a pond,
We saw her body floating.

Durga! I called her angry Durga, a Khali!
I made a temple for her in my heart…
Brave Shabi…in her red bordered white saree
I remember her her floating body.

Chandi, Parmeshwari, Munni, we skipped rope together,
We played marbles and ball, we sang songs for Gouri,
We prayed for kind mothers-in-law, we prayed for fathers-in-law
Who were not greedy. We prayed for husbands
Loving and kind.

We refused to hear the truth,
We refused to think of ourselves as non-human,
Where a woman is worshipped in the temples,
And is trampled in the homes.

I remember struggling women, struggling girls,
The incomplete stories, no stars,
I remember only the dark smoke.

Sexuality

KOSAR SAIRA

Is not a choice
Is not possible
They tell us what to do
They tell us who to fuck
They tell us who will fuck us

They tell us it's our own business
It's people's private business
Well of course that's the case
Why do they then have laws
Laws to
Mutilate, kill
Kill lesbians
Fuck lesbians

My sisters
My sisters, some of us who are not
Allowed a sexuality
Who are not allowed pleasure
Who are not allowed each other
Who are not allowed love

Love between women
Love between ourselves
Love for our own kind.

Sari

SAMANTHA RAJARAM

When the girl reaches eighteen
she wears a sari.
The world then finds a woman beneath
the cloth,
draping and pleating over her body
that will one day collapse with child.

The cloth winds over the midriff, and slyly ignores it.
The midriff soon to be slackened by childbearing
now cinched tight with thin cotton rope
securing a fresh petticoat,
silently entrapping the young, lissome body
now locked in quiet chains of China silk
and starched cotton.

The petticoat slices into young flesh and leaves
the soft abdomen exposed.
Only nine yards, separating the girl's body
from the world—
nine yards and a safety pin, keeping her
from cool escape despite the unforgiving Indian sun,
and its whip-like rays in the afternoon.
Nine yards, of paisley, gold or shiny blue
like the eye of a peacock feather.

She wears white, for innocence
or marriage bonds soon to find her.
Gossamer silk, new nylons called chiffon, waiting
to ensnare her body,
to tell the world she is a woman,
even if she was only

a girl in a skirt
yesterday.

It's Not That I

KAMAL KAPUR

It's not that I
like wearing flowers
in my hair

nor these jewels for ear
finger hand throat ankle

I know myself
to be most beautiful
when naked

It's just that I like
you to linger
removing these

Rag Yaman

PIA GANGULY

Alap

flowering skies
of cotton clouds,
untouched brow of innocence

Jor

peacocks strutting one foot at a time
dropping their crimson teeth
one at a time on the clouds
innocence knocking up its virginity

Jhala

ice flowers on fire, passion drops,
fireworks inside the head
of a stone image of the world,
lights dancing up and down—a whole sunset
dancing on the head of time,
innocence melting in love's caress

alap first stage in musical development, slow
jor second stage, an introduction of more notable rhythm into the piece
jhala third stage, build up in speed and intensity, climax

Dusk in Autumn

ZAVEENI KHAN

A vivid orange sun
quietly peeps through the
branches of a eucalyptus tree.
The ocean wind gently strokes
the whispering leaves
to the rhythm of the waves.

Then slowly the sun sinks
into the ocean to wait
for a certain someone
whose purpling cheeks
speak volumes of secrets.

After hours of
contemplation
the day slowly sheds
her black chiffon sari and with downcast eyes
she descends into intimacy
with the eager sun.

✳

Fissures Of The Past

The Marriage of Minnoo Mashi

QIRONE ADHIKARY

Of course, Minnoo's real name is not Minnoo at all. It's something like Meeni or Monoroma or MadhuChandra, you know, some Bangali name or other. But she really is my Mashi. Or was. Our family doesn't have anything to do with her these days, for obvious reasons. Except for me. I think she's wonderful.

Minnoo was the third girl in a family of seven—three boys and four girls. I never knew my uncles' and aunts' first names. They were all, and still are, Boromama, Mejomama, Chotomama, Boromashi and so forth. Only Minnoo was always Minnoo.

Minnoo's biggest handicap was that she was an intelligent girl in a culture that despises and mistreats its girl children. (But don't all cultures? Minnoo asks. She's like that, sarcastic and sharp-tongued, always speaking her mind.)

Minnoo's mother was my thakurma, my father's mother. Thakurma had barely begun menstruating when her family married her off. She was...what?...thirteen? A wild child, spirited and free, running about outdoors all day and night, barefoot, with her long hair all a-tangle.

They washed her in turmeric and oiled her hair and body, squeezed her into a tight choli and underskirt, its stout cord cutting into her tender waist, wrapped her in seven or eight or nine yards of silk stiff with gold brocade.

They drew decorative designs on her hands and feet with mehndi. They put pounds and pounds of gold jewelry on her. Enormous, heavy bracelets and bangles all the way up her thin sticks of arms. Earrings so long and heavy, her lobes drooped and almost tore—the only thing keeping them whole was the thick gold chain that ran from one earring to the other over her head. Gold, 22 carats, and encrusted with diamonds and pearls—after all, the relatives said, she's so black, better make sure everything she wears shows against her skin.

A thick gold choker loaded with rubies red as blood was fitted around her neck—she looked as if her throat had been cut and she was slowly bleeding a river of gold and red. Heavy, wide and thick anklets encircled her delicate ankles, making it impossible for her to walk.

In fact, it was impossible for her to do much, under all that marital finery. She fainted repeatedly throughout the wedding, from the weight of her jewels and clothes as much as the press of bodies come to see the "little blackie" finally married off at enormous cost to her family.

"The ring through your nose," my grandmother's mother told her, "costs more than your older sister's entire dowry. But what are we to do? Your sister is fair and beautiful, and anyone would want to marry her. For a girl like you, cursed with a black skin, no amount of money is enough to make a man forget what his eyes will see each night."

175

Whereupon her father, laughing, said, "Don't worry, child, he will not see you at night." My Thakurma cried all the way to, and through, her wedding.

Of course, she told this story to Minnoo, as well as to all her other children and grandchildren. And she showed us the wedding jewelry, designed to fit her delicate adolescent body.

It horrified me when I saw it. Oh, it was beautiful enough, skilled filigree work, and I marveled at how tiny her wrists and ankles—and even her neck—had been; but for all that, it looked like the chains worn by a slave.

How could a woman walk under that impossible weight? I asked. "Walk?" My Thakurma was scornful. "What need is there for a respectable woman to walk? Hasn't she a husband and sons to do everything for her, and take her everywhere?"

And, indeed, the bride hardly took a step at her own wedding. She was carried, like a sweetmeat, into the ceremonial place, on a large golden tray. There she was lifted up and placed in her father's lap. The only time she was required to move was when they tied the end of her sari to her husband's shoulder cloth, and she followed him in a tiny circle, seven times around the sacred fire.

Minnoo turned out black, like her mother. What a tragedy, the relatives sighed, lowering their eyes as they tried to calculate the dowry her parents would have to offer. Her other sisters, fortunately for them, took after their expensively purchased father in their fair skin. Of course, all the sons were dark-skinned, but what did that matter? Educate them well, and their value on the marriage market would ensure enough money coming into the family coffers to marry off even one such as Minnoo.

Fortunately, for Minnoo anyway, she was raised like all Bangali girls. Until her periods started she ran wild everywhere. She climbed trees and fell into wells, waded in the river with her skirts hiked up around her waist, caught frogs and tadpoles which she promptly stuffed down her respectable aunties' saris, and for which she was beaten till her bottom peeled. "Ish, baba," she said to me once, "after one of those beatings, you couldn't sit for two weeks. You children, you don't know the meaning of a sound thrashing."

We didn't want to, either.

Minnoo saw her mother's jewelry, the stiff, gold-embroidered wedding saris (the wedding ceremony can go on for days, and each day the bride is dressed in different clothes and jewels); she heard all the tales of the women's lives, her mother's and her aunts'.

The endless stories: of pre-pubertal women married off to men they might never have seen; tyrannical mothers-in-law; spiteful sisters-in-law; lascivious fathers, uncles, brothers and in-laws; womanly honor protected by the esteemed, hoary custom of restricting the woman's movements; the horrendous lives of pardashins; the endless labour of women slaving over husbands, elders, children—their own and others'. And, being an intelligent girl, she asked why. In fact, she asked it so often and so much that they (as all Indian families do) promptly nicknamed her "kenokirtan."

She scandalized the entire extended family (all forty of them) by asking why. When her father read the Ramayana, she wanted to know why Ram was such a creep to make Sita suffer so. And for her inquisitiveness, her bottom peeled for a month.

She scandalized them again when they read her the *Gita*, and she asked why? Why was Radha so stupid as to fall in love with Krishna, who was married to not one, but many others? And why did she stay in love with him when he treated her so badly?

And why was Sati the respected embodiment of Indian Hindu womanhood, when all she'd done was throw herself on her husband's funeral pyre? And wasn't that much stupider than staying alive to avenge him?

Why didn't Sita simply kick Ravana in an appropriately tender spot, instead of letting him kidnap her? Why did she allow Rama to insist on testing her chastity in front of God and the whole world by having her walk through the fire twice?

Why did Chitrangada, the warrior princess, put aside her arms and her martial skills for love of the vain and somewhat silly Arjuna?

So her cheeks, upper and lower, were regularly fluffed with various instruments of punishment—palms, rattans, chappals and so forth, and she spent most of her time on her feet, since her bum was usually too painful to take her weight.

Her parents sent her to school, not because they believed women should be educated, but to get her out from underfoot with all her questions. And in those days, the only schools a well-born woman could safely attend were the convent schools, run by the various nuns.

Let her go drive the nuns crazy, they must have said to themselves, chortling at the thought of the white-clad childless Mothers trying to mother this impossible child.

But Minnoo, as I may have mentioned, was an exceptionally intelligent girl and did wonderfully in school. There was an endless store of books to answer her every why. She was a fast reader, and though her mouth often got her into more trouble than her backside could bear, she survived the experience and learned a great deal in the bargain. One of the things she learned about was love.

What could a bunch of dried-up old sexless virgin spinster nuns know about love? But there's love and love, you know. The love Minnoo found among the nuns was of two kinds: there was the love of the intellect that Mother Sylvie taught her; and there was the love of women, which is another story.

Mother Sylvie was the absolute dried-up old sexless virgin spinster. She was in her late fifties when Minnoo went to the convent to start school. She was French, and had been trained by the Jesuits (thank God?), a fairly open-minded, intellectually-inclined Catholic sect.

Mother Sylvie, with her pensive, gentle face, her wrinkled white hands peppered with brown liver spots and overgrown with twisty blue veins, her sturdy black shoes that laced to the ankle. Despite the tropical heat and attendant foot fungi, her thick cotton socks went up up under her long skirts to God knows where—or maybe doesn't if he's male, for surely no male ever came close to the sanctum of Mother Sylvie's skirts.

Mother Sylvie was the one to whom Minnoo came with her whys and wherefores. And Mother Sylvie was the one who recognized Minnoo's penetrating intelligence, and brought her books—borrowed, begged, scavenged—from distant lands. Under Mother Sylvie's wing, Minnoo learned French, Latin, mathematics, philosophy and a resounding love of learning.

Mother Sylvie is long since dead; the nuns who have replaced her—a narrow-minded, ferret-faced lot—don't seem to give a hang for the whys their students throw at them. They want the girls to learn how to curtsy well, one foot behind the other, toes turned out, heads bowed, skirts raised in a triangle of submission.

They insist the Debating Society stick to topics like "Is it more important for women to have brains or beauty?"; and never notice the contradiction when they espouse home as the ideal place for Womanhood, rather than school or the workforce.

But on to the love of women, of which Minnoo learned perhaps more than her family cared for her to. What she learned about it, I cannot say, for that is Minnoo's business.

For Minnoo Mashi, the high walls of the convent encircled a cool heaven.

The enormous iron gates, with their heavy chains and locks, the outer walls blindingly whitewashed and kept spotless (probably by Divine intervention, since one never saw a scrubber applied), topped with barbed-wire-and-broken-glass salad to keep out, symbolically and actually, the world outside; the cool, dim, shadowy marble corridors inside, with nary a window or other opening (except slits for ventilation) in the outer walls; the endless *sussurrus* of soft, silk skirts rustling around feet clad in soft-soled slippers; the whisper, whisper, whisper of women's soft voices, made even softer by the huge hallways, high ceilings, thick concrete walls that absorbed every sound, nay, even every ray of light that dared wander their way.

While the sun outside blazed, heating the sidewalks to a hundred degrees, and glanced off every glass and metal surface to blind unwary eyes, the convent stayed cool, dark and quiet.

Outside, the world rushed about its business: lorries rumbling by loaded with produce, pineapples from Johore, foot-long green Thai mangoes, pungent jackfruit, thorny, overpowering durians; mosquito buses, named for their annoying, endless noise, carrying loads of ladies to market, men to their jobs, night-shift workers staggering home, loud, happy children; putt-putting motorcycles and the occasional roarer; clunky old cars, mainly Austins and Morrises, mainly grinding and graveling their way down roads filled with potholes, cows, unwary pedestrians, bicyclists, the occasional fallen (and very slippery) fruit or vegetable; honking taxis, aggressive in their desire to earn another dollar before the end of the hour—all combined to set up a din which never once penetrated the iron gates of the convent.

It was as if for the space of some hours, from 6:30 a.m. when the students entered the grounds, to 1:30 p.m. when they left, the world stopped turning. Inside the convent, cool-fingered women, dressed all in white, ministered to the many children they were saddled with; taught them their letters and numbers; fine Swedish Hardanger embroidery, and delicate sewing; the art of cooking onde-onde and mango chaatni.

And the girls! The mynah chatter of little girl-voices, high and sweet, and sometimes shrill, tumbling over one another, no, me first, no, I spoke first, no me, me, listen to me! The sweaty scrambling as they struggled to get into bloomers for their mandated Physical Education period, in which they learned folk-dancing from, of all places, England and Scotland. The whispering of secrets, punctuated by, "My parents would never do a thing like that!" or wild giggling fits.

Minnoo Mashi, in that hothouse filled with blooming young beauties, was like a tigress let loose among the goats. Every naughty thing she could think of, she immediately did, and more often than not inveigled some of the more soft-headed among her classmates into helping her. Weren't the nuns simply scandalized when they found that Minnoo and her classmates, aided by thick straw mats and homemade quilts, had scaled the west wall to steal a neighbor's ripe guavas?

Or when Minnoo set up an "animal shelter," sweet-talked the poorer kids into picking up stray puppies and kittens, bathed and cleaned them in the downstairs bathrooms, tied bows around their necks, then offered them for sale for quite outrageous prices in the little shed behind the school?

She distributed homemade slingshots and gave lessons on how to use them; soon all the little girls were practicing on the boys who teased and irritated them daily from the boys' school across the road. The boys complained to the Fathers; the Fathers complained to the Mothers; and you know whose backside peeled for another month.

She taught them how to shoot rubberbands with a ruler; how to make arrows from splintered bamboo and fit them into the "bow" of ruler and rubberband; and soon the little boys from across the way were picking bamboo splinters out of their sit-upons on a regular basis; while Minnoo's sit-upon, just as regularly, was being rendered otherwise unfit to sit upon.

These, and other such evils, did Minnoo Mashi loose on the hapless inmates of the convent. Can you blame the girls for adoring her?

In all their quiet, well-behaved years there, they had seen no excitement. Most of them were well-off, middle class or better. In their own homes, all their childish spontaneity and vitality had been stifled by parents who only wanted well-brought-up children. Here was a Hera before them, willing to do anything, try any madness, think up any caper.

They followed her like sheep.

Of course, the teachers (who themselves were often on the receiving end of a "crush" or "pash") looked upon this behavior as childish, a phase (in the best Freudian terminology). They'll grow out of it, they reassured each other, watching as the girls competed to carry Minnoo's books to her classroom, or sit next to her, or partner her at Phys Ed classes.

If they knew that steamy letters comprising pages of passionate purple prose were being directed at Minnoo, they never said. Which is just as well, for that is how Minnoo came to experience the love of women, and thereby save herself from the fate in store for her.

For it was in her sixth year at school that she began to menstruate. No one had told her anything about these "women's mysteries" at all. Convinced she was dying of some rare internal condition (maybe cancer, huh? she said to her then-best friend, Saraswati Summawongsi), Minnoo changed. She decided life had to be lived to the fullest then and there, for she might not be around to enjoy it later.

Her pranks got wilder, more daring. She took to climbing ever taller trees, as if she were searching for something up in the heavens. She would run off into the jungle after school and not appear again, until dinnertime.

Needless to say, this drew a lot of attention from the extended family. By and large, their attitude had been: she's a girl, just an extra mouth to feed until a man comes along one day and takes her away, and it'll cost us plenty to convince someone to do that. So, mostly they had ignored her. But now when she failed to turn up promptly at 2 p.m. to do her household chores! "What's the point of feeding that extra mouth?" the relatives cried, "if we can't benefit from that extra pair of hands? And school costs money!"

So a brother was dispatched to fetch her home from school every day. Well, Minnoo was Minnoo. Not about to give in without a struggle. She slipped out the back door; she climbed over the wall; she thought of a hundred different things.

Since Borodada, her oldest brother, could not be spared from his business duties, Mejodada, Minnoo's unfortunate second brother, was responsible for ensuring Minnoo's prompt and punctual presence in the home.

Mejodada was a little slow to begin with. Things were exacerbated by the fact that the nuns permitted no male—not even a brother or father—to enter their hallowed gates. If it had a penis, it stayed outside. So poor Mejodada and his penis remained daily outside the gates, and more often than not returned home without Minnoo, and had his cheeks fluffed.

But slow does not mean stupid. Sooner or later, even the slowest fellow will catch on. So it was with Mejodada. One fine day it finally dawned on him that he might hide himself somewhere and watch for Minnoo instead of stupidly presenting himself at the gate where she might see and avoid him.

Thus, he found her, and having found her, he followed her. And, lo and behold! What should he discover? What carryings-on! That shameless, brazen hussy, Minnoo (who already owed him ten lifetimes' worth of beatings received from relatives), was secretly sneaking off to the jungle to meet her best friend, Kit Lee.

The two girls had discovered an enormous tree with a hollow trunk in some inaccessible spot. There they had made a home of sorts where they brought their favorite books and games. A soft bed of dried fragrant grasses dominated this hidey-hole. And on that bed lay the two girls in their petticoats, arms around each other.

Imagine their surprise when they saw the jug-eared head of Mejodada peering into their—dare we call it a love nest? Were they shocked, furious, upset? As for Mejodada, he was delighted. First, he had caught up with that stupid wretch on whose behalf his cheeks had been regularly fluffed for weeks. Second, the sight of two girls in their petticoats was one a well-brought-up Indian boy might never see in his whole life, for as a rule, young girls did not disrobe where boys or men might see them. And third, the endless possibilities for blackmail! The mere threat of revealing Minnoo's escapade to Mother might result in gifts of money, cups of tea, the best chair in the house. He might force Minnoo to iron his clothes or bring his breakfast, in exchange for his silence.

Or, he might come sometime when the girls didn't know he was there and watch them dress and undress. While he was thinking all this out, Minnoo and Kit were dressing hurriedly.

Kit fled, and Mejodada, sensing that Minnoo was about to follow, leapt on his sister like a young tiger, pinning her by one arm. He proceeded to drag her home for her punishment and his expected reward. But who could imagine Minnoo going quietly? Was she one to give up without a fight?

By the time they got home, it had been made clear to my Mejomama that blackmail was out of the question. Even though he punched her, pulled her hair, twisted her arms and threatened her with severe beatings, Minnoo refused to give in.

She wasn't making tea for this idiot of a brother, no sir! As for ironing clothes! What a fathead! To think that she, who had trouble folding her own clothes, would stoop to ironing his? She kicked his shins, jumped on his instep with both feet so that he had to let go of her arm, punched his nose and threatened to put his eyes out.

"You're mad!" He cried tears and snot, mixing with blood, as he finally dragged her through the front door. He threw her down onto the floor. "Do you know what she was doing?" he said, except it came out more like "Dhu u dough waa thee wath thooig?" because Minnoo had hit his lip as well, and it was puffed out like a puri.

Well, the story was soon out, and the family wasn't sure whether to laugh or be scandalized. To be sure, quite a few of the women pulled the ends of their saris over their faces. Their shoulders shook, their voices trembled. But were they laughing or crying?

180

Mejodada suspected the worst, and shook with fury. His cut lip and bloodied nose were smarting, and the thought of having to explain to his friends that his wild and crazy sister was responsible was, really, too much to bear.

As for Minnoo, she shook with fear and rage. How dare they, how dare they send this stupid lump after her? How dare he spy on her? How dare they laugh at her? How dare they use her to perform all this shitwork, this unpaid labor, and then get angry that she wasn't there to do yet more of it? What would they do to her? To Kit?

The elders, having fluctuated long enough between laughter and tears, sent each child to a different end of the house and locked them in. "Not a word about this to anyone," they said to Mejodada. "Sit here quietly and study. Your father will come in the evening, then we'll talk again."

Of course, father's arrival meant less than nothing, since everyone knew the women made the decisions. The sisters and sisters-in-law and aunts all huddled together in the kitchen, drinking strong gingery chai.

Should they take it seriously, and forbid Minnoo to go to that school? Or less seriously, and simply forbid the classmate? In the end, they decided to say nothing about it to anyone—it was just two girls playing. After all, they had determined from their questioning that no men were involved; how serious could it be? Minnoo was just being rebellious and disobedient, as usual. So they would say nothing to anyone, except the men in the family; and meanwhile, they would look around for a potential husband.

The rest of the children were sent off to their friends' houses to play, having been warned that one word about the day's events would be rewarded with ten strokes of the rattan.

When the men came home from their jobs or errands, they were informed of the hangama, and quietly assented to the decision. Among themselves they laughed. That Minnoo! But to the women, they said nothing. What was there to say? The search for a husband was on, and marriage would put an end to all these goings-on. Minnoo would settle down and become a wife.

Minnoo was not informed of any of this, however. She was released from her prison and warned not to hit her brother again. Mejodada, released from his, tried to repay at least one of the blows he had suffered, but was cuffed soundly by his father and warned to keep his hands off his sister.

Mejodada cried, "But she hit me!" as Minnoo stuck out her tongue and danced away. "You're a boy," his father said, "how hard could a girl hit you?" Mejodada, pointing to his bloody nose and fat lip, was speechless with rage and humiliation. The laughter of his father and uncles only wounded his ego more. He resolved to thrash Minnoo soundly the next time he found her alone, and went out cursing under his breath.

Minnoo, in the meantime, was trying to figure out a way to see her beloved Kit again, without having to suffer the consequences. Kit would be furious, and her brother, of course, would now be spying constantly. It was time to devise a better plan. What her plans amounted to, she never said. But of her mother's plans she was soon to find out.

About this time, her mother and aunts had finally thought to ask Minnoo about menstruation. The resulting uproar had a twofold effect. First, Minnoo realized that she wasn't going to die a glamorous death, with all her relatives on their knees tearfully begging her forgiveness; no, instead she was going to be stuck with this icky, yucky thing, that her mother

politely referred to as her "monthly disease," for the rest of her probably very long life! (Her elders had not seen fit to spring menopause on her at the same time.)

Second, the female elders realized that Minnoo, having attained menarche, was in serious danger of losing that prized feminine quality—her virginity—if not married off pronto, as per custom.

The search for a suitable husband intensified. Now Minnoo, innocent of her relatives' plots, had recently begun to cultivate a cousin that she had hitherto ignored. This cousin, who was actually twice or thrice removed, was a pretty girl—about the same age, height and size as Minnoo, but a little slow.

As a child, Minnoo had at first delighted in putting one over on her, for the girl, Radhika, was rather simple, and, like all the other cousins, adored Minnoo and believed everything Minnoo told her. In the end, it was that which caused Minnoo to stop tormenting her. For Radhika never held anything against Minnoo, never remembered the wrongs done, idealized and idolized Minnoo with a fervor bordering on worship. It was too easy to get Radhika's goat, and what's more, it wasn't even fun.

Now, here she was, guzzying up to Radhika, and her elders were, as usual, torn between pleasure and suspicion. Pleasure that she was taking an interest in a girl mostly avoided by her contemporaries; and suspicion that something was cooking in that naughty head.

Fortunately, they didn't find out—till much too late—what it was. But Mejodada spent many fruitless afternoons following Minnoo (or so he thought) up and down streets from one friend's house to another.

This likeness of the two cousins came in very handy one last time. This final trick of Minnoo Mashi's could only be worked once, though, for it was bound to be discovered, and once discovered, became worthless.

This was the final scandal that caused my Minnoo Mashi to be disowned by the family. Nobody laughed this time. Nobody said, "Ai, that Minnoo!" This time they cut her off without another word.

You see, Minnoo had, with the unwitting help of Radha, continued to see Kit. Secretly and stealthily, the two girls had continued to meet. What went on between them, Minnoo Mashi never said. Only that they both eventually decided they loved each other.

In that day and age, it was simply unheard of that a girl of a good Hindu Brahmin family would remain unmarried unless there were something seriously physically wrong with her. Even mental illness or retardation could not save one from a marriage—arranged by one's elders—to some lunk one might never have laid eyes on.

How was Minnoo to remain unmarried, and at Kit's side?

Kit herself came from a rather conservative Chinese family. Her father had raised her like a boy, but a well-bred boy. Now that she was at puberty, he could no longer pretend not to notice her gender and was thinking of sending her to school in England, where she could continue her studies without attracting unwelcome attention and proving an embarrassment. Few women of any race were educated in those days, outside the big cities.

As for her marriage, if any, Kit's father wanted his daughter to be respectable and well-educated; but she thought he would not force her into marriage with any man she did not want.

The two girls agreed that they could not bear the thought of separation from each other. Nor did Minnoo think she could bear the thought of the marriage that would someday be arranged by her parents. (Little did she know how soon!)

So, with Radhika's help, they continued to meet. As for the future, they decided they would simply wait till Kit's father was ready to send her abroad for further schooling, then Minnoo would try to win a scholarship to the same school, or, failing that, wait till Kit had enough money saved to send for her.

In this way, almost a year passed before reality confronted them again. Minnoo's grades were good, she was doing well in school, and her pranks were limited to "naughty but not excessive," as one of the nuns wearily reported to her father. Her Mejodada's afternoons were spent wearily and fruitlessly following Radhika around in hope of another glimpse of petticoat.

Everybody was getting along fine, minding their own business, except for the local matchmaker. This rather obnoxious but highly efficient old lady had been searching for a husband for the likes of Minnoo, with little success. Upon seeing the darkness of the bride's skin, many a prospective mother-in-law sighed, thought regretfully of the vanished dowry, and returned the photo or portrait to the matchmaker's hands with a remark like, "I can do better for my son."

Needless to say, the better portion of available grooms had mothers who had heard detailed descriptions of Minnoo's character and fondness for pranks. Marry such a wild girl to their son and end up with a devil for a daughter-in-law? They shook their heads and turned the matchmaker down.

Finally, after much diligent searching, this worthy had found a fellow willing to be yoked to Minnoo in return for the munificent dowry paid out by her family. How could she wait to bring the good news home? On her way in the front door, she accosted Minnoo, "Oh, Ma, what a big girl she is! A little dark, but with enough jewelry, who will notice?" and here she leaned forward to pinch Minnoo's cheek, "She'll be the most beautiful bride in this state, I tell you." Glowering as Minnoo struck her hand away, she waddled up the stairs as fast as her bulk would let her.

Minnoo was horrified. She rushed out to Kit's house right away, forgetting brother, cousin, homework and chores. When she came home after breaking the news to Kit, the adults were all sitting around on the main room floor, chewing paans and chattering excitedly.

"So," they cried as she entered, "the bride returns. Enjoy, enjoy as much of your freedom as you can, little one, it'll be gone before you know it. Soon you'll be a little wife, with a big bunch of keys tied to the end of your sari, cooking and cleaning and taking care of your husband."

"And if you have babies," interjected the matchmaker, "be sure they're fair like him, not black like you."

Minnoo glared at them. They only laughed. "What, aren't you coming to see his photograph? What a handsome boy this is, only look!" "Look, a photograph he sent! So your shoshur is not a poor man." "When you go to your rich shoshur's home, don't forget your poor cousins!" Whoever said this last, Minnoo did not know. But, as she always says, she owes them a life debt.

For that's what put the idea in her head, you see. She went along, quiet as a mouse. She was barely fourteen when the wedding was to take place.

Soon the time came for the prospective groom to pay his formal visit. Minnoo, as usual, found a way to see, though not meet him. For she was exiled to the women's quarters, and, at best, might peer at him through a keyhole when he took tea with her parents in the inner courtyard, or in the living room, if she was quick, quiet and careful.

Undoubtedly, Minnoo had already made her plans. Seeing the man her parents had found only confirmed them.

It's possible that if the man had been a little more like Minnoo herself, or if he had been that sweet, tolerant type so common among Bangali men, Minnoo might have put her wild ideas aside and married him. Even she admits it's possible.

But when he showed up, the moment she laid eyes on him, she knew she had to get out of this marriage any way she could. The man was not bad looking, but he was in his thirties, and Minnoo, hidden behind the door, wondered why someone his age would want a bride of fourteen. Then he opened his mouth, and she knew.

He was the only son of his parents, and they were fairly well-off. He was fair, as the matchmaker had promised. But there was a distinctly loutish quality to him that Minnoo could not overlook. Was he stupid? Crazy? Something was wrong with him, something Minnoo couldn't define, but knew in her bones would make it impossible to live with him.

"Education?" he was saying to her father. "Education is not needed for a wife. She can attend music classes or dancing. Cooking classes also okay. But I am looking for a wife and a woman to be a mother to my children, not a degree-wali."

Of course, her father agreed. Effusively.

Minnoo, listening from behind the door, began to fume. As soon as the fellow left, she ran to her father, who, we all agree, spoiled her horribly (when her mother wasn't looking, that is). "But Baba," she cried, "I want to be a degree-wali. I don't want to marry that fat, stupid, hairy fellow."

"There, there, little mother," her father stroked her wild hair back off her face, "a girl's fate is like that. You must marry, and we can't find anyone else who will have you. Besides, all men are hairy. And he's not stupid, just a little…domineering." He looked sad, as if he feared for her. What does it take to tame a wild animal? One must break its spirit. How do you tame a high-spirited child as wild as Minnoo?

Minnoo, who knew and saw and understood far more than even her exaggerating elders thought, lowered her eyes and fell silent. This was the mothers' doing then, she thought, and with them she could not argue. They loved her, but they were afraid for her as well. And rather than let her explore her own wide road in the world, they were cutting for her a path as narrow as their own feet had once trod, in the hope that she would stay safe. And at the expense of everything Minnooish about her. They would rather have a miserable, middle-class Minnoo as a well-fed wife than a daring, madcap Minnoo, happy but dangerously on the edge.

As all parents will and do.

"Baba," Minnoo said in parting, "I will not stop school. And if you try to make me, I will kill myself." She said it in a serious tone, not her usual whimsical, exaggerating, tall-tale tone. Then she looked away so she wouldn't have to see the pain in his eyes.

"But Minnoo, ma, you are going to be married. You are a bride now. How can profane eyes see your face and body?"

"I will kill myself," Minnoo said and walked out of the room. Father went to fetch Mother, Grandmother, Aunties, Uncles. They talked, they argued, they shouted at each other

184

with all the doors shut so the children could barely hear what they were saying, even with their ears pressed to the door.

Minnoo's Mejodada, who had gone to listen at a window, found his hair in the iron grip of their Boromashi, who pulled his head up to her face and said, "Older boy, is this the kind of example you set? Take your cousins and brothers out to the river to play, idiot, or you won't sit on that fat backside for a month. And leave Minnoo alone, or we'll make sure you regret it."

Mejodada, who had been but recently beaten ignominiously by Minnoo (in public, too!) when he tried to sneak up behind her and kick her, was only too glad to leave her alone. Rubbing his smarting scalp, he collected the various children with dire, vague and unspecified threats, and escorted them down to the river, where they rapidly covered themselves and each other with mud and other sundry substances.

The elders called Minnoo in and gave her an ultimatum. She was to quit school immediately, or get the thrashing of her life. She stood before the twelve of them, silent and obstinate.

"Surely God has cursed me for my sins in my past life," her mother wailed, beating her small flat chest with both fists, tearing her hair and weeping. "Don't you see what you are doing to your mother?" her father cried, rushing to his wife's side as she rolled about on the floor, kicking and shrieking.

Minnoo folded her arms and looked down at the floor. "Oh, didi, it's not your sins but mine he is punishing," cried the elder aunt, beating her own well-equipped chest with pounding thuds. "Did any donkey ever have a more obstinate child?" her grandmother shrieked, slapping her face.

Not a tear, not a word, rewarded their efforts. And who had ever known Minnoo to be quiet for a minute? This new Minnoo terrified them. It was as if the lively, noisy, troublesome but loved child they had always known had been taken away and replaced with a stranger. Finally, unable to budge Minnoo, they gave in.

"Never again can we hold our heads up," her grandmother said crossly. "Every one will know that the bride has been seen by all kinds of strange men. If the boy's family calls the wedding off, it's on my fool of a son's head. Do what you want." The other relatives had ceased their crying and breast-beating.

Now that her father's mother had spoken, Minnoo turned on her heel and left without a word. The old lady's word was law, and she had shifted the responsibility to Minnoo's father, who would not oppose his daughter's wish. On the other hand, poor Baba would come in for his fair share of torment at the hands of his infuriated wife and mother.

But Minnoo did not care, for never before had she asked anything of her father, and he knew it. He owed her this.

The new Minnoo continued in her strange behavior, frightening her entire family. She said not a word to anyone. She submitted to having her horoscope read, and being bathed and massaged and oiled and squeezed and squashed in many different ways. The ladies of the family bathed her thick, tangled black hair, oiled it, put herbs and henna in it and braided it. She submitted to all their ministrations. No one teased her. They hardly dared.

"She's growing up," her mother would say, with a worried frown. "She knows she must learn her responsibilities as a wife." So time passed, and everyone, caught up in the preparations for the wedding, stopped paying attention to Minnoo.

Instead of using this golden opportunity to indulge in her usual mischief-making, Minnoo continued in her odd behavior. She went to school every day, worked hard, studied, did her homework and chores, ate, went about her business with a gravity and silence that bored her little cousins, but fortunately escaped her elders' notice.

And she spent nearly every day with Radhika. We can imagine now what they did and talked about. But who knew, then? Only Radhika and Minnoo.

So finally, the wedding day dawned. Fixed by the astrologer as the most auspicious according to the horoscope of bride and groom, it was a bright sunny day with that clean washed feeling that follows a monsoon. A cooling breeze blew in from the sea, heavy with salt, leaving a fresh, bitter coat in every throat and nose. The bride was dressed in her finery and left seated in her room while the relatives went out to meet the groom's family and friends.

The celebrations began, the ritual singing and dancing and teasing, the mock battle between bride's family and groom's, and by-and-by, it was time to fetch the bride. They went in to her and found her sitting exactly as they had left her.

An aunt took each arm, and carefully, they lifted the tender young bride to her feet. With the end of her sari covering her modestly lowered head and face, the bride came with slow steps, anklets jingling, leaning on her relatives.

Was there a dry eye in the house? Cousins, aunts, uncles, and parents, everyone wept as they saw Minnoo, bejeweled and bedecked, almost fainting as she tottered into the room. "A mountain of gold and jewels," a cousin whispered, and was pinched for her pains by some irate elder.

On and on the ceremony went, the purohit reciting the Sanskrit words, ponderous, sonorous, beautiful, even if not understood. Aunts shifted their weight from one buttock to another; cousins stole the shoes of every visitor and switched them around; children picked their noses and cried; elders periodically fainted and had to be revived by the application of cold towels soaked in rosewater. Finally, the big moment came: the bride's veil was raised so the groom could place a sweetmeat in her mouth with his own hand.

The gasp that arose from Minnoo's family was, fortunately, restrained enough that only the groom heard it. What he thought, I do not know. No one in our family discusses Minnoo's wedding; it would be the ultimate in bad taste.

For the bride who sat there, sweating patiently under the weight of her entire dowry, was not Minnoo but Radhika. The cousins looked alike, but not enough alike that their families would not know them. The groom, having only seen the bride's photograph, saw nothing. While feeding his bride, he extended his large yellow teeth to seize the sweetmeat from her dainty fingers, laden with rings of gold. Minnoo's family sat speechless. Where was Minnoo?

At the convent, some miles away, Mother Sylvie was dragged out of bed by the Mother Gatekeeper. "There's a girl out here, looks as wild as a jungli animal. Wants to see you," said the Mother Gatekeeper shortly, returning to her guardianly duties, the massive ring of keys hanging at her belt jingling with every step. Squeezing her heat-swollen feet painfully into their hard black leather shoes, Mother Sylvie walked as fast as she could to the gate.

Should she have been surprised to see Minnoo? Perhaps she was privy to the plan all along. But no, that could not be. That good woman could never have lied for Minnoo, and she would not have countenanced such a prank.

Now Minnoo falls, sobbing, on Mother Sylvie's neck, and Mother Sylvie, conscious that Mother Gatekeeper is listening avidly, although nothing much can be heard through the snorts, sobs, sniffles, wails and grunts of Minnoo Mashi, says, "Come, come, my child, pull yourself together. Let us go to the Chapel and pray for guidance. Then you can have tea in the waiting room and tell me all about it." And she leads a slightly more composed but still red-eyed Minnoo away.

Soon, Mother Superior is rousted. Since Minnoo is under the legal marriageable age, it is something of a scandal. The nuns are in a difficult position, indeed. Something must be done, but what?

"Child," the Mother Superior, a practical woman of great understanding, says to Minnoo, "what are you asking of us? Do you wish to speak with your parents? Do you want the police?"

Minnoo, who has held together under a year or more of various strains, begins to come apart. Being excitable, passionate, tempestuous—in a word, Bangali—she starts telling her story, interspersed with sobs, hyperventilation, hysteria, hair-pulling and chest-pounding. Fortunately, she is flat as a board, or she soon would be.

The nuns calm her with various substances. Tea is brought, then toast, then smelling salts, and finally, brandy. This brings Minnoo to her senses immediately. "I can't drink that," she says.

"Drink it, it will do you good," Mother Marguerite orders. Minnoo raises herself to her full height of five feet and gathers her tattered dignity. "I am an orthodox Hindu," she says primly, "I cannot and will not drink that stuff."

Mother Superior waves Mother Marguerite aside. "Give her some hot tea with lots of milk and plenty of sugar," she says. "Now, child," as Minnoo begins to gulp the scalding tea, "you do not wish to become one of us, I take it?"

"A nun?" Minnoo is horrified, then ashamed at her reaction, more for the nuns than herself.

"There is no shame in this, child. It is a calling. And you have not been called," Mother Superior says. "Shall we send for the police, then?"

"No, no police," Minnoo says. "I want to stay here. I cannot go home now. They will not take me back."

"But they are your parents. Of course they will take you back," says one of the nuns. Mother Superior signals her for silence.

"Why will they not?" she asks sympathetically. "Surely what you have done is not so bad, just a childish prank. They will understand. But your cousin, now…"

"No," says Minnoo, stamping her foot in her impatience, "you don't understand. Once a daughter is betrothed, she belongs to her husband's family, not her own. And I don't want to marry that fat hairy lout. And Radhika does. Want to be married, I mean. And who would marry her, anyway, with her empty head? Except that lout, I mean, he wants an empty-headed wife. But my family cannot take me back. I thought…I do well in class. I could be a teacher. You could train me and I could live here."

"We could not do that without your parents' permission," Mother Superior says gently. "Now go with Mother Sylvie. We must discuss what is to be done," and she ushers Minnoo

and Mother Sylvie out of the room. "Keep her quiet," she says to Mother Sylvie, "we don't want her getting hysterical again and upsetting the boarders."

The upshot of the nuns' meeting is the dispatch of a delegation to Minnoo's family. Minnoo goes with them. They arrive the day after the wedding, which has, according to the fat hairy lout, been consummated with the full cooperation and enjoyment of both parties. The groom's party, fortunately, has already left, bearing away the bride. Minnoo's family has gone through the tail end of the ceremony with faces of stone.

Now, they receive the delegation of nuns with cold hospitality. No one looks at Minnoo or even acknowledges her presence. They give their permission for her to stay with the nuns, who bear her away triumphantly.

And that is how my Minnoo Mashi, a respectable, high-caste Hindu woman, came to be unmarried and living on her own.

Actually she lives with another woman, though that's beside the point. Still, when my mother decided to get me married off at sixteen, only my unconventional Minnoo Mashi dared to intervene.

My mother gave me what she considered the good news at dinner one evening. I was horrified. "I don't want to get married," I cried. "I'm only sixteen!"

"That's old enough to start looking," my mother said coldly. "Meanwhile, we're sending you to boarding school in India. That should stop all this wildness and bad behavior. When we find the boy, we'll bring you back for the wedding."

"I won't do it," I cried. "I won't, I won't!"

"Yes, you will," my mother said. "You'll do exactly what we tell you to. What else could you do, anyway? Are you smart enough to finish school and get a job and support yourself?"

"But I don't want to get married," I said, a little weakly, for really, I had no idea either what I would do with my life. I looked at my father for help, but it was worse than useless. Clearly, they had already argued the issue and Mother had won.

"And how can a girl live if she is not married? Who will care for you? We won't be around all your life, you know. Someone has to take care of you and protect you. You must get married." My mother's tone brooked no argument, but still I tried one.

"Why can't I be like Minnoo Mashi?" I said.

If an elephant had walked in the front door and helped itself to my mother's dinner, the effect couldn't have been more stupendous. There was a thunderous, lengthy silence. Neither of my parents raised their eyes from their plates. Neither said a word. Then my mother looked at me.

"Is that what you want? An unnatural, abnormal life? To be an old maid? What do you think, that two women can protect each other? We spend our whole life working hard to feed, clothe and educate you, and this is our reward? You want to be like your mad mashi? You'll go to hell and burn with her too," and she stormed out of the room, leaving her food untouched.

My brother glared at me. Now you've done it, he mouthed. Father ate uneasily, waiting for Mother's fury to break around his head. I slunk through the kitchen to the neighbors' and called my Minnoo Mashi.

She came right away, for since my Thakurma's death, she visited more often. She walked straight up to Father. "Doesn't experience teach anything, Dada?" she said, then, without waiting for a response she marched into my mother's bedroom. What hangama! What shouting, shrieking, throwing of heavy objects, scolding, screaming and door-banging! It went on for at least twenty minutes. We cowered downstairs, speechless and terrified, Father huddling right in there with us.

"Your mother," he said periodically, shaking his head, "your aunt. What kind of past life did I lead, to be at the mercy of these terrible women?" His eye lit on me as if he wanted to say that I was the cause of the current storm. But my father is too kind. Poor man, he simply can't stand up to my mother, just as he couldn't stand up to his mother. Or his daughters, for that matter.

Mother and Mashi emerged soon after all the noise died down. Mother looked grim, her lips compressed in a straight line, puffing out her chin like a fish. Mashi looked triumphant. Her bun had come apart and curly tendrils snaked over one eye and ear. Mother's face had a thin scratch, and Minnoo Mashi's a couple of bruises. Neither said anything till they reached us.

"Dada," Minno Mashi as usual was the first to get a word in, "the law in this country says a child cannot be married against her will and in any event, not before she is eighteen. I have explained this to my dear Didi, and she has agreed to wait until Probha reaches that age."

My father looked at the ceiling. He seemed fascinated by the progress of a fat-bellied gecko toward a moth.

"I've decided you all need a rest this evening," Minnoo Mashi continued, as if my father didn't exist. "I'm taking the kids to the movies and they'll stay till Sunday night. Come on, kids," she said, picking up her purse.

We didn't need to be told twice. Rushing to our bedrooms, we grabbed pajamas and toothbrushes, books and toys. As I was stuffing my comb into my schoolbag, my mother came into the room. Her eyes were bright and very hard. Suddenly she put her arms around me from behind and hugged me. I was shocked. She hadn't done that in a long time.

When I turned to look at her, she turned away. "Comb your hair, it's so untidy," she said. Her voice sounded funny. Then she looked at me, and I saw she had been crying. "You're growing up so fast," she said. "You're a big girl now." Then she pushed me out of the room. "Go, your Mashi is waiting," she said, and went to her bedroom. I saw my father inside, sitting on the bed. He looked weary and nervous.

I'm never going to have kids, I vowed, as I ran to Minnoo Mashi's car. We rode to her house in silence, but that night, after she had put the others to bed, she took me into her bedroom. "Tonight you can sleep here with Nita and me, okay? Big treat," she said, smiling.

I climbed into her enormous bed, with its cool, white starched sheets and the filmy mosquito netting that hung all around. "Minnoo Mashi," I said, when she had settled in beside me. She turned to face me, giving me all her attention. I felt a little embarrassed, but went on.

"Minnoo Mashi, why was my mother crying?" I asked. Then she told me her story. "She doesn't want you to end up like me," she said, smiling, when she had finished. I wanted to

ask why, but I was too tired. Besides, Nita was there, and I liked her. She always put me in the middle when I slept there, and put her arms carefully around me, as if I were a little eggshell. I put my face in my Minnoo Mashi's fragrant back.

"Thank you for saving my life," I mumbled, as she turned out the light.

"What?" she turned to me again.

"I just said I'm glad you're my Mashi," I said.

kenokirtan keno means why; kirtan means song
pardashins veiled women

Physical Subjectivity and the Risk of Essentialism

SUPARNA BHASKARAN

If women, the poor, the coloured, the ones with cultures (whose cultures are denied, rendered invisible as they are seen as our mark), the queer, are deemed unfit for the public it is because we are tainted by need, emotion, the body.

> María Lugones, *Purity, Impurity, Separation and the Logic of The Politics of Identity, unpublished manuscript, 1992.*

A black woman and a small beige one talk about their bodies. About putting a piece of their anatomy in their pockets upon entering any given room.

> Cherríe Moraga, "Anatomy Lesson," *Loving In The War Years, 1983.*

As a feminist who has lived in both India and the United States, I am usually drawn towards debates on identity, the politics of separation and multiple subjectivities. However, dialogues concerning identity are viewed with suspicion and/or disregarded by some feminists—who identify as postmodern feminists and/or poststructural feminists (and non-feminists)—as being "too essentialist." Further, if modes of theorizing and politics are considered too essentialist, which for some is popular academic name-calling and a way of stratifying "sophisticated feminist work" at the top and "the essentialist" kind at the bottom, the politics of identity is relegated as a flawed and uncritical mode of politics. In this essay I explore the plural meanings of essentialism in relation to identity politics, the multiple facets of feminist subjectivity, and how these issues may relate to the feminist practices of South Asian feminists and feminists of colour.

The Myth of a Woman

I felt that I had come to a frustrating dead end after I had finished reading feminist theory written by certain "poststructural feminists."[1] The works of these anti-essentialist feminists seem to be calling for "nominal skepticism,"[2] and more specifically, a "gender-skepticism."[3] Judith Butler, a poststructural feminist, argues for gender-skepticism or gender trouble, where gender, performance and anatomy are at odds with one another. Further, Butler suggests that it is in the realm of performance—where there is a necessary "dissonance" between gender and performance or gender and anatomy—rather than in identity politics that one can really begin addressing women's oppression.

I found two key points being stressed by the proponents of gender-skepticism. First, anti-essentialist feminists argue that the concept of "woman" is unstable and perhaps the very act of defining and naming a concept "woman" is problematic—problematic because naming would "fix" and "naturalize." For example, the category "woman" in the heterosexual-patriarchal naming scheme would deem it perfectly "natural" or normal or even mandatory for women to pursue motherhood or wifehood. Thus motherhood is considered to be a logical destiny (gets fixed) for women. In other words, natural fact or laws of nature (as prescribed by hetero-patriarchy) carves out roles for women. Consequently, if all feminists accepted the concept "woman," they/we would be claiming that all women are alike and oppressed by similar mechanisms. Second, it is implied that *the* critical alternative to essentialism is the social constuctionist position[4] which asserts that gender or the category of woman is culturally, socially and linguistically mapped by patriarchal power. In other words, anything that is considered to be natural or a natural fact, is socially constructed. Therefore, any act of naming and defining patterns or realities via the concept "woman" or making any connection between female biology and the category woman (as defined by hetero-patriarchy), would be engaging in essentialism or biological determinism.[5]

Getting entangled in understanding feminist politics as rigid either/or scenarios—i.e., the feminist essentialist versus the feminist social constructionist (anti-essentialist)—is problematic and reductive. Feminists (both of the past and those who don't neccessarily identify strongly with poststructural theory) have historically pointed out the workings of phallocentric language, cultural assumptions and systems of meaning. In other words, prior to the popularity of poststructural calls for "deconstruction" and "anti-essentialism," feminists have consistently attempted to critique and challenge (with varying success) the hetero-patriarchal and racially bound notions of what it means to be oppressed as a "woman." Anti-essentialist feminist theory seems to ignore this feminist history and the radical feminist politics of naming, re-naming and embodying concepts with oppositional meanings in radically new ways with multiple possibilities.

My critique of anti-essentialist feminist theory does not intend to ignore some of its contributions—namely its caution against naturalizing identity politics and reductive categories—but often this deconstruction gets lost in a problematic and relativistic contention that all categories are arbitary and any attempt at recognizing meaningful patterns is naturalizing. Such a contention discredits all forms of identity, identity politics and conceptual empowering. Further, the logic of gender-skepticism seems to imply that day-to-day lived oppression is perhaps a problem for some women—poor women, fat women, women of colour, lesbians, women who are not able-bodied—but the immediate problem for poststructural feminists is the fine tuning of their theory of deconstruction and linguistic arbitrariness. In other words, gender-skeptical feminists would be skeptical of categories such as "woman," suggesting that such a concept would erase differences (or homogenize) or rather would erase the "problem of difference" between women. However, for the most part these differences have not been critically explored, and this "problem" would be sometimes justified via disclaimers. In an essay that is not directed specifically at poststructural feminists, María Lugones talks about these disclaimers made by certain white feminists. She argues that they are "noninteractive," that is, "...the disclaimer just serves as an announcement that the

author will not accept responsibility for the effects of her own particular 'social and sexual history' on others."[6]

The connection between language and reality is often contradictory. It is crucial to deepen feminist understandings of the refractions and reflections of man-made and imposed language. Language for the most part has been used to maintain and promote hetero-patri-archy, racism, colonialism, imperialism, poverty and many more interlocking systems of domination. For instance, what does it mean when I identify with the multiple categories in "woman of colour in the U.S.?" The category "woman" is a notion constructed within the hetero-patriarchal universe of discourse, and similarly, being of colour (in the modern sense) is a notion constructed in the Anglo-Christian universe of discourse. Feminists ("of colour" and white) and other persons of colour have challenged the naturalizing assumptions of dominant discourses and have constructed oppositional identities that resist and empower. They resist assumptions such as: women are really women if they become mothers, wives and caretakers of children; or that being dark skinned is representative of being "superstitious" and/or "corrupt." So "woman of colour" in one sense reflects the heterosexist-racist reality, and in the other sense, it reflects the reality of resistance, empowerment and shelter. For instance, radical feminists of all colours claim oppositional identities by removing words such as "woman"..."fat"..."dyke" from the heteropatriarchal-racist matrix and creating new meanings, spaces and radical possibilities with the very same words. These concepts are used simultaneously but with very different politics and spheres of meaning. And the practice of poststructural feminist deconstruction ends up focusing more on draining concepts of all meaning rather than on ways in which patterns of oppression can be discerned through conceptual visibility (or naming) and thus can be demolished.

Women's realities are "refracted" in a world where they are oppressed, and yet it is claimed by patriarchal loyalists that women's naturalized roles as nurturers, peacemakers and self-sacrificers are in actuality morally superior. Our location is refracted by constantly being trained into compulsory heterosexuality—through male-identified women or metro-pole-identified people,[7] patriarchal loyalists and their institutions and, eventually, through our own internalization of these messages. Our paths towards resistance get tedious and confusing when we maim each other with the ammunition of our internalized oppressions. "I have internalized a racism and classism, where the object of oppression is not only someone outside of my skin, but someone inside my skin. In fact, to a large degree, the real battle with such oppression, for all of us, begins under the skin."[8]

A critical understanding of the reflections and refractions of social constructions and language is not something new to feminist theory. Historically, feminists have formulated these issues via the sex-gender distinction. They have pointed out that women have been allocated the domain of nature and restricted by male-defined female biology, whereas men have proclaimed themselves to be above nature and the producers of culture. That is, a woman's place in history has been determined by how her body can serve men: institutions of motherhood, wifehood and marriage were but "natural" goals to be fulfilled by women. The sex-gender distinction, explored by feminists, pointed out the inherent biological determinism of patriarchal discourse and reality.

Most of this earlier feminist "deconstruction" of the nature-culture tension focused on the negativity of female biology (as defined by patriarchy) for women and thus focused on

how women could also be the producers of culture, just like men. Although the sex-gender distinction has been helpful, liberal feminist solutions for "equal rights"—that is, for women to be just like men—have been problematic and inadequate. Among other problems, the politics of equal rights is uncritical and "noninteractive" about the body-desire-mind matrix that maps oppressive conditions for women. Gender-skepticism seems to also carry on this tradition of disembodied somatophobia in the form of anti-essentialist and anti-naming determinism. That is, the critical potential of the female body or the dark body is not explored; rather, the body is limited to a site inscribed upon by the "technologies" of power (such as language).

The construction of women within the sex/gender system needs to be unravelled and rethought outside the "myth of woman,"[9] outside the heterosexual matrix, both as a "collective class" and as "individual subjects." Wittig's conception of "woman" as the myth, and thus a construct of the heterosexual regime, seems to be a helpful point of departure to reconceptulaize womanhood. Class constructions, that is, women as a collective class, provide the lens to locate oppressive schemes. Such a formulation of "women" recognizes that oppression produces categories of sex/gender. Further, the categories sex and/or gender can be understood as mutually constitutive. That is, ideas that construct our desire are genitalia-centric, but these ideas are embodied in our sensual-material subjectivities. Therefore, sex as physicality and sociality is embodied within a reinforcing circuit of meanings and sensations.

The heterosexist culture of oppression constructs dimorphic categories of sex. In response, the social constructionist deconstruction of the naturalness of woman is important, but fails by posing an ambiguous "subject" politics or an ambigious point of reference. As feminists we need to generalize about women's subjectivities, and thus recognize the clever and intricate patterns of oppression that unite us as the binary "Other." Getting too caught up in only finding differences—or the so-called "problem of difference"—within this already constructed Otherness will only strengthen this opposition for its creators. On the other hand, refusing to recognize the critical potential of our different experiences of marginality and privilege will prevent the the meaningful pattern of and the weaving of centers of resistance and community building. It is only through our different experiences that we can begin mapping and naming similar contours of woman-hating, body-hating and darkness-hating. Denaturalizing women within a heterosexual meaning system is crucial, but to de-materialize women fragments positions of emancipation.

Ethnocentric Racism

> They are seen as black, therefore they are black; they are seen as women, therefore they are women.
> But before being seen that way, they first had to be made that way.
>
> Monique Wittig,
> *The Straight Mind and other essays,* 1992.

The familiar phrase from Simone de Beauvoir "One is not born, but becomes a woman" can also be phrased: one is not born, but becomes a coloured/colourful woman.[10] There seem to be some parallels between the sex-gender debates and race-ethnicity debates.

The concept of race is built on and constructed by oppressive conditions of cultural chauvinism/ethnocentrism, and psycho-physical and political domination. "Race" in its modern sense is also initially constructed as dimorphic, often presented creatively by such metropole-identified discourses as: Self/Other; Occident/Orient; White/Ethnic; Civilized/Primitive; Us/Native; Western/Indigenous; Colonizer/Colonized; and Metropole/Colony.

Racism is a form of oppression that constructs physical markers—skin colour, texture of hair, preferred accents, facial features, etc. Ethnocentrism is the culture of the "racialized state."[11] The constructs of race and ethnicity tend to become more nebulous than sexual dimorphism, since its oppressive and multiple physical classifications (oriental, hispanic, negroid, and so on) are always contradicting its original dimorphism (i.e., white vs. non-white). It is in these contradictions that the meanings of race and ethnicity can collapse into each other—for example, some white folks refer to people as "ethnic" when these people "just happen to be" non-white and/or non-western.

Racism and ethnocentrism work hand in hand. As philology would suggest, the modern usage of the word "ethnocentrism" would mean to make the center (centrism) one's own culture (ethnos) for everyone. Or, in other words, ethnocentricism means to view one's own culture or shared understandings and meaning systems as superior to others. This practice of imposing one's standard of being—which is western, white, male, heterosexual, middle class, to name some locations of privilege—also entails constructing the dominant reality as ideal and universal. In the United States the politics of ethnocentric racism is both explicit and hidden and is played out in ambivalent ways. Take for example the practices of the Immigration and Naturalization Service (INS). If one wants to become "naturalized" one needs the intersecting privileges of whiteness, maleness, heterosexualness, and middle to upper classness. The supposed exception to the classist nature of the INS is the "refugee" or "asylum" status—both problematically defined in imperialistic and capitalist terms.

Identity Politics, the Politics of Equal Rights and the Lovers of Purity

Identity politics can be of the "essentialist" kind. Essentialist identity politics can range from the dangerous genetic-blood purifying movements of Nazism, to the anti-imperialist movements that, however necessary, still use a liberal framework that inadequately constructs nationalistic subject identities. Notions of identity in nationalist movements in India employed concepts such as spirit/soul/mind of India and meanings that were produced by the colonial enterprise. The Indian nationalists (usually from elite backgrounds), who were created by colonial "intervention," often utilized homogeneous/unified categories that suppressed marginal and alternative discourses. Geographic areas are naturalized in nationalist politics, since it entails a reconstellation of power holders. This anti-colonial discourse continued to follow the "logic of purity,"[12] and its desire to control, unify, dominate, fragment into neat compartments of divisible or indivisible parts. The lover of purity always constructs *himself* as unified, simple and whole and makes it the vocation of those conceptually erased and controlled to carry on the project of maintaining *him*. The lover of purity promotes essentialist identity politics and the erasure of heterogeneity.

María Lugones posits the radically different "politics of impurity" and "curdled being" as modes of creatively resisting assimilationist politics.[13] An identity politics that takes into

195

account multiple subjectivities, a cross section of different systems of meaning and a non-static positionality (that is, under different locations one can hold different degrees of power) in a transnational world, is the kind of politics I hope for. This kind of subjectivity does not undermine other subjectivities, and does not get retrapped into the categories and conceptual schemes organized by and around the problematic standard of male, white, western, christian, heterosexual, middleclass, and civilized. For these standards are in themselves universalizing and monolithic.

Identity politics that rejects the politics of purity rethinks the processes of centering and re-centering. The process of re-centering entails re-locating or re-positioning your selfhood and peoplehood. People involved in this process do not consider the act of centering as positioning themselves to be superior to other centers or to set a standard for all centers, but view it as an act of rejecting oppressive categories and schemes. It is a permutation of separatisms that are "subtle realignments of identities, priorities and commitments"…"ceasing to be loyal"…"self-preserving recoil" from "systemic misogyny,"[14] ethnocentric-racism, and so on.

The Body as Material Woman-Centered Subjectivity

As women, South Asian women and women of colour, our bodily fleshiness needs to be politicized in its natural-cultural system of meanings. By this I mean that there is a "physical appearance" that oppression consistently molds and maims. A lack of commitment to the "physical appearance" and women's subjectivity—out of fear of engaging in the act of essentialism—and a continued emersion in uncritically fighting categories drains and retards our feminist projects. The assaults on the "physical appearance" of sex persistently confront us through the increasing occurrences of female infanticide, dowry deaths, rapes, battery, and other institutionalized modes of violence, such as the "feminization of poverty" and compulsory heterosexuality for women. "Women's oppression is most complexly tied to our bodies, because patriarchal culture gives women's bodies such variable meanings and submits them to so many controls."[15]

It is crucial to make parallels between "physical appearance" and the experiential-political identity "woman." It is necessary for women to claim a subjectivity that recognizes experiences that oppress and to closely connect these themes to a material arena. This material sphere is that area of physicality that both rejects the oppressive sexual dimorphism of patriarchy and appropriates a reconstructed notion of women's bodies. A notion of women's subjective physicality is necessary to pinpoint dominating mechanisms and the internalization of these mechanisms—thereby providing a historical juncture for resistance.

I use the notion of the body synonymously with the concept of subjective physicality or physical appearance. I use these terms in a way that the physical body is closely intertwined and constituted by awareness, oppression, consciousness, the senses, and language. All these features simultaneously inform one another. I therefore see the necessity to locate "physical appearance" as a dimension of women's subjectivity. The cartography of this physical appearance derives its coherence through the recognitions of patterns (women's physicality that is subject to infanticide, the binding of their clitoris, battery, etc.) and differences (differential body aesthetics and bodily expressions).

196

An issue that needs exploration is the notion of "plural bodies." The conceptualization of the body has varied culturally and historically. Bodies have been constructed as the mechanical body, anatomical body, humoral body, topographical body, and so on. The mechanical and the anatomical body are stereotypically associated with the west. This view begins from the premise of the mind-body split, and sees the body as a machine of interconnected anatomical parts. This notion of the body is alienated further from our subjectivities when it is turned into a commodity. Here the body and body parts (such as breasts, long legs, thin bodies, etc.) are part of a commodity-driven market economy. Women are constrained, dominated and estranged from their own, as well as from other bodies.

The notion of humoral bodies is usually associated with "eastern" philosophies (such as classical Ayurveda in India, Taoist philosophy, etc.), where anatomy is not as explicated in constructing bodies. The "body" is understood as humors (representing elements of hot/cold or sweet/sour, etc.), channels of fluids and processes. Topographical representations of the body attempt to map out pressure points on the physical body that may connect with entirely different body regions/emotions. (This is not to suggest that these notions of the "body" are any less oppressive.)

Although what I have described above is a resource often used by those interested in cultural notions of healing, psyches and the body, multiple notions of the body-desire-mind matrix can be the starting place for colonializing plural aesthetics and desires. I would like to suggest that there are ways that we can explore sites of resistance through our bodies.

La Boca[16]

The body is the site where histories, darkness, lightness, strength, desires, fatness, thinness, the erotic, ableness, thought, emotion, pain, and power reside in multiple ways. It is where one's awareness, consciousness and self (or selves) emerge either to be accepted, controlled or erased.

As I was going through some pictures of Indian iconography, paintings and sculpture, I repeatedly came across representations of the vulva, the uterus and of serpents. Why was it so common for a sculpture to depict or focus on the vulva/womb?...why was it so common to have serpents emerge from vulvas?...and why were women's heads either not present at all or portrayed as multi-headed? Bearing in mind that the South Asian patriarchs of 300 years or 3,000 years[17] have always been committed to woman-hating and compulsory heterosexuality, and thus have attempted to destroy and re-write histories and artifacts of woman-identified or woman-loving evidence, I decided to reinterpret the significance of such iconography and sculpture.

These drawings and sculptures provided me with an avenue of embodying South Asian women's physicality that was radically feminist. The serpent, which is frequently present in South Asian iconography, symbolized to me the embodiment of female serpentine energy, power, thought and scripture. Information about the past, historical events, weather patterns, and correct modes of action is often written in the form of the serpent's wave-like movements.[18] The vulva that represents the female could also be reinterpreted as the critical and radical power of female bodies and sensuality. The combining of the vulva with the serpent, which is often represented as the serpent emerging from the vulva, is a reorganizing of female

197

physicality that empowers female sexuality, desire, eroticism, activity, and intellect, where sexuality and speaking fuse. I see a strong resemblance to what Cherríe Moraga refers to as "la boca"—where the mouth and cunt merge, thereby fusing stigmatized ways of being and acting. These taboo activities—female thought, speaking, sex (lesbian or non-hetero-patri-archal) and desiring—provide avenues to rethink, reembody and rearrange the female body.

Colonizing Markers: Race—Sexuality—Sex

Radical South Asian subjectivity is fundamental to emancipatory politics. But such a subjectivity can come under attack (as in the case of "woman") as being essentialist or binary.[19] This radical subjectivity has a body politic and is critical of the intersections of multivalenced locations. The notion of metropole-identification and colony-identification may be useful in understanding the politics of ethnicity and race in South Asia and outside South Asia. The implicit and sometimes explicit devaluing of dark skin is an issue that confronts most South Asians. Internalized racism and cross-racial hostility is often expressed by South Asians of varying skin colour, hair types and eye colour. In India, advertisements encourage women and men to use "Fair and Lovely" skin creme, skin bleaches, and strong henna in their hair to add an auburn touch. Marriage ads still want Aryan-looking men and women—i.e., fair and sometimes tall (in the case of males).[20] Internationally, throughout the diaspora, different degrees of this internalized racism persists. One of my dark-skinned uncles (who would probably pass as black) warned me about the "niggers" in Brooklyn. Some South Asians, of varying class backgrounds, who settle in the United States often don't want to be associated with "those blacks," yet they have a very good chance of physically being mistaken as black folks.

Alongside the tenacity of internalized racism in South Asian communities, many South Asians outside South Asia are victims of racist attacks, such as: "Paki"[21] bashing in Britain and "dot busting" in the United States. A radical South Asian subjectivity requires working through the rejection of the "ethnocentric racist imagination"[22] and the "straight mind."[23] The logic of purity allows South Asians to be conceptually defined in only two ways: as authentic South Asians or as assimilated South Asians. The "authentic South Asian" may range from being conservative, lazy and poor to being spiritual, brilliant, non-materialistic and religious. By this definition, the assimilated South Asian—including South Asians who may also be living both *inside* South Asia and in the diaspora—pursues the promise of the "postcultural"[24] full citizenship of Anglo life. Or in other words, the assimilated South Asian seeks metropole identification and inclusion into the metropole universe of discourse.

A radical South Asian racial subjectivity entails a commitment to eradicating internal-ized racism, cross racial hostility (differences in privilege and the hostility between people of colour) and metropole identification. This also means that a radical South Asian racial subjectivity needs to deal with rigid binary race logic of the United States. In other words, race is not just about tensions and negotiations between black and white folk, rather racial politics entail further hierarchies of darkness and privilege.[25]

Poststructural (both feminist and non-feminist) deconstruction is helpful, but once again leans towards the abandonment of a coherent and empowered "subject." It is therefore necessary to formulate an emancipatory project that resists colonizing markers of sex,

heterosexuality and race. "Any individual committed to resisting politics of domination, to eradicating sexism and racism, understands the importance of not promoting an either/or competition between oppressive systems."[26] This means claiming identities and identity politics, and reconstructing and mediating them in womanly-colourful meaning systems. Race and sex need to be pulled out of the racist-heterosexual matrix and embodied within notions of physical subjectivity.

Towards "Curdled-Separation"

The interconnections between thoughts of domination and material of domination need to be connected to a politics of resistance of the "curdled sort."

By "thoughts of domination," I am referring to that body of discourse that is male-identified, heterosexist-identified and metropole-identified—or what Maria Lugones calls "the vantage point of the lover of purity" that reproduces systems of privilege. For example, discussions about a "postcolonial" world, within certain circles, emphasize the "post" rather than the contemporary unravellings of the structures (both institutional and psycho-social) of colonialism and absentee colonialism. Further, these theorists claim that peoples from the the geographical third world, who identify strongly with this colonial history, are engaging in uncritical acts of binarism—or essentialism. This thinking is a prevalent form of metropole-identified skepticism.

Colonialism in its 19th and early 20th century forms has reproduced, produced and maintained multiple forms of domination. These forms of domination represent continuities as well as disjunctures. Explicit physical domination is nowadays coupled with even more complicated forms of control, such as those of "soft" institutions (information systems) and transnational capitalist coalitions. In an "information" world, entities such as the media, computers, faxes, and dialogue (between those with privilege) are key oppressors. Certain academic dialogues that solely focus on the inconsistencies of categories such as "woman," "colonial" and "the third world" are highly disempowering to persons who have historically suffered conceptual and physical erasures and violences. Such dialogues continue the project of appropriating the experiences of the less privileged. Even though I claim that my identity is constructed by multiple communities, why am I encouraged to think that there is a crisis of my subjectivity, identity or authorship for my politics? How can there be a crisis over categories that were never intended for my subjecthood?

In creating a crisis of subjectivity, a crisis is created for our bodies. Discourses that continue to deconstruct women or darker peoples directly participate in the material domination of the bodies of women and persons of colour. It is therefore necessary for us to re-embody a revised notion of "physical subjectivity." This means that, as women and as women of colour, we still initially have to hold on to the Phallocratic Universe of Discourse (PUD) or Metropole Universe of Discourse (MUD), the binary standard of our original demarcation as women (female man vs. man) and women of colour (non-white vs. white), until "the standard" is itself de-standardized. Physical subjectivity along with a politics of location provides a shelter for women (both lesbian and non-lesbian) and for racialized women. We need to shelter our bodies and subjective locations within affirming communities. Is there anything like a community for third world women of colour, biological and cultural

199

crossbreeds, women of colour, queers, and multiple permutations of these subjectivities? "But then I ask myself who my people are. When I think of my own people, the only people I can think of as my own are transitionals, liminals, borderdwellers, 'world'-travellers, beings in the midst of either/or. They are all people whose acts and thoughts curdle-separate."[27]

Sheltering ourselves is partly a defensive politics, but it is distinct from a notion of private ownership of body or property. It is defending ourselves from control, erasure and conceptual violence. It is the sphere where the ambiguous, fragmented, hyphenated and grotesque revel in impurity and in multiplicitous subjectivities. Our physical subjectivity and subjective location make our oppression and oppressors less mystifying. Physical subjectivity enables us to speak and express in different tongues when our language and epistemologies become more and more marginalized. Physical subjectivity is one of our sites of struggle, and the meanings we re-embody (such as redistributing and re-sensualizing desire and aesthetics) in our womanly-colourful anatomical-humoral physicality have meanings beyond contemporary circumstances. Socio-physical identities are limiting if one plays no active role in creating them and simply receives them from the binarism of PUD. As the tentacles of our distinctions of origin become economically and politically transnational, it is not *we* who have to keep deconstructing us. Difference among women (non-white and white) needs to strengthen our ties, not strengthen our dominators. My political decision and practice in identifying as a South Asian radical feminist and a radical feminist of colour intends to hold on to a constantly revising, critical politics of identity in the resistance of "curdled-separation."

1. Specifically, I am referring to the works of: Nancy Fraser & Linda Nicholson, "Social Criticism Without Philosophy: An Encounter between Feminism and Postmodernism," *Feminism/Postmodernism,* ed. Linda Nicholson (New York: Routledge, 1990); Linda Alcoff, "Cultural Feminism Versus Post-Structuralism: The Identity Crisis in Feminist Theory," *Signs: A Journal of Woman in Culture and Society* 13.3 (1988); Judith Butler, *Gender Trouble: Feminism and The Subversion of Identity* (New York: Routledge, 1990).

Also, in this essay I employ the terms poststructural feminists and anti-essentialists somewhat synonymously, which is not to suggest that other kinds of feminists practice essentialism.

2. Which means one should be skeptical or critical of their understanding and usage of categories/names. Further, certain anti-essentialists argue that the act of naming would "fix" the potentiality of the entity being named and therefore "naturalize."

3. In the paper I use it to refer to feminist positions such as those of Nicholson, Fraser, Alcoff, Scott and Butler. The term however has been used specifically by Judith Butler who seems to be challenging the "metaphysical foundationalism" of notions such as gender, sex, woman and body. According to Butler, gender is a collage of cultural meanings constructed in a way to fit the fields of compulsory heterosexuality and hierarchy. Further, Butler suggests gender as this artificial cultural construction masks our understanding of the body.

4. This is a position compatible with the anti-essentialist, gender-skeptical or post-structural approaches.

5. "But... to define 'woman' is necessarily to essentialize her," in Toril Moi, *Sexual/Textual Politics* (London: Methuen, 1985), 139.

6. María C. Lugones, "On The Logic Of Pluralist Feminism," *Feminist Ethics,* ed. Claudia Card (Lawrence: University Press of Kansas, 1991), 35–44.

7. I use the term metropole to mean several interconnected but distinct systems of domination. The term metropole is often used to mean the west, overdeveloped worlds, the north, the first world, the colonizer or the central powerhouse of empire. Its opposite being the colony, the underdeveloped world, third world, the south, the east and so on. But the way I use metropole includes interlocking systems of ethnocentric racism, absentee colonialism, and imperialism. By metropole-identification I also mean the construction and activities of one's psychic attention. In some of the so-called "postcolonial" literature a similar sort of poststructuralist skepticism exists that claims that it wants to escape binarism and essentialism.

8. Cherríe Moraga, "lo que nunca pasó por sus labios," *Loving in the War Years* (Boston: South End Press, 1983), 54.

9. A term used by Monique Wittig, *The Straight Mind and Other Essays* (Boston: Beacon Press, 1992).

10. I use colourful to signify all colours that have been made available to us. This includes understanding what it means to be of the colour white and an understanding of the heterogeneity of racism (versus a binary logic of solely black versus white) and cross racial hostility (among people of colour). Additionally, I use colourful with the hope that we may be able to use all senses to understand it, versus just 'seeing' colour. I use the term coloured in a similar manner.

11. María Lugones, "Hablando cara a cara/Speaking Face to Face: An Exploration of Ethnocentric Racism," *Making Face, Making Soul/Haciendo Caras: Creative and Critical Perspectives by Feminists of Color*, ed. Gloria Anzaldúa (San Francisco: Aunt Lute, 1990).

12. A concept explored by María Lugones in "Impurity, Purity, Separation and the Logic of the Politics of Identity," unpublished manuscript, 1992.

13. Ibid.

14. Marilyn Frye, "On Separatism and Power," *Politics of Reality: Essays in Feminist Theory* (Freedom: The Crossing Press, 1982), 97.

15. Iris Marion Young, *Throwing Like a Girl and Other Essays in Feminist Philosophy and Social Theory* (Bloomington: Indiana University Press, 1990), 11.

16. Moraga, "The Long Line of Vendidas," *Loving in the War Years*, 90–144.

17. South Asian history has the added baggage of being written by the metropole, metropole-identified people and nationalists.

18. Versus writing that goes from left to right in straight lines.

19. Being cautioned about binarism is a frequent issue in certain contemporary "postcolonial" theory/literature (specifically, South Asian). This caution is directed against those who may be still using "dualistic" and "essentialistic" categories. For example, if one were to use the category "Indian," is this category simply understood as the oppressed "Other" of British colonialism? If so, one would still be stuck in the binary categories, as constructed by those in power, of Self (British Colonialists) and Other (Indian). The "problem" of binarism is quite similar to the feminist anti-essentialist/poststructuralist concern over naming and fixing the category "woman." However, the scope of my essay restricts me from exploring this any further.

20. For an insightful analysis of the Aryan origin myth see Uma Chakravarti, "Whatever Happened to the Vedic Dasi? Orientalism, Nationalism and a Script for the Past," *Recasting Women: Essays in Indian Colonial History*, ed. Kumkum Sangri and Sudesh Vaid (Delhi: Kali For Women, 1989).

According to Chakravarti, the Aryan myth proved to be a "double edged weapon," used against South Asians. On the one hand South Asians were to make a connection with fairness and their fair oppressors (via the British and Aryan ancestors) and on the other a disconnection by realizing the supposed inferiority of darkness (via the defeated Dravidians and the morally degraded, colonized native culture). The contradictory nature of these identification/mis-identification is still played out among South Asians.

21. Paki is a derogatory racist term for South Asians.

22. María Lugones, "Impurity, Purity, Separation and the Politics of the Logic of Identity."

23. Wittig.

24. María Lugones, "Purity, Impurity, Separation and The Logic of The Politics of Identity." Renato Rosaldo, *Culture and Truth* (Boston: Beacon, 1989).

25. That is, other stigmatized races such as Latina/os, Chicanas/os, Native Americans, South Asians, Southeast Asians and so on.

26. bell hooks, *Yearning: Race, Gender, and Cultural Politics* (Boston: South End Press, 1990), 64.

27. María Lugones, "Purity, Impurity, Separation and The Logic of the Politics of Identity."

Alcoff, Linda. "Cultural Feminism versus Post-Structuralism: The Identity Crisis in Feminist Theory," *Signs* 13.3 (1988).

Butler, Judith. *Gender Trouble: Feminism and the Subversion of Identity*. New York: Routledge, 1990.

Chakravarti, Uma. "Whatever Happened to the Vedic Dasi? Orientalism, Nationalism and a Script for the Past." *Recasting Women: Essays in Indian Colonial History*. ed. Kumkum Sangri and Sudesh Vaid. New Delhi: Kali For Women, 1989.

de Beauvoir, Simone. *The Second Sex*. New York: Penguin Books, 1953.

de Lauretis, Teresa. "The Essence of the Triangle or, Taking the Risk of Essentialism Seriously: Feminist Theory in Italy, the U.S., and Britain." *Differences* 1.2 (1989).

Fraser, Nancy and Linda Nicholson. "Social Criticism Without Philosophy: An Encounter Between Feminism and Postmodernism." *Feminism and Postmodernism*. ed. Linda Nicholson. New York: Routledge, 1990.

Frye, Marilyn. *The Politics of Reality: Essays in Feminist Theory*. Trumansburg, NY: Crossing Press, 1983.

Frye, Marilyn. "The Possibility of Feminist Theory." *Willful Virgin: Essays in Feminism 1976–1992*. Freedom, CA: Crossing Press, 1992.

Fuss, Diana. *Essentially Speaking*. New York: Routledge, 1990.

hooks, bell. *Yearning: Race, Gender, and Cultural Politics*. Boston: South End Press, 1990.

Lugones, María. "Hablando cara a cara/Speaking Face to Face: An Exploration of Ethnocentric Racism." *Making Face, Making Soul/Haciendo Caras: Creative and Critical Perspectives by Feminists of Color*. ed. Gloria Anzaldúa. San Francisco: Aunt Lute, 1990.

Lugones, María. "Purity, Impurity, Separation and the Logic of the Politics of Identity." Unpublished manuscript, 1992.

Lugones, María. "The Logic of Pluralist Feminism." *Feminist Ethics*. ed. Claudia Card. Lawrence: University Press of Kansas, 1991.

Moraga, Cherríe. "lo que nunca paso por sus labios." *Loving in the War Years*. Boston: South End Press, 1983.

Wittig, Monique. *The Straight Mind and Other Essays*. Boston: Beacon, 1992.

Young, Iris Marion. *Throwing like a Girl and Other Essays in Feminist Philosophy and Social Theory*. Bloomington: Indiana University Press, 1990.

bedding

NEEMA VACHANI

I am upset
at
this feeling
that this bed
which is my own
is not
because
you are here

asleep
(while I am not)

who are you
and why
night after night
do we lie together

this is not the security
of lying
between mummy and papa
fast asleep
to dreams
about
big white sheets of paper
that stretch on and on

my imagined memory
and this reality
like the toy shapes that fit one inside the other
and the piece between the couch cushions
leaving an unmatched star

tonight
when I dream

the big white sheets of paper
that go on and on
will loudly c-r-u-n-c-h
and swallow me up

and the chill
of physical intimacy
becomes a fire from my nightmares
a crackle
burst
into flames
which engulf the house

until
I wake
to know
that I am upset
at this feeling
(so alone)
that this bed
is my own
even
when you are here

love supreme/you can name your daughter

RUXANA MEER

i am awake listening to the neighbor downstairs ranting and rolling in the cozy warmth of another winter. underneath my room the sound travels up to me not as loudly as it would down and he's lucky i'm not dancing in my sleep. most nights i'm just trying to turn off the light after it's quieted down. it's wet and damp outside. we've needed the rain for so long. i'm throwing one leg or the other out of the loft to see what that feels like to dangle and also linger even at three a.m. when i should be rushing through my subconscious dreamstate. thinking this is not a bad way to waste the night.

thinking, why is the standard to be scared of one's sexuality while i'm lying on my loft pressing against no one. my fingertips can reach the ceiling where i trace the patterns of humidity. then i say that we should take our sexuality, as powerful as it is to heal us by making us feel good, and know that it is a life giving/love/sharing force and there are no acceptable levels of abuse. tracing the marks of my own, i know the history of this land where this body is concerned. we are told where to go and what to wear when we get there so that we can take it off.

i am just lying here waiting for the neighbor to settle the same way i was lying down that other night and staring when you kissed me and you made sure careful that nothing touched me except your lips. see that is the way i like to be kissed for the very first time by anyone. who knows that i cannot resist a smooth operation when that which is left up to luck chance and fortune works? like when you are having a tarot card reading and it is quite a surprise. anyway it's too late, forget now that i toldja. it's too late for me to get to work on time. it's too late for me to be awake just because you're here. so my eyes close stop wandering in the distant cracks of the ceiling and i realize the paint is slowly chipping into sharp flakes which fall into my bed keeping me awake and dancing around in a commercial and finally resting in your curly hair and when you wake up you don't know what these are.

My Bed Has Big, Warm Arms

MEETA GAWANDE

I sit in this hard wooden chair.
My fingers smashed across my face,
My eyeballs hiding beneath sore lids.

My bed has big, warm arms.

lie down baby. I want to warm you. my swollen hand will press against the small of your back. I will press my face against your cheek. I will never lie to you. I will never hurt you. I will always warm you. lie down baby.

My desk is hard and icy.
The computer hums impatiently.
The smiling face, the rectangles, the flashing arrow.
Parent. brother. paper. project. class. job. application. resume. self.
My hands grip the edges of the desk, my shoulder muscles tighten.
If my neck gives up, my head will fall and explode like dynamite.

In my stomach, the milk is rotting.
A woman has stolen my stomach and hidden it in her basket.
My stomach is in a woman's basket.
She is clasping her hands together
and ramming the basket against my house.
She is laughing sarcastically.
She is crying and running with the basket
and trying to smash herself into the cars that circle my house.
She cries out frantically to the cars,
Help me. Please help me. Take me with you.

A teenager stands on top of the house, screaming down at her.
USE YOUR FUCKING FEET AND WALK!!
DON'T YOU SEE THAT YOU'RE RUINING HER STOMACH?!

I press my dry, swollen eyes against the computer.
My left hand lashes at my right hand,

Trying to force it to touch the keys.
Stop lashing. How will it do anything if you make it bleed?

My bed has big, warm arms.

hello, baby? come lie down now. let me press my face against your cheek. let me hold you with my big, warm arms. I will tell you stories, and you can feel your arms diving through the water, breaking the water perfectly. Your feet will be pointed, legs so straight, shaking and propelling you forward.

You will see the little girl kneeling in her garden, tracing her fingers over each pattern of the flower petals. You will see her scraping the smooth colors onto her rough, sweaty fingers. You will see her smashing the shredded petals across her face.

The horns scream in my ear.
The woman is moaning, exuberant with her self-pity.
The teenager is yelling, her desperation carefully hidden.
My hand is burning, pulsing itself to oblivion.
My stomach is suspended in the air,
waiting for the woman to whip down her arm
and smash the basket against the ground,

Waiting for me to go outside the house and steal it back.

I feel the blood leaving me.

My bed has big, warm arms.

The Devil in the Church

PIA GANGULY

The Devil in the Church
What was he doing there?
He had business.
The accursed were there.
The fornicators. The educators.
The socialites. The pretenders.
The founders of marriage.
The co-founders of divorce.
The conspirators in adultery.
Even God himself,
in laying down rules of conscience
for men he had fashioned
in his own image,
had invited Lucifer to his home,
he came wearing
a pair of earflares
with incised birds' heads.

An Awakening

ANU MITRA

When I was growing up under the bright city lights of Calcutta in the 1960s and '70s, certain names were indelibly ironed onto our consciousness. These names—Sita, Savitri, Devaki, Uddawa, the list continued endlessly—seemed like prized trophies, like a glorious blazon that was both larger than life and worthy of the greatest devotion. As bedtime drew closer, the children of our extended family would huddle closer to Grandmother. From her sweet lips would come forth stories of great chastity, of the virtues of Savitri, and of the selfless action of the prototypical Sitas in all of our collective mythologies.

As I imbibed this daily fare with eyes wide open, I began to wonder about all these legendary women. Was it possible for Sita, the heroine in the the epic of Ramayana, to be perfect at all times? Did she not experience the feelings of passionate desire or intense jealousy or the need for intimacy? Could Savitri's love for Satyavan remain alive even in the face of such terrible odds? And was it really Uddawa's silent, long-term devotion and steadfast love that made her the foremost of Krishna's wives? Were there other aspects of these two-dimensional characters that were being censored out of our storytelling sessions? And, being part of a family with more male children, I personally wondered where all the prototypical male gods had ventured. With the exception of Shiva and Krishna, most others were denied access to Grandmother's quarters.

I did not have to wonder long. I soon figured out that Grandmother's editorial content and style were meant to impress a patriarchal worldview. In her ethos, the men were as handsome as Krishna or as macho as Shiva. They could do pretty much what they pleased because Shiva Himself had taken His abode in them. They were Mount Kailasa in the flesh. The women, oh, the women—they were another matter. They were degenerate and weak and spoke in a language that only the body understood. Later on in life Grandmother admitted that it was because of her daily force-feeding diet of virtuous women that we were able to contain our passions with some semblance of dignity. Without this intravenous hook-up— pervasive and insidious at its best—all might have been lost.

I objected to this fragmentation of our common world. The older I got, the more vocal I became about maintaining that my brothers, like my sisters, were borne of the same flesh. Our origins were similar, as were our destinies. Did it not make complete sense to treat us as one, to recognize that Shiva had made His special abode in us all? What about Grandmother's various readings from the religious texts that made us appear equal? Did this equality exist only in the mind of a strange, faraway, perhaps male God?

The inequities of life became starker by the year. At first, the distinctions were subtle. They hinged on the clothes that we wore (or more likely, were not allowed to wear), or the

manner in which we conducted ourselves in public, or the company that we kept. As the years wore on, the differences that separated my brothers from my sisters assumed enormous proportions. At times, I wondered if we shared the same mother.

It all came to a head in the summer of 1974. I was on the verge of graduating from high school and was deemed, especially by affluent Bengali standards, ready for marriage. This announcement merged from the secret recesses of my mother's room—first in hushed secretive whispers, then in proclamations to the world with much fanfare and the blowing of conch shells. My salvation was to be intimately connected with the destiny of a man whom I would see for a couple of hours. Our respective parents would chalk up the details and make sure that the equations added up right. In this arrangement of the spirit, I would go to the best bidder: the man who had the exact same socio-economic background, the same privileges that money could bring, the same access to the most exclusive schools, and one who, above all, believed that the universe was created for the benefit of men. In this world, women existed as the empty symbols of glory and virtue—like Sita and Devaki—in roles that were transparent to society.

So the mela began. Every Sunday afternoon, for what seemed like an eternity, I would drape my green sari (I always wore my unluckiest color in an attempt to wage this underhanded war of upsetting even the best proposals), slab makeup on my face, wear my grandmother's jewels, and be reminded of the selfless Savitri and the forbearing Sita. All this was a preparation of what was to come. Then, shepherded by aunts and married cousins, I would be chaperoned to a place in the living room that caught the twilight sun as it filtered in through the windows. I would sit under this makeshift spotlight and barely raise my eyes but not quite. Scared to death, I would catch bits and pieces of the prospective players in my life acting our their parts—all preceding the dénouement.

From the far corners of my eye, I would see the parents—the figures of authority and the voices of reason. They saw everything; they judged how I walked into the room, whether my posture was womanly enough, whether my words were to the point and filled with respect and devotion for these unknown people. In the background were the hangers-on, the aunts and uncles from the groom's side who no doubt would proffer the expert advice or the intuitive understanding that would clinch the deal. Further in the background was the groom himself, in sight of his young and recalcitrant wife-to-be, saying yea or nay to his parents' every whim.

At first I felt mesmerized by the loud and fast pulsing of my heart. The scene was so machinated, every step so measured, every word so well thought out. My mouth would be so dry that I was often rendered speechless. The chief protagonists of the drama—the roles of Sita and Savitri—hung like proud effigies in my imagination. I just had to drape their saris to assume their part.

In those early months, my family was proud of me. Perceived as young and beautiful, I had managed to draw the greatest contenders to the game. By behaving in a manner that was deemed totally appropriate, even by Grandmother's standards, I was getting rave reviews. Now, my family had the upper hand and could decide which one of the many suitors was the best for the role.

The heat of the game drew my family in. They opened up the competition to more and more suitors. So every Sunday afternoon, I would go through the motions of displaying myself

before a bunch of cynics and a man whom God had created in his parents' image. Number twenty-five. Number twenty-six. The dealing in the meat market continued. The gains were considerably higher with every move. Thirty. Thirty-one. I had to be quite a success to draw this kind of crowd. Thirty-five. Thirty-six.

When I finally allowed myself to think about the situation, the questions came like the monsoon torrents. There was no escaping. Was there any real success involved in remaining voiceless? What was the total cost of these experiences—repeated over and over again? Wasn't the spirit being wasted and hurt by these meaningless charades? And what about the elements of love and passion and intimacy? Was there a place for these in this most important relationship?

The humiliation of the Sunday parade made me smart. There is no worth to being a woman, I thought to myself. Not all the Sitas and Savitris of yore could convince me that role-playing in the image of women was either fulfilling or fun. I had to do something different. I just could not fit into roles determined for me by Grandmother and her purity stories. There was a fire raging within me.

Sunday arrived as expected. The discussion of whether I should wear green or yellow to mark the beginning of spring dominated the conversation at breakfast. Grandmother took out her antique opal set for the occasion. The preparations progressed as usual for the late afternoon hour. I dressed obediently and tried—as was my practice—to don the roles of Sita and Uddawa. Today, things were different. No matter how hard I tried, I could not kowtow to my revered elders or to the system that had sustained me so long. "There's absolutely nothing wrong with me," I told myself firmly. "Even if those I love make me out to be a contrary pain in the ass, I have every right to live for myself, to live up to my ideals, and to dream of a time when I can be my own person." This mantra kept playing in my head till I really believed what I heard inside me.

At the magical hour of four, the guests arrived. On previous occasions this had been the moment of transformation from a high-schooler to a poised and controlled woman. I was late at the doorway today and the soft and easy transformation just passed me by. I strode in, making direct eye contact with the prospective in-laws and their son. I gave out a shrill, nervous laugh and proclaimed that I really wasn't glad to see them. In fact, by their very presence they were perpetuating a demeaning tradition that brought women to their knees. I had had enough. I demanded an apology from them—directed to me and all the other unknown women they would measure and evaluate and consider—before they took their leave.

Grandmother took the vows of silence for thirty days. Mother stopped speaking to me for bringing this calumny on the house. My brothers turned their faces away. There was a chill in the house which smelled of death itself. I was the demon goddess Kali and the destruction that I had just wreaked spread far and wide. Yet, a feeling of quiet satisfaction for what I had just done came over me. There was no going back now.

Mount Kailasa in Hindu mythology, Lord Shiva's abode

Stop The Insanity

BELLA MAYANI

October
dear god,

...If there really is something out there. I sit alone at the Wednesday matinee. Skipped out of work duties again. Those mundane chores, endless meetings with few outcomes, but mostly people refusing to take a risk. Make a decision damn it! Mostly pushing it up on next week's agenda or interim emergency meetings. Habitual. Stagnant. God I am tired.

The theatre, cluttered with senior citizens who attended the first show. The age of experience. Wisdom. I took another survey of the room. Yes, I was not the only one. Mostly everyone came by themselves. Two thumbs up. The film was an outstanding, dreamy piece. An Italian crew lost during the war. Ship-wrecked on a Greek isla. Two years go by. They're found. No longer non-existent. Their homeland has changed, unrecognizable, split by war, rebuilding, immigrants, boundaries redrawn. The opportunity to return home. A chance to rebuild and establish oneself. Or the time to maintain roots established in the last two years.

What am I searching for? Wooden clothespins clasping my nose shut. The stench of something dying inside. Rotting.

November

I had finished a painting I had worked on in my mind for months. Months of which I could not express myself. My only outlet being the 1990 journals. Or is it that I would not trust someone with my deepest thoughts. If I did, would there be anything left of me? No one quite understands my thoughts. Ascribed to an independent life. Maybe it was the size of my family. More likely the fact that my mother was forty when I was born. A few memories of my childhood and even fewer of my father. Typical Sindhi businessman who successfully built an empire before he was forty. Yet I feel a closeness, a sense of peace when I think of him. Sunday afternoons we sit in the balcony, he reads the paper and I read a book or staring at the bay.

March

I received a letter from my sister, who lives in Washington D.C. Her letters fill me with energy, a replenishing source. She assures me my experiences are real. I wait anxiously for her phone call, just to hear her voice. Does she really exist? Do I make her up in my mind?

I soak in the bathtub in San Francisco, Apt. 206. The oil I splash into the bathtub permeates the steam-filled room. That smell vaguely reminds me of the homemade yellow paste my mother used to put on my sprained ankles. I carefully place my sister's letter on the

floor away from the bathtub. My legs are bent leaving my knees exposed. Goose bumps cover the circle of my knees. Slowly I submerge my body into the tub and wet my face, my hair.

Guilty about being away for so long. Do they know I paint? They are not interested in my child abuse workshops, nor the two years I spent writing my thesis on fertility levels of Panama and India. I can't blame them. My parents don't see a connection between marriage and liberal arts education. My words are too harsh. How can I expect them to understand my work with their experiences. Last summer's Hindi language classes were seen as useful because I would be able to communicate with my in-laws if they are not Spanish or English-speaking. How can I expect them to comprehend my loneliness when I seem surrounded by people? I am isolated. I have a secret life. Unable to share with them.

They just want to complete their duties. After all, sooner or later I will get married so why not earlier and get out of the way for them? But I can't. I can't make them happy. Nervous, anxious, body itching. They don't make me happy.

November

Only one more month before my return to Panama, to my family. I've left the U.S. for now. Traveling through London. My photography has taken off. Black and white. Depth in shades of gray. Today I walked in the same clothes—just a change of underwear, a shower. Alternating shirts. I roam the streets. Focus in on the people waiting impatiently in the line. I met a woman who had been waiting in line for two days. A man rushed by us…he had an appointment. Planned perfection. I just arrive. Pointless to plan ahead if I do not know where I am going.

A woman from Zimbabwe spoke about her life in London. From her deep English accent, I guessed she was born here. She spoke of her last visit to her parent's homeland. I thought of my parent's homeland, Sind, which I have yet to see. In my travels, I usually bump into people from the town of their birth. Someone who lived in the same building or knew his sister-in-law's cousin on her mother's side. The older generation differentiating these Sindhis whose origin was Hyderabad with the ones who came from other towns. Text books define their Indus River Valley homeland as one of the first cities and civilizations.

Sitting in a London outdoor cafe, I remember what I think of my home in Colon. More than my family's vast business ties me to that city. Comfort within sixteen streets and seven boulevards. I walk in the evenings, stopping several times to speak to neighbors I have known forever. Waving at those passing by in cars. Newer immigrants have changed the quaint architecture of this Spanish city, leaving traces of themselves in the new structures. I continue to return…but why?

It rains. I push my face out to the sky to receive the cold water and wind. Clumsily, I cover my weak cafe which has evolved into ice cafe because of the cold London wind. It kills my appetite. I store the remaining money in the travel pouch close to my stomach. I need it for tonight's rent. A temporary roof and I must budget for a meal. It does not worry me. But it torments me that my search may never prove to be fruitful.

At Trifalgar Square. Close in on the florescent cinema sign. *Batman Returns*. In the background cobblestone roads and mildew-covered shingle rooftops. An architectural dream for the romantics. Probably with those English porcelain bathtubs. A woman soaps her body.

The steam heaters clunking while she dozes off above the sound of her street's performers, prostitutes, drug-users, homeless—the people.

This city is filled with people from the world. Not from any particular country. My South Asian friend does not recognize the South Asians. The latest fashions, hairstlyes and English accents leave the superficial traces unnoticeable. Either way, they are of South Asian descent. Walking through the crowded streets and open air markets, I see the South Asian elite frowning at their own people. Maybe for not being quite "modern" or "hip" enough. Maybe for reminding them of a home far away. But I see people. Each one must have a unique story.

What is my story? Why am I afraid to settle, put roots somewhere. Will I be compromising myself? Regrets.

On my last day, I send myself a postcard to my home address to reassure myself that I was actually here. Delirious, insane, spinning with joy.

January

I have returned to Panama, my place of birth. Filled with conga rhythms and beats strange to the body of a foreigner. I feel it in my body. It moves me. I don't have to think of what foot. Left or right. We danced in the hall the size of warehouses. Is it instinct? I question myself. Is this home?

On that block there used to be a park in which I played as a child. Today there is a government hospital. I have given up another way of life. One which may have brought me other opportunities. Variety of scope. Why do I feel a loss? As if I die when I am home. Tangled in my thoughts. Few options for future.

The recent Indian immigrants see themselves as traditional and true Indians. They look down at us Panamanian-born Indians. I hear the whispers as I pass them at social gatherings. But wait until their children are born here. If there is a violent overthrow of government, they will be the first to leave. Years ago, I believed that if that's what it is to be Indian, then I'd rather not be Indian. Now I think there are all sorts of people.

October

Maybe I haven't achieved much in the marriage department, according to my mother. But then again, she is insane. We still live the repercussions of her move fifty years ago from Sind. She is bitter, selfish—tearing me to shreds. Coming from a generation in which you are in purdah until the wedding night and then become a servant for his family and less than human for your husband. I can't retrieve one single experience from my mind that could help me to understand what life was like for her. Only the jazz of that era is familiar—not even the popular Hindi film music. Films, a cultural connection between many South Asians. Bonded by familiar language and actors. I missed out on a transmission of culture.

March

I will be spending the next couple of months traveling through Europe. Mainly to paint and write. Bonding with my intellectually lunatic sister who has been getting several degrees for the last few years. Intellectual, thought-provoking discussion. Reminiscing trivialities of

every day. Decided to let my body hair grow, can't remember what it looks like. Rubbing thighs with the extra body weight.

I had a short conversation with my mother last night. Actually I just listened. She ended the conversation in disappointment and tears. Why is it that marriage is a common denominator? I find that one person is not able to satisfy me spiritually and physically. What constitutes true fidelity? Must I then settle for less? I'd rather risk being alone.

I am finding my days alone in Panama comforting. Weeks of exploration before I return to homebase.

To Sadana

NEEMA VACHANI

The ruby in your eye
a cat's piercing gaze—
I see you naked
standing
beautiful
my breast to your hip
we whisper laugh hold on to the energy
touching
(daring to care)
until the morning
and then
disconnected
your scent on my shoulder
in my mind.

The Visitor

MEETA GAWANDE

All around me is a concrete garden
Overgrown with buildings.
My heart is trapped
Behind barbed wire meshes.

I am a dog in a cage.
vicious. snarling. ferocious.
Trained to protect my master's goods.

I am sad and broken hearted.
The barbed wire is tightly wound around my heart,
Holding it together.
I swing a thorny bat
Round and round my head.

But the scent of a soft, quiet animal
Permeates my cage
And softens my hide.
Is she lured by my eyes? my smell? my fur?
She holds out her hand to me.
I grip it,
But my club comes
Swinging hard.
The animal falls.

Stupid animal.
Did she not see my barbed wire fence
Did she not see my thorny club?

She lifts herself up.

Oh god.
I must have hurt her with my bat.
I must have pierced her with my barbs.

She peels herself from my barbed wire fence and walks away.
She does not run or turn her back.
She merely walks, calmly
and offers me her eyes

Now I live off the juices from her eyes.
I drink deeply
And pray they don't go away.
I have laid down my thorny club
And torn down the barbed wire fence.
She does not come near.
She watches from afar.
I am quiet and still.
I close my eyes only to give her rest.

Sapna

KHADINE SHAH

Thoughts quickly traveling
Like high-powered trains
Upon the many tracks
Rushing across my brain
Many to remember
So many to confuse
Some become derailed
Most never even used
The stations feel cluttered
And often overflow
As the never-ending journey
Fails to reach its goal

Thrka

AARTI KOHLI

Meera collected her wandering thoughts and tried to concentrate on putting in the right amount of salt. She really didn't mind cooking. Besides, when she heard Mom's strained voice over the phone, asking her to start dinner, she took pity. It was probably another day with the 'bitch from hell,' Meera's private name for Mom's boss. Poor Mom, Meera thought, stuck with a woman who knew nothing about programming. "Elizabeth's homegrown," Mom would say. "Sounds like a zucchini to me," Meera finally quipped back. But Meera knew that, after twenty years in the company, Elizabeth had the connections and she was going to make sure that Mom didn't get a promotion. Wonder if I'll have to deal with shit like that? thought Meera as she slowly measured out the dal. She mimicked an icy, stern executive voice: "You have a problem communicating, Meera Khanna." Yeah, right! I'll communicate with them in court, she slammed the lid on the pot.

'Lacking in business skills.' That's what Elizabeth had written with her big bold strokes on the cold sheet of paper Mom had brought home. She could not believe they had given such an evaluation to *her* Mom. Besides, what does a woman who sits in front of a screen all day have to know about business? Meera wondered as she lowered the gas under the boiling dal.

The stuff her parents had to deal with everyday pissed her off. She couldn't imagine the kind of stuff they would have had to deal with if they didn't have college degrees. The onions she was chopping scattered as she pushed down on the knife with force. Some onion juice squirted in her eyes, and squinting, she ran to the kitchen sink searching for the cold water tap. Just as she was wiping her eyes on a paper towel, Papa walked in. "Meera, is something wrong, have you been crying?" Papa asked worriedly as he set down his briefcase. She laughed and pointed to the onions, "It's okay, I was just getting the *thrka* ready." The creases on his forehead disappeared in relief.

"Wah! You've cooked everything. Why don't you go sit down now. I'll take care of the rice, just let me go change," he said as he headed down the hallway. Meera walked over to the kitchen table. She absent-mindedly ran her fingers up and down the oak grain, while looking out into the back lawn. "Wake up, Meera!" she told herself; she still had to finish her trig homework. Besides she wanted to call Anil before Mom got home. She wished she had a phone in her room. That way she wouldn't have to hole up in her parents' room and pretend that she was talking to Jenny. Poor Jenny, Meera thought. Mom thinks she's corrupting me. But Jenny always understood, she had gotten used to Meera's sudden changes of pronouns, "Oh my god Jen, guess what Anil told me today? He's so cute…*She's* so nice huh? Oh hi Mom…"

Often Mom would come in Meera's room complaining loudly, "I don't understand why you have to close the door. Everywhere you go, you shut doors behind you. It's some kind of

disease." As usual Meera ignored the comment. "I have a right to enter your room. Why do I have to knock? What are you doing in there that I can't see?" her Mom would say. What does it matter, Meera thought as she rearranged her dresser. She just can't deal with the fact that I don't want to share everything with her. How can I tell her about Anil, she would never understand, Meera thought with fear as she crossed the hallway and shut her parents' bedroom door and picked up the phone. Anil...she remembered the day she met him.

Jenny ran up to her. "Meera there's a new guy in my English class, I think he's Indian. He's kinda cute! I think he has Spanish next with you." Meera was nonchalant. He's probably a nerd, Meera thought. Why does everyone think I'm automatically going to like an Indian guy? Maybe because they know that those are the only guys who think that I'm pretty, she answered herself. Maybe he wasn't too bad. She decided she would have to wait and see. She slammed her locker shut and rushed to class, hoping to get a seat in the back so she could watch him come in. But he had already been there, sitting alone in the center of the room in Robby's chair.

"Hi," he said shyly as she sat down in the next row, one seat behind him. Perfect location. Cute, she thought, dark heavy lashes attached to big eyes. Seems kind of skinny...The others started trickling in before she got a chance to talk to him. She saw that Robby and Michelle were annoyed that their regular seats had been taken. Oh well, she smiled to herself. "Okay class, lesson Three, Español in the hotel..." Señora Smith started class.

After class he had looked a little lost, "Can you tell me where Room 301 is?" He asked her.

"Oh, you're in Mr. Johnson's trig class too. I'm going there; you can come with me," she offered. They walked in awkward silence, until Meera finally asked, "Where are you from?"

"We just moved here from Queens," he said with a slight Indian accent.

"How long have you lived here?" she asked, truly curious.

"Five years; we came from India when I was twelve."

"You remember India?" she asked.

He was startled by her question. "Of course, don't you?"

Shaking her head sadly she said, "I was born here."

They had talked a lot since then because their science teacher, Mrs. Beasley, had assigned them to the same group for their research project. Jenny and Chris were in their group, but after they left the library Anil and Meera usually ended up staying later and talking. Anil was different from other Indian guys she had met. He didn't pretend that he couldn't speak Punjabi; he even taught her some. He liked being different, he was proud of it, just like she was. On the last day of their science project he said, "You know we could meet here tomorrow...I mean...if you want to...and we could just do our homework or something."

"Sure," she said calmly while her insides turned cartwheels. They started going to the library often. He would meet her there in the evenings after working at his parents' liquor store. Meera told her parents that she was meeting Jenny and other people from her class, and of course, they didn't object.

One day they were at their usual corner table trying to solve a difficult math problem. Meera was bent over the yellow pad saying, "I think that you take this and move it over to the

221

other side." As Anil reached over to compare notes, their heads bumped. "Ouch!" Meera's shout ended in a whisper. Instinctively he rubbed the palm of his hand over the top of her forehead. She could still feel the warmth from his hand after he had awkwardly removed it. Meera had trouble concentrating after that. He had never touched her before. She tried to ignore the current that ran through her body. Anil began, "Okay so we need to solve for a to the third power…" She stared at him, and he stopped talking as she leaned towards him and kissed him softly on the lips. Oh my God, she thought, I can't believe I just did that. He just looked at her and ran his fingers lightly over her face, tracing the curve of her chin. After a few minutes he whispered, "You're so beautiful; I've liked you ever since that day in Spanish." It was impossible for them to do any more work so they decided to go for a walk behind the library. Outside, on the tree lined path, they strolled, stopping every few minutes to turn towards each other.

A month later, as she sat in her mom's room, the scene came clearly back to her. She still remembered how scared she had been that night when she had entered the doorway to her house. Her parents were having tea with the Kapoors, so she couldn't just run up to her room. It was hard to concentrate on what Aunty was asking her. She could only think, they know. They can tell by my face. "Oh, I don't really know yet where I want to go to college…" she had stammered out. After making her escape she sat on her bed, elated and petrified, all at the same time. They would kill her if they ever found out.

She couldn't believe it had only been a month since that day in the library with Anil. They knew each other too well. She was convinced they were lovers in a previous life. "Stop philosophizing, Meera," she told herself as she dialed the liquor store's number. Her fingers tapped the phone nervously as it began to ring. Please God, let Anil answer the phone. A gruff voice answered, "Ello! KC Liquors." Damn, Anil's father. Putting on a high falsetto, she said, "Hi-i, is a-a- aneil there?" She could hear his father yelling, "Anil! oh amrikan kudi hegi hai." Her anxiety turned to amusement as she thought, *that American girl*…if he only knew.

"Hello?" Anil's voice came on the phone.

"Hi, sorry about that. Don't tell your dad it's me. I just wanted to check that we're going to meet at seven-thirty tonight?"

"Yea, fine, bye Jane."

She was still laughing when her mom walked in. "What is so funny?"

"Oh, it was just Jenny telling me a joke."

At dinner Mom and Dad were discussing office politics as usual. Her mind was on Anil. "Meera, Meera! beta can you please check my report for grammar, I still mix up 'a' and 'the,'" her mother was talking to her.

"Okay, later Mom, after I come back from the library," she didn't notice the look that passed between her parents as she put her plate in the sink. "Dad, can you pick me up at ten? I have a lot of homework tonight," she lifted her backpack and headed towards the door.

At the library, she and Anil went for their usual walk before they did their homework. Anil barely said a word, he seemed preoccupied. She waited, knowing that eventually he would tell her what was wrong. They were sitting on a bench when he suddenly turned to face her.

"My father wants me to go to Sycamore Junior College; my parents need help with the store. We're not doing that well," he finally said.

Meera looked at him with dismay. They had been talking about going to the same college. "But," she said hesitatingly, "they know that you're only going to a place where you can get a full scholarship, don't they? Besides he wants you to become an engineer doesn't he?"

Staring angrily off into the trees, he said, "You can't understand—your parents are going to pay for college. You won't have to worry about buying books or groceries. Yeah, my father wants to say, 'my son's an engineer' but in the meantime who's going to take care of the business? No one's going to take my place for free."

Meera sat quietly, knowing that she didn't need to ask him what he was going to do. He had to help his family, there was no choice. She was just beginning to realize how spoiled she was. They walked back to the library in silence.

She watched him, his head bent over his books, worry lines on his forehead. She felt like her insides were shriveling up. I can't lose him, she decided.

"We'll figure something out, don't worry," she whispered to him as she put her hand firmly into his.

Later that night they came out of the library holding hands. It was only nine forty-five so they had a few minutes before her dad came.

"Meera!" She turned quickly to find both her parents coming towards them. Oh no, they've seen us, she thought, fear running through her body.

"You! Go home," her mother pointed her finger at Anil. He slowly obeyed, unsure of what to do. Then she had grabbed Meera's arm and pulled her to the car as if she was a recalcitrant two-year-old, muttering the whole while, "I can't believe this girl. Lying to us the whole time. What a disgrace! What will people say? It is that girl Jennifer's influence, she goes out with boys." My God, Jenny...she must have called while I was here, Meera realized. I forgot to tell her not to call tonight. Damn! There was nothing she could say now, it was too late.

When they got home, Meera ran up to her room. Passing her mirror, she saw that she was shaking. She could still hear her mother's voice screaming downstairs. Snatches of words like "too much freedom" and "that boy" floated up to her room. Meera's tears began to flow as she curled up into a ball on her bed.

An hour later, her mother quietly entered her room without knocking. She seemed even more menacing in her stillness. Meera's tear-stained face was hidden beneath her comforter.

"Get up," her mother said abruptly.

Sitting up slowly, Meera stared at her mother.

"You have lied to us. I forbid you to see that boy. Do you know who he is? He works in a liquor store, I've seen him. It looks so bad. You cannot, you just cannot ruin our good name," she said.

"...but I like him...he's smart and he's nice. What's so wrong about it? I don't understand. I've been so good. Why?! Please!" Meera heard herself begging. She wanted so much to be strong and say 'who cares' to her mother but she couldn't. Doubts crept up on her. I did lie, she told herself. No, they forced me to. She pushed away the doubts; they would have never accepted him.

"Do you know what his parents do? They run a liquor store! They're not even metric passed. He doesn't come from a good family. No, no…you cannot…" her mother continued.

Meera had to respond, "but Mom, how can you be so prejudiced?! Besides, Mrs. Kapoor runs a grocery store and she's your friend. Why is that okay? You're always saying that those people at work discriminate against you and now that's what you're doing to Anil's family. Just because they're not rich doesn't mean he's from a bad family."

"It's not that…they're just not our kind of people. Mr. Kapoor is a professional; he's an engineer. Do you want to be associated with illiterates? If you see that boy anymore I promise you, you will not be allowed to live here. I will put you out on the street, and then I will see who will help you!" her mother said, as she left the room.

Meera sat, stunned. Her mother's words tore at her. I have to leave, I have to see Anil, she decided, I can't stay in this house. But, she thought, how can I go to his house? His parents don't know about us. Besides how was she going to tell him what her mother said? She just couldn't hurt him by repeating those cruel words. No, she had no place to go, she would have to stay here, she realized as she put her face into her hands and cried.

Lying in bed the next morning, staring blankly at the ceiling, Meera couldn't decide whether she could make it to school. She knew that she would break down if she saw Anil. Her father knocked softly on her door. "Are you up?" Pulling the comforter above her head, she remained silent. She could hear him waiting outside the door.

"Meera, you have to get up. You'll be late for school," he tried knocking again, but she refused to answer. She sat up when she heard his footsteps go downstairs. I want to run away so badly, she thought, as she stared outside the window. But where would I go? Who would pay for college? What would she do about books and groceries, just like what Anil had said. I never even thought about it. "I wish I had," she said softly as she looked regretfully at her open closet. The clothes she had bought with her summer job money stared defiantly back at her. Meera headed towards her desk. She knelt and opened the last drawer. Underneath the folders lay the ribbon-tied letters she was looking for. Going back to her bed, she sat down heavily and began rereading Anil's last letter.

"There you go again," she said, as tears started to stream down her face. Fine, she said to herself, I'll pretend that I'm not going out with Anil, if that's what they want. They can't come with me to school can they? It'll just take a little maneuvering, I'll just have to be smarter with my lies.

"Meera, Meera!" her mother was calling her from downstairs. Wiping her eyes, she slowly walked out of her bedroom and stopped at the head of the stairs. Both her parents looked up. "So are you going to school today?" her mother finally broke the silence.

"No." She refused to look into her mother's eyes.

"…All right, then we'll see you later," her mother said as her parents headed out the door, briefcases in hand.

How can they pretend nothing happened? Meera wondered. Not wanting to think about it any more, she went back to her room, crawled in bed, and shut her tired eyes.

The afternoon sun was pouring across her face when a droning noise woke her up. It took her a few minutes to realize that it was the phone. It must be Anil. She ran towards her parents' bedroom.

"Hello?" she said breathlessly, as she picked up the phone.

"Meera? Are you okay? I was worried about you all day. I tried calling during lunch but no one answered," Anil's voice enveloped her.

"I was asleep. Don't worry, I'm fine," she lied forcibly.

"So what happened last night? What did your parents say?"

"They don't want me to date, you know, they think it looks really bad. 'What will people say?' and all that kind of stuff. But I don't care. They can say whatever they want, but I'll do what I want to," she kept the tone of her voice light.

"Are you sure? I don't want to cause problems between you and your parents," he said softly.

"It's too late; besides it's not you," she lied again, "it's the whole dating business."

"Hey listen, I have to go back to work, but I want to talk more. I just have to tell you one thing."

She waited, holding her breath in. He's going to say he can't deal with it.

"I'm willing to lie, sneak around, whatever, to see you. I'm not giving you up...*okay Papa, I'm coming*...gotta go, we'll talk during lunch tomorrow. Bye." He hung up.

"Bye." she whispered to the empty air, as she leaned against the headboard. She was just walking out the door when the phone rang again. It's probably Jenny, she thought as she absent-mindedly reached for the phone.

"Meera, beta?" It was her mother.

"What?" she stiffened.

"Can you make some rice for dinner tonight?" her mother's weary voice asked.

Meera hesitated a minute and finally said, "Okay." She hung up quickly before her mother had a chance to say anything else. When she lowered the receiver she noticed an old framed photograph sitting on the sidetable. It was one of her mother's favorites; Meera's four-year-old hand firmly clasped her mother's index finger. Picking up the photograph, Meera looked angrily at the young girl's trusting expression. Finally removing her gaze, she carefully placed the photograph face down on the table and walked away.

Reading and Writing
the South Asian Diaspora:
Feminism and Nationalism in North America[1]

INDERPAL GREWAL

On the back cover of Bharati Mukherjee's novel, *Jasmine*, the blurb from the *Baltimore Sun* reads "Poignant…Heartrending…The story of the transformation of an Indian village girl, whose grandmother wants to marry her off at 11, into an American woman who finally thinks for herself."[2]

To this reviewer of *Jasmine*, South Asian women are an exploited and oppressed category that serves to construct by contrast the free and independent "American woman". Within this comparison which has its origins in European colonial discourses, India is a uniformly oppressive place for women. In contrast, the U.S. becomes the land of hope, freedom and independence for women. The problem of such a formulation is that it enables the erasure, or the deliberate forgetting, of women's exploitation and oppression in the U.S., and the denial of women's agency in India. Both these erasures are necessary for the formation of "freedom" and "democracy" in the United States as well as in other First World nations. The discourse of "freedom" is essential to the consolidation and ongoing construction of Western state power structures, especially at the present time with the increase in the collection of information on citizens and noncitizens with new technologies, and the corresponding redefinitions of issues of privacy and personal freedoms. The ideology of American "freedom" constructs U.S. nationalism.

Jasmine supports and maintains this discourse of "Americanness" and "freedom" as connected and synonymous even while it can be consumed as a "multicultural" text. It supports the "multiculturalism" that is being embraced currently within liberal U.S. circles; this multiculturalism readily absorbs a text by a "minority" woman, that attacks one kind of racism practiced by the white working class, while remaining oblivious to the more subtle and powerful racism of the upper classes. Affiliating itself with the white upper classes, it speaks of "difference" and "diversity," though it presents diversity in the normative language of the dominant classes. An acceptable form of diversity is presented, within which upper-class minorities and whites align themselves on the basis of class; this version of "diversity" involves acceptance not only of middle and upper class minorities but also of state control by these classes. At present, this notion of "diversity" serves to formulate an image of the U.S. as a nation of "tolerance" that is a model for democratic rights around the world.

Unlike the *Sun*'s reviewer, many South Asians have been concerned with the novel's treatment of South Asian women, immigrants and minority groups, as well as other people of color in the U.S. In order to see such representations as linked to nationalist needs in both the U.S. and India, we need to look at the colonial discourses of essential identities based on gender, race and class within which texts about Asia and Asian women are produced and consumed. These are the global contexts that affect Asians living in the so-called First and Third Worlds, since it remains important for nations in the West to define themselves and their projects in opposition to what is termed the "Third World."

What is suggested by this Western subject formation is that all feminist opposition is defined in the West; for instance, it is believed that if there are feminists in India, they follow the same agendas as those in the U.S. This problematic formulation emerges from a Eurocentrism that ignores any discussion of Third World women's specific exploitations and agendas. For women of Asian origins in the U.S., progressive communities arise out of political coalitions and not from the national essence that is constructed through an authentic "tradition." Such a tradition, though seemingly protective, is often repressive and ineffective against the racist onslaught of white culture of "freedom" and "independence," and a European colonial history in which Asian societies were seen as exploitative and barbaric. This "tradition" colludes with the colonial stereotypes of Asian women as passive and affects both Asians and Asian Americans. It is therefore important to state that it is not America with its much vaunted freedom and equality that makes Asian women into "free" Americans, but that Asian women were active, oppositional, empowered and struggling, though their agendas and struggles were different from those of Western feminists. Alternate and specific histories and accounts of women's lives in Asia affects Asians living in North America for they enable oppositions that do not utilize the questionable structure of First World freedom and equality.

In the aftermath of the Los Angeles uprising in 1991 that followed from the Rodney King case, what we need to focus on are coalitions, within Asian American communities and between minority communities, against racism, homophobia, immigration law biases, sexism and other inequalities. In order to make these coalitions we need to understand the connected issues of state nationalism and cultural nationalism, i.e., how do those South Asians who belong to dominant communities within their nations of origins become politicized as minorities in the U.S.? On what basis do they construct themselves as separate and different? What form does their connection to their country of origin take?

Within the South Asian community and affecting its participation in the larger group of Asian Americans, are the connections between the nationalist politics since the independence of South Asian nations, and the formations of coalitions with other minority groups in the U.S. In the case of Indian immigrants, the effect of decades of nationalist struggle in India resulted in the hegemony of the middle and upper classes, which were English speaking and educated by colonial and Indian education to believe in modernization, development and progress.[3] The dominant culture in India, constructed through such nationalist discourses, required the exclusion of minorities and a belief in the necessity of their assimilating. Power-hungry politicians, millions of disenfranchised peoples and the failure of the secularization project, all contributed to making the communal riots in India that resulted in the deaths of many hundreds of people. We now see the problems and dangers of this hegemonic

culture that leaves out the poor religious minorities and the tribal groups in the construction of the Indian nation.

While for some the belief in modernization leads to a rejection of anything associated with what is seen as "tradition," for many South Asian immigrants (most of which comprised the professional, hence, modernized classes because of the nature of immigration laws after 1965) the belief in a tradition, supposedly static and authentic, remains important for struggles against racism and assimilation. Thus many immigrants to the U.S. who belong to the Indian upper classes are unable to jettison their nationalist luggage, keeping ties to a "home" that is, for them, free of discrimination, and where race seems not to matter. The Indian government, wishing for investments from U.S. immigrants, maintains and nurtures the ties to "home" by creating a category called the "Non-Resident Indian" (N.R.I.) that gives a special financial status to visiting immigrants. Yet this position of dominance in India, together with acculturation in the U.S., where stereotypes of African Americans, Chicano/as and other minorities abound, often prevents any coalitions with disenfranchised groups in the U.S., with other Asian Americans, and with more recent Southeast Asian immigrant groups, and often leads to an uncritical position on U.S. ideology of "democracy" and "freedom."

In what follows, I compare the works of two South Asian women writing in North America to examine how they restructure Indian colonial and post-independence formations in order to align themselves to different communities and different histories in diasporic situations.

In Meena Alexander's recent novel *Nampally Road*, the range of women is impressive. The female characters include a professor and writer, a Muslim woman, a laborer-activist and a doctor.[4] Such a range prevents any simplistic formulation such as oppressed Indian women versus independent American women. The novel's complex representation of India in the Indira Gandhi era, combined with the issue of inclusion and empowerment through affiliations on the basis of gender and class in both India and the U.S., effectively dismantles simplistic colonial constructs of the monolithic Third World woman as victim.

Not unlike some of Alexander's poems set in the U.S., this book is about the relationships across classes: between those who have profited from nationalism and those whose exploitation continues, not by the British, but by neocolonial elites. The book is based on a famous case in which a Muslim woman was raped in Hyderabad by several policemen in a police station. This rape caused riots; the people of the town burnt down the station. In Alexander's novel, they rescue the woman during the riot and try to burn down the tents erected to celebrate the rule of the Chief Minister of the state who sees the state as his private kingdom. The novel focuses on the politics of gender and class, for it is not only about a rape but about the rape of a woman without any power: a poor Muslim woman with no access to power structures, for Muslims in contemporary India have become a disenfranchised minority. Commenting on nationalist politics, it speaks of the power of the contemporary politicians in contemporary India, who are creating little kingdoms for themselves, complete with coopted police and armed secret henchmen. The henchmen wear "three-piece suits and black sunglasses modelled on Papa Doc Duvalier's dreaded Tonton Macoutes"(39); dictators in Haiti

become models for repressive politics in other postcolonies.[5] For these politicians, the votes of the majority population are obtained by increasing control over minorities and women.

In the meantime, the anger and protests against corruption and misuse of power by politicians and the state are seen to require a "containment" necessary to continue the celebrations that would proclaim Limca Gowda a "great leader," another Mahatma Gandhi or Krishna reborn. As the radio announcer says, in what the narrator describes as a "deep, clipped voice, well trained by the BBC Overseas Service people," the celebration is "a historic moment" and that "there is no doubt that all troublesome elements will be subdued. A new world will arise."(75-76) Here Alexander connects the power of such politicians to a neocolonialism that comes from lessons learnt from the British, exemplified by the radio announcer's news report, spoken in the BBC style, in which the poor and powerless are "troublesome elements."(76) Neocolonial elites in India are linked to those in other Third World countries; Papa Doc's terror squads are compared to Limca Gowda's Eveready Men.

While revealing right-wing affiliations, Alexander's narrator focuses also on affiliations between the oppressed. Yet the novel reveals not only the possibilities but also the problematics of these connections. Mira is concerned with the exploitation of the poor and of poor women in particular, but also with the relationship between the poor women and herself as a middle-class person. Although the novel suggests that she tries to understand Rameeza without turning her into a cipher for Otherness, the failure of this attempt in the novel is significant in its betrayal of class relations. Ironically, therefore, one can see the novel as successful in many ways in its examination of the location of the Indian middle-class intellectual and the process of decolonization even while its representation of the gendered subaltern subject, Rameeza Be, is much less convincing. As a college professor and writer, Mira Kannadical questions the lessons of British imperialism, her colonial education, her preoccupation with Wordsworth, and the utter difference between Wordsworth's Romantic Self, which requires an Other to complete its binary structure, and the lives of the poor around her. She questions the ideological effect of her writing, such that in the end her notebooks remain under her bed, her class on Wordsworth untaught, while she is occupied with the rescue of Rameeza Be and the protests that follow. Yet class differences between the elites with an English education and cosmopolitan ties and those disenfranchised minorities, exacerbated within nationalism, cannot be sutured easily.

Alexander constructs a web of struggle that includes India and England, which it necessarily must since the economic structures that give power and privilege to politicians and elites are themselves linked. As a student in London, Mira participates in anti-Thatcher marches. Even though the agenda is different in London, there is a link between the march against Thatcher and the riot against Limca Gowda. Both are concerned with redressing the rights of those without power and working against the politicians for whom people as individuals cease to exist and are linked in the common opposition to the rising power of global economic structures. Alexander presents a politics of location that has a continuity; struggle in India and struggle in London are linked through opposition to similar and connected structures of oppression.[6]

Consequently, for Meena Alexander, the problems of Indian nationalism are very much uppermost, even while she writes poetry about crime and poverty in the streets of New York,

for the problematic of nationalism is the creation of powerful elites and disenfranchised people.[7] It is also about coalitions between the elites and coalitions that must be built in order to oppose the right-wing ones. New York and Hyderabad both have different versions of this nationalist problem; "home" and "abroad" are equally unsettling.

Another set of affiliations is set up by poet Surjit Kalsey. Very different from Alexander, Kalsey writes of the problems of immigrants who come to America because of economic necessity and the hope of bettering their lives, but are disappointed. While Alexander calls on commonalities on the basis of class and gender, Kalsey's work focuses more on race and class discrimination. Such work enables coalitions between people of color; coalitions that are becoming increasingly necessary in the economic recession that pits minorities against each other.

Kalsey, a South Asian Canadian, works on constructing an Indian and an immigrant heritage for poets living in North America. The heritage is not only of poets in India but of the early South Asian settlers in America. In an essay on Canadian Punjabi Literature, she cites as the founding texts the writings of the first immigrants from India.[8] Kalsey's work focuses on the lives of undocumented and working-class immigrants to the U.S., revealing the harshness and difficulties of an existence that is common to many immigrants. In "Siddharta Does Penance Once Again," Kalsey describes the feelings of a young man who leaves his wife behind in order to come to America to make a living. What Kalsey fuses is the structures of experience in India (the traveler is Siddharta in a world of miseries), with the experience of the early Asian immigrants and more recent Asian and Mexican farmworkers. Many of these immigrants had to leave wives and families behind in search of a living. Travel is immigration here, but is also seen as a pilgrimage, leaving what is familiar in search of a mortal salvation. Kalsey portrays their loneliness, their longings to see their loved ones as well as their exploitation as itinerant workers. The worker/speaker of the poem is ironic in his use of the metaphor of pilgrimage for immigration, for this "pilgrimage" has "hermits" who exploit them, and the other "pilgrims" are the immigrant farmworkers: "Everyday they pack us into closed wagons/to dump us into the raspberry, strawberry or blueberry fields." His promises are the promises of many other immigrants, Chinese, Japanese, Filipino or South Asian:

> I'll come home very soon
> or I'll apply for your immigration very soon
> so that with you own eyes you can touch that "holy Tree"
> under which, doing penance,
> I've found the path to salvation from hunger...(26)

Kalsey presents the plight of the farmworker within the background of racism in America. The sad irony is that this search for a mortal salvation creates divided families, alienation and sorrow. Yet the experiences presented in this poem sets up affiliations across many communities of color, for many Asian and Mexican and African American's shared the same experience that the farmworker in the poem speaks of. These affiliations occur on the

basis of race as well as of class. More importantly, the poem does not present India and America within the free-unfree binary, for such a binary does not exist for an immigrant who is a farmworker.

As shown by the work of Alexander and Kalsey, South Asian and South Asian American politics of location moves between nationalist politics of contemporary India, colonial discourses and new affiliations demanded by immigrant contexts. Despite different agendas in different locations, the transnational nature of these struggles implies a linkage among various contexts. Faced with neocolonial alliances between colonialists and elites, struggles for self-determination and against exploitation also form oppositional coalitions. Meena Alexander and Surjit Kalsey are two examples of South Asian women who bring to their work different but linked affiliations to the communities in which they live and move.

Bharati Mukherjee's novel *Jasmine*, on the other hand, makes distinctions rather than affiliations among the working classes and those who are not in privileged positions. Not only does this narrative participate in the problematic discourse of Indian nationalism, but it also prevents any coalitions on the basis of another kind of history: that of immigration to America, thus foreclosing the problematization of U.S. nationalist ideology. The characterization of other U.S. ethnic communities reveals that this text does not participate in any formation of Asian American communities struggling against racism, sexism and stereotypes of Asians as backward and barbaric. Moreover, the stereotyping of a minority community from India, the Sikhs, reveals a disinterest in participating in the formation of an Asian American anti-racism coalitions for it ignores immigration history. Sikhs, who are described in the text as fanatics and terrorists, formed the majority among the first South Asians to come to the U.S. They and other South Asians were important in contributing to the struggle for Indian independence, as well as in providing a history of South Asian presence in the U.S. that can be built upon to provide coalitions with other Asian Americans.

Yet by ignoring such histories, *Jasmine* not only cannot connect newly arrived immigrant communities to the earlier ones, but it also cannot present the struggle against racism as one that has a history with all the communities that history created and can create. Mukherjee's protagonist, Jasmine, outside such a history, is consequently presented as an anomaly among Asians and Asian women and outside all preexisting contexts and communities of struggle.[9] Without history and community, Jasmine's struggle is that of the Euro-American feminist striving for individuality. Thus the only "freedom" that *Jasmine* reveals is that of being part of and valorizing the dominant power structure. But more problematically, this so-called "freedom," gained at the expense of Asians and other people of color, is taken as empowerment. For Mukherjee, as she has said recently, insisting on being called "American" is political intervention, rather than seeing herself as Asian-American or even as Indo-American. Instead of dismantling the hegemony of the term, "American," she wants to be included within it.

In light of Mukherjee's statements, it is not surprising that what seems most important to the protagonist of the novel, *Jasmine*, is becoming part of the dominant, white, upper class group. This is done at the expense of Asian women, South Asian minorities, other Asian cultures and groups and other people of color. Such a formation testifies to the ways in which

nationalisms, though seemingly in opposition, collude in order to become powerful; some Indian elites, gaining power through nationalist struggles in India, make alliances with the white, upper classes as immigrants in the U.S.

Moreover, Mukherjee's narrative of a simplistic religious conflict presents communalism as a manifestation of natural antipathies between people who follow different religions rather than as a colonial construct that is being redeployed for particular reasons by various politicians today. Communalism, as Gyan Panday has suggested in his important book, *Communalism and Nationalism in North India*, is a colonial construct that enabled state control in the guise of mediating religious divisions. According to Panday, "Communalism…is a form of colonialist knowledge…The paradox is that the nationalists have done more than anyone else to propagate its use."[10] In effect, communalism as religious difference, was constructed as the Other of modernity and nationalism; therefore, it was necessary for the emergence of India as a nation. Indian nationalist claims for the Hindu character of the Indian nation and of Hindu nationalism (and conflicts in response to this claim) occurred concurrently with the positioning of the Indian nation-state as the keeper of law and order, just as the colonial state had been.

If we see "communalism" in this more complex light, we have to be aware of the way in which divisions on the basis of religion were much more than what they appeared to be, and to see religious differences as being utilized and mobilized for many reasons by many people in power and by the state. Class, caste, regional, gender divisions that are changing and historically specific reveal that these entities are as constructed as is the nationalist history of India. Without such complexities—which have to be ignored if a narrative is to be presented in terms of "freedom" and "unfreedom," in which the nation is unproblematized— we have a narrative of stereotypes. Thus, just as all Palestinians or Iranians are seen as terrorists in the West, all Sikhs are terrorists in Mukherjee's work. What is unproblematized is this Hindu nationalist structure of the innocent Hindu vs. the terrorist Sikh. This structure, and other similar ones, are currently being utilized by right-wing politicians in India to advance their own power much as the English used what they had termed "communal" divisions. Hundreds of people have died in this new mobilization of "communalism," and the Hindu vs. Sikh division is only one of many being utilized in India at the present time. Unfortunately, the nationalist legacy and the rhetoric of colonialism and Western "freedom" that enables the designation of certain groups as "terrorists" adds not only to the present ethnic strife in India, but it elides the way in which the unrest of the minorities in India is to a large extent the response to the consolidation of power in the hands of the dominant Hindu elites, to a greater centralization of state power, the diminution of the rights of minorities and to the unfulfilled promises of nationalism to the poor in India.

Consequently, to keep to an unquestioned discourse of communalism is to be faithful to the controlling right-wing power structures and to the extension of the power of the state in India. Such a narrative also extends the power of those in the U.S. who are all too ready to dismiss all nonChristians as fanatics and terrorists.[11] Such racist discourses enable the extension of state power over minority and white working-class communities in the U.S. as well.[12]

Jasmine's claim to the reader's interest and attention seems based on the notion that she is unlike other Indian women—that she is active, a risk-taker and adventurous. Mukherjee has called these qualities being "American," claiming that many "Americans" live in other parts of the world.[13] Thus Jasmine is implicitly "American" from the very beginning, so that, unlike other Indian women, she has the sympathy of many American readers. Since she is supposedly an anomaly among Indian women, she is represented as a rebel, one who can act according to her desires. Such an agency is, however, miraculously unexplained, because what is revealed to the reader is that women are so oppressed in India that such an agency is impossible. Jasmine has the "scrubbed-rawest hands" because "I boiled the river water three and four times, when everyone else just let the mud settle before drinking."(39) She is also the only one with the courage to face a mad dog, while other women crawl away terrified. Since she is so anomalous, no one understands Jasmine. Infant girls are thrown in wells, others have various terrible fates. Jasmine is the survivor, unlike all the others who live miserable lives. This is clearly a First World fantasy of Third World women's lives. Thus Jasmine says, "My grandmother may have named me Jyoti, Light, but in surviving I was already Jane, a fighter and adapter."(35) In this text, a "Jyoti" cannot be a fighter. One has to be Jane, a European American, to be one.

Trinh T. Minh-ha has called this portrayal of an anomalous Third World woman as a representation of "specialness" rather than one of difference.[14] Trinh suggests that this kind of formation creates a division "between I-who-have-made-it and You-who-cannot-make-it" and it has unfortunate consequences in the preservation of one's identity as special at the cost of other women; it leads to a "double game: on the one hand, (I shall) loudly assert my right, as a woman, and an exemplary one, to have access to equal opportunity; on the other hand, (I shall) quietly maintain my privileges by helping the master perpetuate his cycle of oppression."[15] This representation of Jasmine's "specialness" seemingly enables a denunciation of racism in the U.S. (which is likely to lull criticism of the book from minorities and liberals who welcome other minority voices), at the same time as it suggests, problematically, that racism should not be directed against Jasmine because she is different from other women of color.

We search for what is called the "genuine foreignness" that makes all white men she meets fall in love with her. But all we find is submission and mystery in the guise of independence. Thus Jasmine's freedom simply implies her ability to change herself according to the wants of the dominant culture. Her power is to make people aware of her oriental mystery, to long for Otherness that she embodies, to make them want something Indian at their dinner table every day. Difference is reduced to curry—one that can be consumed by the dominant classes.

If this narrative is one of "specialness," then what is problematic is Mukherjee's own position within the U.S. and the agenda of liberal "multiculturalism" within which this novel is consumed. *Jasmine* works on the level of monolithic representations, for instance, of what it means to be an "Indian woman," or what it means to live in a "typical" Indian community in the U.S., by focusing on what it means to be an "anomalous Indian woman." While many authors who are not writing about white America have to struggle against what has been called the "burden of representation,"[16] the success of this novel depends on it being seen as representative.

It is not surprising, therefore, that other nonwhite communities are also presented as representative, and Jasmine has little solidarity with them. For instance, when she arrives in the U.S. and is walking the road looking for help, it is not the Mexican farmworkers who help her, but a white woman. The men in the fields are "Short, thick, darkskinned men with vaguely Asian features"(115); a little boy among them points a toy gun at her, which looks similar to the Uzi carried by the so-called Sikh terrorists. He sprays her with imaginary bullets while she is gasping for water. Like the Sikhs, the Latinos in the fields seem violent and threatening to Jasmine.

It is the white woman, Lillian, who rescues her and who becomes the model of what Jasmine yearns to be. She is described as "a facilitator who made possible the lives of absolute *ordinariness* that we ached for"(117)—this ordinariness never available in Asia but present in an upper middle class white existence in Manhattan. The other refugees in Lillian's house are never described as individuals, nor are they named; they are "the Kanjobal women" who teach Jasmine how to make tortillas while she teaches them how to make chapatis. This is as far as we get in terms of solidarity with other people of color. Lillian, on the other hand, teaches them how to be domestics, but she too, amazingly enough, sees Jasmine as different from "the Kanjobal women." So in her "brisk, direct way," she says "Jazzy, you don't strike me as a picker or a domestic."(120) We wonder why the others were seen as appropriate for domestic work, while Jazzy is sent off to Lillian's daughter in New York as a "very special case."(120) After Lillian is busted for harboring undocumented persons, Jasmine sees this woman for whom the only future for women of color is as domestics, as a heroine: "She represented to me the best in the American experience and the American character."(121)

The lives of other South Asian immigrants are presented as empty and pathetic in comparison to Jasmine's, since she is full of hope and desire, and the South Asian immigrant family she stays with seem not to have such feelings. We are told they have "retired behind ghetto walls," because they chose to live there.(129) Flushing, New Jersey, seems like Punjab to her, and of course, this is a derogatory comparison.[17] Jasmine, immured in the immigrant ghetto, is oppressed by the boredom of such an existence. Since this life does not qualify as that of the "absolute ordinariness" that occurs only in a white middle-class existence, she would often find herself "in the bathroom with the light off, head down on the cold, cracked rim of the sink, sobbing from unnamed, unfulfilled wants."(131) It is, of course, not possible to present the immigrant "ghetto" as a place of pleasure, comfort and community, one that immigrants would intentionally or actively seek out and prefer to live in. Nor does it even suggest, as in the case of Chinatowns, that in a climate of racism, the "ghetto" may be the only haven.

What the novel suggests is that since life in India equals violence, the "ordinary" life Jasmine searches for is only available within middle-class existence in New York. The text does not present the "ordinary" in India. This ordinary life, available within all classes and in many places, cannot be represented through the tourist's gaze. This is because the tourist can only see in comparison with the West, and within this comparison, places in Asia only can be situated in relation to modernity. A homogeneous Third World thus appears, where women seen are seen only as exploited and oppressed. What is not visible in touristic novels such as *Jasmine* is the representation of lives in the so-called "Third World" as normal,

234

ordinary, with all the pleasures and pains that ordinary life contains.[18] Mukherjee's work reveals the Third World as barbaric and the First as civilized; its success in the U.S. depends on keeping to this problematic assumption. In *Jasmine*, life in India is anomalous, strange, unnatural; none of its characters have any pleasures in the details of living. And it is not only India that is viewed through a tourist's lens, but also Vietnam, as becomes apparent in the section of *Jasmine* that concerns the young boy, Du, Jasmine's adopted son. Du is presented as the perfect Asian, because he has endured terrible privations and tragedies but survives to become a computer whiz. Thus, in seeing what they have in common, Jasmine says:

"Du's doing well because he has always trained with live ammo, without a net, with no multiple choice. No guesswork: only certain knowledge or silence. Once upon a time, like me, he was someone else. We've been many selves. We've survived hideous times. I envy Bud the straight line and smooth planes of his history."(190)

To live in Asia is to live in a combat zone, a zone of warfare; consequently America, as its opposite, is the place where, in contrast, Lillian Gordon's "absolute ordinariness" can become possible. It is never possible in Asia.

Mukherjee's novel seems written for Euro-American audiences with the gaze of a Euro-American tourist, and not of one who has lived in India or comes from India. Like the work of V.S. Naipaul, *Jasmine* represents South Asia with the tropes and ideologies of Western hegemonic structures. Its portrayals of women in India are especially problematic because, without present the complexity of state formations, regional politics and contemporary power structures as they impact upon gender relations in India, the novel does not help in the formation of feminist agendas different from those of bourgeois feminists in Europe and North America.

On the other hand, a reading of Meena Alexander's novel, *Nampally Road*, gains immensely from a knowledge of specific events that occurred in India in the eighties, from knowing well how politicians function there, as well as from a concern for lives of women in different classes and communities. Alexander's work is, unfortunately, not as well known as Mukherjee's. Its complexity prevents it from functioning as a representative text describing "the Indian woman" or "the South Asian immigrant experience," as does *Jasmine*. Perhaps it is for this reason, unfortunately, that it will not be a bestseller in the U.S.

1. This essay was written with the encouragement and help of Sukhminder Grewal, Ruth Frankenberg, Caren Kaplan, Lynn Wardley, Tani Barlow, Lydia Liu, Margot Stange and friends from Narika.

2. Bharati Mukherjee, *Jasmine*, (New York: Fawcett Crest, 1989).

3. For more on this topic see essays in *Rethinking English*, ed. Svati Joshi (New Delhi: Trianka, 1991).

4. Meena Alexander, *Nampally Road* (San Francisco: Mercury House, Incorporated, 1991).

5. One final note about the Rameeza Be case and the power of the police and the state: After her case became a cause, the police framed and arrested Rameeza for enticing girls for prostitution.

The judge convicted her but did not pass a sentence. He ordered her release on probation for one year, during which she was directed to prove her good behavior. (Report in *Manushi*, January 1978).

6. More on what can be called "transnational" struggles appears in the Introduction to *Scattered Hegemonies: Postmodernity and Transnational Feminist Practices*, ed. Caren Kaplan and Inderpal Grewal, forthcoming (University of Minnesota Press, Spring 1994).

7. Meena Alexander, "City Streets," and "Poem on Amsterdam Avenue," *Toronto South Asian Review*, (Fall-Winter 1987–88).

8. Surjit Kalsey, "Introduction," and "Siddharta Does Penance Once Again," *Contemporary Literature in Translation* 26 (Spring 1977).

9. And in a way she is—few works with an Indian background have so few cultural references to India that are not negative stereotypes. A novel by another South Asian living in the West, Salman Rushdie's *Midnight's Children* (Great Britain: Jonathan Cape, 1980; New York: Penguin Books, 1991), is a good contrast. In that novel the language is imbued with the rhythms and vocabularies of Bombay streets and Bombay films; in Mukherjee's work, the action could occur anywhere which is exotic and terror-ridden. For a forthcoming essay on this aspect of Mukherjee's work see Fred Pfeil's "No Basta Teorizar: In-Difference to Solidarity in Contemporary Fiction, Theory and Practice," *Scattered Hegemonies: Postmodernity and Transnational Feminist Practices*, eds. Caren Kaplan and Inderpal Grewal.

10. Gyananendra Panday, *The Construction of Communalism in Colonial North India* (Delhi: Oxford University Press, 1990), 6.

11. This has already been happening. Sikh men, who wear turbans, are often taken for Iranians, for the Ayatollahs also cover their heads similarly. Sikh men have been racially harassed on U.S. streets during upsurges in anti-Iranian sentiment.

12. For more on the working of U.S. power through discourses about "terrorists" and "fanatics" (often Muslims), see Edward Said and Christopher Hitchens, *Blaming the Victims* (London: Verso, 1987), and *After the Last Sky: Palestinian Lives* (New York: Pantheon, 1986). An excellent example of how "diversity" is utilized by U.S. conservatives is the nomination of Clarence Thomas to the Supreme Court. For essays that examine "diversity," state power, racism and sexism see *Race-ing Justice, En-gendering Power*, ed. Toni Morrison (New York: Pantheon Books, 1992).

13. This was a comment made in Mukherjee's talk at a conference on "Asian American Cultural Transformations: A Literature of One's Own" at U.C. Santa Barbara, April 26, 1991.

14. Trinh T. Minh-ha, *Woman Native Other* (Bloomington: Indiana University Press, 1989), 86-87.

15. Ibid.

16. Ella Shohat, "Can the Non-Subaltern Speak? Cinema Studies, Multiculturalism, and Questions of Representation," unpublished paper.

17. This is a popular stereotype of people from Punjab that is endemic in many parts of India that see themselves as more "cultured" and "civilised." Punjabis are often seen as without any valuable traditions, as too ready to ape the West, as vulgar. The Punjabi language is believed to be without any literature worth reading.

18. Other touristic works are those by V.S. Naipaul. See *A Bend in the River* (New York: Knopf, 1979); *An Area of Darkness* (New York: Vintage, 1981); *India: A Wounded Civilization* (New York: Vintage, 1977).

Becoming Agents Of Our Identity

ZAINAB ALI

I was nine months old, enclosed by the strength of my father's arms and the salty air of the Bay of Bengal. My parents were moving to the United States, and were here, in Madras, India, obtaining their visa. They were breaking their confinement, promising—hoping—all the while to keep their religion, their heritage, their contact to family and friends left behind. Severed. Hyphenated over the Pacific Ocean and in their new identity. Indian-American. A Western merger. Artificial. The only purity that remained was coiled in that place in their hearts where McDonald's, televangelism and *Vogue* magazine—all that lay literally and symbolically behind the hyphen—could not violate.

"Taxi!" I screamed. My parents turned with both delight and surprise.

"Say it again. Say it again," Baba persisted in Urdu, bouncing me in his arms, while Amme picked my year-and-a-half-old brother from the concrete to her softness, then pointed to me for my brother to see.

"We say it so much here, that must be it," she said, still pointing and watching my brother, her voice in the low tones she speaks when talking to babies. My brother gripped her saree, watching the cars and rickshaws drive by on the road, his tongue swirling around his tiny index finger in his mouth.

"But what a coincidence, and how appropriate. We are going to America for the first time, and her first word is in English." Baba began his open-mouthed, all-teeth-showing-and-back-arched laugh that leaves his face so innocent. "America...and English!" he repeated, still in Urdu, laughing. "Who would have thought? Huh? Who would have thought with us living in Hyderabad, the heart of Urdu-speakers?" He became talkative as he does when he's excited. "Meri beti!" He held me close, still bouncing.

"Taxi!" I screamed into his hair.

I remember a time in fourth grade, when I went to my teacher after class:

"I'm sorry but I can't say the Pledge of Allegiance because I'm Muslim." My teacher's eyebrows narrowed and the skin on her forehead crunched into lines.

"Oh," she managed to finally say.

I realized she didn't know what to say to me because she hadn't dealt with a situation like this before. But I was Muslim and I was determined not to commit a sin simply because I attended an American school.

"Well then," she said. "I guess you can remain sitting while the rest of us say the Pledge."

"Thank you!" I exclaimed. I was grateful she hadn't made a fuss and had allowed me the freedom to practice my religion.

That night I told my mom about the great feat I had accomplished in school that day. "You did what?" she asked in disbelief.

"Yes," I beamed. "I told her that I would sit while the rest said the Pledge."

"Oh, honey," my mother sighed. "We need to have a talk." She took my hand into hers and sat on the sofa. Then she sat me down next to her and looked into my eyes. "Listen, honey. Mommy thinks that you're very strong for standing up for what you believe in, but I think it's okay for you to say the Pledge…"

"But Amee…" I blurted out. I couldn't believe my ears; what was my mom saying?

"Shhh. I want to explain something to you, honey." And for two hours that night, my mother explained that religion and nationality are two separate things: It's okay for me to say the Pledge because I am an American citizen, which means that I am devoted to this country without my citizenship infringing on my religious life. I finally understood.

But for the next two days, I continued sitting during the Pledge because I didn't have the courage to tell my teacher that I was wrong. Finally, three days later, as the students stood to say the Pledge, my teacher walked over to my desk—where I sat with eyes lowered—and asked me to stand.

"Okay," I excitedly replied, then stood and pledged. I never asked her who told her it was okay for me to say the Pledge; she never told me either. I can just imagine her telling the principal and the teachers having a meeting to discuss whether this small, Muslim child should and can say the Pledge.

This is the first of many incidents in which I have felt like I am sitting on the border of two cultures and religions. This position invariably forces me into feelings of disjunction because I must choose between two cultural practices. Nevertheless, it would be wrong to assume that I am able to choose to which side of the fence I want to jump: I have no choice. Rather, I am disjointed from both my Islamic culture and my Urdu language, and my—yes, it is *mine* also—Western culture and English language. Which do I use to express myself? Which becomes my identity?

At certain times, such as the Pledge incident, my identity becomes that of Islam. Other times, however, I become confused and disoriented, and overcompensate for my differences in order to assimilate. This paradox of simultaneously getting closer to and further away from discovering my identity in both cultures occurs because I am an "orphan" who is on the fringe of two socio-cultural orders. I had to deconstruct these social mores in order to bare and discern my identity.

For instance, I remember studying nutrition and the four food groups in the sixth grade. "Okay, class," my teacher chirped, her smile reminding me of the good witch in the *Wizard of Oz*. It was bright, wide and friendly. She lifted her long red-painted index finger and continued: "Today we will go around class to see what each of you had for breakfast. We can then see if we are all eating nutritiously. I'll go first. I had Nutri-Grain Waffles, coffee and orange juice. Jen, you go next and we'll continue around class from aisle to aisle." At that time, I never thought that such a small exercise would cause so much anxiety.

"Well, I think I had orange juice too, and—oh, I know—I had oatmeal."

"Very good, Jen. Did you hear that, class?" our teacher trumpeted. "Jen had a very nutritious breakfast. We're proud of Jen, aren't we class?"

"Yes, Mrs. Peterson," we replied in unison, some boys in back giggling nastily at Jen.

"Alex?" Mrs. Peterson continued.

After about five people had shared their breakfast experiences, I realized that my breakfast was completely different from the rest. If I told them, would the boys then laugh at me? Would Mrs. Peterson and the rest of class be proud of me? After all, no one would even understand what I had for breakfast; it was so...*Indian*. Panic set in, my eyes grew bigger as each student replied: cereal, or toast, or pancakes, or—as most did—oatmeal. I didn't even know what oatmeal was! Should I pretend that I had it anyway? Should I lie in order to keep the friends that I had so they wouldn't be scared of my differences? After all, I didn't want to be different, my *parents* were.

I stared at Mrs. Peterson, the smile on her face now resembling that of the Wicked Witch of the North. Her laugh no longer flowed, but cackled. She was out to humiliate me, I thought, and I knew she could if I let on to my breakfast.

"Zain*aab*," her voice squawked my name, mispronouncing it as she had throughout the school year. But now I was angry at her mispronunciation and her attempts to make me lose my friends.

I held her gaze and said emphatically: "Spaghetti."

Her face wrinkled, her smile washed away in my words, and I knew I had won. The boys in the back were awestruck. "Wow," they thundered. "That's so cool. I wish I had parents as cool as that. You're lucky."

I smiled triumphantly. A simple lie allowed me to keep my friends and become even more popular in my class.

"That's very good, Zainab," Mrs. Peterson weakly uttered. "Mark," she called on the boy behind me, "how about you? What did you have?"

"Well, nothing as cool as spaghetti," he began. And my thoughts wandered. I was thankful that I had not told the class that I really had an omelet and toast. They would have thought that I was weird.

Now I realize that Anglo-Americans also have omelets for breakfast—and I'm sure some student might have said it in class, but I was too terrorized to listen. This terror forced me to overcompensate—to lie—in order to express universality in customs and practices.

During the Gulf War, as I walk through campus to get to my class, I cross paths with another student who watches me approach. When I am within earshot, he says, "Oil-rich bitch! That's our oil, you *Shit*-ites better give it back."

I continue walking, pretending I have not heard him. "Oil-rich bitch!" He repeats his words over and over until I cannot hear him. Even when his voice stops, his words resonate through the walls of my body.

Throughout the day, I think of different ways I could have confronted him. I imagine telling him it's *not* America's oil, but the Middle East's; that Saddam Hussein is not Shiite, but Sunni; that not all Muslims support him: my own family dislikes him for his massacre of Iranians. I wish I told the student that the U.S.—his own people—gave Hussein the power to attack Kuwait; that whispers are being heard about the U.S.—his people—encouraging this attack on Kuwait. I wish I had explained to him about the real 'dirty politics' and dirty

dealings with the Middle East. I wanted to ask, "Why is the U.S. there helping Saudi? Why did they turn away from the Iranians? The Palestinians?"

I know these are simple thoughts, but I know he must begin with the basics if he is to consider the many branches of this tree.

Yet, I said nothing to him. And I gave him nothing, not even a look.

Two years later, a bomb explodes in New York. I am watching a roundtable discussion on CNN analyzing the reasons for the terrorist action.

"These fundamentalist Muslims cannot be allowed in the United States anymore," one man says. "The more Muslims we bring into America, the more terrorist actions we'll see."

"I disagree," a woman reporter on the panel says. "Not all Muslims are like those involved in this bombing."

"This has to be linked with Iran," another panelist interrupts her.

I turn the TV off and lay my head against the back of the couch in an attempt to relax. "Muslims not allowed in the U.S.," a voice keeps repeating in my mind. "Muslims no longer allowed in the U.S."

I shake my head, trying to shed these thoughts. I think of the millions of people watching the show, nodding their heads in agreement. Some, perhaps, will go out tomorrow to ensure that Muslims can no longer immigrate to America. They will never know how we feel, I think. The media never asks how we feel.

Nor does the media tell the complete truth. I know those millions watching CNN right then will not hear of the suspicions that some of the "fundamentalist" Muslims involved in this bombing emigrated during the war between Afghanistan and what was then the Soviet Union. The U.S. supported Afghanis enough to provide them with weapons and unlimited entrance into the U.S. without visas simply because they had a common enemy.

The people here will never see the Iranian streets lined with dead children's bodies as Saddam Hussein killed them with poisonous gas in the Iran-Iraq war that the U.S. supported. They will not feel the coarseness of cheeks after the tears have finally dried. They will not understand why this man suddenly became this day's U.S. enemy when he tried to take over Kuwait.

No, all people here see is that hundreds were injured, twenty killed, as the fundamentalist lunatic Muslims-who-should-never-have-been-in-this-country-in-the-first-place bombed innocent people.

They will then turn their TVs off, grumbling that the world has gone mad, that it was not like this when they were growing up, and who makes these damn immigration laws in the first place? Those damn *Moslems* must be stopped. They will ask, who brought these people here in the first place? Who gave them the right to pollute our country, our world?

They will never once think to look at my palms. To see that the lines resemble theirs. That skin covers bone. That the darkness in their eyes is reflected in mine. No, they will know only to rush away and hide behind the lens that fragments the whole.

So my brownness scares them. As do my saris. My chicken curry. My call to prayers. From the safety of this lens, they pit Black against Red, Yellow against White, Brown against Brown, me against my past. I begin to feel as though this arm is not mine, these eyes should not be black, this hair is not straight, these legs are not a pair. I fall apart, walking two different

directions. Then they put me back together, leaving out a fingernail here, a belly button there and erasing my nose. But I am nonetheless, reassembled.

Every now and then, a memory flashes, making me ache. I grab these memories, these blades of time, and layer them on top of McDonald's, televangelism and *Vogue* magazine.

Then with these memories, I re-member my pasts with my futures, my Indian with my American, my Urdu with my English. I will not allow them to again fall through the cracks of memory. And it is through re-membering, repasting, that I, too, keep my memories coiled in that place in my heart where mainstream America cannot violate.

In The Belly Of The Multicultural Beast I Am Named South Asian

NAHEED ISLAM

South Asian is a category fast catching on in academic and literary arenas. However, some of us have remained invisible in the new name, devoured by the multicultural zeal.[1] The ideal of multiculturalism assumes that everyone placed in these categories has equal space and voice within and between them. But a new hierarchy has emerged in which certain voices have been privileged and have developed their own hegemonic power. Multiculturalism participates in this process by its uncritical approach to the positioning of subjects and groups within the new categories.

Living on the margins of marginality, I first welcomed this term that hinted at recognizing my origins. It was like being at a neighborhood mela—and getting a sense of belonging to a larger community. But why would I be South Asian when I could be Bangladeshi? And the Tripuras, Shantals and Chakmas living within the borders of Bangladesh, brutally suppressed by the military, may choose to distinguish their identity from that nation-state. Why have we created this quagmire? We are trying to create a single space while ignoring the politics of positioning and our fluid positions within a complicated nexus of gender, class, race, religious, cultural, sexual and national positioning. And who is making this new box for me in the governmental mis-interest in my racial and ethnic naming? Who does it make visible and who does it negate?

South Asia consists of Bangladesh, Bhutan, India, Maldives, Nepal, Pakistan and Sri Lanka. While we use this term with some ease even within the region, what ties these nations together? It is a region of vast cultural, linguistic and religious diversity within and between national boundaries. These nation-states were created by the somewhat arbitrary wills of colonial powers and the specific interests of local elite (shrouded in nationalistic or religious rhetoric). These South Asian nations have developed their own nexus of power based on the imagined divisions of the West in addition to, and in interaction with, the local political and economic and social divisions. India and Pakistan are the regional superpowers and play an active role in the struggle over distribution of resources and territory. We must examine how these regional political dynamics transplant and transform themselves in the American context.

The very name India has retained the aura of the undivided empire that was the "jewel in the (British) crown." The colonialist nostalgia for the glamour of the raj has always kept India visible in the West. It is seen as the "memorable" moment of direct Western rule of Asia. Despite the divisions into national boundaries, Bangladesh, Pakistan and India are in some

ways perceived as larger (undivided) India. And Bhutan, Maldives, Nepal and Sri Lanka are either made invisible or seen in the context of their political and economic connections to India. For example, South Asia Studies departments in the U.S. focus their courses and research on India while claiming to "study" the whole region. They are taught by predominantly white and male faculty.[2] My own review of the South Asia Studies departments in the U.S. shows an emphasis on Ancient India Studies. Moreover, the recent addition of the India Chair to South Asian departments, first initiated at U.C. Berkeley, best illuminates the positioning of India in the South Asian context. The India Chair is created from donations by the well-to-do in the Indian American community, with support from the Indian Embassy. It is presented by the department as creating a connection between the academic community and the Indian American community. The India Chair position shows clearly which community within the South Asian countries has the economic power and infrastructure to purchase visibility. It is visibility defined by the privileged of the First and Third world.

The "Other" South Asian countries are invisible even within Indian political organizations. When a massive cyclone hit Bangladesh in 1991, killing hundreds of thousands of people, I frantically contacted many South Asian organizations for help. One offered their sponsorship but no active help. A few individuals volunteered their services. But for the most part my calls were never returned. Silence also followed from many Indian American political activists that I had worked with to form a South Asian coalition. I don't remember a single one of them asking me about what was going on in Bangladesh despite the relatively heavy news coverage of the events. However, these very same people have long spoken of the need for regional cooperation as well as showing interest in acknowledging the interlinked fates of all the nations in the region.

An Indian American community organizer once told me how she had thoughtfully used South Asian, instead of Indian, in the title of her presentation. Another gesture of "inclusive" politics. I vented my anger on my well-meaning friend. I pointed out that her presentation was on the Indian community and did not warrant being called South Asian, that the noble gesture claiming to include and represent the region made me and other non-Indians invisible. I wanted to know why Indian Americans wanted to claim the term South Asian when they were speaking only of themselves. The term is not even used by members of the different communities for self-reference. People within the communities refer to themselves as Bangladeshi, Nepalese, Sri Lankan, etc. It is only within political organizations and academic circles that the term has found currency. She was offended and made defensive by my angry response. While she conceded to some of my points, it was with a "will you never be satisfied!" note.

Similarly, a student-organized conference titled "South Asian Perspectives on Development" focused almost entirely on India, with one paper from Nepal. A white male professor and myself were the only other non-Indians on the panels. The forum should have been called "Indian Perspectives on Development" or "Development in India and Nepal." If Indian Americans want to speak of India they should do so, rather than presenting themselves as legitimately speaking for our collective interests and experiences.

In the U.S. the Indian American community has been developing its own politics. It is not a homogeneous community and many of its segments are struggling with the hegemony

within it. But Indian Americans are the numerical majority (with the largest immigration compared to other individual "South Asian" countries) with a large professional class trying to transform their economic power into power in the U.S. political system. They have accepted the term South Asian and are trying to shape it to their interest. There are a number of problems with this category. I wonder at the politics of an "ethnic" rather than "racial" category. According to the legal history of the U.S., people from Bangladesh, India and Pakistan were considered white/Caucasian until it was used by a Sikh American to contest his denial of citizenship.[3] The courts repealed the status stating that while people from India were Caucasian, they were not white and therefore were ineligible for citizenship. Indian Americans[4] had struggled to be labeled white in order to claim the privilege and protection provided by that racial category. Since the court's decision, as well as the eventual gaining of citizenship through other changes in immigration and naturalization laws, Indian American community leaders have lobbied for an ethnic category.[5] Ethnic categories give the illusion of parity between all ethnic groups such as Irish American, African American and Asian American. It tries to neutralize the reality of racial politics and recreate the imagined ladder to success.

The use of the term "South Asia" has become interchangeable with the term "India." Some Indian American groups have made a deliberate policy statement to acknowledge the inclusive nature of the term. But the easy shift of the tongue between the terms makes one wonder at the commitment to ensure all of our visibility and interests. I have worked with numerous political organizations claiming a South Asian membership. The majority of the participants tend to be Indian American with some Bangladeshi and Pakistani members. The rest of the region is almost never represented and there are disturbingly few questions raised about this absence. Despite many discussions on the use of the term in sweeping generalizations and its interchangeability with India, these problems resurface in old frustrating ways. And this experience is shared by many other people and organizers from the region.

My own experiences so far have left me skeptical of the community we are trying to build. We must recognize at present there isn't an existing South Asian coalition or community. While I continue to work with others of South Asian descent on certain issues, I also emphasize the need for our different communities to organize themselves. In the complex political web, there are possibilities for collaboration. Ultimately, the fate of a coalition depends on the struggle of each community to voice their issues and on the commitment of Indian Americans to examine their own hegemonic role in the region and in the U.S.

1. Multiculturalism is an institutionalized liberal discourse and a part of the postmodern philosophical genre. It claims to displace the master narrative and respond to the political pressure of the civil rights struggle, feminism and decolonization by equally dividing the academic curriculum and social benefits between newly codified cultural/political groups.

Here I agree with Cornell West's argument that multiculturalism pacifies the middle class and is consumed without critical engagement. Cornell West, *Beyond Eurocentrism and Multiculturalism*, vol. 2 (Monroe, ME: Common Courage Press, 1993).

2. Often, non-white faculty members are either visiting professors or regional language instructors. Those who teach the languages are hired as lecturers and usually on a contract basis. Therefore almost all the tenured positions are held by white faculty members.

3. United States v. Bhagat Singh Thind, 261 U.S. 204 (1922).

4. While the legal battles for this categorization were made by Indian Americans, the interests were possibly shared by Bangladeshi and Pakistani immigrants. But due to smaller numbers and lack of developed political and community organizations, they were unable to represent those interests. Therefore, when I say that Indian Americans wanted to be labeled white, I am only referring to the legal and recorded history. I am not aware of the position held by Maldives, Nepal and Sri Lankan communities.

5. The 1986 U.S. Census created "Asian Indian" as a new category. So now the choices for me are between the "nearest to home" (i.e. Asian Indian) or "other" category. And this is not so much a criticism of the Indian American community efforts to create a box for themselves as the problem of the taxonomy of racial and ethnic categories in general.

Tesha's Peace

TESHA SENGUPTA

Her grandfather holds her face in his bony hands and she struggles to meet his eyes lost behind thick-powered glasses. He refuses to speak Bengali, insisting that she will understand his English better. She tells him she can understand, but he continues anyway.

"You're an American now." He smirks at his own joke.

"I'm no more American than the last time I was here." She tries her best to enunciate so he can hear her better.

"You have an accent," he laughs but knows he's hit a soft spot.

"I know." She's annoyed with his humor.

"Your father should have stayed here, with me." Her father had told her to expect her grandfather's disgruntlement.

"He misses you, but America…he must live in America now."

"You should learn to be more Indian."

"I should learn to be less American." She stands up and crosses the room to sit near the window. A layer of dirt covers the windowsill and with her index finger she writes her name in it.

"You've become darker, not a good sign. Fair women have better marriages."

"I know." She remembers all the times she resisted going to the beach in preparation for this visit. She stares out the window, noticing the young children, barely clothed, playing with the water pump. She sighs and turns back around to face her grandfather.

"Your sister is a good girl." He motions towards the door and she knows her sister is within earshot.

"I know."

"Are you a good girl?" He laughs again, thinking he's made a joke.

"No." She's glad he can't always hear her.

"Your sister is very fair, that's good."

"I know."

"She's more Indian than you; she dresses more Indian."

"I know."

"You should wear a salwar, then people will know you are a real Indian girl."

"I know."

"You should try to be more Indian."

"I should try to be less American. I know." Realizing that she cannot avoid an argument, she excuses herself to fix the dinner table.

246

She stands in front of the bedroom mirror. Lifting her hand, she touches the image in the glass and looks away. She fingers the locket her grandfather gave her and knows he is right, she has gotten darker. She slips off her clothes and puts on the salwar. Looking up, she notices the eyes staring back at her, so unlike her own. And then she realizes she doesn't know if the eyes that stare back *are* her own.

"Your grandfather loves you." Her father holds her face in his hands. "He's only kidding with you."

"No, he's not."

"Well, maybe you should wear more Indian clothes. Then people will know you really are Indian." He pours himself another cup of tea.

"It won't matter, people on the streets still stare at me as if I don't belong."

"You don't. I mean, you're a foreigner to them." He smiles, leans back in his chair and rests the teacup on his lap.

"But I'm not a foreigner, I'm an Indian citizen." She rises, pushing her chair back noisily in frustration.

"That doesn't matter. People here think you're a foreigner." He stirs his tea so the sugar will dissolve.

"But I'm not."

"But they think you are," he laughs and takes a long sip from his cup. "So what?"

"I know." She stands and paces the green tiled floors.

"India isn't your home anyway."

"But neither is America." She allows her voice to get louder.

"Yes it is."

"No it isn't. Home isn't a place, it's a feeling; America will never be my home." She knows her father will never understand but he nods in feigned sympathy.

"Yeah, I know," he smiles stirring his tea again, hoping the sugar will dissolve.

"I can't call India my home and I can't call America my home." She stops pacing, walks back towards him and sits down.

"I guess you're homeless," he laughs at his own joke. She leans forward and sighs, staring into his tea, noticing that the sugar still won't dissolve.

She lies down and stares at the cement ceiling above her. The cot is hard and she feels the blanket her grandmother made for her scratching her arms. She hides her head below the sheets and breathes in the smell of fresh wool, trying to wrap herself in it. Her legs will feel cold, and when she sits up to reach for her book she sees that the blanket isn't big enough to cover all of her.

Her sister is brushing her hair in the mirror. Turning around, she rests the brush on her lap and stares at her. "Do you think Grandfather hates Dad for leaving?"

She looks up from her book. "Of course not. He's just a little...*disappointed*."

"Do you think he's *disappointed* in us?"

"Maybe. Probably. Who cares?"

"If you had been brought up here in India, you wouldn't talk about your grandfather that way." Her older sister laughs at the family cliché.

"Shut up." Smiling, she crawls to the edge of the bed, facing her sister.

"Hey, I'm the elder and you're not suppose to talk to me that way." Her sister echoes her father's words perfectly. They laugh and her sister lifts her brush and turns back around.

"Do you think you'd ever want to come back?" She slides off the bed and joins her sister on the dresser stool.

"I don't know what there would be to come back to," her sister meets her eyes in the mirror. "Do you ever get the feeling that you don't belong?"

"Every day. Believe me."

"Me too. I use to be embarrassed to wear pants on the street. But then I was thinking, I should be proud of who I am. I don't have to change, do I?" her sister says.

"No, but then how will you belong?"

"I belong. I know I belong." Her sister's insistence is reassuring.

"How do you know who you are?" she turns her back to the mirror.

Her sister holds her face by the chin and turns her forwards again, "Look, who do *you* see in the mirror?"

"I see me."

"Exactly."

The Strength
That Mends Her Soul

Pieces

SUNITA VATUK

Margarita had us write our pieces
"sin analisis" first
knowing it would all drop
into place once
they were all there.
So Ochoa's coup of sorts,
his role in counterinsurgency,
went into the pile;
the restructuring of the FMLN in the typewriter.
We hope it will fall into place once the pieces are there.

I met a man without ears
in a dark church that he never went out of
it was perfumed with bodies and disinfectant
it took days to get the smell out of my nostrils.

They cry every time
(I cry)
everyone cries every time they tell their stories
except the babies fighting and scrambling under desks and benches.

I thought that was news (living in that dark church
not ever leaving)
and it seems the smart reporter for the best of newspapers probably
knew it too.
When there was news that might prevent a beating or save a life
the friendlier ones promised to "talk to my editor about it."

Some days I see fissures in the world and
the tape that holds together the pieces
my life: glass from my grandmother's shelf in the window
glued to scraps of khadi, smudged with the grime of an el train
the smell of perfumed shit.

The Battle Cry of an Ex-Battered Ex-Wife!

HUMA DAR

I am not half of a couple,
 not the better half,
 not the fairer half,
 not the weaker half.
I am whole
I too am human
You do not own my soul
You could not!
You do not own my body
You can not!
You do not own my mind
You dare not!
You do not own my destiny
You will not!

Not a million beatings, no searing pain
can flog my spirit or smother my voice.
No torture, no assault, no chain
can shackle my mind in fear again.
 No! Never ever again!

The day I killed my fear of your violence
with my own bare hands
 was the day I was born again.
The day I told the world of your misdeeds
 was the day I found my voice again.
The day I stood up for my rights in the courts
 was the day I discovered my feet again.

Beware!
For every Pharaoh, a Moses!
Until I save my children, myself, and this world from you
I will never rest again!

Cloud 26:
"Will you play my hand?"

RINI DAS

Flakes of wry cynics play on
At the bridge table.
You have the sense of stargazing
Nailed to the ground.
Or maybe otherwise.
Who knows.

I look into your toes, and see
That the virtual is original;
And the real in sleep
Surrogates the desire in our loss.
The loss of faith and the simple
Overtones of trust.

Do endure the space, while
Tyme revolves on with
A torso, stuck and edged with
Randomness.
"Why, may I ask?" you say.
"What happened to the lined
Pillows and the fractions we shared?"

Gopal Nights

KESHINI KASHYAP

There is something in the scent of a mortal sun-skin
Which reminds her of an awakening
From the depths of slumber and
From Gopal nights of her past
Sweet, pallid years
She assumes the form of Ganga and cascades from his hair
From his glorious blue-black skin
Into the depths of an ashram
Once and for all

Aroused by a scent, a mouth, a body,
She discovers answers to a thousand questions
The strangeness of her soul, her heart, her will
She says she is the ocean queen
The goddess of saltiness and strength

Gopis of the past nights call—what were
The paths of red clay and stone taken
Followed and wept over?
She could not love the rocks of her dreams
Just as one cannot make a lover of the wind
A god
An immortal
She cries
And asks him kindly not to hold her in his matted locks
She unleashes the water
For the night to share and make joy in her earthy salt

Death Is The Spring
In Every Dancer's Toe

KAMAL KAPUR

Oh Krishna
your pellucid eye
I saw roiled
with confusion

when you returned
unexpectedly after having gone
and saw me dancing
naked on the banks
of the Jamuna

and saw how it wasn't
a dance of sorrow

(though there's
no denying death
is the spring in every
dancer's toes)

saw how I howled with joy
at the river's rush and roar
its raging lust to pass

eternally

and beat my chest
as if a hollow drum
and made some music there

my eye was pellucid
that day, O Krishna

in which I saw

how every anguish is a door
before which the weak weep
but whose knob your lovers seize
and enter
countries where death is the tongue
of delight

Pati Dev

PUNAM LUTHRA

My father always said he was blessed by having three daughters, three devis born into his house. We were our dad's mandir and he never made us feel that we were a burden. But, ever since I can remember, our relatives have questioned my parents about how they expected to provide daj for not one but three daughters. I have been told that one of the reasons we came to America was that my parents wanted me and my two sisters to have a good education and therefore, in their eyes, lead a prosperous life. Although my family left India when I was only six, my parents constantly reinforced that we were Indian women and we were going to marry Indian men. The yearly trips to India, the language, the meals, our religion, the decoration pieces, the pictures on the wall, and the constant family discussions reinforced the unsaid. I grew up idolizing our culture, our religion and our people. Mom recited myths, sang songs about the women of Gita and the Devatas on the white horses. I saw great marriages full of love and respect. We were told that we would carry on the tradition of arranged marriages and how our husbands would bring us love, prosperity and, foremost, security.

I always knew I would get married but I kept putting it off to pursue my career. It was only after Dad expressed his wish to see me, his eldest daughter, married that I began to seriously consider it. Dad's health had deteriorated because of a car accident that left him paralyzed, and my mom's health was just as uncertain due to colitis. I felt obligated to carry out their wishes.

Mom called me at work one day. She said some distant friends, who had agreed to mediate, had found a boy for me. The family saw my bio-data and photograph and were anxious to meet me. My parents asked me to come home the following weekend and meet the boy and his family. Though I wavered, I pictured my dad and had no choice but to agree. I asked my mother the standard questions about him. I was adamant that one or two meetings were not enough for me to make a decision. My family said that they and the mediators had more experience than I did. Still, they reassured me that I would have some time to get to know him.

His name was Sanjay Gupta. He and his family came for tea, the traditional meeting time for such occasions. I sat in a separate room away from the living room where Sanjay and his family were. I became more curious as I listened attentively to what was going on in the other room. My heart raced when I heard the mediator praise Sanjay. I was beginning to feel uncomfortable about the entire situation. I felt like I was going to be on trial and that he had the power to accept or reject me. When the mediator came to ask me if I was ready, I wanted to run. She primped my hair, straightened out the last pleat in my chunni, that one dropped pleat might be a cause for rejection, and made sure I looked perfect. I just tried to smile.

I walked into the room and folded my hands and said, "Namaste." My chair was purposefully stationed right in the center of the room. I was a showpiece to be seen. I really had no more strength to stand. My breathing was strained and my legs gave out. I was happy I landed safely in the chair. Soon, the conversation began and I managed to make everyone laugh. Sanjay, my prospective husband, was laughing the most. I got the courage to look at him when no one else was looking. He was smiling at me. He was six foot, well groomed, innocent-looking, soft-spoken. After just one meeting he had charmed me.

A few days later, Sanjay asked me out for the evening. I accepted, as I accepted all his invitations after that. We both knew that the purpose of our dates centered around the possibility of marriage. This was not just a casual date. He proposed soon after we began to see each other, and I said yes.

Although I still didn't feel like I knew Sanjay well, I convinced myself that he was perfect for me. As my relatives continually reminded me, I had to move forward. I forced myself to put aside any doubts. Why put my parents through any more anguish, I thought. They could be relieved of one burden and die in peace seeing me established.

Wedding plans began seconds after my announcement. I saw peace and relief in Dad's face. Everyone was happy, it all seemed worth it. Dad asked Sanjay's mother if she had any expectations. She was silent for a minute, collecting her thoughts, then she said "I only want the wedding to be something to remember, the arrangements have to be perfect." Dad reassured my future mother-in-law that the wedding would be nothing short of spectacular.

Relatives from both sides came from India for the marriage. It was more and more exciting for me. By now, in my naivete, I had created Sanjay into a perfect man. I was even looking forward to getting married. In retrospect, I had no choice to build a bond with Sanjay because the decision had been made, and there was no turning back. I was expected to develop feelings, so I did. My beliefs were so strongly ingrained that somehow I did not let myself hesitate.

My parents had been waiting for the day of the Sagan to welcome their new son and to join our families. As was traditional, Dad had happily given each of the family members gifts of cash, clothing and gold. Therefore it came as a surprise to my mother when Yadav Mama pulled her aside and asked her if we had discussed the dowry demands, because he sensed some unhappiness. She told Yadav Mama that all the Guptas wanted was a beautiful wedding and we were carrying our their wishes. Meanwhile, my mother-in-law, Raj, and her sister were sitting beside me and discussing other weddings. I heard dowry being mentioned several times, but I did not pick up the hints. They would say, "I went to so-and-so's wedding and they gave the groom a house and a car, his life was set. It was so cute!..." I thought it was just conversation. My attention was focused on Sanjay, but he did not say much to me. I convinced myself that he must be nervous being the center of attention.

I returned to my parents' house to get ready for my new home. I hurriedly packed my clothes because the wedding was in three days and I still needed to complete the preparations. In the rush, I almost forgot that my birthday was three days before the wedding. I was in heaven when Sanjay asked me to come up so we could celebrate my birthday together. When I arrived, Sanjay had flowers and balloons and gift after gift. I felt so lucky to have a man who cared so much. However, towards the end of the night Sanjay began snapping at me. I thought

258

he was tense because the wedding was so soon. I had just moved my suitcases into 'his' home, so I assumed he was probably grieving the loss of his freedom.

We had planned that I would stay the night because we needed to get up early to finalize the arrangements. He gave me his bedroom and said good night. I closed the door and fell on the bed happily exhausted, forgetting his tension. I thought, this house is my mandir now, where a new life was about to begin for me. Sanjay knocked on the door. I thought he had forgotten something. I opened the door and without warning he lunged forward, grabbed me by the neck and threw me against the wall. My head hit the wall with force. He held me in place by the neck and the weight of his body. Then, he pulled out a measuring tape and measured me. I was in complete shock. Not knowing how to react, I could not help but to cry. He released me after keeping me wedged against the wall for what seemed like an eternity. In the middle of my hysteria, I begged him to tell me why he had done this. He responded by saying, "I wanted to know how tall you were." His attitude was nonchalant and he ignored my emotional state. He just walked out of the room leaving me crying. I cried all night. However, by morning I decided that I should put the incident behind me. It would never happen again. He is nervous, I told myself, forget it all. He had been so wonderful up to now, why blow one incident out of proportion, especially two days before the wedding.

The next morning Sanjay woke up with a smile on his face and he seemed excited about visiting the wedding site. I pretended as if nothing had ever happened. I had thought about telling my family and even calling off the wedding, but I knew it would bring shame upon us. All my relatives and friends had already begun to fly in for the festivities. All I could feel was that the family name would be smeared by the community. In my confusion, I didn't even want to acknowledge that Sanjay had actually done this. I decided that I had to cope with the situation by forgetting it ever happened. Sanjay was going to be my husband and I couldn't blemish his image, in anyone's eyes, especially my own. Foremost, I had a loyalty to him. His shame would become my shame. I decided I would never tell anyone. It was a secret I would die with. Early in life I saw how Indian women put their husband, their families and their children before themselves. They bore the burden of maintaining the family name at all costs. But a husband could do no wrong because he was the God.

The wedding day arrived. I had worked so hard to make sure that Raj's wishes were to be carried out. Our home was full of festivity that day. There was a suitcase of gifts for Sanjay and his parents. I saw my father stuffing envelope after envelope with numerous amounts of one hundred dollar bills, a now familiar sight at all the wedding ceremonies. We were blessed to have the opportunity to be generous.

Our guests were eagerly anticipating the arrival of the baraat. When Sanjay and his family arrived we were informed that they insisted on seeing Dad before performing the Milni. However, Dad's lack of mobility due to the wheelchair made it very difficult to go down the steep driveway. Only after half an hour did they concede to come up so the Milni ceremony could be performed. I later learned that the family had wanted Dad to go down because they were going to demand a house and money or they would withdraw their offer for marriage.

After the Milni, Sanjay and I sat in a gazebo while the pundit prepared for the fire ceremony. Because Sanjay had seemed confused during the Milni, I explained that it was a ceremony uniting two families as one. And more significantly, when we put garlands on each

other we accepted each other as husband and wife. To my confusion and surprise he became angry and yelled, "Why didn't anyone tell me that Milni meant marriage?!" I stayed quiet, thinking that anything I said might provoke him. The pundit was escorted to the mandup, the fire ceremony was ready to take place. Sanjay brushed off my uncle when he came to take us to the mandup. Hurt and embarrassed by his arrogance, I quietly said, "Sanjay everyone is waiting, we should go." He responded by shouting, "I'll go when I'm ready to go!" His reaction made me cry. Seconds later he jumped up and walked to the mandup without me. I followed a few steps behind. This entire incident became symbolic of my life with my Devata.

We took our rounds around the fire, and we made our vows. Sanjay repeated the words, but I did not know whether he knew their significance. He was abrupt with me and my family at the wedding reception. Family and friends noticed his unnatural behavior but they all kept silent because it was too late. They did not want to hurt my new family or me. Relatives heard Sanjay's family telling each other that there was probably nothing else coming to them, other than what was at the wedding. I had to delay my cake cutting ceremony because Raj was drunk and we had to wait for her to sober up.

My family became very emotional when the Doli was ready to leave. Sanjay and I entered the limo which was to take us to my new home. No sooner had the doors shut when Sanjay began complaining. We entered our new home with Sanjay shouting about his back. Without even turning towards me to say goodnight, he lay immobile all night. He was still angry and I was too afraid to ask why. Maybe he is tired, I told myself, things will be better in the morning. I decided the wedding had been beautiful and now I was Mrs. Sanjay Gupta. No one could take the pleasure of those words or Sanjay from me.

Before leaving the next day for our honeymoon, we made the traditional visit to my in-law's home. I pictured that Sanjay's family was going to receive me with warmth and smiles. I had another mother now who would nurture me and call me her daughter. But when I arrived at Raj's house, all I felt was hostility. In the entire time I was there, there was no mention of the wedding. It was as if it never happened and therefore, I never happened. Sanjay and Raj kept eyeing each other as if they needed to talk, it seemed as if I was in their way. I felt like an outsider, not a daughter.

On our way to the airport, I was very quiet. Sanjay asked me what was wrong. I was hesitant but Sanjay insisted that I be honest with him. Finally I asked, "Sanjay, what was wrong at the wedding? Did I offend your family? Why was your mother so aloof?" He responded to my honesty by blaming me, "It was all your fault, you can't do anything right!" Then he withdrew and punished me further by refusing to speak to me. This became a very typical reaction. He would badger me for the truth, but he was too insecure to listen to it. He considered it an attack. I was always made to feel bad for upsetting him, and soon I learned to apologize even when there was no reason.

On the honeymoon Sanjay asked why title papers to a house were not given. He then repeated that his mother had warned him that if a house was not given in the daj, my parents would never give him one. I was thrown off guard because this was the first time I had heard such demands being voiced. He said he knew through the mediators that Dad had property and since he was the first son-in-law, he deserved and was entitled to the papers. I was completely stunned. But it all made sense now, his reaction, Raj and her family's reaction,

the taunting, the distance. He ordered me to ask my parents for the property. I refused. Sanjay began torturing me, first by denying any sort of relationship or romance on the honeymoon. When I still did not give in, he resorted to slapping me and inducing fear.

Once we returned from our trip, Sanjay would continually pester me to ask Dad for the property. I refused and the beatings and emotional torturing began. One morning I was kicked out of bed with both of his legs and at such force that I flew onto the floor. Another day he picked me up and threw me across the floor so I that I landed bottom first. Many times he propelled me against walls, purposely, so he could hear the sound of my head hitting the wall. Daily the violence escalated and no matter how much I tried to be perfect for him, I could not escape his wrath. I could never predict what would set him off; even the slightest motion could evoke his rage. Two weeks into our marriage he repeatedly threw a telephone at my head. Sanjay used anything within reach, cups, pillows and other items as a weapon. My only response was crying, but soon I learned that it only intensified his anger. After a few weeks, I learned to run to anywhere in the house, up and down the stairs, to escape him in hopes that he would calm down or even have less energy to beat me once he caught me.

One time I locked myself in our bedroom, waiting for him to calm down. Instead he kicked in the door, splitting it in half. Coming close to my face he said, "Ugly bitch!" and repeated the chant until he foamed at the mouth like a mad dog. I realized then that there was no escape and the only way to react to his anger was to quietly endure his rage. It was as if there was an internal "on-off" switch, which I was a victim to. One second he would be laughing and the next he would be yelling. His behavior was unpredictable and I lived in constant fear. I did notice though that once he had beaten me, he was able to relax. Afterwards, he would sleep like a baby.

His rage had become extremely violent; there was no stopping him and I would let the beatings happen shielding not my body, but my mind away from the pain. I was thrown from a flight of stairs because, according to Sanjay, I was rude to his mother. She saw my bruises and when I asked her what I was doing wrong she would say, "You treat my son so badly, you're trying to separate us..." When I denied their accusations, he would take me home so he could abuse me. Once while he was tearing my clothing to shreds, he yelled, "You have no respect for what a husband is. You have to listen to me. You're not Indian," and he continued his barrage until he temporarily paralyzed me. I suffered in silence so no one would ever know of the beast that lived inside him. His hands around my neck, choking me, was symbolic of his desire to take away any remnant of my consciousness. The monster's existence was enhanced by the fact that he justified all these incidents because he was "Pati Dev."

I was expected to make extravagant meals made from scratch. For example, I would get up early in the mornings and make enchiladas. My tortillas, beans, salsa were all from scratch. Then there was breakfast of fresh squeezed orange juice, crepes, hash browns, etc. These were the easy meals; dinner was much more extravagant. During the first four months of our marriage when I worked, he purposefully increased his expectations so that I would not be able to meet them. Because I had to work within his inconsistent constraints, I was unable to hold down the job he 'allowed' me to have. By the end of the marriage, I was not allowed to work and had no access to money (in which, detailed accounting and receipts were kept). The worst part was that I was not allowed to speak or have any contact with my family.

Somehow after the wedding, I was to cut off my relationship with my family. They were now evil, according to Sanjay, because they disrespected him by not giving him a car or a house. He and Raj made me feel crazy for loving my family. But I was afraid to speak up because there would be more arguments. I could not let the relationship end in divorce. Instead I forced my feelings within, while longing for contact with my family, if only to keep my sanity.

After a year of torture I gave in to the pressure, I conveyed Sanjay's demands for dowry: a Mercedes, a house, cash, a trip around the world and, finally, sole control over my dad's property. My father asked me what he should do. I was so saddened by the fact that he was actually willing to give into all of Sanjay's demands, jeopardizing the family's future just to save my marriage. And even if my family fulfilled the demands there was no assurance that the marriage would last, especially because he constantly threatened to divorce me.

I felt that if Sanjay wanted to stay with me that it should be because he loved me, not because of the financial gain. Despite the abuse, I still felt dependent on him and I convinced myself that what he was giving me was love and security. Besides he assured me that no one would ever consider me as a whole human being again if he divorced me. "You're used, you've been tainted. No one's going to marry you again when I divorce you!…" It did not matter that his mother had been divorced three times; he felt justified in his hypocrisy. I would never be equal to his mother, who could do no wrong, in fact he wanted me to fulfill the role of the stereotypical, traditional Indian wife. He lived in denial of his mother's divorces and continuously lied to me about his family while condemning mine.

Within a few months of marriage I had seen numerous doctors, jumping from one doctor to another so no one doctor would become wise to my situation. Often Sanjay would accompany me to the hospital to be sure I did not say anything. Declared anorexic, I was loosing not only weight, but my mind. Sanjay continued to tell me that I created all the problems. Sanjay's family was perfect. I was crazy and I could not do anything right. They openly discussed the option of institutionalizing me. I was terrified that they might be able to manipulate me into an institution, similar to what they had done to Sanjay's brother. They suggested that I divorce Sanjay so they could maintain their appearances in the community. Sanjay would then have a chance to remarry and get the dowry that I was not providing. I felt that divorce and death were synonymous with each other. My chances for remarriage within my community would become very difficult. I was 'used,' not the pure Indian bride that everyone wanted. Six months after our marriage, he began saying, "You're so ugly, why don't you commit suicide? Go ahead…"

By the end of my marriage, I could not discern between his reality and the truth. His constant threats of divorce were encouraged by other women who said that Sanjay was a good catch. His abusive tones over my appearance and depiction of my self-worth as Zero made survival difficult. But I continued within my marriage because I had two younger sisters that had to be married. If I was divorced their chances for marriage would become difficult within the community. My parents had suffered so many tragedies in his life, I could not inflict any more agony. There would be so much shame that my family and I would have to endure. My family would have to bear the burden and consequences of divorce along with me.

Was I not a Devi? Our entire mythology, culture and thinking revolves around the goddess in the Vedas. Every object, whether animate or inanimate, is associated with the

female gender. No prayer is complete without a woman. Ideally, the culture and religions are all so beautiful, so deep. Why must they be tainted by such hypocrisy?

I faced the hypocrisy daily in my life with Sanjay. My love and devotion was all one sided. Fourteen months after the marriage Sanjay filed for divorce. Even before I knew, my in-laws drove to my parents house and informed them that we would soon be divorced. It was a bombshell for my parents. I was the last to learn of the divorce. I begged Sanjay not to file for divorce but he laughed at me. He informed me that he was going to remarry within a year. I had not even been served the papers and he was already talking of remarriage.

When I thought of the impending divorce I could only think that I had let everyone down. I had let Mom, Dad and most of all my husband and his family down. I lost the only and the most important thing in my life. How could I continue on with life? I didn't know how I would ever show my face to the world. I didn't know what more I could have done to save my marriage, still thinking that somehow I would have been able to. For fourteen months I endured his pain and torture, both of the mind and body. I felt when we separated no one would believe my side of the story. I was confused whether I wanted him to leave me to face the shame.

Before we separated Sanjay and I had an argument that went out of control. The abuse had escalated to the point of animal rage. He told me he was going to kill me. I had no doubts that he would carry out the threat. I lived in enough terror to know that this was an unusual situation so for the first time I called the police. I managed to lock him out of the house so I would be safe until the police came. They quickly arrested him when they arrived. One of the police officers handed me a card. It was of an abuse shelter. Up to this time I never told a soul of the abuse. It was the first time someone said, "You are not crazy, he is."

Sanjay was one of the first Indian men to be prosecuted. Luckily, the court system was very good to me. I was relieved that the truth was out and someone believed me. From that time on, I knew that I needed to share my experience. I had to go through this type of pain so I could help other women in abuse situations. Now, I speak out boldly in the community. I found that battle continued after my divorce when my community turned their back on me when I asked for help. All my fears came true, there was no sympathy for me. My mother-in-law had status in the community, she had friends and connections. I was made out to be the crazy one and the liar. It hurt me that my community turned away from their daughters.

It takes a lot of courage to defy your community, to speak the truth to deaf ears. A scapegoat is always a simple and easy solution. They deny the evidence and the woman's pain and tears, and so they deny the woman a chance to heal. Women like me have only one option. We need to fight back but there is no way to do it alone. I speak to the community, but it saddens me when they call the victim a liar. As an Indian woman I sacrificed my life in the most violent manner. I endured the violence because I did not have the resources to survive. I was victimized twice, once by my husband and second by the community. I continue to survive only because of the love of my family and friends. Justice will come to me when people not only hear, but listen to and believe my story.

we're not mean,
we're just hardheaded

RUXANA MEER

emerging from insecure positions within the context of our own ethnic communities
as girl children muted someone always asks
can't you control what comes outta your mouth?
to give depth to the intellectual pursuit of happiness followed so effortlessly by the
surrounding dominantly white student body
examining the circumstances forming the basis of our marginalization
we got permission to do this and call it our work
knowing the importance of being self-reliant as a female child.

you better shut up precious
or i'll knock your head off your shoulders
it'll roll down onto the ground and those birds will eat it
how you gonna knock someone's head off and say you didn't do it?

people don't get used to violence and abuse
not my mama either
after my years of childhood
she finally got permission to go outside and play
woman will get out when
she sees her daughter driving the getaway car
she doesn't believe it happened to her own life
so every detail unravels the plot

she finally gave herself permission
she said write about what girls have to know
is not a sleeping beauty and the beast story
and someone else/a woman who supposes her own self
the model of female independence tells her
alla these years while the going was good you was with him
now that it's not so good you left him
but it wasn't even all that
there was nothing left over
the family is still hungry and no hunger is easy

the whole day pacing back and forth
the lioness has surprising strength/the food freshly killed
without regret
each mother passes on the strategy for survival
so i don't lose how to be beautiful without lies
or get bitter waiting
when i don't want to kiss a beast outta kindness to make him better
don't havta
i got a permission slip right here in my pocket

now you show me yours
who took it from you?
show not tell
do not be afraid
say that you will never leave yourself woman
do not be nervous
show me you know you have permission to be here
ask him to get out of your house
when he blames you/defines you
tries to throw you through the threshold
then tell me your secrets
do not be afraid
say you gotta cry now
show yourself your beautiful big threatening mouth
our collective visibility and individual stability
means our differences
are like tissues to wipe each tear
at the point of departure

we are not just good performers
from the import love film industry
but extra large scientific magnifying glasses staring
using the sunshine to burn a hole straight thru
whoever is about to knock her head off is in trouble
because we got permission to turn people in
to the proper authorities/which is us/at this time

how you gonna say we sneak around
when you stole the knob to the front door?
we got our maps on our bodies
street names after street walkers
coming after a whole bunch of protective

services who don't detect anything wrong while it is going on
while in the meantime you got your hands up her shirt
so you don't realize/we're coming back/now you hear us singing

you wrote us off in a language of forgery
we got a note that say to get our baby sisters
we got permission to stay up all night if we have to
we do our homework together

my parents talked about school
so much because no one can take away your education it is everlasting
so don't look at us you'll never regret it
what about the irreversible side effects?
coming back talking a million miles an hour not saying anything
so young and so seriously worried

who's the hottest?MEEEEEE i'm the hottest
who want to cover their body in water?MEEEE
who want to drink cold juice?MEEEEE

old enough to go out by ourselves/be alone/meet
when we give ourselves permission to be unsupervised/unadulterated
to hear what our stories sound like after all this traveling.

Mississippi Masala *and* Khush:
Redefining Community

DHARINI RASIAH

The South Asian American community is on the verge of a new identity, one that is a response to the growing numbers in the community, the increased violence that has been focused on South Asians and the intersection of diverse immigrant experiences. Very few scholars have attempted to place South Asian Americans within a conceptual framework as immigrants in America, and many who have perpetuate the perceived homogeneity of the group as a wealthy, educated, professional elite. Two films by South Asian women, *Mississippi Masala* (1992) and *Khush* (1991), attempt to redefine the community by presenting a broader, more complex analysis that shifts the focus to working-class, lesbian/gay and women's voices.

South Asians have been subjected to stereotypes not unlike those used to define other Asian Americans by the mainstream media. The people of this 'model minority' ethnic group are alternately defined as economically successful or as exotic and mysterious foreigners steeped in their Eastern traditions.[1] Though the Immigration Act of 1965 invited many South Asian students and professionals into the country (for the benefit of the U.S. economy), there are countless numbers of other South Asians residing here who don't fit this category. In order to create one story that can easily be placed within immigration history, scholars have seldom pointed to the disparities within the South Asian immigrant experience. This homogenizing denies the diversity within group identity and contributes to the creation of false assumptions. Barbara Christian points to a disturbing lack of thoroughness among scholarly writers and researchers in their attempts to create a new theory that includes previously underrepresented ethnic groups:

> Constructs like the center and periphery reveal that tendency to want to make the world less complex by organizing it according to one principle, to fix it through an idea which is really an ideal. Many of us are particularly sensitive to monolithism since one major element of ideologies of dominance, such as sexism and racism, is to dehumanize people by stereotyping them, by denying them their variousness and complexity.[2]

As the community grows and as interethnic confrontations become inevitable, it is critical that the differences are identified and that the image of South Asians as solely a privileged group dissipates.

Film is a medium that has come to represent the social and political identity of communities and can challenge existing ideologies. Though the film industry has generally been open to the recent influx of minority works, filmmakers are often forced by the pressures of producers and market audiences to create generalizations and perpetuate stereotypes in order to sell their work. *Mississippi Masala*, directed by Mira Nair, is the only film about the South Asian American experience that has reached the mainstream American audience. Though Mira Nair presents some generalizations about South Asians and African Americans, in an effort to unite the communities, she focuses on one particular Indian family with the intention of representing the normally invisible experiences of women and the working class, as well as introducing the South Asian immigrant experience to an American audience.

Set in rural Mississippi, the film explores the interracial relationship between Mina, an Indian woman, and Demetrius, an African American man, in the context of growing hostilities between the two groups. Though the relationship itself is somewhat superficial, it is a tool for Mira Nair to reconcile the differences between the two communities by describing the antagonism and anticipating an increased tolerance. Bagla explains,

> While the length and directness of the love scene might offend the sensibilities of some Indians, these same people will not be able to deny the similarity between Demetrius' family relationships and those that exist in an Indian household.[3]

The South Asian community has not reacted uniformly to the film. The problem lies within the representation of the community that is depicted. Some are particularly offended by the very nature of the stereotypes—emasculation of the South Asian male, exotic images of the women, the prevalence of the greedy businessmen, etc. Others appreciate Mira Nair's attempt to introduce the issues, however distorted, to mainstream America. Inarguably, the film's greatest merit is its critically-timed release that begins to examine and deflect the growing anti-South Asian sentiment among other ethnic communities.

In an effort to depict the prevalence of multicultural experiences among South Asians and the possibilities for interracial communication, Mira Nair recognizes the phenomenon of multiple migrations within the South Asian diaspora. "Mina is the masala, the Indian born in Africa, raised in England, living in Greenwood. 'My parents are my home,' she says."[4] Her parents have strong attachments to Africa where they were born and raised but realize that their expulsion from the country was directly related to their race. In explaining to Mina the difficulties of interracial relationships, her father states,

> "You know why we left? Because after 34 years, it all came down to the color of my skin. That's why we left...People stick to their own kind. You're forced to accept that when you grow older. I'm only trying to spare you the pain."[5]

The rootlessness that South Asians often feel because of the lack of attachments to South Asia negates the notion that there exists a single South Asian identity that descends from one specific geographic location. The complexity of multiple migrations and interethnic

conflict in Africa creates a further depth to the South Asian experience. Mina and her parents find themselves expressing as deep a connection to Ugandan culture as they feel to their Indian identity.

In the context of a white and often hostile society, South Asians are increasingly forced to examine interethnic conflict. There are several growing white supremacist groups who target South Asians; the most visible is named the 'Dot Busters.' But as the white power structure, through the media, continues to perpetuate stereotypes of people of color, interethnic conflict takes place between members of different communities of color and is exacerbated on a working-class level, while white society remains unscathed. In *Mississippi Masala*, an Indian hotel owner remarks to Demetrius,

> "Black, brown, yellow, Mexican, all the same. As long as you're not white, means you're colored. Isn't that so? You are a good man. All us people of color must stick together. United we stand, divided we fall."[6]

When the South Asian community does not recognize its own multiplicity of experiences, especially the existence of the working class, there is no basis for unity among themselves nor for union with other ethnic groups. The South Asian community is no longer dominated by the professionals who were targeted by the U.S. government in the 1965 Immigration Act.[7] South Asians now comprise a large portion of the work force in the service sector: restaurants, motels, and convenience stores. In New York, over fifty percent of the taxi drivers are South Asians.

Though *Mississippi Masala* begins to examine the economic framework of interethnic conflict in the U.S., it ignores the grim details of this conflict and focuses on the similarities between the African American community and the South Asian American community. Mina embodies a mixture of associations. She defies the expectations that have been rigidly placed on South Asian women by the community as well as by white society. This dark-complected character challenges the universal standard of beauty: that lighter-skinned women are the ideal. She also solidifies the fact that there is a working-class South Asian experience. She is depicted scrubbing toilets in their family run motel as well as dancing in cornfields with her African American boyfriend (both fully outfitted in ethnic clothing). *Mississippi Masala* offers to the South Asian community a very different representation in film than they most commonly see in Indian Hindi films.

Gita Sen argues that Indian women in film have been forced into a position of powerlessness:

> The growth of the film image of Indian woman-as-sex-object presents however a paradox for our argument that the commodity form is less responsible here for the sex objectification of women. Commercial Indian film has precisely been using female sexuality in order to sell a commodity—itself.[8]

South Asians worldwide have been heavily influenced by the Hindi film, a form of communication that reaches a wider audience than any other medium. Because American

society expects immigrants to conform to a white-European cultural ideal, the South Asian immigrant community turns to these films as a reinforcement of traditional thought and images. What they see are images that celebrate the sexualized and submissive role of women, as well as the wealth of the elite. Transposed to the U.S., these images perpetuate the same message: South Asian people must maintain a traditional society that preserves the illusion of the idealized world they left back in their homelands. Women in the films come to represent this cultural link. Images of women that reject the assigned roles have marked an implicit betrayal against the community which has relied on the preservation of tradition.

The changing images of South Asian women in film are largely a result of women filmmakers emerging from the community. Their films require a refocusing on its structure. Every frame represents a meaningful vision, one of redefinition and innovation by the filmmaker:

> Making films from a different stance supposes 1) a re-structuring of experience and a possible rupture with patriarchal filmic codes and conventions; 2) a difference in naming—the use of familiar words and images, and of familiar techniques in contexts whose effect is to displace, expand or change their preconceived, hegemonically accepted meanings.[9]

While Mira Nair uses more conventional techniques—though with a centering on the South Asian woman—in *Khush*, Pratibha Parmar explores the issue of sexuality through experimental camera work and offers a visually stimulating film.

The conservatism that permeates the South Asian community is deeply rooted in tradition. Nair and Parmar attempt to redefine the community in order to promote positive changes within the structure of South Asian society. Often when South Asians emigrate from their country of origin they attempt to preserve the culture by rigidly holding to the values that were prevalent at the time of their departure. But in reality, society in South Asia has changed and in many ways has become more permissive, while the immigrant communities remain generally unwilling to accept a non-heterosexual, middle-class existence. As *Mississippi Masala* points to the realities of class differences, *Khush* brings to the surface issues of sexuality.

Khush presents lesbian, gay, and bisexual issues and even further creates a more diverse definition of the South Asian community. It also offers a sense of solidarity to those who might be in the process of exploring their identity.

> *Khush*, (an Urdu word meaning ecstatic pleasure), deals with moving coming-out testimonies from South Asian lesbians and gay men living in Britain, North America and India, who speak of the pain of being ostracized from their deeply traditional communities and the exhilaration of discovering their sexuality.[10]

In order to preserve the integrity of the community, many South Asians have repressed homosexuality as one of the many acts of protection from the severe racism against their community. This repression is intricately linked to the history of colonialism in South Asia, and as the community begins to reject the past injustices of British rule, the men and women

270

in *Khush* suggest that a return to a pre-colonial South Asian value system is necessary. As they recount their stories of discrimination from within the community, they are often able to describe in detail the violence perpetrated against South Asian people as they become the targets of racism and homophobia.

In South Asia there is a general acceptance of displays of affection (though not sexual) between the same sexes. There is also a large lesbian and gay community in South Asia; in India, there "are over eighty million lesbians and gay men...more than the population of Great Britain."[11] South Asian art reflects a two thousand-year-old history of the glorification of homosexuality, and only with the mass destruction of these forms of expression by British colonialism has doubt been cast over the acceptability of an alternative sexuality. The British have significantly imposed their moral principles on South Asian values by destroying those images that have shown explicit homosexual acts. *Khush* explores the various art forms that have escaped colonialism and according to one, "this expression of sexuality is critical for South Asian gays and lesbians. We need our own definitions of gay because our history is different."[12] Others argue that the word 'lesbian' is rooted in western language (lesbos) and is further alienating to the community.

Khush addresses both the mainstream South Asian community as well as those gay men and women who are afraid to expose their identity. The pressures of South Asian society dictate that one get married, have children and maintain an upwardly-mobile lifestyle. For South Asian gays and lesbians, this becomes more problematic:

"After I went to my cousin's wedding and saw how it united the family, I found myself thinking about finding a nice Indian man I could cut an arrangement with. He'd have his girlfriends and I'd have mine. I couldn't believe I was thinking this after being out and happy for four years!"[13]

Due to the constraints of immigration, South Asians in the diaspora have become conservative and inward-looking which necessitates the institution of marriage as a central process in preserving identity. For many, especially the immigrant and first generations, it is of great importance to retain the culture as they adjust to their new environment. *Khush* offers South Asians some insight into why gay South Asian men and women are forced to hide their sexuality. It also offers some reassurance that homosexuality and the preservation of tradition do not have to be diverging values. According to one woman, her preference for South Asian women is steeped in her love for the people and culture.

Khush proves that racism in the U.S., as well as in other white hegemonic cultures, has largely defined the responses South Asian gays and lesbians have elicited in their coming-out processes. South Asians have commonly settled in white neighborhoods, creating a link between community survival and repression of sexual identities. "The daily racism my family experienced in Canada's suburbs and in school was incredible...The issue was survival and that meant acting as straight as possible and even as white as possible."[14] Growing up in white communities, South Asian gay men and lesbians often depend on the support they can get from their family, who share, at least, a commonality in heritage that becomes of immediate importance in the face of white racism. The bonding in communities becomes an act of protection. As one gay man explains, "for an Asian man to come out, he needs to be

able to deal with the racism on his own because his community isn't going to accept him."[15] For South Asian women, *Khush* is particularly empowering. *Mississippi Masala* does not fully diverge from the more traditional aspects of the expectations of the woman as mother, nurturer and carrier of tradition. But *Khush* presents women as fully autonomous, having overcome male authority disguised as conformist societal pressures. Pratibha Parmar is continually creating powerful images of women through her films, particularly within the South Asian community, by examining the process of self-determination. Parmar's ability to create this low-budget film rested on the fact that her funding sources and producers did not adversely affect the film's content, as often is the occurrence in mainstream films.

Finally, the differences in class are isolated in *Khush* as a legitimate measure of group diversity. As *Mississippi Masala* gives some definition to the meaning of the working-class South Asian experience, *Khush* further examines this reality:

> We need to confirm the class issue in our representation of homosexuality. Because middle-class concepts and sensibilities are so prevalent, it becomes easy to define ourselves accordingly.[16]

In her article, "Sexuality, Lesbianism and South Asian Feminism," Anu articulates one aspect of the connection between class and lesbianism:

> "On a more day to day basis, many South Asian lesbians are compelled to submit to a heterosexual marriage. A few who cannot face the prospect and feel they have no options have been known to commit suicide together…The only women who stand a chance are those whose class position enables them some degree of control over their lives."[17]

Out of economic necessity, working-class South Asian lesbians and gays have challenged the forces that perpetuate divisions in society:

> "For me, being a lesbian is a fight against homophobia and a fight against the system that creates homophobia and that system is a class system. It's imperialist, it forces people to have to migrate to other parts of the world because of its own economic and other whims. It's a system that's racist and that is responsible for the racist incidents my family has experienced, as have all people of Asian and African descent. It is critical that I extend myself beyond my middle-class privileged experience so we can all come together, regardless of class, and change this system."[18]

Khush attempts to bring some resolution to the misconceptions many South Asians perpetuate in order to protect the community from racism. The film realizes that race is often inextricable from class and sexual differences.

A new consciousness permeates South Asian women's films, one that has been articulated by other women of color filmmakers. These films are necessarily built upon a

rejection of the powerless images of women perpetuated by mainstream Hindi films and by British and American-made films that glorify the colonial relationship. In seeking to shift the central voice to that of the woman, women of color have theorized that the first step is a dismantling of the patriarchy. bell hooks believes we "are taught that our relationships with one another diminish rather than enrich our experience."[19] Films by women about women reject this ideology, create an intimacy between the filmmaker, her subjects and her audience and offer a reconstruction of society. *Mississippi Masala* and *Khush*, to varying degrees, attempt to address the changes in the South Asian American community as well as bring to the surface realities that, however submerged, have always been present.

1. Edward Said, *Orientalism* (New York: Vintage Books, 1979), 222.

2. Barbara Christian, "The Race For Theory," *Cultural Critique* 6, 59. Also, "The Race For Theory," *Making Face, Making Soul/Haciendo Caras*, ed. Gloria Anzaldúa (San Francisco: Aunt Lute, 1990).

3. Bagla, "The New Masala," *India Currents*, February 1992, 17.

4. Dana Sachs, "East Meets West Down South," *San Francisco Chronicle Image Magazine*, 9 February 1992, 18.

5. From *Mississippi Masala*.

6. Ibid.

7. Joan Jensen, *Passage From India* (New Haven: Yale University Press, 1988), 280.

8. Gita Sen, "Subordination and Sexual Control," *Review of Radical Politics and Economics*, 16 (1984), 133.

9. Trinh Minh-Ha, *When the Moon Waxes Red* (New York: Routledge, 1991), 151.

10. Hema Nair, "South Asian Films By Women: 'Making It Personal,'" *Ms*. III. 3, 68.

11. From *Khush*.

12. Ibid.

13. Ibid.

14. Ibid.

15. Ibid.

16. Ibid.

17. Anu, "Sexuality, Lesbianism and South Asian Feminism," *Anamika*.

18. From *Khush*.

19. bell hooks, *Feminist Theory—From Margin to Center* (Boston: South End Press, 1984), 43.

The Graves Of Academe

INDIRA KARAMCHETI

Yankees live on familiar terms with their dead. Tombstones push up through the soil like teeth through gums. Graves dot the New England landscape, ubiquitous as mosquitoes after a rain, plentiful as salt on french fries. Death here is a casual matter.

Partly, it's just that there are so many dead here, so many mementos asking, no, demanding that we remember those who were but are no longer. Live elbows jostle for space with dry funny bones, living cheeks rub against jawbones with a calm bordering on contempt. "Living cheek by jowl" has a new, if macabre, meaning here. Graves are everywhere, in unexpected corners, poking up in the midst of the daily business of living.

There seem to be no clear boundaries between where the living live and the dead reside. To my newly transplanted Californian eyes, used to the strict segregation of like from unlike—shopping malls and tract homes, for example—there's something dauntingly, undiscriminatingly democratic in the motley mixing of the houses of the dead with the homes of the quick. Death should be set aside, at a remove from where we, who still can, move in our various comings and goings. Cemeteries, in my experience, are supposed to be some distance from business districts and residential areas, at the end of dead-end roads, landscaped in funereal trees like yews and weeping willows that grow nowhere else. You behave in certain solemn ways there, as you wear certain solemn clothes there, that you don't employ anywhere else.

In my experience, the dead are treated with as little fear as any other group in the general population. There are, it is true, a few large, orderly cemeteries like the ones I'm used to in California, with rows of gravestones like orchards waiting for harvest. But there are also smaller, disheveled ones, casually planted in someone's backyard, leaning up against a fence, standing still in hot forest clearings throbbing with cicadas. A friend of mine has just moved into an apartment in Middletown, where I now live. She loves her place and I love it, too. She loves the newness of it, the rich hardwood floors, the fresh paneling still smelling of sap. She loves her new kitchen because of its newness: new wallpaper, all black appliances, gleaming black tile counters and stainless steel sinks. I love it because of her kitchen window, into which graves grinningly peer, watching her toast bread in her shining black toaster oven, chattering companionably about the freshness of the vegetables in her sink, wishing her goodnight as she wipes off her gleaming counters. I still remember my shock when I first noticed that what I had previously assumed was a vacant, if somewhat littered lot next to her apartment building, in fact, contained the remnants of some dearly departeds' remains.

I have grown increasingly fond of New England graveyards since I've been here. I came to Middletown a year ago, hired by the English department of Wesleyan University to teach

274

postcolonial literature, or, as I sometimes like to think of it, p.c. lit. Although I came to the east coast most recently from California, I am a native of India, born and brought up there until the age of seven. Trained in the U.S., I teach material outside of the western literary canon—literatures from the colonies and former colonies of Africa, Asia, Latin America and the Caribbean. Wesleyan University is a small prestigious liberal arts college with exceptional, mostly highly privileged students and a longstanding tradition of political liberalism. It is committed to understanding and enacting multiculturalism; I feel welcome here both for what I teach and for what I am.

Admittedly, that welcome takes forms both wonderful and puzzling. A great deal of joy has been lavished on me since my arrival. When I walk down the street I am greeted on every side with smiles. Initially I wondered whether there were something comic about my self-presentation, but have since grown more confident that I am just inherently likable. My mere presence causes pleasure. I think this Californian "have a nice day" smiliness—surely uncharacteristic of the New England Scandinavian winter (how's this for climatic stereotypes?)—is a reaction to my "multicultural-ness." I am a "person of color," and as such, an occasion for joy. Sometimes I feel that I stand in for all the "other" people of the world and am inundated with a global multicontinental welcome, foiled of its proper destination. When I and my husband—a man of color—go for a walk with our children of color, we leave a tidal wake of joy behind us.

I take refuge from all this gladness by going for walks alone in the local graveyard attached to the Wesleyan campus, just to sober up. The cemetery is named Indian Hill Cemetery, an appellation which gives me an appropriate, and appropriately ironic, pleasure. I like being an Indian walking among the dead, none of whom are Indian, in a place named for Native Americans who were not Indian, despite the name, and none of whom are here either. The dizzying convolutions of this "Indianness" that isn't, tickle me. But by the time I have passed through the black, wrought-iron entrance gates, wound up the gently curving road, and arrived at the top of the hill to the grass knoll with its 360-degree view of the Connecticut hills, I feel I have understood something, something important about being an Indian woman working in the groves of U.S. academe.

The presence of these dead teaches me something. This cemetery isn't a memorial to the past; it is an incarnation of the strength and power of this society. The graves, their aesthetic styles, their disposition—all replicate in miniature this culture's internal structure. The older plots, especially, reveal its organization and its hierarchies. In a typical family plot, a tall, phallic obelisk memorializes the father; mother takes her place modestly behind and beside this erection, in the form of a smaller, flatter plaque; the children, usually dead at pathetically young ages, are ranged behind her in a series of baby tombstones that pop out of the ground like kernels of popcorn. There are even two monuments that are miniature mansions, complete with formal entries, to indicate the social class of their inhabitants. The cemetery is segregated; the ethnic groups have their own residential areas. There are no "Indians"; the Jews occupy a separate section; I doubt there are any African Americans here. The various aesthetic styles of the graves testify to the worldliness of this place of the dead. There are family graves adorned with elaborate Celtic crosses, others with streamlined art deco monuments. My favorite, just for its sheer whimsicality, is an art nouveau family: each

275

grave is marked with sections of a log cast in cement. The grooves of the bark, the tendrils of ivy trailing over the log, the rings in the cross-section, are all faithfully rendered in gray cement. There's even a cement bench, looking like a split log, for the visitor to sit on while he or she reflects upon these felled segments of the family tree.

This is a culture that does not want to let the past go, that tries to recast mortal flesh into stone. There is a great fear of losing that past, and a great desire to transmute it, to hang on to it somehow, to make the dead part of the experience of living. But the culture I come from, and to some extent represent, does not bury or otherwise attempt to preserve its dead; we burn the past. We erase the physical evidence that we once lived; we allow the flesh to evanesce. Loved or unloved, rich or poor, our dead are reduced to ashes and dust; that dust in its turn is left to the wind to be lifted and dispersed.

This difference, between a culture that fixes its past around it in visible form and one that looses its spirits to the breath of the wind, allows me to understand something about what I am and represent, what I'm doing here at Wesleyan, in both its difficulties and its importance. In a sense, I speak for those cremated ashes; I'm being asked to summon up the presence of the dead, or at least of the absent, the Indians, the Africans, the poor, the colonized, those who live in all those brightly colored and distant lands. Universities are, of course, another kind of mausoleum where the cultural past is buried and preserved for remembrance, meditation and ceremonial viewing. In the classrooms where I teach, the spirits of the dead speak in sepulchral tones from books great as tombs, tolling their own names: Shakespeare, Donne, T.S. Eliot. Their company has grown: names like Pyncheon, DeLillo, Morrison, Walker are now also sounded. The canon has expanded and I am being invited to expand it further, to inter my unconventional dead—Shoba De, Tsitsi Dangarembga, Efua Sutherland, Hanif Kureishi—in the graveyard. But this is both difficult to do and inherently false.

The cultural artifacts of other societies are not always possible to recover. They may be as evanescent as flesh turned to dust: oral stories, folk tales, stories whispered into the wind. Of course other cultures have their own ways of memorializing their pasts, their traditions, their genealogies. But we can only recover and accommodate what works in our own systems, what can be used in a literary canon, taught in the classroom. What cannot be fitted into those spaces remains as ungraspable as ashes floating in the air. Translating one culture into terms understandable by another is a cultural mixing of genres, as motley and undiscriminatingly democratic as the mixing of the dead and the living.

In my teaching, I am always conscious of the difficulty of accurately, vividly, translating the artifacts of another culture into Western terms and of the distortions that inevitably accompany such attempts. And I am also aware that at another, perhaps more powerful level, what my students come to me for has very little to do with what books I assign or what is said about them in the classroom. As an Indian woman teaching in a department of English, despite myself, I am the single, central, constantly reread text in my classroom. My students study me for clues, decipher me for cultural understanding, look to me for cultural references.

I stand in a peculiar relationship to what I teach: as a "foreign" woman, I am both the subject matter and the most reliable guide to that subject matter. As an Indian, I am one of "them," as much the real thing as an Indian Coke. This idea of my "otherness," my cultural difference, is the basis of my authority: I must know what I'm teaching because, after all, I

am the pukka, the gen-u-ine article. As a woman and as an Indian, I am simultaneously completely known to my students and an impenetrable mystery. I represent the extremes of glamour and squalor, the exotic woman, the pampered idol of orientalist fantasy; and the eternal victim, the oppressed Third World female doomed to poverty and ignorance, subject to being burned alive at both ends of the marriage bed, as a bride or as a widow. I can speak with an almost genetic authority.

This is of course very much a borrowed authority. Neither I nor anyone else can deliver a representative, authentic Third World woman to academia or elsewhere. Even in India, there is no such thing as *the* Indian woman—there are only Indian women. And the individuals are far more interesting than any assumed stories of authenticity. I am, in fact, if judged by the standards of glamour or squalor, as inauthentic as Coca-Cola. I am the third generation of academics in my family; my great-grandfather was smart enough to amass a fortune as a civil servant—under the British. The women in my family, far from being uniformly silent and oppressed, are voluble and eccentric. My great-grandmother, in fact, was such a powerful personality that my grandfather finally took refuge from her in complete silence: he refused to speak to her for at least ten years before she died. It drove her crazy, if not to her cremation pyre (she wasn't that crazy). My immediate family immigrated to the U.S. when I was seven; I grew up in fairly privileged circumstances as a faculty brat in California. In fact, most of my life has been spent on university campuses.

My authority, of course, ultimately derives from my academic credentials, from my training in the groves of academe and my ability to speak the language of academia. But I do have a scholarly and a cultural authenticity, a more complex one than the fairly simple model of "otherness" described above. As a woman, as a mother, as a nonEuropean, as a specialist in nonEuropean literary texts, I am myself the demonstration of the kind of mixing of cultural and professional genres that is increasingly "us," not "them." This is one face that we ourselves see when we look in the mirror—a motley garb composed of familiar elements combined in unfamiliar ways. One term for this is multiculturalism. Another way of thinking about it is that the graveyard is learning how to make room for the living, not the dead.

I am left with two thoughts. How difficult it is to accomplish this mixing of cultures—how unequal are the weights, the physical presences of the monumental graveyard and the cremated dead. And second, sitting in the center of the green knoll at the top of Indian Hill Cemetery, surrounded by these massive, marble and granite markers rearing up into the sky, I am conscious of how small a space I occupy, how lightly my footsteps weigh upon the ground, how little room I take up in comparison to these dead.

Author's Note: I first became familiar with the term "yogini" after reading the work of Giti Thadani, writer and photographer from India. Giti is doing a feminist lesbian reinterpretation of Hindu iconography and texts. She describes the yoginis as mythological beings who are the "superlative form" or "multiple transformations" of Goddess Kali—each form manifesting different aspects of the Feminine self, but belonging to the spectrum of "independent, unconquered, non-domesticated amazon." The story that follows was inspired by a waking dream. It was imagined for an audience of children.*

The Two Yoginis

V.K. ARUNA

There was a baby elephant named Rani who was always straying away from her family. She would wander off by herself when the others grazed near the lake, and discover new places to visit or strange fruits to eat. Yet, Rani never got lost because she knew when to turn back. And her mother, Vinodhari, kept a watchful eye so that no harm would come to the young one.

Rani's family traveled in a group. She had four cousins about her age, five aunts, two grandmothers, and a mother. Her father sometimes came with them but he usually lived alone and Rani seldom saw him. Unlike the other mothers, Rani's mother was patient with her baby elephant because she too had been a wanderer when she was a calf. Besides, she enjoyed the stories Rani brought back from her escapades in the forest.

One day, Rani ventured too far and forgot the way back. She kept moving further and further till she could no longer smell her mother's familiar scent, and she lost her sense of direction. Vinodhari searched everywhere for her baby elephant. The family helped, spreading out across the hillsides. But Rani was gone. The herd had lost their baby elephant.

For many days Rani wandered around in panic. The forest paths she had used before vanished; all around her trees and vines with giant green leaves blocked the light. As she crashed and fought through the dense undergrowth, creatures much smaller than she sprang out in front of her, startled by the intrusion. But Rani, who had always depended on her mother's protection, was equally startled by the sudden appearance of wild boar, snakes and flying foxes that seemed ready to attack her. She did not know how terrifying she could be; she had no idea how large she was.

After many days and nights, Rani learned that the animals could lead her to watering holes; that tendrils hidden among the vines made good food; that snorts and squawks were creatures making way for her and growls were meant as a warning.

Then, just as she was feeling less afraid of the forest, and the idea of being alone became familiar, Rani found herself in a meadow. She had never seen a meadow before, and for obvious

reasons. The meadow was on the other side of the forest, a long way from the lake where the elephants grazed.

Rani could hardly recognize what she saw in this new place—ferns that looked like palm trees dividing the forest from the meadow, flat open land that spread like an ocean, tall grass that waved like dainty fingers, pinkish purple and vermillion flowers that grew among the grasses. Everything seemed strange and magical at the same time. Rani's sense of adventure was awakened once more.

But the meadow was not necessarily a safe place because there were poachers and hunters living in the area, people who killed elephants for money. Rani had never seen a poacher or a hunter, but her mother had cautioned her about men with parangs, blowpipes and spears. However, in her excitement about discovering a new place, she forgot all about hunters. She lifted her tired legs and ran through the tall grass and wild flowers, and with each move forward, the forest fell further behind, till finally there was no forest at all.

Suddenly, Rani stopped. Looking right at her was a girl child. At first she had not seen her because the girl wore a flowered dress that made her seem part of the meadow. Then the girl turned and Rani saw that she was a living creature.

The girl's name was Chitra. She came to the meadow whenever someone in school made her cry. Chitra had never seen a live elephant before, only in picture books, and once at the zoo when she went to the city to visit her uncle and aunty.

When Chitra saw Rani, her first impulse was to scream, but the elephant reached out with its trunk and sniffed the toffee that Chitra was sucking. And then she saw that the elephant was trembling. Chitra took the toffee out of her mouth and handed it to the elephant. Rani hesitated for a few seconds, then curled the tip of her trunk around the sticky brown glob that smelled so tempting, and raised it to her mouth. Chitra watched Rani for awhile. She felt less frightened and decided to talk to the elephant. This might seem strange for a girl to do, but Chitra often talked to animals and they talked back to her. That afternoon, for instance, she had been talking to a magpie when some girls came by and made fun of her. That's why she had fled to the meadow, to be alone, where she could watch the dragonflies and bees racing through the flowers.

It did not take long for Chitra and Rani to become good friends. Chitra wanted to take Rani home, but Rani suddenly remembered what her mother had taught her. She said no. Chitra knew all about Rani being lost and wanted to help. Finally, they both sat down and thought about what could be done. Then Rani piped up, "Maybe you could hide me."

"Where?" Chitra asked.

"Some place where no one will think to look for me. Do you know of such a place?" Chitra puzzled for a long time. Then she clapped her hands.

"I could hide you inside me," she smiled. Rani thought the girl was crazy. But Chitra was wild with excitement. "We could do it. Together, we could make it happen. If I think hard about you and you think hard about me, and we really really try, you could make yourself small and come live inside me. What do you think? Let's try, let's try!" She jumped up and down, her eyes flashing like jewels in the sunlight. Rani decided she had nothing to lose. So the baby elephant and the little girl stood up in the meadow, stared into each other's eyes, and wished hard. They stared so long that their eyes began to smart, and tears rolled down their faces. Still, they did not stop wishing.

Then it happened. Chitra felt a wiggle inside her stomach and Rani disappeared. From that day, Rani and Chitra lived together and no one knew about the baby elephant inside the little girl. No one noticed anything different or strange about Chitra except that she did not run away to the meadows anymore. And the other girls in school found that they could not say nasty things to Chitra like they used to because Chitra was not afraid of them any longer. In fact, she got into more scraps than they ever did and eventually became their leader.

Years passed. Chitra grew up and became a wildlife photographer. She traveled all over the world and Rani went with her. While Chitra matured and turned into a beautiful woman, Rani remained a baby elephant.

Chitra gave Rani first choice on assignments, took her to the best restaurants, indulged in exquisite baths and perfumes. Rani gave Chitra wild ideas and taught her not to be afraid; she helped Chitra find the meadow within herself.

Just when life seemed to be going smoothly, Chitra fell in love. The woman came from Australia, a horseback rider with reddish brown hair and the smell of cigarette smoke in her clothes. She left her country and moved in with Chitra. Rani was not happy. She complained about the intrusion but Chitra laughed, "Don't be so jealous. I need other friends." Rani realized that Chitra was all she had and there was no place else for her to go. If Chitra asked her to leave, Rani would once more become a lost baby elephant without a home. So she learned to share her friend with the new person in Chitra's life.

But little by little, the horseback rider took over Chitra's thoughts, time and home, squeezing Rani out till she did not seem to exist. Rani threw a tantrum. She ranted and raged inside Chitra for three days and three nights, making Chitra sick with chills and fainting spells. When that did not work, Rani trumpeted for three more days and three nights till Chitra was confined to bed with horrible migraine headaches and nausea. Finally, Rani rattled the insides of Chitra's rib cage so fiercely that the Australian thought Chitra was insane, and took the next plane home. Chitra checked herself into a hospital. But the doctors could find nothing wrong.

The night after her friend left for Australia, Chitra heard the voice of another friend she had long since neglected. By the next morning, she was as good as new. Chitra learned from that day never to forget that she was not just one but a part of two, and that if she took a lover, she was not still two but a part of three. At the same time, Rani learned that she could not hoard Chitra for herself, for although she was still a baby elephant, Chitra was a grown woman who would meet other women and fall in love. Thus, the two friends found a way to live together and became inseparable companions for life.

Then suddenly something changed. Rani began missing home. Chitra brought gifts and treats to appease her friend but nothing worked. Rani was inconsolable. Finally, they decided to look for Rani's family in the jungles and zoos of India. Chitra used her job to travel. Rani went with her. For many months, they went in and out of places that elephants might be. But the search proved useless. Rani was not able to locate the elephants who were her family.

One day, a friend of Chitra's invited her on a trip to the hills of Orissa. Chitra had never been to Orissa and thought that the journey might help take Rani's mind off her search for home. She accepted her friend's invitation.

The first night in Orissa, Chitra woke up in a sweat. Her body was feverish, her head was on fire. Rani was just as restless, but her restlessness came from wanting to get out of Chitra's body. Until now, Rani had never felt the need to leave. She liked being with her friend. But on this night, the inside of Chitra's body had become a cage with no door, a room with no air. Chitra talked to Rani, urging her to calm down, but the baby elephant refused to listen. She wanted to get out. She wanted to find her own home.

Chitra realized that she had to let her friend go. Without a sound, she rose from her bed and left the house. The chilly night air felt good against her burning skin. As she walked, the tempest inside her quieted down. The clouds drifted across the half moon and crickets shrieked into the night.

Chitra and Rani then did what a little girl and a baby elephant had done many years ago in a meadow hundreds of miles away. Only this time, they could not stare directly into each other's eyes, so they conjured up visions of each other in their minds, imagining the meadow at the edge of the forest with dragonflies buzzing in the sun. They imagined the eyes that each looked into with tears pouring from them. Then the visions of Chitra and Rani met and embraced each other. And the night creatures roaming among the trees grew silent, so silent that even the dew could be heard descending over the hills.

Chitra did not see Rani emerge from her. Neither did she see her go. All she sensed was a sudden wind swirling inside her as if someone had opened a door. She heard the rush of a distant waterfall. Her fever broke and Chitra felt a sudden tiredness. As the clouds slipped back to reveal the moon again, she called out softly, "Rani." But there was only silence.

Two years passed. Then five, then ten. Chitra worked frenziedly, made new friends and fell in love. But things were not the same. She could not stop thinking about Rani. She could not stop missing her friend.

One day, Chitra came home from a job assignment overseas and found a letter from her friend, the archaeologist who had invited her to Orissa. As she unfolded the letter, something slipped from the thin onionskin pages and fell to the floor. Chitra bent down to pick it up. She found a picture of an elephant-headed woman made of stone.

From the letter Chitra learned that her friend had come upon the ruins of an ancient temple, half concealed in the dense forests of Orissa. Inside the temple, she found ten stone carvings of beings that were part human, part elephant. One of the sculptures, taller and bigger than the rest, sat surrounded by a circle of smaller sculptures—all of them female. After careful study and many trips to the site, Chitra's friend realized that she had actually uncovered the Elephant-Headed Goddess and her lost community of elephant-headed women from thousands of years ago.

Chitra wondered about the photograph she had received. She held it under the light and looked closely at the stone carving. Its belly was like an earthenware pot resting on strong muscled legs. The feet were adorned in intricate anklets and planted firmly on the ground. Ears like young plantain leaves rose on either side of the figure's head, and a trunk curling ever-so-slightly nestled between two full and rounded breasts.

But it was the sculpture's eyes that held Chitra's gaze. They seemed to carry a half-smile that she recognized so well. Chitra knew this was no stranger. This was a photograph of Rani, no longer a baby but a stunning elephant-woman.

That night, Chitra lit a candle and stared at the stone image for a long time. She let her mind enter the space behind the photograph; she let it carry her back to the place where she had felt Rani leave. She listened for the sound of the distant waterfall. For a long time she sat remembering that night—looking for clues that would help her solve the mystery of her vanished friend, searching for something that would ease the ache of not knowing where she was.

Suddenly, she was there—along the same forest path on which Rani had been lost...by the lake where the baby elephant had grazed with her family...beyond the hills where springs gushed over shiny black rock...to a time when a young elephant-headed woman, restless for adventure, asked the goddess for the gift of departure. And in the grey coolness of the forest temple, Chitra felt the sadness of the goddess as she watched her young companion leave, even as she felt the warmth of that day in the meadow when a trembling baby elephant reached out with her trunk.

Chitra heard the candle flame crackle inside the pool of wax. She touched the face of the stone sculpture in the photograph. Her friend had finally gone home.

* This definition is from a book-in-progress by Giti Thadani about pre-vedic goddess myths, sites and worship practices.

Plonk In The Middle Of

KAMAL KAPUR

Plonk in the middle of
thoroughfares cars honking
in traffic jams heat and smoke
the thought of you stirs
some root unseasonably thrusts
its stem out of my
nipples and flowers

※

My Feet Found Home

The Landscape of a Body

GITA SRINIVASAN

In Salman Rushdie's *Midnight's Children*, Dr. Aziz is made to carry out a series of medical examinations by peering through a seven-inch hole cut in a sheet that swathes the body of a young woman. Her father's sense of modesty demands that she not flaunt her body for strange men, doctor or not. Aziz becomes fascinated over years of such consultations, over the glimpses of stomach, shoulder, ankle. He falls deeply in love with a woman who, "glued together by his imagination...accompanied him on all his rounds."*

This image rises up before me as I reflect on identity and meaning: the landscape of a body. A geography, a map of the skin. When I was young my German Jewish mother, with landscapes and diasporas of her own to draw around me, made a film about the sandhya prayer ritual in India and narrated the smoky daybreak scenes in her cool, quiet voice. In rare moments, my Madras-born father would tell me of pulling on new clothes in the Diwali dawn and I could smell them, cotton and coal. In my nine-year-old mind's sensuous eye, India was a place that happened in the morning.

Later as I grew the afternoons came, and then the dusks, and I became aware that I collected glimpses up inside of me. I traveled. In a Jakarta bus terminal the Indian ticket vendor drew me aside to tell me I must visit India, because You Know in India you put the money (he gestured with the coins in his hand) you put the money in the water and it sinks! I imagined the ocean. He contemptuously rattled the Indonesian change so I could hear how flimsy it was. An aged woman of South Asian descent, completely deaf, sat next to me on the bench in a Singapore home for the elderly. Looking into my face, she suddenly seized hold of my nose; India nose, she said. Like mine. She wouldn't let go. In Bali, a Hindu tour guide sat me down in his dusty roadside office. There, among the ads for Package Deals, Bus Tours, Days of Sightseeing, he spoke quietly in fervent tones, impressing upon me the importance of going Back. Of visiting the temples. For myself, and also, his glance silently said, for him. For others I could not see. The stories are endless, the stories of image collectors—for none of the people who spoke to me had ever been to India.

Indias of the mind follow me. Always these moments of longing shared with strangers, in which the images wash through me. It is in the largeness of such moments—the way they open up and connect me to others—that I have come to recognize in these Indias the yearning for all return. For wholeness, for a sweetness in the mouth, for the beginning. For words that make echoes, for all that has been loved and forgotten. A yearning to stand up on the land. India is the name for that which has gone and left its traces on the bodies of men and women. In Trinidad they touched their chests to show me, when words failed, the mark of its passing.

They held out arms and slapped to make the veins stand out; they said, *My blood took you in. Your Indian people and mine planted sugar cane. Maybe we are related.*

To collect images, or even to invent them, yet not let invention change the nature of the believing: this is what it means to bear witness to those experiences which lie in between, as I do; to those radical disjunctures in culture and consciousness which seem to yet be impossibly contained in lives. Sit up straight like a Brahm-Jew! my mother admonished us at the kitchen table.

My cousin Gopi in Bombay tells me I'm an American but my sense of smell is Indian. And in Trinidad, people looked at me longingly and said I had eyes like the star girls in the Hindi films. If you're from India, they said, for the belief was strong in them, at least you could sing us a song. In Trinidad I would recite my name as if it were a story. Tell it again. When the Indian bank teller in Port of Spain had to write my name over and over filling out the forms, she drew the letters slow with a kind of reverence, impressed that both my first and last names sounded real, like-from-India names. She looked at the letters and my face watchfully, I felt like a living memory. I had been glimpsed in a name. A pair of eyes, a nose. The glimpses of stomach, shoulder, ankle, of history, of geography, of identity.

sandhya prayer Hindu evening prayer

diwali Hindu festival of lights that celebrates the return of the mythical hero Rama to Ayodha

*Salman Rushdie, *Midnight's Children* (Great Britain: Jonathan Cape, 1980; New York: Penguin Books, 1991), 23.

Origins

DINAZ ROGERS

We Parsi-Zoroastrians are one of the most unique people that inhabit this earth. Or so I was told by family, and as a child this is what I believed. I still do.

Parsis—I remember as a little girl transposing the letters of that beloved word, so it became Paris to me. For a brief time I believed that my ancestors had run away from France, till one day the storytelling began. Those wonderful stories came to us from all directions: grandmothers, grandfathers, father, mother, aunts, uncles and neighbors and of course a few adored older cousins. Twice-told tales that one never tired of.

But then our heritage is twice blessed—the proud Indo-Iranian legacy. "You see we had to run away, mind you, not as cowards but as descendants of the brave soldiers, citizens and of course the priests of the last Zoroastrian king, Yezdergard III, the last ruler of the Sassanian dynasty of Iran," my aunt stated with pride evident in her voice and eyes. Oh, what a marvellous orator she was, my father's first cousin, married to one of my father's brothers.

"Between 640 and 649 A.D. our Iran was overwhelmed and conquered by the invading armies of Khalif Omar in the conclusive battles of Qadisiya and Nihavand." The little ones and the not-so-little ones around her gasped. With her sharp wit and self-assured manner my aunt was an imposing woman. We were deeply in awe of her and her M.A. in Philosophy. She had written a few books and had translated from Farsi into English and Gujarati.

Her rich voice continued its dramatic narration. "But before Iran's fall Syria was demolished by the Arabs and like dominoes they fell to the sword—Jerusalem, Caesarea, Palestine, Iraq and Egypt. Spain would have to wait another hundred years to be reached through North Africa." My aunt cleared her throat, "But you know..." dropping her voice to whisper, she looked around, satisfied that we were her eager listeners, "our ancestors, the Persians, put up a great fight against the invaders. The conquest of our madar vattan Iran (mother country Iran) took such a long time because we were a solidly united nation and we were steadfastly Zoroastrians. After a time, realizing things would never be 'normal,' that this too shall *not* pass, our ancestors fled to the mountains of Kohistan in Khorsan in Iran."

Scanning her captive audience, my aunt looked over her glasses that were halfway down her nose and stated, "As a matter of fact, that was the region called Parthia in ancient times." And she added, "Don't forget that most refugees, our ancestors, came from a region called Pars."

The story continued. "After a century of hardships, they fled to the port of Hormuz, Islamic religious persecution nipping away at their heels. Thence they set sail for the west coast of India."

Much later, I learned that Iran unfortunately was ripe for such a heart-wrenching conquest and conversion. The once-glorious House of Sassan was, in its later years, in a state of decay from within, as evidenced by its weak kings, haughty and disloyal generals, the devastating wars with Rome to the West and the cruel marauders from the East. (Geography has indeed shaped the histories of Iran and India.) Avarice, famines, plagues and dissatisfaction were eroding the nation's vigor. But the unkindest and most mortal blow was dealt when the pure and simple teachings of Zarathushtra (Zoroaster) were replaced by intolerance and unbending fundamentalism. The country was like a fragile house of cards—the gates opened—and a gust of wind in the form of the Arab armies blew in, collapsing the glory that was the Zoroastrian Iran.

"After a brief stay on the island of Div, off Kathiawar on the western coast of India, we landed in Sanjan seventy miles north of Bombay," my aunt explained, beginning the story of our life in India.

"Tell us about Jadhav Rana and the milk and sugar story." I was anxious, not just to hear the tale beloved to all Parsis, but to hear the way my aunt told the tale. Her marvellous voice alone captured one's attention.

"Just imagine the shock of the inhabitants of coastal Sanjan when these tall, differently-garbed people came ashore. But remember, India in those days was not India as it is today. India was in reality made up of small and large kingdoms ruled by kings and maharajas, each nation a kingdom unto itself and at war among themselves. And so the request for refuge went to the then king of the kingdom Jadhav Rana, the Hindu king of Gujarat."

At this point the narratives diverge slightly, depending upon the storyteller, but my favourite was my aunt's version.

"This king of Sanjan was war weary. He did not need any strangers camping on his land. To indicate that his own overpopulated land could not absorb any more, he sent a cup filled to the brim with milk. One of the wise priests on the ship, understanding the polite refusal but at the same time realizing the gravity of the denial, put sugar in the milk." Tears were threatening to spill over from some of our eyes.

"'Just as sugar mixes with milk and sweetens it,' the priest explained, 'so shall we. Adding more milk to the cup would be a waste, as the milk will spill over. But we will be the sugar to your milk. We'll sweeten your lands with our words, deeds and allegiance, if only we will be allowed to practice our faith in peace.'

"Iran had by that time been converted to Islam, and oh how I can imagine the pain those brave souls, my ancestors, must have felt! Beginnings, especially ones in far-off lands are always risky, but the fact that during all those intervening centuries the Parsis of India have survived is a testimonial to the spirit of those pioneers!"

"Wonder if they celebrated?" Her son, Faredoon—my cousin—was curious, running ahead of the narrative.

"They must have—with a Jashan, a thanksgiving prayer ceremony—but I'm sure that some, still haunted by thoughts of their motherland, were not ready to cheer out loud," thus the mother answered her son's query.

My aunt's voice went out into the beautiful Sunday morning as all of us, with heads covered with black caps (called topis in Gujarati), sat on the porch of the Madresa. We had

gathered for our weekly religious classes where we were taught prayers in the ancient language of the Avestha, received an explanation of our religious rituals, and heard stories from the Shahnamas.

"The conditions our ancestors had to agree to in exchange for some land and religious freedom were: Sharing the knowledge of their own faith; that we adopt the Gujarati language as our mother tongue; we women would wear the sari, the Indian women's garb; surrender all weapons; and hold our marriage ceremonies after sunset." There was a dramatic pause. "And so the small amount of sugar stayed in the milk of human kindness—Mother India— continuing to sweeten the milk, as we have indeed and will continue to do so forever. Giving much to the country but never asking for much in return—the most ideal refugees any country could ever wish for!"

I was sobbing, moved by the theatre of it all—much to the amusement of some of the older boys—I would cry at anything.

"Yes, today we speak Gujarati, wear saris, still hold marriage ceremonies after the sun goes down, are very pacifistic and perform our religious ceremonies, faithful to those that were performed in ancient Iran. If Mother India is a dramatic word, no one understands or feels that word more than we Parsis of India do—or as our ancestors must have felt.

"When about five centuries or so after our ancestors arrived in this new Motherland (you see, India was our Israel), the armies of Mahmud Bagada, or according to another source, the Muslim general Alaf Khan, attacked Sanjan, Parsis fought alongside of the Hindu compatriots. But they lost to the invading armies and fled, taking their holy fire with them.

"A threatened massacre was averted in 1425 when the Portuguese governor of Thana, twenty miles north of Bombay, demanded that the Parsis convert to Catholicism or be killed. The Parsis, pretending to acquiesce, asked for one last time to celebrate their religious rituals, and as the celebrating continued with the entire town present, the Parsis with their holy fire fled the town.

"Thus in their flights and peaceful migrations, the sacred fire moved from place to place too, because the fire is a very sacred symbol to the Parsis, just as the cross is to the Christians. Wherever the Parsis went, the fire went, and a new fire temple—we called our house of worship Agiyari—would be built," Aunt concluded.

Madresa a Parsi word for a religious institute of the Parsis

maharajas heads of princely states

shahnamas an account of a Muslim king's reign told in the form of a prayer

English Our (M)other Tongue; Nurturing The Cultural Divide

SONALI PERERA

In *Decolonising the Mind,* Ngugi wa Thiong'o observes that "language, any language has a dual character, it is both a means of communication and a carrier of culture."[1] This is not a particularly novel idea. British Imperialists have long been aware of this useful concept. And in making English the sole medium of instruction in colonial schools, they utilized this intrinsic duplicity of language to create yet another perfect paradox of colonialism. Focusing specifically on the British colonization of Sri Lanka, I have found that the study of English acted as a unifying agent in the face of the language differences of a pluralist society. It also became a divisive wedge transmitting harmful Western political ideals along with the inescapable contagion of elitism and racialization (both cultural by-products of colonialism.)

Although theorists often speak in a formulaic manner about the related effects of colonialism upon the extensive range of British colonies, it is necessary to carefully examine factors that differentiate between and complicate general formulas. In view of the current ethnic crisis between the majority Sinhalese and minority Tamils, there are those Sri Lankans who nostalgically recall the "tranquil" colonial past, in which the island-wide medium of instruction was English, and schools were "modeled on British public school lines" fostering a "public school ethos [that] produce[d] an elite unified by certain traditions, aspirations and norms... [T]his facilitated and maintained a social discourse between the Tamil and Sinhalese, between Christian, Buddhist and Hindu..."[2] This idyllic situation was largely true of the school that I attended, for the brief shining moment between its inception in 1908 until the emergence of latent linguistic nationalism in the neo-colonial 1950s. However, my personal experience of St. Bridget's Convent did not measure up to the elusive British ideal.

Although the school was originally run by Irish nuns, from the late 1970s to the middle 1980s (during which time I attended the school), the entire administration was Sinhalese with the notable exception of Mother Superior. She was a brittle porcelain figurine summoned all the way from England to lend sanction, simply by her presence, to the missionary credo that gave rise to our school and to hymns such as:

> What though the spicy breezes
> Blow soft o'er Ceylon's isle
> Though every prospect pleases
> And only man is vile!...[3]

292

A "separate peace" was created and hermetically sealed in by our whitewashed convent walls from the outside adult world of ethnic riots. And it is true that Catholic, Buddhist, Hindu and Muslim schoolgirls all sang to "dear St. Bridget, Erin's glory."[4] But following the advent of the Tamil and Sinhala linguistic movements in 1950, separate mediums of instruction were established, segregating Sinhalese and Tamil students, who then met only on such rare occasions as weekly elocution class. Instruction in elocution was a privileged addition to our compulsory study of English. Notably, we came together to correctly pronounce our vowel sounds and learn poems by A.A. Milne one week, and those of Tennyson, the next.

"Contact between Sinhalese and Tamil students was reduced to a minimum, and the social distance served in time to convert difference into enmity and confrontation, and to create distrust, dislike, and fear."[5] The colonizer might strongly contend that this state of affairs had nothing to do with colonialist education policies, but rather could be attributed solely to the "Swabasha" (National Languages) movement. And indeed eloquent Tamil politicians, such as G.G. Ponnambalam, feared the ramifications of the Sinhala Buddhist revival. Ponnambalam contended as de Silva notes, that "a Sinhalese Christian can become a Sinhalese Buddhist, but a Tamil cannot become a Sinhalese...Implicit in all his arguments was the belief that the English language provided a neutral medium for fair competition between the two communities."[6]

"It is the final triumph of a system of domination when the dominated start singing its virtues,"[7] affirms Thiong'o. It is true that at face value the English system seems to exude the mission schools' promised "Balm of Gilead," but lulled by their hymns and anthems, we often fail to take into account the many ways in which the British and their language policy are responsible for the ethnic tensions straining the island apart. Language as the "carrier of culture" explains the wide cultural divide between Sinhalese and Tamils. Cultural norms transmitted by the English also contributed towards the systematic widening of this chasm.

As Stanley Tambiah notes, many "progressive" British notions of politics and government were not ideally suited to the pluralist society and complex ethnic problems of Sri Lanka.

> Universal franchise, territorial electorates and majority politics no doubt worked against the interest of minorities, who would have preferred quotas and special constitutional protection. But these same phenomena of democratic politics also eroded traditional bases of leadership and power and produced deep divisions within the Sinhalese society itself, which had repercussions for the Sinhalese-Tamil relations.[8]

When in 1950 the British finally gave up the governmental reins, they handed them to an aggregate of Sinhalese and Tamil politicians who were exclusively English-educated Catholic school alumni. This move inevitably contributed to the development of a resistance against urban nationalist politicians. This social movement was headed by a rural elite drawn from the villages and comprised of schoolteachers, ayurvedic physicians and newly rich merchants. These activists "were all educated in the Sinhalese language...and therefore spurned by the English educated...because they wished to conserve 'traditional' culture and customs, [and] were hostile to the spread of a 'Western' style of life exemplified by western clothes, western films, western sex mores, western recreations and so on."[9]

This movement, headed by the incensed marginalized village elite, soon evolved—with the lingusitic revolution of 1956—into the powerful "Swabasha" movement, which introduced the problematic notion that to be truly Sinhalese (and synonymously Sri Lankan), one must both be Sinhalese *and* practice the "Sinhalese religion," Buddhism. In response to this threatening ideology, the vernacular-educated Tamils sought to construct their own version of linguistic nationalism—harking back to the 1920s policies of Ponnambalam Ramanathan. Ramanathan, a Tamil politician, to safeguard minority interests, vehemently opposed the granting of universal suffrage. He emphasized "the virtues of a separate Tamil identity, of a Tamil nationalism to be fostered in collaboration with the British, and if necessary, in opposition to Sinhalese nationalism."[10]

Thus in selecting and designing an elite saturated with English cultural ideals—who would undoubtedly carry on where the Raj left off with its democratic policies—Britain assured the continuance of the ethnic crisis well into the future. It is also important to consider that in acting to preserve their mercantilist concerns on the island, the British can hardly be excused as subtle, sideline contributors to the Tamil-Sinhalese problem, but rather should be recognized as blatant instigators. British importation of Tamil laborers from India to work on the coffee plantations established in the 1830s, introduced yet another element of plurality to an already precarious situation. "The separation of the plantations from the villages as physical and ecological spaces and as European-owned enterprises helped to prolong the social distance between Sinhalese peasants and Indian laborers."[11] In addition to bequeathing a problematic cultural legacy of majority rule politics, Britain further compounded the existing problems by creating a more pluralist society.

In retrospect, surveying the damage done by the colonizer and his "gift" of an English education, Padraic Pearse surmises that in Ireland "it is because the English education system...has deliberately eliminated the national factor that it has so terrifically succeeded."[12] He suggests that a new education must necessarily "lead Ireland back to her sagas." This mood of cultural nostalgia, however, does not function constructively in postcolonial Sri Lanka. The "Mahavamsa" chronicle composed around the fifth century A.D. by Buddhist monks of the Mahavihara fraternity "simultaneously presents the dual destiny of the Sinhalese people to conquer, unite and rule the island of Sri Lanka for the preservation and glory of the Buddhist religion and the necessary expulsion of the Tamil invaders from South India..."[13] Tambiah notes that many politicians indeed went "back to the sagas" to recontextualize and reactivate them according to their own political aspirations.

Sri Lankans then seem to be faced with the unhappy prospect that there may be no solution to the escalating ethnic problem that traces its roots back to the tangled machinations of British colonial policy. But yet again, a sympathizer of pragmatic colonialist politics may reiterate that the nationwide study of English kept linguistic nationalism, and consequently the ethnic crisis, in abeyance. Could the solution then encompass going back to English as the medium of instruction in schools? (Not necessarily the English of the colonizers, but a hybrid English, a patois English—the receptacle and transmitter of a new culture encompassing aspects of both vernacular Tamil and Sinhalese?) This notion, however, would undoubtedly be dismissed as dangerously naive by militant nationalists on both sides. The English language, however extensively modified, would still remain intrinsically English and in a colonial aftermath would still be associated with the elitism of the colonizer.

It is not difficult in postcolonial retrospect to sort out the subtle genius of British political methods of "divide and conquer." But it is slightly harder, though vitally necessary, to understand the abstract concept that racism is a structural, not aberrational, part of colonial society. Many of the current glaring differences between Tamils and Sinhalese are a direct consequence of British cultural notions of racialization and "otherness" permeating into the fabric of a mutually oppressed pluralist society. Frantz Fanon explains the situation by affirming that "collective autodestruction in a very concrete form is one of the ways in which the native's muscular tension is set free."[14] Simple recognition of the insidious underlying dynamics of the colonizer's English education might well be the first step towards unifying the Tamils and Sinhalese against a common enemy.

ayurvedic the ancient art of medicine and of prolonging life that originated in South Asia

mahavamsa great ancestry/dynasty

amahavirhara great Buddhist monastery

1. Ngugi wa Thiong'o, *Decolonising the Mind* (London: J. Currey; Portsmouth, N.H.: Heinemann, 1986), 13.

2. Stanley Tambiah, *Sri Lanka—Ethnic Fratricide and the Dismantling of Democracy* (Chicago: University of Chicago Press, 1986), 76.

3. H.A.I. Goonetileke, *Images of Sri Lanka Through American Eyes* (Colombo: International Communication Agency, Embassy of the U.S.A., 1976), 139.

4. School Anthem of St. Bridget's Convent in Colombo, District 7.

5. Tambiah.

6. K.M. de Silva, *Managing Ethnic Tensions in Multiethnic Societies: Sri Lanka, 1880–1985* (Lanham: University Press of America, 1986), 81.

7. Thiong'o, 20.

8. Tambiah, 68.

9. Ibid., 69.

10. de Silva, 207.

11. Tambiah, 66-67.

12. Padraic Pearse, *The Murder Machine and Other Essays* (Dublin: Mercier Press, 1976), 22.

13. Tambiah, 70.

14. Frantz Fanon, *The Wretched of the Earth* (New York: Grove Weidenfeld, 1963), 54.

Boundaries

HERSHINI BHANA

My poem is about this fucked-up African/Indian/Kansan,
angry in California
It talks of women who run in place and write of
lost braids and even more lost children
It whimpers of aching feet and the only fingers to
heal them being thousands of spaces and telephone calls
away
It whispers of mothers with round backs and long
hands that dig deep between legs for loneliness
It tells of wanting and wanting and never being
sure
It screams of dislodged food in toilet bowls
scrubbed clean with tears
It sobs of losing and losing and being tired of
losing

My poem is about boundaries and
my poem is about a lack of boundaries.

Storm

GAURANGI KAMANI

settled in the traps
choked in kerosene
nibbling at the sweetened dough

maria maria they are coming!

crossing eyes
gasping frenzied under covers
I have to scream but
is it real/there/brown long

the juicer turns like a slug
the orange flesh is stranded on a point
while inside the wheels are grinding bodies
which crawl in the night
creaturing

in another time hummed into another mantra
you will lie soft and full small and sleek
under wings of gossamer dull and gold
sensing darting retreating

the bad luck is when they fly up your dress

those
cockroaches

The Rings Around Anna

DINAZ ROGERS

Rings! Pinkish and reddish rings are what I noticed when I first met Anna. No, not red or pink rings of sparkling rubies around her short and stubby fingers, but faint and at times more prominent rings around her face and exposed parts of her body. That is, if she let any part of her body be exposed to stares of the curious. An occasional hot gust of wind would lift her dirty old ankle-length skirt to display those strange rings around her stubby legs.

And I wondered and I watched.

I was intrigued rather than shocked, as were some in this dusty little town, about the rumors and gossip regarding Anna and her family.

"The Lida family likes to dig up the earth. Have you noticed how they always look dirty?" Sylva Foxx asked.

"They hate birds! They shoot all the birds in sight. They've chopped down every tree and shrub. Even the fence posts and all the fencing have been taken down." Robyn Byrd was furious. "They've even done something to their chimney so that no bird could possibly build a nest."

"Oh now, don't ruffle your feathers," Liv Fisch joked.

I did not see actual feathers, but Robyn's legs were, or were they not, scaly? I dismissed the thought as a reaction of my naturally suspicious nature and an overactive imagination. Logic told me scaly skin was due to the hot dry weather of the desert, made more severe because of that unfortunate accident over yonder at the…

"No!" I spoke my thoughts aloud.

The others who were chattering around me did not pay any attention. I scanned their faces. I tried putting their names to match the general physical features of their bodies. There were Woody Sapp and Stuby Goetz. Just look at Winnie Pigg's snout, er…I mean nose and…"Oh never mind, you," I chided myself. I was a stranger in a strange town. I was a scholar, a wanderer, travelling from one broken-down town to another, trying to gather what was left of the country and civilization for the "Society for the Restoration and Preservation of Arts and Literature of the Eve Before the Destructions." Names, names of towns I knew not, neither did the inhabitants of these almost ghost towns. Life other than human was almost nonexistent in this town. What was left of the birds was taken care of by the Lida family rifle.

Anna Lida was hacking away at a wooden sign swinging from the roof of the porch. THE LIDAS, the family sign, now lay on the dusty, broken-down porch.

"Why did you do that?" I questioned. "Written signs are becoming a rarity and writing a lost art…well, almost…don't you know?"

She did not speak.

"Don't you know the art of writing is dying?" I repeated with a mild touch of irritation. "We have schools only in big cities far away. No one to teach us writing and reading here," I persisted, hoping to elicit a verbal response from Anna Lida.

A gust of very hot wind blew in our faces. Anna held on to her skirt.

"May I see your parents?"

Anna squirmed. Her expressionless little eyes were almost lost in her reddish-brown, moist and soft pudgy face.

Did she hear me? Did she have ears? Rumors about the Lidas being deaf were attributed to them having no ears. I looked for them on Anna's exceptionally small head. I peered into the darkened house for Anna's strange sisters, or was it her sisters with strange names? Archia, Polycha, Oligoa and Hirudia. All I could detect inside was darkness and the smell of freshly turned earth.

"They say," I pointed out with a vague gesture toward the dilapidated little village, "your parents, your grandparents and your sisters have not been seen by the town for a long time."

Anna's body seemed to wriggle. She looked limp—no backbone or any kind of supporting structure, or so it appeared.

Books. I needed books to read up on something that was bothering me. Only books had the answer; only they held the secrets.

Meanwhile the rings around Anna's body were deepening and no one knew…

It would take me months to travel back to Big City to look for a library. I knew I could read and understand the written word, unlike most of the scattered denizens of the planet. Where had I read all about this? Where? Where? Must have been in those schools.

I was beginning to feel weak and strange. Had I spent too much time in these backwood villages? Maybe I should have heeded the warnings of my Big City friends and never have come to these remote places.

I felt as if my mind were turning senile. But I was too young for that—or was I?

No one knows what day or month or year it is. Or maybe just a few who control the government know everything. There are so many rumors about what happened. That accident, miles away from Big City, started it all. Then paranoia and fear set in and nations bombarded nations with disastrous results, wiping out all that had been accumulated during the tenure of civilization. How long ago this happened, no one knows.

Books! I had to leave this arid town. Travel to Big City. I felt that I, for some strange reason, was changing…more like regressing. What was it? My mind or my body? Had I overstayed in this nameless village?

It took me forever to reach Big City. It did not take much time to reach the neglected building some called the Library. I read books on religion. One whose name evades me now talked about rebirth, for the sorrows and sins of the present condemned one to reincarnate into a lower animal form. Religion, now considered an absolute philosophy in this almost

lawless and chaotic time, gave me a fascinating insight into what the distant or maybe the not-too-distant past must have been like.

I read books on geography, history and assorted subjects. Then I read books on biology. Through yellowed and crumbling pages I read about the orderly arrangements of living things, with regard to their similarities, relationships and evolution. With much interest I devoured pages about Linnaeus, a Swedish naturalist, and his Animal Systematics—about phyla, genera and Latin names.

I felt weary. Why was I doing this? What was it that I was looking for? I began going down through strange-sounding names…Phylum Porifera, Phylum Coelenterata, till I stopped cold at Phylum Annelida. In parentheses the authors explained that the Latin "annelus" meant little ring. Best known examples: earthworms and leeches. I read on and found that Phylum Annelida was broken down into classes: Class Archiannelida, Class Polychaeta, Class Oligochaeta, Class Hirudinea. I shut all the books and shut them hard. I could hear the pages within them crumble. I had a fleeting urge to eat those yellow tidbits of paper.

I began to realize what just might be happening in those remote villages. Have you? I am scared. Are you? My heart is sinking as I begin to dwell on the diverse subjects, such as self-fulfilling prophecies, reincarnation and even being simply scared. But then my name is Eugene Roache. What's yours?

Predicaments of the Hyphen

KAMALA VISWESWARAN

The offices of the Indian Consulate, Paris
June 1991

Trying to get a tourist visa to travel to India, I am called again to the counter, surveyed, finally asked, "Are you of Indian origin?" An immediate freezing, and then a slow stammer, "I don't know what you mean. I was born in the United States; my father is Indian, that is he used to be...now he's an American citizen..." my voice trails off. I begin again, unable to control the pitch of my voice, a register too high, "Why do you want to know? What difference does it make?..."

I am cut off before I can make a proper offensive. "Just one moment, please be seated," says the consulate official coolly as she turns from the window. A few minutes later I am informed that the Consul General would like to speak with me. Would I wait until 5 p.m. when the Consul has finished with his meetings? It is only 3:30 p.m. I wait. At 5:30 p.m. I am told that the Consul has already gone home for the evening, and am asked to return the following morning.

The next morning my appearance causes a stir. I hear variously in French, English and Hindi the same question and confirmation, "That's her?" "That's the one." In the next few minutes, half a dozen people enter the booth on one pretext or another. I am made to repeat why I had not been able to obtain a visa for visiting India before leaving New York; how I'd left it until the last minute, how the Indian Embassy in New York had been closed because of Rajiv Gandhi's assassination, the last three days in May before I left for Paris.

The consulate official frowns at me and studies my application. I look down and find penciled in large letters across the top: NO PROOF OF INDIAN ORIGIN. Further down the page in red ink I can make out the scrawl: "Applicant became hostile when asked about her origin. Refused to answer question in a straightforward manner."

I look up. The consulate officer fondles my passport, then stamps it aggressively before delivering a short lecture on applying for visas well in advance of departure. I never see the Consul General, nor am I told why I was made to wait.

*　　*　　*

Certainly the question, "Where are you from?" is never an innocent one. Yet not all subjects have equal difficulty in replying. To pose a question of origin is subtly to pose a question of return, to challenge not only temporally, but geographically, one's place in the present. For someone who is neither fully Indian nor wholly American, it is a question which provokes a sudden failure of confidence, the fear of never replying adequately.

301

The consulate official's questioning highlighted, in a brief moment, a series of contradictions about how we understand and talk about identity. By "origin" was she referring to my parentage, place of birth, or both? If she meant to emphasize my parentage, was it because I "looked" Indian, thus invoking concepts of "race" and "blood," which I am usually at pains to dispute? Did it matter that one parent was Indian by birth and the other not? Was it important to know that both were American citizens? Did it matter what I called myself, or with what culture(s) I claimed affinity? For me, race, nationhood, culture and identity were as surely entangled in the consulate officer's question as she had seen it to be "straightforward."

I am aware of a potentially productive conflation of second-generation with post-colonial subjectivities. Airports and consulate offices are increasingly marked as the sites for the enunciation of post-colonial identities.[1] Airports, of course, mark the geographical space of liminality, while consulates and embassies signal (at least) the discourse of citizenship and rights in foreign territory. At such sites arrival and departure scenes are immanent, but suspended by what is now departmentalized as "International Relations." Although there are obvious similarities between second-generation and post-colonial positionings, I think it makes sense to underscore further points of contact, to mark those differential, though contradictory, predicaments of the hyphen.

Hyphe-Nation

When I was growing up, no discrete identity existed that I could claim. Faced with a questionnaire, I never knew which box to check, "Asian," "White," "Other"? I was among the first-born to that second wave of Indian immigrants to the U.S. which began as a trickle in the early '60s when immigration restrictions were relaxed. As Gouri Bhat notes, the date of our parents' arrival in this country is important because it limited our cultural options.[2] This slice of the second generation was raised without "Indian friends, Bharatanatayam dance classes, Karnatic music recitals, Hindu temple societies, or Hindi films," because the large Indian communities of Los Angeles or the San Francisco Bay Area, Dallas or New York, were not firmly established until the mid-seventies.[3] Bhat argues that "Indian-Americans have had no distinctive creative voices of their own, probably because that generation of [second]-wave immigrant offspring is still maturing, now swelling the college ranks."[4]

The increasing currency of terms such as "Indo-American," or "Indian-American," even given the maturing of a generation seeking its voice, does not reassure me. Rather it signals for me the continual virulence of identity politics in the United States as newer groups rush for their hyphens, even as some groups begin to abandon them, as still others, such as U.S.-born or immigrant Puerto Ricans, have never adopted them.[5]

The Indian-American hyphen retains the imaginary of the nation-state, its mobile diaspora with increasing (if complicated) choices about whether to go or stay. It is a hyphen that signals the desire (and the ability) to be both "here" and "there." Yet the post-colonial nature of this particular hyphen should not obscure other processes of hyphen formation. For example, in the African-American context, the notion of a "diaspora" with "a land of return" is problematic. Such a notion must be located equally in post-civil war "repatriation" schemes launched by whites to return American blacks to Africa, and in the social movements of Marcus Garvey and others who viewed this return as a form of empowerment.[6] Then too

there is the fact that few Anglo-Americans recognize the political etymologies of the words "Native American" or "American Indian." Five hundred years after Columbus, too few "Indian-Americans" recognize how their hyphen participates in the erasure of those on this continent long before Columbus got lost.

I do not mean to suggest that claiming the hyphen has not also been difficult or without worthy elements of struggle. For there are other, more derogatory ways of naming my generation. We of the alphabet soup[7]—the ABCDs (American Born Confused Deshis); the ABCDEFGs (American Born Confused Deshis Emigrated from Gujarat); with HIJs (Houses in Jersey)—are the ones Salman Rushdie satirizes in *The Satanic Verses*, the ones who cannot properly pronounce their own South Asian names:

> "There was a TV reporter here some days back," said George Miranda. She said her name was Kerleeda. I couldn't work it out.
>
> Zeeny interrupted. "He doesn't know what freaks you guys turn into. That Miss Singh, outrageous. I told her, the name's Khalida dearie, rhymes with Dalda, that's a cooking medium. But she couldn't say it. Her own name. Take me to your Kerleader. You types got no culture. Just wogs now. Ain't it the truth?"[8]

If Rushdie's caricature of South Asians in Britain rings true, so also does Bhat's account of attending a Hindi language class at the University of Texas: "wall to wall ABCDs" with slack-jawed West Texas drawls.[9]

There were, however, other reasons for not knowing who I was; it was not simply the lack of some ready-made identity when I was growing up in the '60s and '70s. There was also the fact that my father rarely spoke of India, except to punish one of his willful daughters: "If we were in India you would never speak to me like this!" Nor did he ever speak to us in Tamil, his mother tongue. It was only later that I learned that an Indian birth would not have prevented English being my first language (given trajectories of a certain South Indian caste, the privileges of an aspiring class). I use the term "first language" deliberately. Although English was my mother's tongue, I cannot bring myself to call it my mother tongue.

Bharati Mukherjee speaks of being born into a class that does not live in its native language.[10] And I puzzle over the relationship between post-colonial South Asian friends who are illiterate in their mother tongues (What must it be like to be so supremely literate elsewhere, but to stumble through intimate geography in a Madras or Delhi, unable to read street signs, buses, store-fronts?) and someone like me speaking with a clumsy tongue, who after years of language study, can read and write enough Hindi to tell whether the bus is going to Janakpuri or Chanyakpuri and enough Tamil to skim the newspapers and write to my grandmother. Are we "Midnight's Children," post-colonial and second-generation: born that some might speak, and others to read and write; that some be deaf or dumb, and others blind?

Meena Alexander speaks of a "treasured orality," a "cherished illiteracy" in her mother tongue, Malayalm. She records memories: A Scottish tutor who over and over makes her say "duck duck," "pluck pluck," "milk milk," "silk silk";[11] her "split sense of writing in English."[12] And finally, in spite of her attempt to ironize the "privilege of illiteracy," a sense of rage:

303

Come ferocious alphabets of flesh
splinter and raze my page

that out of the dumb
and bleeding part of me

I may claim
my heritage.[13]

* * *

For a post-colonial critic, writing about an "over-there" enacts a certain similarity with the anthropologist's "Being There"—the act of writing about one place from another. And yet, as Nasser Hussein argues, the act of "going home" subjects the post-colonial critic to a particular vulnerability, a loss of the immunity that exile affords.[14] Thus Salman Rushdie confesses, "…however I choose to write about other-there, I am forced to reflect the world in fragments of broken mirrors…I must reconcile myself to the inevitability of the missing bits."[15]

This fractured or hyphenated identity marked by the geographical site "over-there" is also marked temporally by the term "post-colonial." As Hussein continues,

> Hyphens are radically ambivalent signifiers, for they simultaneously connect and set apart; they simultaneously represent both distance and connection, belonging, and not-belonging. What is even more curious about a hyphenated pair of words is that meaning cannot reside in one word or the other, but can only be understood in movement. "Post-colonial" then suggests a movement away from and yet a vital connection to colonialism.[16]

Hyphenated identities in the U.S. share with post-colonial identities, "a movement between cultural identity and nation-states,"[17] revealing important limits about the specification of difference. For it is not possible to hyphenate all identities. If it seems strange to speak of Bengali-Indians (or Bengali-Americans), Punjabi-Indians (or Punjabi-Americans), Tamil-Indians (or Tamil-Americans), it is not absurd to note that a Gujarati Samaj, a Singh Sabha, Tamil Sangam or an American Federation of Muslims from India (AFMI) finds potent expression on American soil.

The hyphen enacts a violent shuttling between two or more worlds. Trinh T. Minh-Ha, however, argues that "the challenge of the hyphenated reality lies in the hyphen itself: the *becoming* Asian-American; the realm in-between, where predetermined rules cannot fully apply."[18] Minh-Ha continues,

> [T]he *becoming* Asian-American affirms itself at once as a transient and constant state: one is born over and over again as hyphen rather than as fixed entity, thereby refusing to settle down in one (tubicolous) world or another. The

hyphenated condition certainly does not limit itself to a duality between two cultural heritages.[19]

All identities are intrinsically coalitional, in that they seek to establish grounds of affinity. The term Asian-American, however, is a deliberately constructed coalitional identity, an inclusive political term of solidarity for those of diverse Asian backgrounds which attempts to distance itself from the logic of nation-states. Other coalitional identities such as "South Asian" or "women of color" function similarly.[20] It is important to recognize though, that coalitional identities are by nature unstable, and may also, as in the case of "becoming Asian-American," set into play a necessary set of exclusions when talking about affirmative action criteria and the specific histories of different immigrant groups in the United States.

The hyphenated ethnic identity in the U.S., however, has more often than not marked a move toward the center. The hyphen in "Indian-American" then, must be seen not simply as a conflict of identities, but as a political signifier, not merely as Bharati Mukherjee has put it, a form of "ghettoization," a "temptation to be surmounted."[21] Thus hyphenated identities have typically signaled a politics of assimilation in this country, at least formally different from experiences in Canada or Britain, where South Asians may form part of a coalitional identity termed "Black."

In fact, the place of South Asians in the U.S. has often been to work against coalitions with people of color. "Affirmative action alibis,"[22] South Asians are often unwitting or willing mediators between the white power structure and other communities marginalized by it. We find it easier to condemn the racism that is sometimes directed against us, than the hypocrisy and racism in South Asian communities directed against other American people of color.

Indeed, I wonder if the unwarranted attention given Dinesh D'Souza's book *Illiberal Education*[23] isn't related to the politics of the hyphenated Indian, many of whom are members of a large and increasingly powerful business community anxious to prove to the conservative interests who run this country that it too stands for the same liberal values of "competition" and the "free market" ready to emphasize that the "race" recorded on some South Asian passports is still "Aryan."[24]

A recent article in *Indian American* magazine, an emerging voice of such hyphenated interests, reports triumphantly that Indian small businesses in San Francisco qualify for the "Minorities and Women Business Enterprise Program," allowing them to compete with well-established firms for lucrative public contracts by taking ten percent off a minority bid.[25] In order to be considered, the Indian community had to present evidence of historical discrimination in California. This, no doubt, was done by pointing to two groups settled in the state in the early 1900s: the "Mexican-Hindu" community of the Imperial Valley[26] and the Sikhs of Yuba County, many of them agricultural workers or small orchard owners. (Other Sikhs have been more recently employed as low-paid cannery workers in Stanislaus County.)[27] The irony of the Indian victory in San Francisco should not be lost. The less well-off Sikhs of Yuba county may never be in the position to benefit from such Affirmative Action policies,[28] yet Indian businessmen are not only given preferential treatment in the United States, but as NRIs (Non-Resident Indians), they are also awarded higher rates of interest to invest in India. Thus even as they proclaim historical victimization, they enact the power of

privilege. The hyphen is indeed an ambivalent signifier, for it includes under its umbrella first-generation immigrants, both citizens and non-citizens, and second and third generations born on American soil, born as well to different experiences of racism and discrimination.

<p style="text-align:center">* * *</p>

I wonder at the ease with which Bharati Mukherjee can proclaim "I am an American,"[29] words which were forced back down my throat in grade school, words I was never permitted to say with any amount of certainty. How is it that Mukherjee's post-colonial transition from "graduate student to citizen"[30] remarks neither upon a process of immigration long problematic for India, nor upon second-generation subjects who have often found the promises of unmarked citizenship elusive at best?

Kalpana Vrudhula's poem, "Do not belong to this or that, but I am here" expresses some of the ways in which second-generation Indians handle the presumption that they are not American:

> "Are you from India?"
> "No, my parents are."
> "Oh, How exciting! You know I saw the movie Ghandi. I thought it was great…Have you been?"
> "Oh, Yes, of course!"
> (I've only gone once, I was already 23)
> "The guy I work with is from India. You must know him? his last name, uh…let me think, oh yes, Patel?"[31]

Vrudhula is effectively able to convey the ignorance with which most white Americans view India through her repetition and variation of these lines throughout her reflections. Her continual polite reply to the ignorant questioner: "Oh, Yes, of course" is a means of underscoring both the nature of the question and her own (lack of) response, for she is not able to say, as the title of the poem suggests, "No, I'm from here."

Yet if second-generation Indian voices are coming to terms with citizenship, Americanness and cultural belonging, they must also face questions of race, and in ways that immigrant parents have not often been forced to confront. Indeed, I would argue that race is perhaps the most crucial juncture distinguishing South Asian post-colonial from second-generation subjectivities. That is, second-generation writers must reconsider not only their relationship to white Americans but to American people of color as well. The second stanza of Vrudhula's poem painfully manifests what Mira Nair's film, *Mississippi Masala* (1992), portrays so clearly about racism in the Indian community (whatever else might be said of the film).

> "Say baby is you mixed?"
> "Mixed?"
> "You know, I knows you black, but you're sometin' else too?"

"No, I'm not *mixed*."

"Yes you is. You're black 'en?"

(Why the hell should I answer this guy?

I could, but he probably would ask me

what tribe anyway).

"Come on baby, what else is ya?"

(Ah...The bus).[32]

Here Vrudhula repudiates an attempt to establish affinity on the basis of color. Instead of the polite replies proffered her other interlocutors, she provides no information at all to her black questioner, responding instead with a stereotype that is far more offensive than her questioner's attempts at conversation.

Gouri Bhat's essay, on the other hand, attempts sustained reflection on the complexities of color and identification both within and outside of the Indian community, showing both a willingness to recognize points of contact with other communities of color, and an unwillingness to use color as a means to appropriate the experiences of those less privileged. She calls the Indian-American child's benign sense of difference "the form without the content of prejudice."[33] And although there is room for disagreement on the levels of racism that immigrant and second-generation Indians face in the United States, the very unevenness of the community's exposure to racism points largely to the protections afforded by class privilege. As Bhat writes,

> In the classrooms of radical discourse, the darkness of my skin is like a badge of honor. I am marked as an Empath. Guilty and solicitous white male scholars tip-toe around my privileged understanding of cultural texts. And I think: I was not raised in the barrios, in the ghettos, under the British colonial empire, so how is my color a window?[34]

* * *

My Illinois birth certificate registers my mother's race as "white," and my father's as "Indian." The very appearance of the category "race," and the responses it elicits, somehow surprise me. And yet in California miscegenation laws remained on the books until 1951, with the result that most Punjabi men in the Imperial Valley formed families with women of Hispanic origin.[35] "Men and women applying to the county clerk for a license had to look alike, and most often it was Hispanic women who satisfied that requirement. Many a license application had 'brown' and 'brown' in the blanks for 'race'..."[36]

Yet I cannot forget that my childhood in Fresno (as the daughter of an immigrant who arrived in the U.S. in 1960) was not that of Kartar Dhillon's, whose father arrived at the port of San Francisco in 1899, and whose family faced life-threatening racism. As Dhillon recounts, "My mother was sure she would die after surgery. A doctor told her she would have to go to the county hospital in Fresno to have a tumor removed. Her first sight of the doctor in the hospital confirmed her fears. 'That man does not like Indians,' she told us. 'He is the one who

let Labh Singh die.'"[37] Dhillon's mother was right. She did die a few days after the surgery. The year was 1932.

Second Wave, Second generation

The accounts of women from the second wave of Indian immigration to the United States, are of course, markedly different. They traffic hugely in the idioms of class privilege, and unless one is knowledgeable about conditions of the everyday in India, it is easy to mistake such markers for the generalized oppression of women in India. Thus when Bharati Mukherjee proclaims: "I was born into a religion that placed me a Brahmin, at the top of its hierarchy, while condemning me as a woman to a role of subservience," and later says without a trace of embarrassment, "I'm a person who couldn't ride a bus when she first arrived..."[38] It is easy for an American audience to misunderstand that the sheltered life evoked here refers not so much to being shut away, as to the privilege of being driven from one place to another. Likewise, in Indira Ganesan's 1990 novel, *The Journey,* the narrator reflects upon how her mother weathers the transition from a small South Indian village to the United States. She wondered, "as a young girl who had family and servants to cater to all her needs, a woman who had never been to the market by herself," how her mother could leave for America to bravely face supermarkets, kitchen appliances and car washes.[39] Ably conquering self-service America, the narrator's mother does not lament the loss of servants in India.

I do not mean to suggest that all narratives that mark later periods of Indian immigration to the U.S. are so steeped in the language of adjustments to material, rather than emotional conditions; or that all such transitions are easier rather than difficult. For there are many different stories of arrival and survival. If the extent to which race is addressed by the subjects of first-generation narratives is inflected by class positioning, second-generation subjects, because they have been interpolated from early childhood into the racialized structure of U.S. identity politics, are compelled to confront race in their narratives. A recent documentary by Indian feminist Indu Krishnan, *Knowing her Place* (1990), poignantly addresses some of the emotional crises of identity among second-generation and immigrant Indians in the United States. The film opens with a middle-aged woman naming the pain of a "second generation immigrant child": "It takes a long time to figure out where you belong."

Krishnan presents a dramatic subject, a woman who oscillates continually between the questions, "Are you Indian," and "Are you American"—never able to answer either. Vasu, the wife of an NYU mathematics professor, is tortured by this question-cycle which enacts a vicious attack on her fragile hold on selfhood and identity. In order to escape the endless repetition of these questions, Vasu attempts suicide while the documentary is being made.

Vasu's family had moved to New York when she was a baby, and her childhood was effectively American (she avidly describes her passion for "rock and roll"). So too was the racism she experienced at age seven or eight: children who spit on her to see if the "dirt" will rub off. Although her family returned to India when she was twelve, she spent only four years in India, returning to the U.S. at age sixteen with a husband. Yet those four years, the years of adolescence, must have been as formative as her American years, deepening what Vasu calls "the dualism within her." She movingly, if obliquely describes her experience of puberty, shut away for several days in a dark room as is the custom among orthodox groups, part of

308

her knowing this was unacceptable in the country she had left behind, and part of her accepting the isolation: afraid, and at the same time understanding that it was impossible to ask questions.

Before returning to India at age twelve, Vasu entertained the hope, encouraged by her father, that she might attend the Sorbonne. Her hopes were cruelly dashed, however, upon her father's death when she was fifteen, the event that provokes her early marriage. Vasu tells her audience, "My feeling about marriage is very bitter…I just didn't want to get married at sixteen."

As a historical subject, Vasu's particular experience of immigration to the United States falls between two major waves of Indian immigration to American shores, one at the turn of the century and one later in the '60s.[40] Yet perhaps it is Vasu's very particularity as a subject that instigates experiences of identification across very different audiences. Although she is in her mid-forties, since Vasu's childhood was American she speaks to a second-generation, college-age audience. Her being trundled off to India at age twelve also signals the powerful gender differential that marks second-generation experiences in South Asian communities. Girls are more restricted than boys, not allowed to date, and to this day, may be sent "home" during the teenage years to ensure a protected environment and proper marriage. The response of Vasu's mother to the question, "What would happen if boys and girls dated?" ("They would…slowly start kissing…") usually marks a point of heartfelt laughter among audiences, yet it also dramatically underscores the different way in which female, as opposed to male, second-generation subjects "return home."

Vasu is, however, also an adult immigrant to the United States, and this aspect of her identity—named by the filmmaker, but not Vasu herself—provokes another range of identifications, including the complicity of Krishnan herself in erasing certain questions about post-colonial identity by subsuming it too quickly into its second-generation counterpart. However, the particular dualism of Vasu's historical positioning says something about the nature of second-generation identities in general: pointing to an oscillation between post-colonial and racialized American subjectivities.

The film generates strong responses from three other (not always distinguishable) groups of people—South Asian women, South Asian mothers, Anglo-American mothers. It is not uncommon to hear from a cousin's mother-in-law or an Indian friend's aunt that Vasu's sense of an unfulfilled life, her plight in raising (male) children, and lack of sympathy from her husband resonate powerfully with their own experiences. It is also not uncommon to hear older Anglo-American women in the audience (particularly those who have parented teenagers) say that the film engages their experiences as well. And it is true that Vasu's interactions with her teenage sons—lack of respect, being taken for granted—are not atypical of mothers' experiences in a variety of cultural and historical contexts. The film then speaks powerfully to that generation of women who were first emboldened by Betty Friedan's *Feminine Mystique*,[41] revealing that the middle-class woman's "housewife dilemma" is far from resolved.

Although it is Vasu's middle-class status that enables different groups of women to identify with her across cultural space, it would certainly be wrong to reduce Vasu's conflicts to an American "housewife's dilemma." Although Krishnan's own focus unwittingly plays to this interpretation (ordering Vasu's life into a therapeutic narrative: identity crisis, attempted

suicide, counseling, increased self-confidence, new job, functional subject, functional family), Vasu's own diagnosis of "cultural schizophrenia" is a compelling one.

Vasu plays the Indian daughter when she visits her mother at home in Madras, and the dutiful Indian wife at home with her husband in New York; with her two sons, she struggles to be an American mother. For holidays she prepares elaborate American meals, rather than the sambar or rasam she prefers to cook. (At a Thanksgiving meal her younger son says a mock grace: "Thank you Vishnu for this food…" then complains that the roast is too mushy.) Her older son dates, plays in a rock band, and has his own apartment at age seventeen. He too says that his mother's cooking doesn't suit his "utility function."

This is perhaps the axis that should have been more thoroughly explored by the filmmaker. Vasu's children appear as cardboard examples of assimilation to the materialist values of the Reagan era. The older son, explaining that he couldn't live in India because he wants to be comfortable and happy, says, apparently without an ounce of self-consciousness, "Money can't make you happy but if someone gave me a million dollars right now, I'd be the happiest guy in the world." Later when he is asked "Do you feel Indian or American?" he says "Both" too quickly, then challenges, "What's the conflict? I am how I am. Just like Popeye says, 'I am what I am what I am.'" Vasu's younger son tells her, too, that even if she went from Queens to India, then back to Queens, she "has no conflict."

Why is it that Vasu's children so strenuously resist acknowledging her conflict? (Her husband resists too, but at least acknowledges that "the conflict may be real for the person experiencing it.") Is it only a matter of patriarchy in the household, or is this a juncture the filmmaker might have probed more deeply? What is it that Vasu's children, and by extension, Krishnan herself, repress?

What is advanced by the film is the fantasy of assimilation (and indeed, as "new ethnics," Indians seem to be among the recent "model minorities"). What is repressed is the question of the children's American-ness, precisely because it is assumed. The children assume it, possibly because the fear of not being fully American is very powerful. Vasu's comment that she knows what her older son feels when people call him Go-pal instead of Gopal is telling. Krishnan herself assumes the children's American-ness because she continually presents "Indian" and "American" as essentialized identities, never broken down into further specific-ity. (During the scenes filmed in India, for example, the voice-over never identifies that the language spoken is Tamil, or the community, Brahmin.) Thus in Krishnan's eyes, the children must be American because they lack Indian markers: language, religion, appreciation of food, etc. I suspect that if Krishnan had probed deeper, she might have unearthed second (in this case, third) generation sensibilities that are not articulated in the film.

To Krishnan's credit, the hyphenated identity, "Indian-American" is never offered as a solution to Vasu's dilemma. Vasu herself never articulates it as a possibility. Instead the film closes with an affirmation of Vasu's duality: she has not chosen, nor can she ever choose, one culture over the other. "Growing up in two different cultures, or coming from one to another, is like moving two directions at once; or being in two places at once." The final words of *Knowing Her Place* remind us that one definition of biculturality is not being "home" in either place.[42]

deshi native, local

samaj society

sabha meeting

sangam organization

Vishnu one of the three gods of the Hindu trinity

1. See for example, Gayatri Spivak, *The Post-Colonial Critic: Interviews, Strategies, Dialogues* (New York: Routledge, 1990), 65, 91.

2. Gouri Bhat, "Tending the Flame: Thoughts on Being Indian-American," *COSAW BULLETIN* 7 3/4 (1993), 1–2.

3. Ibid., 2

4. Ibid., 4. The original quote is "...that generation of first-wave immigrant offspring is still maturing..." The word "second" is an author insertion.

5. See for example: Jose Limon, 1985 for discussion of terms Chicano vs. Mexican-American; Rosa Linda Fregoso, and Angie Chabram, "Chicano Cultural Representations: Reframing Alternative Critical Discourse," *Cultural Studies* 4.3 (1985), 3–12; A. Juarbe, Rina Benmayor, C. Albarez, Blanca Vazquez, "Response to Poverty Among Puerto Rican Women," *Report to Joint Committee for Public Policy Research on Contemporary Hispanic Issues of the Inter-University Program for Latino Research* (Hunter College, CUNY, 1992); Rosa Torruellas, Rina Benmayor, A. Goris, A. Juarbe, "Affirming Cultural Citizenship in the Puerto Rican Community: Critical Literacy and the El Barrio Popular Education Program," *Centro Cultural Studies Task Force, Language and Education Task Force* (Hunter College, CUNY, 1991).

6. See Stuart Hall, "Cultural Identity and Cinematic Representation," *Framework* 36 (1989), 68–81.

7. This is not a unique phenomenon for second or third generation groups. ABC, for example, is also slang for "American Born Chinese."

8. Salman Rushdie, *The Satanic Verses* (New York: Viking Press, 1988), 54.

9. Bhat, 4.

10. Bharati Mukherjee, "The 400-Year Old Woman," *San Francisco Review of Books* 16.3 (1991). See also Nita Kumar, *Friends, Brothers and Informants* (Berkeley: University of California Press, 1992).

11. Meena Alexander, "Language and Shame: Reflections on My Life in Letters," *IKON* 12/13 (1992), 20.

12. Ibid., 21.

13. Ibid., 23.

14. Nasser Hussein, "Hyphenated Identity: Nationality Discourse, History, and the Anxiety of Criticism in Salman Rushdie's *Shame*," *Qui Parle?* (Summer), 8.

15. Cited in Ibid., 11.

16. Ibid., 10.

17. Ibid.

18. Trinh T. Minh-Ha, *When the Moon Waxes Red* (New York: Routledge, 1991), 157.

19. Ibid., 159.

20. As Chandra Mohanty writes, "'women of color' often used interchangeably with third world women is a term which designates a political constituency, not a biological or even a sociological one. It is a sociopolitical designation for people of African, Caribbean, Asian, and Latin American descent, and native people of the U.S. What seems to constitute 'women of color' or 'third world

women' as a viable oppositional alliance is a common context of struggle, rather than color or racial identification." Chandra Mohanty, "Cartographies of Struggle," *Third World Women and Politics of Feminism,* ed. Chandra Mohanty et al. (Bloomington: Indiana University Press, 1991).

21. Mukherjee, 57

22. Spivak, 62.

23. Dinesh D'Souza, *Illiberal Education* (New York: Free Press, 1991).

24. In 1923, the U.S. Supreme Court disallowed the claim of a Punjabi Sikh to be considered a member of the Caucasian race. From Baida Nath Varma, "Indians as New Ethnics," *The New Ethnics,* ed. Saran and Eames (New York: Praeger, 1980), 29.

25. Sunita Sorabhji, "Indians Win Minority Status," *The Indian American* (September 1991).

26. Karen Leonard, "Pioneer Voices From California: Reflections on Race, Religion, and Ethnicity," *Sikh Diaspora,* ed. N. Gerald Barrie and V. Dusenbeery (Columbia, MO: South Asia Books, 1989); and *Making Ethnic Choices* (Philadephia: Temple University Press, 1991).

27. Marcelle Williams, "Ladies on the Line: Punjabi Cannery Workers in Central California," *Making Waves: An Anthology of Writings By and About Asian American Women,* ed. Asian Women United of California (Boston: Beacon Press, 1989).

28. "One can say that earlier Indian immigrants, living mainly in the Fresno Valley of California...maintain their cultural identity...but have not quite access to the primary group network of power holders in American society. Their position is lower-middle-class....As compared to them, the newer immigrants of the 1960s and 1970s are in the upper-middle to upper-class structure of the occupational ladder." From Varma, "Indians as New Ethnics," 38.

29. Mukherjee, 57.

30. Ibid., 56.

31. Kalpana Vrudhula, "Rentike cheddah revadi, Nenu Ikkada unnanu," *COSAW Bulletin* 7 3/4 (1992), 10–13.

32. Ibid.

33. Bhat, 3.

34. Ibid.

35. Leonard, 134.

36. Ibid, 121.

37. Kartar Dhillon, "Parrot's Beak," *Making Waves: An Anthology of Writings By and About Asian American Women,* ed. Asian Women United of California (Boston: Beacon Press, 1989), 214–215.

38. Mukherjee, 56. See also Kumar, *Friends, Brothers and Informants,* 13.

39. Indira Ganesan, *The Journey* (New York: Knopf, 1990), 44–45.

40. "Indians can be classified as new ethnics because their migration to the U.S. started first as a trickle in 1885 and reached its peak of 5,000 immigrants in San Francisco in 1910...In 1922 there were 2,600 Indians in the U.S. but in 1940 only 2,400 were counted. Of the more than 3,000 Indians in 1950, the student population was 1,500. In 1946 rigid immigration laws gave India an annual quota of 100, which was not changed until the Immigration Act of 1965. Then started the second wave of immigration." From Varma, "Indians as New Ethnics," 29.

41. Betty Friedan, *Feminine Mystique* (New York: Norton, 1963, 1983; New York: Dale, 1974).

42. Spivak, 83.

Fly Me to the Moon

SUNITA VATUK

"My dear sister Sunita,
On that particular day when you left India
your Bhabhi left this world."

Maybe it takes a soul to hold a plane aloft.

We come from the airport
in a car with dying headlights.
Now my father writes
"My dear Ashok,
Today as your parents leave the United States
your American Nani left this world."

I listen.
Sound stops and time stops. I go off
looking for the place to start it again.
Tim, wrapped in the darkness
of our drive can't leave his room.
The bathroom very cold.
The living room cold,
my father sat alone.

I used to wish that I could stop time.
And wondered, what effect on my lifespan,
would oil freeze in my car
so I'd have to walk everywhere
till I turned it back on.

In Fazalpur in a corroded cardboard box there's a picture
of her sent back to them
my father's first New Year's in America,
their memory of a meeting that can never happen.

Tauji reaches over and crushes a button on my kurta.
"That's how we had to live."

Brother/sister in Hindi there is no distinction between cousins and siblings; therefore, a female cousin is a sister, male a brother

Bhabhi brother's or cousin's wife

Nani mother's mother

Tauji father's older brother

kurta traditional shirt, often of handloom cotton

To Motiba and Grandma

SHEELA BHATT

South Side Pittsburgh Pa.

The South Side of my childhood is no longer the ghetto for Eastern Europeans that it was when I lived there in 1975. But we still go there just to visit relatives and see the old house on Sarah Street that both my mother and I lived in as children. It was Pappap and Grandma's house and my mom spent the first twenty-five years of her life running around those streets with her sisters and brothers and all of our Serbian and German relatives. I can just imagine what it was like for them because even in 1975, when we first lived there, the air of the 'old world' was still very present. My mom and dad used to take us to Barsotti's, the bakery run by an Italian family, and buy the saltiest bread ever. My brothers and I would walk to the malt store, run by a Jewish man, and buy gum and Coke and read comic books. South Side was an exciting inner city playground for my brothers and me. But, most of all, I remember us surrounded by my mother's relatives who strongly identified as Serbian and always reminded us of our Serbian roots. Though they didn't speak to us in Serbian or force us to eat Serbian food, during the short time we lived in my mom's native South Side, we had a strong dose of the culture.

My dad used to tell us stories about when he first came to this country in the 1950s and found a job at U.S. Steel. He said that Pittsburgh was a place alive with culture and industry and economic prosperity. Sarah Street is one block down from J&L Steel—now just a closed-down, empty, desolate blight on the community. The collapse of the steel industry also saw a change in the makeup of the residents of South Side. The Yugoslavs and Poles, and other 'old world types' got older; there were no new generations because there was no industry. Instead, over the past twenty years, young professionals have moved in and converted many of the old homes and warehouses into refurbished living spaces.

The first time I saw the South Side I was six years old. The five of us, my parents, two brothers and I, had just returned from India. I had completed first grade at a convent school in Rajkot. Only a year earlier we'd been living in Los Angeles when my parents decided to move back to India for awhile; my father wanted to expose us to Indian life and he wanted us to know his parents. But it was clear, after one year, that my parents would be more successful professionally in the U.S., so we came to Pittsburgh. Though we stayed at my grandparents' house only six months, while deciding on the next move, my memories of South Side are still very vivid.

During those months we began to build a strong relationship with my mother's relatives—just as we had with my father's in Rajkot, Gujarat—and I began to be conscious of my cross-cultural heritage.

315

My parents have always made clear to my brothers and me that we are both Indian and American and should be proud of both. They took us to church and temple, taught us English and Gujarati, and forced us (at that time they really did have to force us) to visit India with them every three years. Yet we also spent all the American holidays with our Serbian relatives in Pittsburgh.

Mixing up the cultures was evident in all aspects of our lives. Even our family home in India, built on top of my grandparents' home, is a blend of my mother's Western tradition and my father's Indian style. While both the downstairs and upstairs have very traditional Indian features, like the jhula or punka, one particular amenity installed in both homes was ultimately American: the Western toilet and bathtub. My parents tried to create an environment which was generally very Indian in order for us to adapt to small town Indian life, while simultaneously attempting to create a balance between both cultures.

We moved from South Side in 1976 and spent the next seven years moving from Illinois to Connecticut to Ohio to upstate New York where I went to high school. Because we moved so much, we always felt that our roots were in the places where our relatives lived: Pittsburgh and Rajkot. We called those places home. We never really belonged where we lived; we never stayed long enough

I look back now at the things I have always taken for granted and realize how unique the experience of being bi-cultural is. I used to think it was strange that I was related by blood to people who lived ten thousand miles away from each other and had never met. But I never thought, until I left for college, that it was that strange to have one set of cousins who were blond-haired and blue-eyed suburbanites and another set who were one hundred percent small town Indian. They all loved me and I didn't think of myself as brown or white in front of them. I thought of myself as a part of whichever side I was with at the moment and I still do—regardless of my increased awareness about color and race.

Being bi-cultural has its painful side. When I reentered the U.S. school system in the second grade, I was faced with a great humiliation—because of my accent I was forced to take remedial English classes. I was retaught phonics because my pronunciations weren't American English pronunciations and I was forced to go to special classes because I had a lisp. Every day, I used to pretend to be sick because I was so embarrassed by who I was and by my academic inadequacies. Though my parents were aware of my problem with school it did not occur to them that it stemmed from insecurities related to my differences: color, speech and even culture. They were confident in their identities and they were confident that they had done the right thing by instilling Indian culture in us. I was sure I was doomed for life.

During junior high I became friends with a Black girl from up the street. We were in the same grade and we took the same bus every day. Soon we were inseparable (and are still close friends). We could always count on each other to hang out, play sports and work during the summers together, picking strawberries on a farm near our houses. We used to joke around with the other students that we were cousins because she was part Indian. Not knowing the difference between Native American and Asian Indian, they believed us. I still remember the confidence their ignorance gave me. Somehow it allowed me to be proud, to

feel 'one up' because of my color and difference. I think back now and realize it was one of the only times I *chose*, along with my friend, to point out my difference.

I was defined as 'Indian' by my classmates because I was brown. In young people's eyes, color makes a great deal of difference. Because my mother is a White American I was allowed to feel that much closer to my peers who were white, American and 'popular.' But even if I was accepted in their eyes as 'American' because of my mother, I was still always going to be seen as brown first. I think all non-white people who are brought up in this country face this same dilemma: being colored and, therefore, not 'really' American. But, this was further complicated for me by the fact that my mother was seen as very much an American and very much a part of this culture and system.

Straddling both cultures had its awkward and confusing moments for my brothers and me. I have many memories of our doing strange things when my friends' families seemed to be following the normal American etiquette. For example, on Thanksgiving, we would eat Indian food, along with vegetarian stuffing, mashed potatoes and cranberry sauce (Of course, we kids would have liked to have had a more traditional meal on Thanksgiving like all of our friends!) Or, even worse, my brothers, with my father, once had to change their Brahmin sacred thread (in front of onlookers) on a beach in Santa Cruz. Every year they would change their thread on a certain day near a body of water—whether it was an ocean, lake, pond or even a stream. Unfortunately, that year the closest body of water was one of the biggest tourist beaches in California. It was a totally humiliating situation for my brothers and me, but my dad didn't even notice. They had nothing on but shorts and a sacred thread around their chest. They had to sit and pray and perform the proper ceremony, standing up with their hands holding the sacred thread up to the sky. I was designated as the photographer (I got off easy). The photo memories of that time are extremely funny now, but, when I was fifteen, it was a traumatic experience!

Except for these few moments, I generally took our ways for granted. The blending of our Indian and American traditions was masked at home because we were all together. In college, however, my status of 'half-n-half' felt like it stood out more. Many other students were making distinctions about their identifies—usually around race/ethnicity or class background. When I started to figure out 'who I think I am,' my bi-racial dilemma really surfaced. Because bi-racial people were not visible at all on my campus, I felt like I had to be either White or Indian. Organizations, and even social groups, all seemed to be oriented towards 'single race' identities: African American, South Asian American, Chicano, etc.

Initially, I got involved with white activist organizations because they were the most visible on my campus. Soon, however, I realized that I didn't want to surround myself only with white liberals. I often felt alienated and removed from their world view. I could not afford to be a radical hippie. Many of these people could ultimately rely on their upper-middle class backgrounds—something I could not do—and live their life in any manner they pleased because of racial and economic privilege in this country. Also, since most had not been confronted with economic and racial discrimination, race and class were often the tokenized afterthought issues—in order to 'diversify.' These issues were not personal to them. So, while they were discovering their identity as radicals/liberals, I completely reevaluated the way I had begun to identify myself.

Still, I didn't go out of my way to participate in South Asian organizations because I didn't feel any strong affinity to South Asian American people either. My best friends in high

317

school had been either White or Black and I had never had an Indian-American friend outside of school. My affinity with India stemmed from my tie to the country and our home and family there. Because we moved often and the places where we moved to did not have strong Indian communities, my parents had stopped going to, or hosting, Indian parties (much to my brothers' and my relief). So, we had even less contact with the Indian community here in the States. We still had our Gujarati lessons and cultural lessons but this happened inside the home. Our social life happened in our neighborhoods and at school. We grew up much more Indian and American than Indian-American.

I also had no desire to go to Indian functions or meet Indian men. (Though from the time I was sixteen, my dad's relatives had been collecting bio-data on good Gujarati Hindu boys for me to marry!) I didn't feel like I would fit in. I was not fully Indian; I was not brought up the same way as kids whose parents were both Indian; and I had insecurities about being different from the norm. Often during college, my roommate's Indian-American friend would invite me to functions held by the campus Indian-American organization. I always said no—graciously of course—while inwardly flinching at the mere idea of subjecting myself to a college student's version of the Indian parties of my youth. I have enough memories of those parties: all the kids watching Indian movies, eating Indian food, pretending we were in India when we weren't. Meanwhile the adults would gossip and talk nonsense to each other. Saying no was easy.

But during my junior year I had a chance to rethink all of this. I took time off and went back to India to travel through the country with my jikaka and Benifaiba (my father's brother and sister). I saw the country through my relatives' native eyes, as well as through my foreign ones. I also lived in our family home with my motiba and relatives in a way I had never been able to when we had gone as a family. I reacquainted myself with my old childhood friends and wondered why I had never developed any close friendships with Indians in the U.S. I found out for myself why my father loves India, and I returned to the States wanting to preserve my Indian heritage. I realized that I needed to seek out people, outside of Indian-American social clubs, who had experiences similar to mine.

The year I returned to the U.S., I met and developed a group of South Asian American women friends—outside of any formal South Asian organization—because of our similar political and social interests. Though we were in the same university, we had been in very different social and political circles and had never realized that there were other South Asian Americans like us out there. Many of the women that I am closest to now have, like me, spent very little time with South Asian Americans—the most visible of whom are part of the conservative Indian American community. (Because my women friends were not just from India, I began to realize the exclusionary qualities of the term "Indian American." This compelled me to consciously redefine myself and my community as South Asian.) But these women have made me want to be a part of South Asian American culture here in this country. With encouragement from them, my family and my non-South Asian friends, I have also lost a great deal of my inhibition to assert my dual identity. I now feel very strongly about acknowledging and respecting both parts of my heritage.

Still, being bi-cultural/bi-racial is complex and, often times, alienating. My white friends and 'people of color' friends have limited interaction because the groups deal with

very different issues and approach life in different ways. I, in turn, feel I lead two separate lives—though equally fulfilling. Yet, like so many who come from mixed backgrounds, I often feel forced to choose one group over another. However, I know that I can and will discover a way to better integrate the two parts of me, just as my parents have always hoped. When they named me Sheela, my brother Jay and my other brother Sunil (which could be shortened to 'Neil'), they had a specific reason in mind. They wanted our names—and us—to 'pass' in either culture. They succeeded in their attempt to create a multi-cultural upbringing within the home. Unfortunately the acceptance and understanding one gets at home does not always translate into the outside world.

Increasingly I am meeting bi-racial/bi-cultural people who identify as such and feel proud of who they are. It has been encouraging for me to share experiences, or even just to get to know others like me, just as it is empowering for South Asian Americans to have our own support networks. Also, I think that bi-racial/bi-cultural people have a unique perspective on the inter-racial strife within our multi-racial/multi-cultural society. And I hope that we can, in our emerging visibility, begin to affect the racial prejudice that comes from the fear, ignorance and segregation from one another.

Making a Space for Women in the Third World: Displacement and Identity in Suleri's Meatless Days*

RASHMI SADANA

In *Meatless Days*, Sara Suleri's spirited collection of dense autobiographical tales, Suleri writes about her family in Pakistan. Several of her tales are devoted to the women in her life: her Dadi, her mother, and her sister Ifat. This collection focuses on women not as one entity, but as individuals. As she writes about these individuals, Suleri is aware of the ghost-like presence that women in the third world seem to have, and she even writes that "there are no women in the third world."(20) While comprising half of the physical existence of the third world, women's individual and separate lives in that world do not exist, nor are they considered unless they are closely tied to some international political issue or event. Women are essentially seen through politically focused binoculars. While certain problems are magnified to educate the collective Other World, the individual is of little or no consequence. What remains is a distortion of reality. When Mother Teresa is sick, we may only then remember the women (and men) she has helped in Calcutta; when Benazir Bhutto becomes the first woman prime minister of an Islamic nation, we think that the average woman's life in Pakistan has changed. Perhaps it is only when Bhutto is later dethroned and charged with power abuse and corruption that we realize that she is one persona in Pakistan, not representative of women in that country.

Suleri, a Yale English professor, explains the political enigma of the third world at the outset of *Meatless Days*: "When I teach topics in third world literature, much time is lost in trying to explain that the third world is locatable only as a discourse of convenience...not located precisely where you're sitting." (19-20) However, as Suleri recounts the physical and psychological displacements of her family members, she shows how individual identity is inextricably linked to history and place, no matter how "unlocatable" they may seem to be.

In *Meatless Days*, Suleri gives women a space for expression. Suleri and each of the women in her life has experienced some form of displacement spurred by physical migration, and this forms the basis of her narrative. By focusing on individual lives, domestic quarrels and obligations, and personal tragedy, Suleri shows how women's identities are much more than expressions of their societal roles as mothers, wives and daughters. Grandmothers are not all kind creatures whose sole purpose is to comfort the younger generations. Just as mothers do not always have the right answers, and may themselves be struggling to form their own identities outside of their roles as benevolent Mamma. In her consideration of the intricacies, complexities and conflicts in the lives of these women, Suleri chronicles them as real individuals living in all of their idiosyncratic absurdity. Throughout *Meatless Days*, Suleri

320

rejects the politically cast identity of third world women, and focuses on the irrelevance of the state's definition of women. In a sense, her tales are stubborn—they don't fit neatly into most conceptions about Pakistan, politics or third world women.

Suleri's juxtaposition of the state and the individual, and the disdain that each has for the other, is particularly evident in her sentimental, yet vivid depiction of Dadi. Even during the tumultuous times of Partition, Dadi is unconcerned with the workings of the state. Suleri writes that "Dadi was peeved" by independence and resented it "for the distances it made." (2) In writing about Dadi, Suleri injects neither nostalgia nor valorization in regard to her grandmother's life. Instead, she portrays Dadi as a self-centered old woman consumed by the passions of food and God. And it is in this sense that Suleri rejects symbolic identities of women. Suleri places value on the reality of women's lives. Dadi is neither glamorous nor friendly, nor is she particularly caring. But the tragic element of Suleri's account is not that her grandmother did not live up to Suleri's expectations, but that Dadi as an individual is a displaced person within her own societal and religious structure. Suleri describes Dadi's physical migration in cultural terms when she writes: "When India was partitioned in August of 1947, she moved her thin pure Urdu into the Punjab of Pakistan."(2) It is ultimately the loss of her cultural milieu that prompts Dadi to resent "independence for the distances it made."(2) Suleri resurrects the importance and significance of this displacement when she comments upon the unimportance of Dadi's death. Dadi's death is upstaged by the death of Zulfikar Ali Bhutto. Suleri shows how Dadi is casually forgotten as the national agenda takes the spotlight. Suleri writes of Dadi's death,

> It happened in the same week that Bhutto finally was hanged, and our imagina-
> tions were consumed by that public and historical dying. Pakistan made rapid
> provisions not to talk about the thing that had been done, and somehow,
> accidentally, Dadi must have been mislaid into that large decision, because she
> too ceased being a mentioned thing. (17)

Unlike her characterization of Dadi, Suleri's remembrances of her mother and her sister, Ifat, are laden with grief and sorrow. At first, it seems that she is expressing her own sense of personal loss at their deaths, but the sorrow is ultimately a tribute to their displaced lives. Suleri's mother was a white Welsh woman who emigrated to Pakistan after marrying Suleri's father. Like her mother, Ifat is initially displaced by marriage. By marrying "an army man," Ifat takes a step closer to the state and to what Suleri sees as symbolic support for Pakistan. She writes that "Javed (Ifat's husband) signified to Ifat a complete immersion into Pakistan."(140) By religiously committing to memory everything from the rules of polo to the history of the army, and by learning the customs and dialect spoken by Javed's family, Ifat seems to take on a new identity with her role as wife. However, Suleri shows that the essence of Ifat, her sister, was unchanged. Ifat's true identity is not altered when she moves away from her family; nonetheless, Ifat becomes estranged from the family because of her marriage to Javed—a symbolic marriage to the state more powerful than her individual identity. Suleri describes the displacement's eventual toll on identity when she writes, "So in the end there was no place where Ifat could return: in each room she was new."(143)

Ifat's identity is caught between myth and reality. Women are encouraged to relate to religious and national identities, but these larger identities are ultimately irrelevant when it comes to the concrete issues of women's rights and opportunities. In reference to Benazir Bhutto, Suleri notes that even with a female Prime Minister, the psychological revolution had little to do with the socio-economic realities of the majority of Pakistani women. For this reason, it seems, Suleri chooses "meatless days" as the central image in her collection of stories. Suleri explains that the Pakistani government designates two days a week as meatless days in order to conserve the supply of livestock. (31) But instead of conserving meat, people hoard it before these designated days and feast on "anything fleshy" during the "meatless days." The irony of this response to the government's proclamation serves as Suleri's prime example of the uncontrollable gap between symbol (or myth) and reality.

Though her autobiographical pieces mostly pertain to women's identity, Suleri shows how similar forces of displacement and identity are at work in the life of her father. Suleri's father defines himself through his political writings, making his theories on the government's policies his only form of self-expression. As an individual, his identity collides with the state, and he is ultimately engulfed by it. Suleri refers to her father's career as "the longest romance of his life" and as being "tempestuous." It is his political passions that estrange him from his family. After the war of 1971, when her family learns of the atrocities of the army's actions in Bangladesh, Suleri describes her conflicting reactions with those of her father:

'I am not talking about the two-nation theory,' I wept to my father, 'I am talking about blood!' He would not reply, and so we went our separate ways, he mourning for the mutilation of a theory, and I—more literal—for a limb, or a child, or a voice. (122)

It is with this strain of literalness that Suleri writes her account. In order to question national identity and the symbols that attempt to define that identity, Suleri boldly uncovers the displacements of her own family members. Using dense and highly literal prose to examine the truths in her family's lives, she shies away from lyrical images that would provide reader accessibility. The result is a sometimes choppy, and almost always slow reading of *Meatless Days*, but Suleri does not compromise her desire to show the grit of daily life and the intensity of raw emotion. Her aim appears to be to cut through the haze of the imaginary Pakistani national identity and find the limb, the child or the voice.

In doing so, Suleri also draws an interesting parallel between the complexity of identity and the representation of language. Suleri discusses her mother's displacement in terms of language when she writes, "Mamma's Urdu was an erratic thing, with sudden moments of access into idioms whose implications would throw her audience into gasps of surprise." (41) Her mother's imprecise language skills are much like her mother's inability to gauge the subtle workings of Pakistani society. Something has been lost in translation, and her mother seems to be living in a kind of linguistic no man's land. That Suleri's mother holds a Pakistani passport is inconsequential; this official piece of identity bears no relation to the reality of her immigrant experience as a British woman in Pakistan. Suleri explains the non-acceptance of her mother into Pakistani society:

There were centuries' worth of mistrust of Englishwomen in their eyes when they looked at her who chose to come after the English should have been gone: What did she mean by saying, 'I wish to be part of you?' Perhaps, they feared, she mocked. (163)

Suleri's own migration to the United States serves as the larger displacement and backdrop to her autobiographical accounts. Her perspective as a South Asian in America lays the foundation for her questioning of cultural identity. Suleri's confusion about the nature of the word *kapura* (testicles) shows her insecurity about her own cultural identity. Her mother had taught her that the word meant sweetbreads. When Suleri is confronted with her misuse of the word as she is preparing sweetbreads in New Haven, Connecticut, she writes, "Natives should always be natives, exactly what they are, and I felt irked to be so probed around the issue of my own nativity."(22) By bringing herself into the ambiguous immigrant equation, Suleri shows the endless possibilities of migration and displacement in the modern world. Each member of her family has migrated—either from India to Pakistan, Great Britain to Pakistan, or Pakistan to the United States. Suleri shows that it is not the distance traveled which is significant, but the individual's personal experience and relation to place by historical or personal connection.

In a sense, Suleri's account has little to do with the plight of many third world women. She does not address poverty or violence against women, for example. Instead, she considers the artificial, or perhaps, intellectual space that the term "third world" occupies in modern parlance. The negative image of corruption, disorganization and general chaos that seems to so easily define anything "third world" is shown in this very personal collection to be the least important aspect of people's lives. In addition, there is nothing exotic or fantastic about her portraits. Instead, Suleri focuses on the subtle and almost unnoticeable effects of displacement on the people she knows best, the women in her family. Ultimately, history and the individual are not only intertwined, unable to untangle themselves and live happily apart, but it is the individual who must surrender to history. Suleri writes of her mother's life, "I am curious to locate what she knew of the niceties that living in someone else's history must entail, of how she managed to dismantle that other history she was supposed to represent." (164)

If Suleri appears to shed a dreary pall over the postcolonial world of migration and displacement, she also makes a substantive analysis of the emotional consequences of such a world. In the case of Suleri's sister, Ifat makes no easily definable migration—she moves within her own society. Though her essence remains unchanged, her "immersion" into Pakistan by marrying an army man literally overpowers her identity. Similarly, Dadi's identity is overrun by the whims of an imperial map maker and a bitter religious war whose only temporary cure is mass migration. Both Ifat and Dadi live in the somewhat ominous shade of the state which claims to create their identities. While Suleri and her mother are not caught in the definitional strong arm of state politics, they experience the birth pangs of being cultural outsiders in a new world. Where language and history become all important, the common holds that bind a culture are ruptured as these women live in non-native lands. As individuals, their identities are the essences of their migrations. Though it is apparent that history, language and state politics are the guiding forces of individual experience, Suleri

portrays the essence of individual identity as something in constant struggle with, and in opposition to, these dominating forces.

dadi father's mother

* Suleri, Sara. *Meatless Days*. Chicago: University of Chicago Press, 1991.

A French Woman of Tamil Descent in Réunion Island

MARIE-CLAIRE SAVRIAMA

An important part of the Indian Diaspora still lives in Réunion, a small island in the Indian Ocean. Réunion, previously a French colony, became a French Department in 1946. Its economy was based on sugar cane plantations. The multicultural population—Europeans, Africans, Hindu and Muslim Indians, Chinese and Malagasy people—is all under the control of the French Administration. My ancestors, who were practicing the Hindu religion, came from India to this Island in the last century. An Indian woman in the French cultural context of Réunion today is expected to uphold many traditional values and, at the same time, confront many cultural changes. I am the fourth generation from Tamil descent born in Réunion Island and I was raised practicing Hindu and Christian religions, as well as Indian and French cultures. Since I have been living in the United States, I have realized how unique this situation is.

In the eighteenth century, the economy of the Island was based on the sugar cane plantation. The abolition of slavery of people from Africa in 1848 led the white landowners to recruit new laborers by contract to work for them on their plantations. That policy resulted in the immigration of many Indian people from the French Indian settlements in the Tamil Nadu (mainly Madras). The majority of people of Indian descent are of Tamil background. A mistaken denomination in the nineteenth century led foreigners to call all the people from South India (Tamils included) "Malabars." This term has been attributed to contract workers coming to Réunion and has been maintained as a definition of the identity among them. To avoid any confusion, in this paper I will use the term "Indian" (even if this term did not exist at the time of the immigration in the Island) instead of "Malabar."

The principal immigration wave took place in the middle of the last century and stopped officially in 1881. Initially, the engagement contract lasted for five years and the laborers intended to return to their country after this period. Many were obliged to go on working after the end of their contract because of their debts. Most of the landowners did everything to keep the Indians working on their plantations. They paid them little by little, sometimes much later than expected. More often, they gave them vouchers allowing them to buy what they needed. If the workers were fortunate enough to finish their contract and get their wages, they often had to wait many months to embark on a boat and return to India. The perpetual postponement of their departure, which kept the immigrants in a state of insecurity, often obliged them to spend all their money and finally to request a new contract either with their

former landowner or another. These particular circumstances, coupled with the occasional voluntary decisions to stay in Réunion, formulated the Indian community in the Island.

The vast majority of the Indian immigrants were from different castes, each expecting a better life or hoping to return home with enough wealth to begin a new life. The daily life of these immigrants was very hard. Not only did they work ten to twelve hours a day, they suffered from exploitation within the hierarchy created by the white landowner and his supervisors. Despite the contractual commitments they had signed, specifying, among other things, that they could practice their Hindu religion, it was almost forbidden at the beginning. The workers soon realized that the French Administration wanted to convert them to the Christian religion. However, their strong faith in Hindu gods gradually was recognized and accepted. They were allowed to build Hindu temples and practice their religion with their fellow believers. Because of their physical closeness in the sugar cane plantations and in the camps, the caste system became irrelevant for the Indian immigrants and their descendants. Nowadays, people of Indian descent in Réunion do not know the caste(s) of their ancestors and their peers. All are "Malabars." Meanwhile, if the meaning of the caste system has been forgotten, hierarchical positions of families are still crucial.

The intended policy of the sugar cane planters was to bring an Indian labor force to Réunion Island. Very few Indian women, perceived to be physically weaker than the men, were brought to the Island. There were approximately four Indian women for every ten Indian men. This explains why a great number of Indian men could not marry Indian women and had to marry women whose ancestors were mostly of European or African origin. There is a large population who have Hindu names without any specific adherence to Indian culture. The Indian immigrants who could find an Indian woman to marry were able to maintain their culture and transmit it easily to their offspring. The continuation of marriage within the community is an important way of understanding the Indian culture on this Island today. My ancestors, originally from India, have strictly intermarried among Indians, which has been a key element in preserving the Indian culture in our family.

My sisters and I live in a society in which the dominant cultural model is French. Except for our long hair, we do not explicitly show our traditional "Indianness." We don't wear the sari, except occasionally when going to the temple to pray. We don't even speak Tamil. Our way of being, nevertheless, is full of typical Indian habits which have been unchanged for more than one hundred years on this Island. Like our parents and grandparents, we were sent to church to learn the Christian religion in order to be French. This imposed integration through the adoption of the dominant patterns in the Island (religion and clothing) didn't prevent us from acting in an Indian way. As a young girl I was not allowed to speak to non-Indians just because, according to my parents, "they are different." No more explanations were given to me. I realize now that my parents scorned the non-Indians' physical and moral "impurity." Their concern about pollution (they touch everything, eat meat whenever they want, do not go to the temple...) underlies this irrevocable separation.

Though the general cultural model of the society is quite Western, my parents—and especially my mother—have maintained the Indian tradition through their daughters. When I was seven years old and had to go outside the home, I realized that the way I had been raised was not the only way. Very early I learned not to ask questions. I still remember my mother

saying "Things are like that because they have always been like that…" For example, I was not allowed to sleep during the day; after 6 p.m., I was not allowed to go outside the house, to comb my hair or cut my nails. My mother just told me that these acts were "not auspicious." There was no inquiry, but rather a total obedience and an emulation of the daily acts of my elder sisters. Respect for the past, the elders and tradition was expected of me.

In my family, the birth of a girl is not as coveted by the parents as that of a boy (because a girl is not allowed to conduct the ritual for the ancestors due to her regular impurity). For my sisters, this acceptance of unfairness was the way we lived. But for me, even at that time, I didn't accept that unfairness and each time it was possible, behaved like my brothers. I used to help my father when he did odd jobs instead of being with my mother in the kitchen or in the house. Nevertheless, the link between my mother and me has always been very strong from birth and our deep relationship is indelible. As a baby, I was weaned very late and slept in my parents' bed until I was able to walk by myself. My mother took special care to protect me from every sort of bad influence: from jealousy and the "evil eye," although unconscious, of the passer-by and sometimes even the extended family itself. The constant suspicion of "others" led to a need of protection which was physically expressed by a little red dot that my mother put on my forehead. Very early I was taught how to preserve myself from the "others," who were everyone outside the family's home.

As a young girl, I learned to separate things. I separated myself quite easily from my brothers and soon stopped playing with them; this was one of the many things I didn't question. I separated myself from the constant threat of the outside world. I was not allowed to play with non Indian children. I separated my Hindu religion at the temple from the Christian one which I "showed" to non-Indians as a good French Christian should. However, I learned to invest most of myself, as my parents did, into the Hindu religion. Despite the fact that I and my sisters were more likely to be given a Christian first name—Marie—one fact that remained typically Indian was, and still is, the choice of the first letter of our middle name. When a child is born in our family my father, who is a Hindu priest, used to consult his astrological books to find out which letter our name must begin with in order to be auspicious and to protect us during our lifetime. Each time a problem occurred it was the Hindu religion that my whole family would resort to. This basic complete separation has followed me all my life.

An experience of this separation came at the time of my first menstruation. This event no longer is a religious ritual, but it is the object of a certain dramatization. My mother took me into her room and told me simply not to be afraid. I was expected to be more careful. I learned that I would not be allowed to go to the temple during my menses because I would then be considered as "impure" in front of God. Thus I entered into the women's world. I could not approach my father and my brothers. As my relation to them became more distant, I was also more careful with men on the outside and even avoided any kind of closeness to them in the street.

My mother insisted then on the decency expected of an Indian girl. Any of my deviant behavior with respect to avoiding boys and men would be considered a threat to my family's honor. In the Indian families of Réunion Island, honor is a common propriety and depends on the behavior of all the members. The strong identification with my family led me to

consider the consequence of my action before acting. My sisters and I respected the norms of honor by preventing ourselves from having pre-marital relations. My parents never spoke about it but we knew. Even though the whole family was protecting my sisters and me, my mother was responsible for our virginity and was judged accordingly. By protecting our chastity, they maintain their own honor and reputation. I must admit that even now it is hard to think of any sexual relationship outside marriage.

Marriage is in fact the only institution which allows sexual intercourse between a man and a woman in the Indian system of values. It was expected that the ideal husband for me would be a man who was also a Hindu and who had at least the same social status. The pressure of society has led Indians to integrate the Christian marriage practices at church. This does not mean a complete loss of Hindu principles and practices. Choosing the day of the wedding according to the birth dates of the betrothed is one of the Hindu practices which is maintained.

Unlike ten years ago when Indian parents were still arranging marriages, now in Réunion we have the freedom to choose our own spouse on the conditions of money, education and family. However, a certain ritual of meeting between the suitor and the girl's family is maintained. What matters for my parents is that my sisters and I will have everything in our own families that they have given us at home and that we will be able to live what they consider to be a happy life.

After having raised all her children well, my mother became more respected than ever. My mother was taught by her mother to be responsible for inculcating her daughters with the proper values. Her duty as a mother will end when her own children are married. She often says, "I have done my duty in front of God." For me, she has been the perfect mother. Yet my mother, who wanted me to be highly educated, did not anticipate that I might question her traditional way of raising me. My parents do not understand that I am not married even though I have still chosen to preserve the basic good Indian values I learned from them.

For me, the challenge now is to deal with two systems of values. Between my South Indian origin and my upbringing in Réunion, I have the opportunity to take what I want from each one. The challenge is not an easy one, but I know that the experience of taking the best of both cultures is certainly worth the effort.

Sunsets

SUSHILA GAWANDE

When I was just a little girl I saw a beautiful sunset on the Sabarmath River. I just admired it.

As an adolescent I went to see the sunset just to get away from the hectic routine of school and homework and that was about it. Mind was still empty, thoughtless.

When I got married and had children we saw beautiful sunsets on the banks of Florida, Hawaii, Kanyakumari and still, with my empty mind, it had an awesome beauty.

But one day children grew up and left the nest and I look at the beautiful sunset, admire it and smile to myself knowing I have seen something more beautiful than that and you know what it is? My children's faces.

A Marriage Proposal

ANU MURGAI

The first time Priya heard about it, it was March and pink flowers were blooming in the roundabout on Shanti Path. Someone who knew someone else who happened to know Ma had heard that the Mehtas in Punjabi Bagh (the ones who owned a chartered accountancy firm) had a son of marriageable age. They had been asking about Priya, questions about her age and where she was studying. Ma told Papa and they both thought that it was a family with a decent reputation. Priya was a good girl—pretty and intelligent; one could only wait and hope. Ma told Priya, just in case.

The phone call transformed rumor into fact a week later. Mr. Mehta informed Priya's father of his overwhelming respect for Priya's family and his profound longing for the admission of one member, Priya, of this very respectable family into the ranks of his own household. He invited the Vedis for dinner on Saturday. "Let the boy and girl see each other," he said. "Let them decide for themselves."

All this was not important. Not important for Priya anyway. The whispers and the phone calls were immaterial; they had planted themselves in the background ever since she graduated from high school. What grew remained in shadow; Priya could not see the link between a mundane phone call and the vast plains of the future that shone in her eyes.

What is marriage really like? she thought. Oh, she knew the facts of life and all that...but what did all this mean? She leaned forward and watched her hands outline her eyes in kohl. (Ma was scolding Sona; she wanted her to wear a "frills and bows" dress. Papa was humming to himself as he stood in his underwear in the bathroom, shaving.) Marriage was nobody; marriage was nothing. Her cousin got married four months ago. Since then, the sun had crept into her eyes, her arms jingled and jangled with twinkling bangles, her lips flirted with the world.

Sometimes marriage stood behind Priya's shoulder, his breath ruffled the ends of her hair, his shadow fell across her body.

Ma was calling everybody to the car; Priya rearranged her chunni and combed her hair again.

Throughout the drive, Ma leaned close to the window, squashing her nose on the glass, peering into the streets as if a thick fog covered the car. "That's the house," she said. "Stop the car, Pran." The family's actions were punctuated by her voice. "Roll up the windows. Don't touch your hair, Priya. Sona, you must sit next to me all evening. Did you roll up the windows?" She looked around the street to make sure no ruffians were waiting to steal their car.

The door was opened by a maid. The family crowded into the corridor; Ma hastily patted her hair (she had a phobia about disappearing hairpins) and Papa tugged at his pants. A woman—that is, a woman's backside—blocked the end of the corridor. "She must be Mrs. Mehta," thought Priya. She had short, black, bouncy hair, one side of which extended a fashionable distance from her ear. The maid timidly tapped her on the shoulder; she turned around.

The front did not match the backside. God had glued together two different casts. A large stomach, lined with tiny wrinkles, thrust itself outwards from under the thousand-rupee sari. It was all of her, it advertised itself, distorting her center of gravity to the degree that she walked at a slight angle to the ground. She murmured a word or two in greeting; Priya heard her own name waft into the air.

Priya was smiling; her mother was smiling; Mrs. Mehta was smiling; they were led into the drawing room and there was another woman standing there. "My sister-in-law," Mrs. Mehta's voice rumbled behind Priya. The woman smiled; she had a sparrow-like face—a tiny nose and grey hair-twigs peeping out of the round bun. Her eyes were magnified by square black frames. "Please sit down," she said, and Priya liked her.

Ma was sitting on the sofa on the other side of the room, her back upright, her mouth smiling a readiness to begin a polite conversation. Papa was already talking to his father (and where was *he*?); his father looks like any father, she thought, except Papa. "Priya, meet my son, Ranjan." She looked up into Mrs. Mehta's dark blue printed saree, then they were all standing up, then he was sitting down in the chair next to her; Mrs. Mehta had already joined the others across the room, leaving the two of them alone.

She didn't know what to think.

He looks like his father, his shirt is nice.

"Where are you studying?"

Okay voice, nice smile, he must be from St. Columba's.

"LSR," she said, looking at his shirt buttons. "Economics Honors."

He was smiling again. "What year?"

"Third year. My exams are in June."

"What are you planning to do after that?"

She looked at his buttons again. "I don't know." Maybe I should sound more decisive. "I was thinking about a graduate degree."

"IIM? XLRI?"

Am I supposed to say something to that? Why do you think I'm here? You know what I'm going to do next!

She sat silently, smoothing her hands on her salwar, waiting.

"Are you here because you want to be here?"

She had to look at him now.

Brown eyes, big nose.

"Nobody forces me to do anything," she said (a little too quickly, she thought). "I am allowed to make independent decisions."

"Okay," he said, leaning back.

She rearranged her chunni; he looked at the roof.

"Look," he said. "I can't think of anything that will get more than a one-line answer from you. What should we do?"

"I don't know," she said and they laughed.

Mrs. Mehta was holding court. The maid put a tea tray down on the table in front of her and tiptoed from the room. Mrs. Mehta poured tea into a delicate porcelain Hitkari cup with tiny pink flowers printed on the saucer.

"Milk and sugar?" she asked Ma. Papa looked satisfied; he and Ranjan's father had stationed themselves beside a bowl overflowing with cashew nuts. "Please have some more," said Mrs. Mehta.

"In our Hindu tradition," she said, "the comfort of a guest is very important."

"Yes, yes," murmured Ma.

"In America," continued Mrs. Mehta, "they expect the guest to look after himself. He has to help himself from the fridge and even wash all the dirty dishes after dinner." Papa reached out for more cashew nuts and popped one into his mouth. "Yes," he said, and bit the cashew nut. "Indians are famed for their hospitality." The sister-in-law patted her hair and said, "Sudama gave Lord Krishna all the food he had, even though it meant that his family would starve."

Ranjan's father passed around the bowl. A fruitseller's singsong voice wavered in the distance.

"In America," said Mrs. Mehta, "children grow up very quickly. What kind of childhood do you have when you must replace your dolls with bottles of perfume and bright lipstick at thirteen?" She paused to dip her hand into the orbiting bowl. "They spend all their college years looking for a husband. They have no time to have fun, to play or to study."

The bowl returned to the table. Two fragmented cashew nuts lay at the bottom. Mrs. Mehta looked at Ranjan and Priya, who were talking softly.

"Ranjan," she said. "Can you help me in the kitchen?"

Papa and Ranjan's father were entangled in an argument on the future price of Reliance shares when Ranjan came back. The sister-in-law was saying something to Ma. Her grey blouse had wet patches under the armpits. A bra strap peeped out boldly on one shoulder.

Ranjan had a smile on his face. Mrs. Mehta stood next to him, her hand on his arm. His father's stomach deflated with a hiss. The sister-in-law sat up suddenly.

Ma looked at Papa, then at Priya. She smiled.

The orange sulphur lights on Ring Road carpeted the street in a glow. Sona had given in to sleep; her head shook gently in tandem with the movement of the car. Priya took off her sandals, tucked her legs underneath her and watched Motibagh vanish into the night.

Ma turned around to look at Priya. "His family is reputable. The sister-in-law was telling me that her uncle's father-in-law was that famous writer...I don't remember his name but he wrote something quite large, four hundred pages or so. Ranjan took a third in Delhi in the Chartered Accountancy exam. He is doing very well, you know. He has only worked for a year and already, he has a Maruti car. What do you think?"

"I don't know," said Priya softly. She pictured him in her mind. "He is nice…funny," she said. "Nice shirt."

As they were getting out of the car (Ma was coaxing an irate Sona to sleep in her bed instead of the car seat), Priya remembered about the dinner. "We are going to eat dinner at the Hyatt on Tuesday," she said.

Suddenly, her life made way for Ranjan. Trifling events such as exams rested on the wayside as Ranjan stalked the corridors of her mind. She would be standing in a crowded DTC bus, hemmed in by several bodies swaying to the rattle of the bus and he would appear. In a trice, her view would be blocked by his face. She could see tiny grooves spreading from his lips to his eyes as laughter coursed through them. Before she could blink, the vision vanished.

The next few weeks ticked by. Priya could do nothing with them—with the hours, with the thoughts, with everything she did. She could not file them under any of the many categories in her mind; she could not dismiss them; they were lodged uncomfortably in the center of her heart.

The first dinner marked the beginning of those confusing weeks. Several questions scurried across her mind as she followed Ranjan into the Hyatt's imposing edifice. Where should I keep my purse, on the table or on the chair? What if I have to eat with chopsticks? I hope I don't drop anything on myself…Should I pull out the chair myself? If the waiter pushes it in too quickly…She pictured herself sitting on the carpet, underneath the table, while the waiter and Ranjan towered over her…She shivered and almost tripped on her stilettos. I must be very careful, she decided.

But she enjoyed herself. They talked about Rajiv Gandhi, dogs, his job, Intershoppe (he dropped some sweet and sour pork on his shirt; it left a brown stain), Anil Kapoor, his temper, her moods. He reminded her of Vivek, her cousin, his back flung against the chair, his legs sprawled under the table, one hand in his pocket, the other resting heavily on the table. He had square, serious hands with short nails. Sometimes he would question her, leaning forward until she could see the stitching on his shirt buttons and the curly hair whitened by talc on his chest.

They went to see a movie at Chanakya, to Lodhi Gardens, to dinner at the Orient Express. Sona came with them to the amusement park, Appughar. He called her up often; sometimes they would talk for half an hour.

Often she felt his hand hovering behind her back. It would come closer and closer…sometimes it would brush lightly across her blouse and stay still. Once she was walking out of the movie theatre and she stopped to look for him. He was behind her; he touched her back and gently pushed her forward.

Grandma came to visit them. She was installed in a large chair. Tea and warm pakoras appeared in front of her. She sent everybody away, except Priya. "That's the person I've come to see," she cried, patting her on the cheek. She leaned back against a cushion and said, "You are an adult now, Priya. You must make your own decisions. Why don't you accept their offer of marriage? Your parents don't want to push you into anything yet…the Mehtas call up every day."

"Twice," said Priya.

"Almost every day," repeated Grandma. "You are getting older every day. He is a good choice: wealthy, decent...He came third in the Chartered Accountancy exam. We shouldn't let go of a chance like this. You may regret it all your life."

"I'm thinking about it," said Priya.

She got up to go but Grandma waved her hand in the air. "Young people should make decisions quickly instead of dilly-dallying or shirking the matter. We need to make arrangements for the wedding. Why don't you tell your parents today?"

"Arrange your own wedding," retorted Priya. "Leave me alone!" She flung the pakora in her hand at the wall; for a moment it remained there, and then, fell to the ground. Priya rushed out of the room. It took the family an hour and several pakoras to pacify Grandma. Ma was going to drive her home when the phone rang.

Priya knew it was Ranjan.

The crisp evening had refreshed the stale air. It was dark when they reached their favorite haunt: the Chinese restaurant at the Hyatt. They got a table right next to the large glass windows with a view of the swimming pool.

As usual the waiter poured water into their glasses; as usual Ranjan took out his wallet from his pocket before sitting down. The waiter laid the menus beside their plates; Ranjan opened his to the page on chicken dishes.

Two years from now Priya could be sitting here, in this very room, across from Ranjan.

Ranjan turned the page. There was a stain on his shirt; a hair-strand peeped out of his nose.

Two years from now...

We would make good parents, she thought. The future was clear to her now. It was only two months ago that she had been dreaming into the future, dreaming strange things: a shadowed man, a shadowed house, a kaleidoscope of colors, constantly changing, always beautiful. Life is not like that, she thought. My future was written in my past; I borrowed it in everything that I did, in everything that my parents told me to do, in school, in college, in the clothes that my parents bought for me, in what they taught me. Now I have to pay it back. My future was already signed for; my family held it in their hands. The waiter brought two bowls of soup; obviously, Ranjan had ordered for her.

Maybe the fight with Grandma had upset Priya. Maybe the heat of the afternoon had agitated her mind. Whatever the reason, she had an uncontrollable urge to box Ranjan on his nose.

"I don't like your shirt," she said, leaning forward, halfway across the table; her elbow knocked over his soup.

His eyes bulged; he dropped his spoon to the ground. Thick droplets of soup scattered on his thigh. Priya began to laugh.

Ranjan wiped the spots with his napkin. He stared at her and then smiled.

They were walking to the car when he touched her arm. She turned to face him and his arm slid around her waist. He kissed her.

334

Priya woke up when the sun had touched the top of the neem tree with a gauzy orange film. It was Sunday; she could stay in bed awhile. She drew the bedsheet up to her chin. She heard the dull thud of a newspaper landing on the balcony.

She had liked what he did last night. It was nice.

Ma opened the front door for the maid. Priya heard the clanking of the milkcans being carried into the kitchen. The sky stretched itself further into the room, planting a sunlit stripe across the bed.

His shirt had a warm, coarse feel to it. His hair was soft...she remembered his smiling eyes.

Ma was in the next room now, pleading in a loud voice that Sona wake up and take a shower. It was time to get up.

Priya found Ma on the balcony, as usual. "A mother's life is defined by her children," she said. "You will understand when you have your own." She peered into Priya's face; she was gathering dreams of grandchildren in her daughter's eyes. "You must decide soon, Priya bete," she said quietly. "The Mehtas are getting impatient. He is nice, trustworthy, dependable...he will be faithful to you all your life. Do you want to marry him?"

Priya did not know what to say. Her mother's voice had a pleading note; she wanted to cry.

"I have to go inside now," said Ma. "Papa's come back." She gently pushed Priya's hair away from her eyes. "Try to comb your hair sometimes," she said.

The sun rays had captured the treetops and were hiding behind the water tank on the roof across the street. The park was already in shadow.

He is nice, she thought. She remembered the words whispered in her ear last night. He's better than any of my cousins; he listens to me. She thought of the way he looked at her. Ranjan was not potbellied like her cousin's husband. He liked English movies.

Yet. She wanted something. It was in the air; she wished she could just reach out and lock it in her fist.

She checked her thoughts immediately. Here she was, in the midst of making the most important decision in her life, and all she could think of were fairy dreams. I can't keep waiting for the unknown to happen. Besides, I don't even know what I want; I've never been in this situation before.

Grandma, Ma and everybody else have seen these things several times. They are probably right.

· Priya announced her decision at the dinner table. Papa rushed to the phone to tell the Mehtas the good news. Ma hugged Priya. Sona giggled. Papa called Grandma as well, and she appeared at their door with a massive box of sweets (and Grandpa) an hour later. She stuffed a ladoo into Priya's mouth, saying, "I am glad that you are adult enough to realize what's good for you." Then she patted Sona and said, "Learn from your sister." It was decided that the engagement-cum-thaka ceremony would be held this weekend at the Taj Hotel; the Mehtas wanted the marriage to take place as soon as possible.

The Mehtas were an hour late, as was to be expected. Papa had enough time to finish his argument with the caterers. Ma was giving elaborate instructions to the man they had hired to film the party. The Vedi clan gathered around Priya, who was seated in one of the two sofa-chairs placed near a wall. Grandma sat in the chair next to hers, regaling the crowd with a narration of The Story: the Priya-Ranjan match. "We even let the two of them go out alone to restaurants and movies and whatnot. We ignored the conventions of society," she said. "Things have changed since my time. In the modern world, you must let the boy and girl meet each other and decide for themselves."

The video camera man was already waiting by the door when the Mehtas entered the room. Mrs. Mehta came into the room first, with Ranjan. She walked royally, in small steps, flashing a smile at the bystanders. She was dressed in a green banarasi sari with a large magenta border. Her neck was hidden by a glittering band of gold. Gold earrings swung gaily from her ears, almost touching her shoulders. Ranjan looked handsome in a blue suit. Ranjan's father, displaying a benign smile, was shepherding his herd through the door. The sister-in-law, her face awash with anxiety, purse clutched in her hand, was greeting Grandma earnestly. Following them was an amorphous mass of people.

Ranjan was escorted to the chair next to Priya's to an accompaniment of merriment and laughter. Ranjan's father enveloped Priya in a bear hug and whispered in her ear, "Welcome to the family." Mrs. Mehta stroked Priya's hair, flashing yet another smile, and straightened her chunni. The sister-in-law touched her shoulder timidly and smiled at her.

Mrs. Mehta opened the gifts they had brought for Priya. (She had waited for the video man to position himself so that he could focus on her.) She laid a gold chain bedecked with rubies around Priya's neck. "Ranjan, stop staring at her like that," said one of his friends. "You will be seeing her every day for the rest of your life." Ranjan hurriedly turned his face away and the crowd erupted in merriment. Priya threw her head back and began to laugh.

"Don't laugh so loudly," Mrs. Mehta's voice hissed in her ear. Priya turned around. Mrs. Mehta was standing behind Ranjan, her hands resting on his shoulder. "If you open your mouth so wide, a bee will fly into your throat." She stuffed a ladoo into Priya's mouth. "Besides, a young bride should be shy." She scrutinized Priya's face. "I will get you a green sari," she said. "Green becomes you." Priya tried to speak but the ladoo was stuck in her throat. Before she could say anything, Mrs. Mehta had moved away and Ranjan was holding a ring in his hand. She barely felt the cold metal slide onto her finger.

I like my laugh, she thought. That is one of the best things about me. I can laugh even if I am unhappy. She looked at Mrs. Mehta. You give out your smile as a reward, she thought. You open your mouth and display those yellow slanting teeth at moments orchestrated as carefully as an S.D. Burman song. You don't even laugh. I can do what I like about my laugh!

Ranjan was introducing all his friends to her. The crowd directed its energy towards eating. Ranjan and Priya were left alone with his friends and her young cousins. "Priya bhabhi," said one of Ranjan's friends, "you have caused me a lot of trouble." "How?" said Ranjan, frowning. His friend leaned forward. "Usually, Ranjan's letters were my newsletters on the goings-on of the Mehta household. Now, his letters are incomprehensible. The only word that I can recognize in them is Priya, perhaps because it appears twice on every line." Priya began to laugh as Ranjan pretended to punch his friend in the stomach.

336

Mrs. Mehta was staring at her. From across the room, she had heard Priya's laughter. Priya looked up to see Mrs. Mehta's eyes concentrating on her lips. She stopped laughing.

Ranjan leaned across and whispered, "Do you want to meet my friends and me for dinner tomorrow?"

The ring glinted as the car turned the corner. The spark of light jolted Priya out of her fatigue. A new life. This ring would bring something different, something...Mrs. Mehta's voice resounded in her ears; Ranjan's smile appeared before her eyes. The car rolled to a stop.

Grandma collapsed into a chair the moment they reached home. She sent Sona to get her a glass of water. "People will be talking about this party for days," she said happily. "Well done!" This was directed at Priya's parents, who were busy unloading the gifts and food from the car. "Sit down, sit down," said Grandma to the room at large. "We have to discuss the wedding arrangements."

Priya had already sat down. She watched sleepily as the family gathered together. They ignored her. After all, there were several things to be done; a wedding is no laughing matter. Grandpa would ask the priest at his Samaj to perform the wedding ceremony. Papa would talk to one of his friends about renting a room at a hotel. Grandma and Ma decided to go to Anarkali's to look at wedding lahengas next week. Also, Papa had to arrange for money to buy jewelry. "They didn't even mention a dowry," said Grandma. "All they wanted was our beautiful child. Not only that, the poor boy wants the wedding to take place as soon as possible." Priya fell asleep.

Everybody seemed to be busy. They were always talking about things to be done. Ma had even stopped standing on the balcony in the evenings; instead, she would talk to Priya about the clothes that had to be bought. And Priya? She was taken to Anarkali's; the shopkeeper spread a dazzling array of saris and lahengas in front of her. She chose a red and green lahenga with gold jariwork. She could only listen and obey; like ants, the minutes themselves were busily building the walls of her future.

Papa told Ma that the engagement had affected Priya positively. She was mature and poised now. She never giggled during a polite conversation; in fact, she had not burst into fits of laughter in a long while.

The hotel ballroom had been decorated; the podium on which the ceremony was to take place was outlined in red and yellow flowers. The waiters, decked in red uniforms, stood behind a table arrayed with a variety of dishes. The priest was snoring in a corner of the hall. Priya had come back from the beauty salon; her mother helped her with her wedding lahenga. The mirror reflected a glowing face. The lahenga fell in swirling folds around her feet.

"They've come." Sona was standing in front of her sister, staring at her. Ma arranged the chunni to cover Priya's hair. They began to walk to the hall where the wedding party had already arrived.

She could feel her mother's touch on her arm. Her head was weighed down with happiness; the chunni framed her vision. Her eyes could only see the red rim of her lahenga; it moved with every step she took, the gold threads glinting in the light.

The soft strains of the shehnai, proclaiming a wedding, wafted in the air. Memories from several years permeated her mind. Every morning, she had woken up to this music on Vividh Bharati radio...

Papa was sitting on his bed, with his papers and pens spread out around him, anxiously watching the clock. "Hurry," he told Priya. "You will miss the school bus." She was standing in front of the mirror, padlocking her hair with a hairband. Ma was shaking Sona in an effort to wake her up and send her to the bathroom. The notes of the shehnai carpeted the air, waiting for sunlight to walk into the room.

"The bride looks beautiful." "Her face is radiant." Words of praise reached her ears; her eyes were lowered to the ground. "Priya, you look like a fairy." Sona's hand clutched at her arm for a moment and then disappeared.

They had reached the stage. "Here is the garland, Priya." She looked up for a moment. Ma was holding out a garland of red, white and yellow flowers. There was a sea of faces around her. Her eyes feasted on Papa, fingering his tie, Grandma, smiling at her, Sona, fascinated by Priya's lahenga, and Ma, her eyes filled with tears. She lowered her eyes again.

"Ranjan, stand on tiptoe," said his friends as she attempted to garland him. "That's it! Don't make it easy!" Priya stretched her arms out; the garland finally fell around his neck. "Priya, move away quickly!" her cousins exhorted her. "Make him struggle!" The garland came into her vision. Ranjan's hands were trembling slightly. She moved away just as he let go of the garland; it fell to the floor.

Priya laughed. She looked up and Mrs. Mehta was standing to one side. She stopped laughing as the garland encircled her neck.

Lakshmi

VASANTHI VICTOR

My grandfather had passed away. It said so in this letter from home, in black and white. It was written by Mother who matter-of-factly moved on to other news about the rest of the family in India. This unexpected jolt took me back into the past—his death had triggered some old memory long since wiped out by the conscious present. My parents had come from the state of Kerala and I remembered visiting there in my childhood. On these occasions I visited my grandfather and step-grandmother as well as innumerable uncles, aunts and cousins.

It was a great change for us those days to go from our house in the city to a remote village in Kerala. There was no electricity or running water in the homes. But almost every household had its pond which supplied water for washing and bathing. Some of those ponds were used to breed fish. We children enjoyed playing at the pond's edge since none of us dared to swim in its murky waters. Or we played in the sand that covered the front yard. It was freshly swept in the early hours of the morning by a woman who came in each day to do the chores.

The sound of the ocean could be heard in the distance and a ten-minute walk brought one to the beach. Here fishermen still lived in huts made of woven palm leaves that were dried and tied together. Their floor was nothing but sand on which they spread mats to sit and sleep. Their livelihood depended on the catch of the day. These sturdy men left in their long canoes to spread their nets in the pre-dawn hours and returned at mid-morning with gleaming, slithering fish which their wives carried in baskets balanced on their heads to the gates of surrounding homes. Sometimes their children ran ahead to announce the catch of the day. I remember old women saying, "Twenty years ago there were more fish than you could eat in a week on any single day. Now you can count the fish on your fingers, just like those coconuts hanging on the palms."

Coconut was used for everything—as oil for frying or as hair oil on our heads. Nothing like fish curry done in coconut milk or meat fried with coconut slivers. My aunts grated it to mix with vegetable dishes. Some men carried out the task of climbing palms to gather the nut. Grandfather usually had them climbing for tender young coconuts as a special treat for us. We delighted in feasting on the big bananas, the jackfruit and mangoes that grew nearby.

In Grandfather's house the main room where visitors were received also contained his bed. This is where he was to be found when he was not out working or tending to business. At night, after the evening meal, we congregated around his bed and listened to stories in the semi-darkness of the oil lamps. The glow of the lamps attracted bugs and mosquitoes so that we could never sit still, but kept slapping our bodies to kill the insects. One of our favourite

stories was about the man returning home at nightfall, on foot, by way of the beach. There was no transportation so most people walked ten to fifteen miles a day while they went about their business. At the time there was a tale going around about a crooked lawyer who had met a violent death. His ghost was supposed to frequent this particular stretch of oceanfront. He waylaid unsuspecting travelers and scared them out of their wits. Some said he wore his lawyer's robe, others that he appeared headless or with a walking stick. Whatever his attire, they swore they had seen him and came back frightened and panting from running.

This man was more skeptical than others and, refusing to be scared by such tales, set out as usual. On his journey home he carried a sack of dried peppers on his back. As he made his way in the falling twilight, alone with no soul in sight, he was reminded of the lawyer's ghost. Except for the sea there was no other sound, maybe a solitary gull or two. In the growing stillness he suddenly heard a rustling sound; the faster he walked the louder it grew. He began to think it was the swish of a cape behind him and turned a few times to see who was following. He saw nothing. All the same, as he approached the spot of the last sighting, he hurried even quicker. Louder and louder was the swish behind his back, until he was running, sure that the ghost was chasing him. He reached home in a state of anxiety and fear and ran a high fever during the night. It was only later—after he had recovered and in the light of bright day—that it dawned on him: he had been scared witless by the sound of the dried peppers on his back. He told his wife and children about what had really happened and soon the whole village came to know about his escapade. He could never walk among them without it being recalled by one or the other, and the village children laughed behind his back.

The children heard many stories from Grandfather but none as funny as this one. Sometimes in the afternoon when the household was napping, they got into his wallside shelves and went through his books and personal belongings. It was rumored among the family that he hid money in the pages of his books and forgot about it. On one visit, my brother found forty rupees in a book that he had casually opened. He was too honest to keep the money and gave it to Grandfather. However, my other relatives didn't think twice about deceiving him, and as he grew older, his sons stole most of the property and wealth that he had acquired through hard work and diligence. He never walked without his cane now and his feet were flat, knobby and twisted from all the walking he had done in his lifetime.

He had been married three times. His first wife had been our grandmother. She died when their children were still young, the last a toddler. It was while traveling to attend the funeral of a relative on another island that death had snatched her. I had been told she was a kind and charitable person and people remembered her good deeds. She had gone by canoe, accompanied by a relative and two servants, when a sudden storm struck and they capsized in the raging water. When news of the tragedy reached my grandfather, he cried and wailed in sorrow. For months he could not be consoled, but some of the elders eventually persuaded him to marry again for the sake of his little children. The woman he wed was his wife's younger sister. Perhaps it was because she resembled his former wife, or his wife's family had reasoned their daughter's children could best be looked after by their aunt rather than a stranger. Whatever the reason, the marriage was a success and she bore him ten children in the course of twenty years. Though all the children did not survive, it was a large family.

Grandmother number two was a strong and capable woman who ruled her family with discipline and will. She was ambitious for their futures and realized the value of education.

340

As her children grew, she made plans for each of them. One was to be a doctor, the other a lawyer, one an accountant and so on. Under her urging and influence Grandfather was persuaded to donate funds to erect a schoolhouse where all of the children could attend. Among them were children from neighboring villages who did not have such a facility. It was a grand schoolhouse, one made of stone and brick. Grandmother could hear the lesson recital from where she stood inside the compound walls. At that time, the teachers believed the louder the students recited, the better they learnt their lessons. A few years after it was built, she died of smallpox.

In a place where vaccinations were unheard of, smallpox was a mysterious and fatal disease. People believed it was a curse wrought by a cruel goddess, and in her fury she went home to home wreaking havoc until entire villages were afflicted. They cowered in their homes not knowing when she might descend on them and prayed feverishly, burning incense to keep her away. When struck, they still prayed in their misery to be spared and some miraculously survived, their flesh scarred for life. One of our uncles carried the pox marks; they said he was lucky to be alive. None of her children died, and Grandfather was a widower again with many young children.

The third time he married he must have been in his fifties, though he couldn't remember and no one was sure of his age. There were no birth or marriage certificates. His wife was much younger and from a distant town. She had given up on any man marrying her and was considered an old spinster at age thirty-eight. She was tall and gawky. Her protruding teeth gave her a seemingly insipid look, but this was not really the case. She had seized the offer to marry an aging widower with ten children and travel far from her family to live in comparative ease and luxury. It rescued her from being a poor woman who was only tolerated because of her usefulness in doing chores around the house. At home she was nothing more than a servant, here she was its main keeper.

Everyone hated her for invading their territory. Grandfather's sons and daughters, some of whom were grown, could not bear to see their mother replaced by this ugly and stupid creature. They did not want her turning their father's attention away from them. They did not understand what he saw in her and why he felt he had to marry again. Certainly she was not going to bear him any children, nor did he want any. Some of his friends and family snickered he was too randy for his age and that's why he had taken another wife. He himself thought she would be the comfort of his old age and when none of his children would care, he would have a wife to take care of his needs. Later, he doubted himself in taking such a step. It was too late, Grandmother number three was here to stay.

I was one of the few who did get along with step-Grandmother. She tolerated my presence and allowed me to tag along on her daily rounds. Each morning she was up before the rest of the household to supervise the milking of the cows she kept. These cows were regarded as one of her eccentricities by her stepchildren. She had named each of the cows and spoke to them like they were her own children. It may or may not be true that she took better care of them than her spouse. Later, she could be found tending the store that supplied essentials to the labourers who were employed by Grandfather. Here she kept a strict eye on the debit and credit ledger as most of our customers had very little cash to pay for goods. I was especially favoured because Grandmother gave me goodies to eat, as well as coins to add

to my growing collection of small change which I kept in a can. The can was locked up in the store at closing time because she didn't want my cousins to find its treasure.

My cousins envied my favoured status since they were not so lucky. At the evening meal when all the members gathered around the table in the large kitchen, they teased me for growing rich at such an early age. They hinted that one day soon it would be found. Then where would I be? In fact, among my uncles and aunts, one trusted the other so little that each kept their belongings under lock and key in old wooden almirahs. These almirahs were brought by the daughters-in-law as part of their dowry and each took special pride in her piece of furniture. Everyone examined the wood and kind of workmanship displayed and pronounced it good or bad accordingly. Grandmother had brought her own and its contents were still a mystery because she took great care to open it when no one else was around. Some of her stepchildren grew so curious that they began spying on her at all times of the day and night. It was on one of these occasions, much later in their lives, that one of my uncles came on her exercising in the nude, her body glistening with oil in the light of the moon coming through a window.

When this report spread among the family, they were stunned. It was strange even for someone as eccentric as her. Women were never known to exercise in those parts, let alone in the nude by moonlight. Among us grandchildren, it conjured up visions of an old lady dancing eerily in the pale moon, to some hidden god in a forgotten ancient ritual. This vision still danced in my eyes as I reached back into the past.

When Grandfather became ill and had to remain in a hospital for weeks, the enormity of the bill so struck his wife's prudent nature that she never recovered from the shock and hastily preceded him in death, or so it was related by her enemies. He died a few months later, his back covered with bedsores from being confined so long with no one to care for him but a young compassionate grandson. He might have been in his late nineties or past one hundred, no one could be sure. In his days he had walked tall and proud, built a thriving business from scratch, and raised enough children to create a future generation that spread to many corners of the world.

In my distant home, I can almost hear the whistling of coconut palms in the breeze. And if I closed my eyes and was absolutely still, there is Grandmother smiling her buck-toothed grin—her hair grey and tightly wound, big gold hoops dangling from the top of her ears, her ear lobes stretched and torn from heavy jewelry, empty and gaping holes. Those same lobes I had pulled and felt as a child because they were soft to the touch and curious. I remember asking, "How come they are so big?" But Grandmother only laughed and said, "Go mind your own business, child. I have things to do."

"Will you be bringing the cows again tonight?"

"Yes, Lakshmi."

"Can I come with you?"

"No, it will be dark and I can't watch out for those stupid cows and you at the same time."

"I promise I will be good and walk right behind you."

"And step into their dung and come crying home. No. It's better you go in, they will be beginning their evening prayers soon."

"But Grandma…"

"Shush, child. Go, go on in, before someone comes looking for you. I think I hear your mother calling."

Pressing on with youthful optimism, "Okay, but tomorrow will you teach me to milk the cows?"

I never did learn how to milk those cows, but watched from a safe distance their swollen udders being pulled and stretched to give a steady stream of milk—by Grandmother's strong and capable hands, while she soothed and coaxed those animals with talk. From the way they stood, yielding and pliant, it was easy to believe her. They were like great big children, letting her do as she willed, trusting her closeness, her love.

Yes, Grandmother had been a loving soul. The others couldn't see it and never gave her the chance to belong. So she turned her attention to the cows, and when I came visiting, thought I was special. A kindred spirit, trying to belong and not belonging. Apart and a little withdrawn—she could see, from the way I watched. I had nothing to do, and time heavy on my hands. So Grandmother had picked me to be her favourite. I reminded her of herself, when she was a little girl. Grandmother had found me, so to speak. Now I would have to find myself.

Pondicherry Beach

SAMANTHA RAJARAM

In the morning, the beach gleams refreshed,
like a polished cat's eye stone suddenly held to light,

Illuminated by the ravaging sunlight
there are no people, no living flesh devouring that
brilliance,
only the breathing curve of ocean waves throwing themselves
or delicately cleaving to the sand.

At night the emptiness has cooled;
a collection of people emerge, selling pistachio ice cream
and young coconuts, sweet with thin water and pearly meat to
be scraped from inside.

Every moment, capricious waves and
driftwood arrange themselves as they will never be again,
leaving tomorrow morning empty,
but full of gold and cerulean.

At night the path of a hundred people
studying others, or selling, or speaking in untroubled
voices—
And an old man, sitting on the ledge
gazes with poor eyes, the small end of that
blue expanse—

The beach becomes a thousand places:
where silence leans sweetly into the horizon,
where the waves selflessly offer their moonlight-sweetened
black patina at night,
while the rhythmic strain of their work continues and ends
on packed sand or rocks.

The iridescent belly of a shell,

the warm sand being trampled,
the crystalline body of sand crabs—
in palms, or underfoot, like the rest,
they endure, unseen.

The Red Tears

RATMALI GUNARATNA

Sitting next to the airplane window, I cried. Not knowing anything but Sri Lankan culture and traditions, I was scared to immigrate to another country. Living in Sri Lanka for fifteen years, the experiences I faced have shaped my life, and helped me survive through the difficulties of adjusting to a new country. At times I cried like a baby because of all the destruction I've witnessed but I learned to grow through it all.

I will always remember July, 1983. Those first two days changed my life and the lives of many Sri Lankans. It was another hot day and it felt like volcanoes had erupted. I held my aunt's hand tightly. I was nine years old, my white uniform was dirty with dust and ashes. My eyes were full of tears; I was tired of being pushed around in order to get onto the crowded bus. Through the shattered windows of the bus, I saw Colombo. The capital city was on fire. The air was filled with smoke from burning stores.

Even though I was a little girl, I knew about everything. Everyone was talking about it. The Sinhalese people were destroying jewelry shops, restaurants, hotels and even the lives of the people. A day before, Tamils had killed thirteen Sinhalese soldiers in the northern part of Sri Lanka. My eyes and my mouth were wide open and I was afraid of all the people around me who carried big sticks and knives searching for Tamil people. Being Sinhalese, I knew I was safe, but I was worried about Tamil people who were in our bus. This was the first time in my life I saw violence and hatred, yet I was happy to see the kindness and care a few people showed for each other from both races. I stared at the street and wondered why all these innocent people were being hurt. I could not understand how people could hate each other so easily.

Next day, walking through the silent streets I saw the bones of a dead person, nothing there but the smell of death. I heard people saying they burned a Tamil doctor; I figured out this must be him. In my mind I tried to understand why they killed a doctor. Sri Lankans had always worked together, loved each other, taken care of each other. As a child I thought the hate would end in one day, like when I fight with my cousins. But there was no peace now. I heard that Tamils were taking revenge on soldiers in the north, bombing their trucks and killing innocent people including little children and monks.

Even though I was living in the capital city and didn't see that much violence, I still felt the mourning of all the people and I saw the sadness in the eyes of Sri Lankans. All of our lives started to fall apart. In the North and Colombo there was not school every day. Education started to disappear for the younger generations and the economy went downhill. Nobody knew who to blame or what to do. Because of the anger, revenge and hatred, all of us were trapped.

346

Almost nine years later, I still feel the pain of civil war. All the dead bodies of Tamils and Sinhalese are gone, but their spirit and sacrifice will always remain. All Sri Lankans, Tamil and Sinhalese peoples' contribution to Sri Lanka made us a powerful island; we defeated the English, Spanish and Portuguese. Now it's time for us to come together and be a powerful nation again. As long as we keep our memories of the dead sons and daughters of Sri Lanka, they will be alive.

Hardwar

PREETY KALRA

heads in
lotus fire
flowers floating
in the river

the river
that wades
for the dead

hear the bodies
moving water
woman man
pushed against
each other
immersed in
the weight of
the people

only the motion
submerged
released
no sense of
direction
sky and
land
have become
one
body
and spirit
merge

feel the ashes
face against face

these are
ashes of
my people

A Photograph

DHARINI RASIAH

I have a memory
of Sri Lanka.
I am four,
watching Thambi passed from aunt to cousin to grandmother's arms.
I wait on the steps
restlessly
and turn to Bobby-Mama who shows me
the big watch he wears on his wrist.
His smile comforts me among the unfamiliar faces
gathered to greet us
on our first trip back.

My only memory
of Sri Lanka
of my uncle—
the last of the family
to leave a country
that forced him into a life as a refugee.
From England, Canada, to California—
with each move came a new home for my family,
a new life more removed than the last.
While he
in Madras
helped the Tamils
living in the camps
who could not return to the country
that was no longer their home.

I ask my mother for a story,
of my uncle—
a link to my past—
but she hesitates to reveal his life
and risk his protection
for the luxury
of a poem.

I look at the photograph
she gives me instead,
of a young girl
wearing a watch that catches the glare of the camera's flash.
Her uncle is sitting behind her on the steps
of her grandmother's house,
beneath the reflection of the trees in the windows.
The distance of this past—
before Jaffna was destroyed—
makes me question
if this memory was ever
my own.

Defining Genealogies:
Feminist Reflections on Being South Asian in North America

CHANDRA TALPADE MOHANTY

My local newspaper tells me that worldwide migration is at an all-time high in the early 1990s. Folks are moving from rural to urban areas in all parts of the Third World, and from Asia, Africa, the Caribbean and Latin America to Europe, North America and selected countries in the Middle East. Apparently two percent of the world's population no longer lives in the country in which they were born. Of course, the newspaper story primarily identifies the "problems" (for Europe and the USA) associated with these transnational migration trends. One such "problem" is taking jobs away from "citizens." I am reminded of a placard carried by Black and Third World people at an anti-racism rally in London: We Are Here Because You Were There. My location in the USA then, is symptomatic of large numbers of migrants, nomads, immigrants, workers across the globe for whom notions of home, identity, geography and history are infinitely complicated in the late twentieth century. Questions of nation(ality), and of "belonging" (witness the situation of South Asians in Africa) are constitutive of the Indian diaspora. This essay is a personal, anecdotal meditation on the politics of gender and race in the construction of South Asian identity in North America.

On a TWA flight on my way back to the U.S. from a conference in the Netherlands, the professional white man sitting next to me asks: a)which school do I go to? and b)when do I plan to go home?—all in the same breath. I put on my most professorial demeanor (somewhat hard in crumpled blue jeans and cotton T-shirt—this uniform only works for white male professors, who of course could command authority even in swimwear!) and inform him that I teach at a small liberal arts college in upstate New York, and that I have lived in the U.S. for fifteen years. At this point, my work is in the U.S., not in India. This is no longer entirely true—my work is also with feminists and grassroots activists in India, but he doesn't need to know this. Being "mistaken" for a graduate student seems endemic to my existence in this country—few Third World women are granted professional (i.e. adult) and/or permanent (one is always a student!) status in the U.S., even if we exhibit clear characteristics of adulthood, like grey hair and facial lines. He ventures a further question: what do you teach? On hearing "women's studies," he becomes quiet and we spend the next eight hours in polite silence. He has decided that I do not fit into any of his categories, but what can you expect from a *Feminist* (an *Asian* one!) anyway? I feel vindicated and a little superior—even though I know he doesn't really feel "put in his place." Why should he? He has a number of advantages

351

in this situation: white skin, maleness and citizenship privileges. From his enthusiasm about expensive "ethnic food" in Amsterdam, and his J.Crew clothes, I figured class difference (economic or cultural) wasn't exactly an issue in our interaction. We both appeared to have similar social access as "professionals."

I have been asked the "home" question (when are you going home) periodically for fifteen years now. Leaving aside the subtly racist implications of the question (go home—you don't belong), I am still not satisfied with my response. What is home? The place I was born? Where I grew up? Where my parents live? Where I live and work as an adult? Where I locate my community—my people? Who are "my people"? Is home a geographical space, an historical space, an emotional, sensory space? Home is always so crucial to immigrants and migrants—I even write about it in scholarly texts, perhaps to avoid addressing it as an issue that is also very personal. Does two percent of the world's population think about these questions pertaining to home? This is not to imply that the other ninety-eight percent does not think about home. What interests me is the meaning of home for immigrants and migrants. I am convinced that this question—how one understands and defines home—is a profoundly political one.

Since settled notions of territory, community, geography, and history don't work for us, what does it really mean to be "South Asian" in the USA? Obviously I was not South Asian in India—I was Indian. What else could one be but "Indian" at a time when a successful national independence struggle had given birth to a socialist democratic nation-state? This was the beginning of the decolonization of the Third World. Regional geographies (South Asia) appeared less relevant as a mark of identification than citizenship in a post-colonial independent nation on the cusp of economic and political autonomy. However, in North America, identification as South Asian (in addition to Indian, in my case) takes on its own logic. "South Asian" refers to folks of Indian, Pakistani, Sri Lankan, Bangladeshi, Kashmiri, and Burmese origin. Identifying as South Asian rather than Indian adds numbers and hence power within the U.S. State. Besides, regional differences among those from different South Asian countries are often less relevant than the commonalities based on our experiences and histories of immigration, treatment and location in the U.S.

Let me reflect a bit on the way I identify myself, and the way the U.S. State and its institutions categorize me. Perhaps thinking through the various labels will lead me back to the question of home and identity. In 1977, I arrived in the USA on an F1 visa—a student visa. At that time, my definition of myself—a graduate student in Education at the University of Illinois, and the "official" definition of me (a student allowed into the country on an F1 visa) obviously coincided. Then I was called a "foreign student," and expected to go "home" (to India—even though my parents were in Nigeria at the time) after getting my Ph.D. Let's face it, this is the assumed trajectory for a number of Indians, especially the post-independence (my) generation, who come to the U.S. for graduate study.

However, this was not to be my trajectory. I quickly discovered that being a foreign student, and a woman at that, meant being either dismissed as irrelevant (the quiet Asian woman stereotype), treated in racist ways (my teachers asked if I understood English and if they should speak slower and louder so that I could keep up—this in spite of my inheritance of the Queen's English and British colonialism!), or celebrated and exoticized (you are so

smart! your accent is even better than that of Americans—a little Anglophilia at work here, even though all my Indian colleagues insist we speak English the Indian way!).

The most significant transition I made at that time was the one from "foreign student" to "student of color." Once I was able to "read" my experiences in terms of race, and to read race and racism as it is written into the social and political fabric of the U.S., practices of racism and sexism became the analytic and political lenses through which I was able to anchor myself here. Of course, none of this happened in isolation—friends, colleagues, comrades, classes, books, films, arguments, and dialogues were constitutive of my political education as a woman of color in the U.S.

In the late 1970s and early 1980s feminism was gaining momentum on American campuses—it was in the air, in the classrooms, on the streets. However, what attracted me wasn't feminism as the mainstream media and white Women's Studies departments defined it. Instead, it was a very specific kind of feminism, the feminism of U.S. women of color and Third World women, that spoke to me. In thinking through the links between gender, race and class in their U.S. manifestations, I was for the first time enabled to think through my own gendered, classed post-colonial history. In the early 1980s, reading Audre Lorde, Nawal el Sadaawi, Cherríe Moraga, bell hooks, Gloria Joseph, Paula Gunn Allen, Barbara Smith, Merle Woo and Mitsuye Yamada, among others, generated a sort of recognition that was intangible but very inspiring. A number of actions, decisions and organizing efforts at that time led me to a sense of home and community in relation to women of color in the U.S. Home not as a comfortable, stable, inherited and familiar space, but instead as an imaginative, politically charged space where the familiarity and sense of affection and commitment lay in shared collective analysis of social injustice, as well as a vision of radical transformation. Political solidarity and a sense of family could be melded together imaginatively to create a strategic space I could call "home." Politically, intellectually and emotionally I owe an enormous debt to feminists of color—and especially to the sisters who have sustained me over the years. Even though our attempt to start the Women of Color Institute for Radical Research and Action fell through, the spirit of this vision, and the friendships it generated, still continue to nurture me. A number of us, including Barbara Smith, Papusa Molina, Jacqui Alexander, Gloria Joseph, Mitsuye Yamada, Kesho Scott, and myself, among others met in 1984 to discuss the possibility of such an Institute. The Institute never really happened, but I still hope we will pull it off one day.

For me, engagement as a feminist of color in the U.S. made possible an intellectual and political genealogy of being Indian that was radically challenging as well as profoundly activist. Notions of home and community began to be located within a deeply political space where racialization and gender and class relations and histories became the prism through which I understood, however partially, what it could mean to be South Asian in North America. Interestingly, this recognition also forced me to re-examine the meanings attached to home and community in India.

What I chose to claim, and continue to claim, is a history of anti-colonialist, feminist struggle in India. The stories I recall, the ones that I retell and claim as my own, determine the choices and decisions I make in the present and the future. I did not want to accept a history of Hindu chauvinist (bourgeois) upward mobility (even though this characterizes a

353

section of my extended family). We all choose partial, interested stories/histories—perhaps not as deliberately as I am making it sound here. But consciously, or unconsciously, these choices about our past(s) often determine the logic of our present.

Having always kept my distance from conservative, upwardly mobile Indian immigrants for whom the South Asian world was divided into green-card holders and non-green-card holders, the only South Asian links I allowed and cultivated were with Indians with whom I shared a political vision. This considerably limited my community. Racist and sexist experiences in graduate school and after made it imperative that I understand the U.S. in terms of its history of racism, imperialism and patriarchal relations, specifically in relation to Third World immigrants. After all, we were into the Reagan-Bush years, when the neo-conservative backlash made it impossible to ignore the rise of racist, anti-feminist, and homophobic attitudes, practices and institutions. Any purely culturalist or nostalgic/sentimental definition of being "Indian" or "South Asian" was inadequate. Such a definition fueled the "model minority" myth. And this subsequently constituted us as "outsiders/foreigners" or as interest groups who sought or had obtained the American dream.

In the mid-1980s, the labels changed: I went from being a "foreign student" to being a "resident alien." I have always thought that this designation was a stroke of inspiration on the part of the U.S. State, since it accurately names the experience and status of immigrants—especially immigrants of color. The flip side of "resident alien" is "illegal alien," another inspired designation. One can be either a resident or illegal immigrant, but one is always an alien. There is no confusion here—no melting pot ideology or narratives of assimilation—one's status as an "alien" is primary. Being legal requires identity papers. (It is useful to recall that the "passport"—and by extension the concept of nation-states and the sanctity of their borders—came into being after World War I.)

One must be stamped as legitimate (that is, not-gay-or-lesbian and not-communist!) by the Immigration and Naturalization Service (INS). The INS is one of the central disciplinary arms of the U.S. State. It polices the borders and controls all border crossings—especially those into the U.S. In fact, the INS is also one of the primary forces which institutionalizes race differences in the public arena, thus regulating notions of home, legitimacy and economic access to the "American dream" for many of us. For instance, carrying a green card documenting resident alien status in the U.S. is clearly very different from carrying an American passport, which is proof of U.S. citizenship. The former allows one to enter the U.S. with few hassles; the latter often allows one to breeze through the borders and ports of entry of other countries, especially countries which happen to be trading partners (much of Western Europe and Japan, among others) or in an unequal relationship with the U.S. (much of the noncommunist Third World). At a time when notions of a capitalist free-market economy seem (falsely) synonymous with the values attached to democracy, an American passport can open many doors. However, just carrying an American passport is no insurance against racism and unequal and unjust treatment within the U.S. It would be important to compare the racialization of first-generation immigrants from South Asia to the racialization of second-generation South Asian Americans. For example, one significant difference between these two generations would be between experiencing racism as a phenomenon specific to the U.S., versus growing up in the ever-present shadow of racism in

the case of South Asians born in the U.S. This suggests that the psychic effects of racism would be different for these two constituencies. In addition, questions of home, identity and history take on very different meanings for South Asians born in North America. But to be fair, this comparison requires a whole other reflection that is beyond the scope of this essay.

Rather obstinately, I have refused to give up my Indian passport and have chosen to remain as a resident alien in the U.S. for the last decade or so. Which leads me to reflect on the complicated meanings attached to holding Indian citizenship while making a life for myself in the USA. In India, what does it mean to have a green card—to be an expatriate? What does it mean to visit Bombay every two to four years, and still call it home? Why does speaking in Marathi (my mothertongue) become a measure and confirmation of home? What are the politics of being a part of the majority and the "absent elite" in India, while being a minority and a racialized "other" in the U.S.? And does feminist politics, or advocating feminism, have the same meanings and urgencies in these different geographical and political contexts?

Some of these questions hit me smack in the face during my last visit to India, in December 1992—post-Ayodhya (the infamous destruction of the Babri Masjid in Ayodhya by Hindu fundamentalists on 6 December 1992). In earlier, rather infrequent visits (once every four or five years was all I could afford), my green card designated me as an object of envy, privilege and status within my extended family. Of course the same green card has always been viewed with suspicion by left and feminist friends who (quite understandably) demand evidence of my ongoing commitment to a socialist and democratic India. During this visit, however, with emotions running high within my family, my green card marked me as an outsider who couldn't possibly understand the "Muslim problem" in India. I was made aware of being an "outsider" in two profoundly troubling shouting matches with my uncles, who voiced the most incredibly hostile sentiments against Muslims. Arguing that India was created as a secular state and that democracy had everything to do with equality for all groups (majority and minority) got me nowhere. The very fundamentals of democratic citizenship in India were/are being undermined and redefined as "Hindu."

Bombay was one of the cities hardest hit with waves of communal violence following the events in Ayodhya. The mobilization of Hindu fundamentalists, even paramilitary organizations, over the last half century and especially since the mid-1980s had brought Bombay to a juncture where the most violently racist discourse about Muslims seemed to be woven into the fabric of acceptable daily life. Racism was normalized in the popular imagination such that it became almost impossible to publicly raise questions about the ethics or injustice of racial/ethnic/religious discrimination. I could not assume a distanced posture towards religion any more. Too many injustices were being done in my name.

Although born a Hindu, I have always considered myself a non-practicing one—religion had always felt rather repressive when I was growing up. I enjoyed the rituals but resisted the authoritarian hierarchies of organized Hinduism. However, the Hinduism touted by fundamentalist organizations like the RSS (Rashtriya Swayamsevak Sangh, a paramilitary Hindu fundamentalist organization founded in the 1930s) and the Shiv Sena (a Maharashtrian chauvinist, fundamentalist, fascist political organization that has amassed a significant voice in Bombay politics and government) was one that even I, in my ignorance, recognized as

reactionary and distorted. But this discourse was real—hate-filled rhetoric against Muslims appeared to be the mark of a "loyal Hindu." It was unbelievably heart-wrenching to see my hometown become a war zone with whole streets set on fire, and a daily death count to rival any major territorial border war. The smells and textures of Bombay, of home, which had always comforted and nurtured me, were violently disrupted. The scent of fish drying on the lines at the fishing village in Danda was submerged in the smell of burning straw and grass as whole bastis (chawls) were burned to the ground. The very topography, language and relationships that constituted "home" were quietly but surely exploding. What does community mean in this context? December 1992 both clarified as well as complicated for me the meanings attached to being an Indian citizen, a Hindu, an educated woman/feminist, and a permanent resident in the U.S. in ways that I have yet to resolve. After all, it is often moments of crisis that make us pay careful attention to questions of identity. Sharp polarizations force one to make choices (not in order to take sides, but in order to accept responsibility) and to clarify our own analytic, political and emotional topographies.

I learned that combating the rise of Hindu fundamentalism was a necessary ethical imperative for all socialists, feminists and Hindus of conscience. Secularism, if it meant absence of religion, was no longer a viable position. From a feminist perspective, it became clear that the battle for women's minds and hearts was very much center-stage in the Hindu fundamentalist strategy. Feminists in India have written extensively about the appeal of fundamentalist rhetoric and social position to women. (The journals *The Economic and Political Weekly of India* and *Manushi* are good sources for this work.)

Religious fundamentalist constructions of women embody the nexus of morality, sexuality and Nation—a nexus of great importance for feminists. Similar to Christian, Islamic and Jewish fundamentalist discourses, the construction of femininity and masculinity, especially in relation to the idea of the Nation, are central to Hindu fundamentalist rhetoric and mobilizations. Women are not only mobilized in the "service" of the Nation, but they also become the ground on which discourses of morality and nationalism are written. For instance, the RSS mobilizes primarily middle-class women in the name of a family-oriented, Hindu nation, much like the Christian Right does in the U.S. But discourses of morality and nation are also embodied in the normative policing of women's sexuality (witness the surveillance and policing of women's dress in the name of morality by the contemporary Iranian State). Thus, one of the central challenges Indian feminists face at this time is how to rethink the relationship of nationalism and feminism in the context of religious identities. In addition to the fundamentalist mobilizations tearing the country apart, the recent incursions of the International Monetary Fund and the World Bank with their structural adjustment programs which are supposed to "discipline" the Indian economy, are redefining the meaning of post-coloniality and of democracy in India. Categories like gender, race, caste/class are profoundly and visibly unstable at such times of crisis. These categories must thus be analyzed in relation to contemporary reconstructions of womanhood and manhood in a *global* arena increasingly dominated by religious fundamentalist movements, the IMF and the World Bank, and the relentless economic and ideological colonization of much of the world by multinationals based in the U.S., Japan and Europe. In all these global economic and cultural/ideological processes, women occupy a crucial position.

In India, unlike most countries, the sex ratio has declined since the early 1900s. According to the 1991 census, the ratio is now 929 women to 1000 men, one of the lowest (if not *the* lowest) sex ratios in the world. Women produce seventy to eighty percent of all the food in India, and have always been the hardest hit by environmental degradation and poverty. The contradictions between civil law and Hindu and Muslim personal laws affect women— rarely men. Horrific stories about the deliberate genocide of female infants as a result of sex determination procedures like amniocentesis, and recent incidents of sati (self-immolation by women on the funeral pyres of their husbands) have even hit the mainstream American media. Gender and religious (racial) discrimination are thus urgent, life-threatening issues for women in India. In 1993, politically-conscious Indian citizenship necessitates taking such fundamentally feminist issues seriously. In fact, these are the very same issues South Asian feminists in the U.S. need to address. My responsibility to combat and organize against the regressive and violent repercussions of Hindu fundamentalist mobilizations in India extends to my life in North America. After all, much of the money which sustains the fundamentalist movement is raised and funnelled through organizations in the U.S.

Let me now circle back to the place I began: the meanings I have come to give to home, community and identity. By exploring the relationship between being a South Asian immigrant in America and an expatriate Indian citizen in India, I have tried, however partially and anecdotally, to clarify the complexities of home and community for this particular feminist of color/South Asian in North America. The genealogy I have created for myself here is partial, interested and deliberate. It is a genealogy that I find emotionally and politically enabling—it is part of the genealogy that underlies my self-identification as an educator involved in a pedagogy of liberation. Of course, my history and experiences are far messier and not at all as linear as this narrative makes them sound. But then the very process of constructing a narrative for oneself—of telling a story—imposes a certain linearity and coherence that is never entirely there. But that is the lesson, perhaps, especially for us immigrants and migrants: i.e., that home, community and identity all fall somewhere between the histories and experiences we inherit and the political choices we make through alliances, solidarities and friendships.

One very concrete effect of my creating this particular space for myself has been my recent involvement in two grassroots organizations, one in India and the other in the U.S. The former, an organization called *Awareness,* is based in Orissa and works to empower the rural poor. Their focus is political education (similar to Paolo Friere's notion of "conscienti- zation"), and they have recently begun to very consciously organize rural women. *Grassroots Leadership of North Carolina* is the U.S. organization I work with. It is a multiracial group of organizers (largely African American and White) working to build a poor and working peoples movement in the American South. While the geographical, historical and political contexts are different in the case of these two organizations, my involvement in them is very similar, as is my sense that there are clear connections to be made between the work of the two organizations. In addition, I think that the issues, analyses and strategies for organizing for social justice are also quite similar. This particular commitment to work with grassroots organizers in the two places I call home is not accidental. It is very much the result of the genealogy I have traced here. After all, it has taken me over a decade to make these

commitments to grassroots work in both spaces. In part, I have defined what it means to be South Asian by educating myself about, and reflecting on, the histories and experiences of African American, Latina, West Indian, African, European American, and other constituencies in North America. Such definitions and understandings do provide a genealogy, but a genealogy that is always relational and fluid as well as urgent and necessary.

This essay is dedicated to the memory of Lanubai and Gauribai Vijaykar, maternal grandaunts, who were single, educated, financially independent, and tall (over six feet) at a time when it was against the grain to be any one of these things; and to Audre Lorde, teacher, sister, friend, whose words and presence continue to challenge, inspire and nurture me.

Search For My Tongue

SUJATA BHATT

Days my tongue slips away
I can't hold on to my tongue
it's slippery like the lizard's tail
I try to grasp
but the lizard darts away—
mari jeebh sarki jai chay—
I can't speak—I speak nothing.
Nothing.
 Kai nahi-hoo nathi boli shakti
I search for my tongue—

parantu kya shodhu? Kay?

hoo dhodti dhodti jaoo choo
But where should I start? Where?
I go running, running,

nadi keenaray pohchee choo, nadi keenaray
reach the river's edge.
Silence—
 Akedum shant
neechay pani nahi, oopur pakshi nahi—
below, the riverbed is dry. Above,
the sky is empty: no clouds, no birds.
If there were leaves, or even grass
they would not stir today,
for there is no breeze.
If there were clouds
then, it might rain—
Jo vadla hoat toh kadach varsad aavay
jo varsad puday toh nadi pachee aavay
jo nadi hoy, jo pani hoy toh kaeek leelu leelu daykhai
if the rains fell
then the river might return

if the water rose again I might see something green
at first—then trees enough to fill a forest.
If there were some clouds that is—
jo vadla hoat toh
Since I have lost my tongue
I can only imagine
there is something crawling
beneath the rocks, now burrowing down
into the earth when I lift the rock—
 jyaray patther oopadu
the rock is in my hand, and the dry
moss stuck on the rock
prickles my palm—
I let it drop
for I must find my tongue.
I know it can't be here
in this dry riverbed.
My tongue can only be
where there is water—
pani…pani…
hujoo yad chay paylee chokri
"thunda pani…meetha pani…" bolti bolti aavti—
mathay kallu matlu, hathma, pittulno pyalo
oobhaylee gaadi baju aavti
bari taraf hath lumbavenay pani aapti
unay hoo, ateeshay tarsi
mota mota ghuntada layti pee jati
hujoo yad chay paylee chokri
Even water is scarce.
There was a little girl
who carried a black clay pitcher on her head,
who sold water at the train station
she filled her brass cup with water—
stretched out her arm to me,
reached up to the window, up
to me leaning out the window from the train,
but I can't think of her in English.

II

You ask me what I mean
by saying I have lost my tongue.
I ask you, what would you do
if you had two tongues in your mouth,
and lost the first one, the mother tongue,
and could not really know the other,
the foreign tongue.
You could not use them both together
even if you thought that way.
And if you lived in a place where you had to
speak a foreign tongue—
your mother tongue would rot,
rot and die in your mouth
until you had to spit it out.
I thought I spit it out
but overnight while I dream,

munay hutoo kay aakhee jeebh aakhee bhasha
may thoonky nakhi chay
parantoo rattray svupnama mari bhasha pachi aavay chay
foolnee jaim mari bhasha mari jeebh
moddhama kheelay chay
fullnee jaim mari bhasha mari jeebh
moddhama pakay chay
it grows back, a stump of a shoot
grows longer, grows moist, grows strong veins,
it ties the other tongue in knots,
the bud opens, the bud opens in my mouth,
it pushes the other tongue aside.
Everytime I think I have forgotten,
I think I have lost the mother tongue,
it blossoms out of my mouth.
Days I try to think in English:
I look up,
 paylo kallo kagdo
oodto oodto jai, huhvay jzaday pohchay
ainee chanchma kaeek chay
the crow has something in his beak.
When I look up
I think:
 aakash, suraj

and then: sky, sun—
Don't tell me it is the same, I know
better—to think of the sky
is to think of dark clouds bringing snow,
the first snow is always on Thanksgiving.
But to think:
 aakash, usman, aabh
mathay mota kalla kagda ooday
kagdanay mathay suraj, rojay suraj
akepun vadul nahi, atelay varsad nahi
atelay anaj nahi, atelay rotli nahi
dhal bhat shak nahi, kai nahi, kooch be nahi
matra kagda, kalla kagda—
Overhead, large black crows fly.
Over the crows, the sun, always
the sun, not a single cloud
which means no rain, which means no wheat,
no rice, no greens, no bread. Nothing.
Only crows, black crows.
And yet, the humid June air,
the stormiest sky in Connecticut
can never be:
 aakash
chomasama jyaray varsad aavay
aakhee raat aakho dee varsad puday—vijli jai
jyaray ma rasodama gheenay deevay rotli vanti
shak halavti
Ravindrasangeet gaati gaati
saonay bolavti
the monsoon sky giving rain
all night, all day, lightning, the electricity goes out,
we light the cotton wicks in butter:
 candles in brass.
And my mother in the kitchen
my mother singing:
mono moro meghero shoongay, ooday chalay deek de gontayro pani…
I can't hear my mother in English.

III

In the middle of Maryland
you send me a tape recording
saying;
 huhvay aa ake vaat toh kahveej padshay
bhalaynay bahr kootra bhasay, bhalay dhobi aavay
bhalay shakvali aavay, maray aa vat toh kahveej padshay
bhalay tapali aavay, bhalay kagda kaw kaw karay
bhalay rickshano avaj aavay
maray tanay aa vat toh kahveej padshay
You talk to me,
 you say my name the way it should be said
apologising
for the dogs barking outside
for the laundryman knocking on the door
apologising because
the woman selling eggplants
is crying door to door
 reengna...reengna...
but do you know
how I miss that old woman, crying
 reengna...reengna...
It's allright if the peddlar's brass bells ring out,
I miss them too.
You talk louder, the mailman comes, knocking louder,
the crows caw caw cawing outside,
the rickshaw's motor put-put-puttering...
you say:
 Suju bhen huhvay tamaray matay tabla vagadu choo
you say; listen to the tablas—
listen: dha dhin dhin dha
 dha dhin dhin dha
listen dha dhin dhin dha
 dhinaka dhinaka dhin dhin
 dhinaka dhinaka dhin dhin
 dha dhin dhin dha
 dhinaka dhinaka dhinaka dhinaka
 dha dhin dhin dha
 dhinaka dhinaka dhin dhin
I listen I listen I listen
 dha dhin dhin dha
I hear you I hear you

363

dhinaka dhinaka dhin dhinaka dhinaka dhin dhinaka dhinaka dhin
listen listen listen
Today I played your tape
over and over again

 dha dhin dhin dha
 dhinaka dhinaka dha

I can't dha I can't dha
I can't forget I can't forget
 dha dhin dhin dha

Author Biographies

QIRONE ADHIKARY is a writer of South Asian descent who mostly writes fiction, though she has been a copywriter, journalist, scriptwriter, and other media hack. Her work is used to teach college students about Third World writers writing in English, and includes feminist folk tales for children, two cookbooks, short stories, and an unpublished novel. For the past ten years, she has lived in California with her two cats, Faridah Peeples and Ramon Rivera.

ZAINAB FATIMA ALI is a 1992 Loft Inroads participant who studied with David Mura. Her recent creative essay on multiculturalism, "Becoming Agents of Our Identity," has been published in an anthology and is being taught to Minneapolis college students. Her most recent work, "Daddy," has been published in the *Inroads Anthology*. She is presently writing a novel-length memoir.

V.K. ARUNA is a nonimmigrant Black Feminist Lesbian of dual Tamil heritage, born and raised in Malaysia, currently living in the Washington D.C. area. She writes, speaks and performs creative works on issues of racialism, domestic violence and the concept of community for South Asian Lesbians living in exile outside and within their geographical "homes."

FRANCIS C. ASSISI is a freelance writer who has contributed to a variety of publications including *India-Abroad*, *India-West*, *India Currents* and *News India*. He now lives in India and is completing a book on Indian immigrants in the U.S.A.

HERSHINI BHANA, born and raised in Durban, South Africa, immigrated with her family in 1989 to Lawrence, Kansas, due to political pressures. She is currently studying women's literature of the African diaspora at the University of California, Berkeley in the Ethnic Studies Graduate program.

SUPARNA BHASKARAN was born in Calcutta, India. She came to the United States as a university student and is presently in the Graduate Anthropology programme at Michigan State University. She roots her graduate work and political thought in her involvement in different feminist communities. Her research explores the politics of race and sexuality in South Asian cultural politics and feminist politics.

SHEELA BHATT currently lives in the Bay Area and is doing her Master's in City Planning and Public Health. She plans to work directly with people as a community health care worker. She thanks her mother for being such a strong role model and guiding force in her life.

SUJATA BHATT was born in 1956 in Ahmedabad, India. She has an MFA from University of Iowa in Iowa City. This poem is from the collection *Brunizem* (published in 1988) which won

365

the Commonwealth Poetry Prize for Asia. Her two other collections are *Monkey Shadows* (1991) and *This Stinking Rose* (1994). She is living in Germany and working as a free-lance writer and translator.

RADHIKA SITA CHARI was born in the U.S.A., the first daughter of parents who had just emigrated from Andhra Pradesh, India. Currently she is living in Washington, D.C. and is actively involved in social justice work.

HUMA DAR is a Kashmiri woman, born in Pakistan in 1963. A mother of two children, Huma is currently a student of Computer Science at U.C. Berkeley. She enjoys a passion for her children, life and adventure—her proudest achievement to date being the recovery of her son from Pakistan, a year after his kidnapping from Berkeley.

RINI DAS's birthplace and the first twenty-two years of her life were spent at Calcutta, India. She has been around and in the U.S. since then. Mathematics sustains her, and she loves doodling and talking along all kinds of dimensions.

SAYANTANI DASGUPTA is a freelance writer living in New Jersey. Her articles have appeared in *Ms. Magazine* and *India Currents Magazine*. She is also writing for the upcoming *ONward Magazine*. Sayantani graduated from Brown University in 1992 with a degree in public health. She has worked at the American Foundation for AIDS Research and is particularly interested in Indian AIDS policy and women's health care delivery. She will be attending John Hopkins Medical School in Fall 1993.

SHAMITA DAS DASGUPTA is a mother, psychologist and community worker. She is one of the founding members of MANAVI, an organization for South Asian women in the U.S. Her research interests are in the areas of psychology of women, issues and concerns of South Asian immigrants, and violence against women. At present she is affiliated with the Women's Studies program at Rutgers University, Newark, NJ.

MAYA DEVI is in her twenties and currently resides in Chicago.

PARIJAT DESAI was born in New Delhi, India and grew up in Houston, Texas and Aurora, Colorado. She studied cultural anthropology at Stanford University and she plans to choreograph, fusing Indian Classical and Modern dance techniques.

Originally from India, **CHITRA BANERJEE DIVAKARUNI** lives in the San Francisco Bay Area with her engineer husband. She teaches Creative Writing at Foothill College, where she is a director for the annual multicultural Creative Writing Conference. Her work reflects her interests in travel, women's issues and the immigrant experience.

LALITA GANDBHIR, born in 1938, has lived in greater Boston since 1965. She has published stories and poems in several journals and magazines including *Massachusetts Review*, *Toronto South Asian Review*, *Spotlight*, *Poetry India Midfest International*, *Journal of South Asian Literature* and *Eve's Weekly* in Bombay. She has published three short story collections in India. Gandbhir works as a physician.

PIA GANGULY was educated at Presidency College, Calcutta and U.C. Irvine. She embodies the spirit of a cross-cultural pollination of ideas and visions. Currently she lives in Anaheim

Hills and is the profile editor of *India Currents*. Her book of poems, *Head of a Woman* is due to be published in September.

SUMEETA GAWANDE was born in Brooklyn, New York and raised in Athens, Ohio. She was a community organizer in Oakland, California, and is currently living in Newark, New Jersey, developing her legal tools with the hopes of making the world a better place. She envies people who can answer the question, "where's your home?" with one word, and she's really proud that both she and her mother are part of this anthology.

SUSHILA G. GAWANDE was born in India, in Ahmedabad, a town then dominated by the Independence Movement. She was raised by her mother because her father died when she was only five years old. She came to America when she was a medical intern. She met her husband in New York City and has two children. She feels privileged to have the opportunity to know two cultures very well: Indian and American.

gracepoore is a South Asian feminist writer, videomaker and activist. She has been working on domestic violence issues since 1985. She founded SHaKTI PRODUCTION, an all-women research and video production team. Her writing has been published in *Conditions Thirteen* and *Response* in the United States and *Her World* in Malaysia.

INDERPAL GREWAL is Associate Professor of Women's Studies at San Francisco State University. She writes on topics including travel, imperialism, international feminism, South Asian writers and Asian American cultural formations. She also serves on the Boards of the Asian Women's Shelter in San Francisco and of Narika, a referral service for South Asian women.

RATMALI GUNARATNA was born in Sri Lanka and immigrated to the United States when she was fifteen. She graduated from Berkeley High School and is planning to attend New York University in Fall 1993.

MINAL HAJRATWALA is a recent graduate of Stanford University. She is a writer and a journalist and lives in Northern California.

NAHEED ISLAM is a Ph.D. student at the Sociology Department at U.C. Berkeley. She specializes in development studies, race relations and sexuality. She is currently working on an oral history project with Bangladeshi women in L.A. and plans to do her dissertation with the Bangladeshi community in L.A.

PREETY KALRA is a third year student at U.C. Berkeley. She is studying Ethnic Studies and wants to combine her experiences from this field to immigrant women and health care. She hopes to practice medicine in community-based clinics and eventually spend time working in Delhi.

GAURANGI KAMANI has been asked whether she is from Afghanistan, Bengal, Bolivia, Brazil, Chile, Ecuador, Egypt, Ethiopia, Fiji, Goa, Gujarat, Guyana, Hawaii, Iran, Israel, Kerala, Maharashtra, Mauritius, Mexico, Pakistan, Peru, Puerto Rico, Punjab, Spain, Trinidad, Turkey, Venezuela. She lives in Northern California.

KAMAL KAPUR and her husband, Donald Powell, live with their two cats, Chua and Pari, in San Diego, where she teaches writing at Grossmont College. She is the author of a book of poems, *Radha Sings*, and several plays, two of which won national awards in India.

INDIRA KARAMCHETI is an associate professor at Wesleyan University in Middletown, Connecticut. She has written on post-colonial authors such as Salman Rushdie, Anita Desai and V.S. Naipaul and is presently working on a book titled *Post-Colonial Theory*.

KESHINI T. KASHYAP is a third-year student at U.C. Berkeley. She recently co-created the video, "A Crack in the Mannequin: Three South Asian Working Women In America," which has been shown in various film and video festivals in North America. Keshini loves India very much, as well as America, and would one day like to make sense of life between cultures.

TEHMINA KHAN is a Hyderbadi Muslim who grew up in the Bay Area. She studied Literature at U.C. Berkeley and spent her junior year in Cairo, Egypt. She currently teaches English as a Foreign Language and is pursuing a career as an independent filmmaker. Her first film, *In the Last Passage*, is a twenty-minute documentary collage about the Palestinian experience. She is presently working on one experimental film and one dramatic film, as well as a compilation of her writings.

ZAVEENI KHAN is a native of Sri Lanka who has lived in the U.S. for eleven years. At present she is the Director of the Multicultural Center at the University of California, Santa Barbara. She received her B.A. in English Literature from California State University, Long Beach and her M.A. in Education from U.C. Santa Barbara.

AARTI KOHLI was born in Chandigarh, India in 1971, and immigrated to the U.S. at the age of seven. As a graduate of U.C. Berkeley who has been involved with the Bay Area South Asian community, she sees the rifts that are currently being created as a result of class, caste and regional differences. Her fictional short story was written for all young South Asian women, especially for sister Gauri.

KIRAN ALELIA LALL weaves her life with threads of dramatic art, mythology, Tarot readings and Raja Yoga. Her father emigrated from New Delhi, India and her mother emigrated from Port of Spain, Trinidad. Both Kiran and her younger brother began life in San Francisco. Kiran holds a Bachelor's degree in Dramatic Art from the University of California, Davis.

PUNAM LUTHRA, born in India, immigrated with her family (Shan, Santosh, Swapna and Sangita Luthra) to San Luis Obispo, California and is now planning to get a degree in law. A woman's advocate, she speaks on the taboo issues of spousal abuse, dowry and divorce in the South Asian household. She can never thank her family, friends—especially Richard Birdsall and Hussein Khan—and the justice system, that overwhelmed her with love and support, enough.

LATIKA MALKANI was born in Bombay and raised in the suburbs of California. She most recently worked with the Asian Immigrant Women's Advocates and presently studies law. She thanks her mother for teaching her about courage and self-respect.

LATA MANI comes from an extended family whose roots and canopy resemble an ancient banyan tree. Among the gifts her family has bestowed upon her are a formidable army of aunts

and female cousins and a conviction that resistance to social injustice is the bedrock of an ethical existence. She currently teaches Women's Studies at the University of California, Davis, and is active with the Asian Women's Shelter, San Francisco.

BELLA MAYANI is the youngest in a family of five children. She is a first-generation born in Panama of Sindhi parents who left Sindh during Partition. She received her Bachelor of Arts in Sociology from Mills College in Oakland, California. She is currently working in an import-export business in Panama.

RUXANA MEER is a Pakistani Muslima working in Oakland. Strength to all the women who've made this possible.

ANU MITRA is the director of Communications at Union Institute, a University for working adults based in Cinncinati, Ohio. She has a Ph.D. in English and Women's Studies from the University of Rochester. She spends her free time playing make-believe with her husband and two children, ages four and two, and dreaming up impossible dreams.

CHANDRA TALPADE MOHANTY teaches feminist, anti-racist and Third World Studies at Hamilton College in Clinton, New York. She is co-editor with Lourdes Torres and Ann Russo, of *Third World Women and the Politics of Feminism*, (Indiana University Press, 1991) and with Jacqui Alexander, of *Movements, Histories, Identities, Third World Feminisms, a Reader*, (forthcoming from Basil Blackwell). She is a member of the Board of Directors of Grassroots Leadership of North Carolina, and of Kitchen Table, Women of Color Press.

ANU MURGAI was born in Newark, Ohio in 1967 and moved to India with her family when she was two years old. She lived in Bihar in a small town till she was fourteen, and then moved to Delhi. In 1986 she came to the U.S. to begin undergraduate studies at Swarthmore College, and is presently completing an MBA degree at the University of Chicago Graduate School of Business.

ROSHANI NASH was born in Bombay, India. She came to study in the U.S.A. and graduated from Colorado Women's College in 1970. For many years, Ms. Nash commuted to Hollywood to work in film and television. She now lives with her husband John, daughter Ariana and dog Ginger in San Francisco. "Nadia" is excerpted from a longer work in progress about growing up in India.

SAJANI PATEL is a high school student in the small city of Upland. She is one of the ninety-something members of her family. Her goal is to bring Amnesty International to her campus as a club and highly wishes that people will take interest in it. During her free time she enjoys drawing, listening to music, and writing. She dedicates her short story to all women of color who have felt neglected in this cruel world.

SONALI PERERA, born in 1971, is a native Sri Lankan who immigrated to the U.S. in 1985. She recently graduated from U.C. Berkeley with honors in English, having completed a thesis on issues of post-coloniality and gender. She eventually hopes to engage in graduate work in the field of post-colonial studies.

PREM PRASAD has received a Ph.D. in Social Welfare from Columbia University. Currently she teaches at Sussex Community College in Long Island. She is also a writer and a poet who has been published in many journals and newspapers.

NATASHA PRATAP is an undergraduate at Stanford University majoring in English with Creative Writing. She has just spent her junior year at Oxford University and will be graduating next year. Having grown up in Bombay, she enjoys writing stories set in India.

PREETY's writing is based on her experiences within the working class of the South Asian community. However, she does not want to project that physical and psychological abuse occur only within a particular class. She knows that it transcends these boundaries and hopes that more South Asians are open to giving support and understanding to one another.

SAMANTHA RAJARAM was born in Long Island, New York. She left New York and lived in Wyoming with her family for almost ten years. As an elementary school student, she published poetry in the local newspapers—a hobby she hopes to continue in the future. She has lived in the Bay Area for the past five years but is currently majoring in English at UCLA. Samantha hopes to attend graduate school for a degree in English in a few years. Her parents are from Madras and Pondicherry, India, which she visits every two years.

DHARINI MANOJI RASIAH was born in Colombo, Sri Lanka and is now a resident of California. She is currently pursuing her Master's in Asian American Studies with an emphasis in film and video at UCLA. Her work with South Asian women includes production of a video, *A Crack in the Mannequin*, and volunteering with Narika. She hopes to continue her commitment to women of color issues through visual communication.

DINAZ KUTAR ROGERS was born and raised a Parsi in Bombay, India. She obtained her M.S. in Biology from Montana State University and a Teaching Certificate from Oregon State University. She lives in Albany, Oregon, with her husband and two daughters.

ROSHNI RUSTOMJI-KERNS has lived, studied and worked in India, Pakistan, Lebanon, U.S.A. and Mexico. Her articles and short stories have been published in journals such as, *The Journal of South Asian Literature*, *The Toronto South Asia Review*, *The Massachusetts Review* and *The Literary Review*. She guest-edited a special issue of *The Journal of South Asian Literature* on South Asian women's writings on the immigrant and expatriate experience. Her background is in Comparative Literature and Mythology and she is a Professor Emeritus of Sonoma State University.

RASHMI SADANA was born in Toronto and grew up in Los Angeles. After graduating from U.C. Berkeley in 1991, she took off for India to go backpacking in Kerala and hang out with family in Delhi and Bombay. She then researched and wrote three chapters for Fodor's *The Berkeley Guides* in southwestern France and on the island of Corsica. Rashmi is now living in London and working on a Master's degree in South Asian Post-colonial literature and history at the University of London/School of Oriental and African Studies.

KOSAR SAIRA is a Black, Pakistani (Mirpuri), working class lesbian, living and working in England. She works part-time for the Law Centres Federation, and is reading law with a view of becoming a lawyer. In her spare time she is an artist working in a number of media, including photography, painting, poetry, film and video. She also writes short stories and is currently working on her first novel.

MADHURI SANGHVI is a sometimes writer and an all-the-time thinker. She has big plans for combining the two in the future.

RUPAL SANGHVI graduated in May 1993 with a Bachelor's in Political Science and Women's Studies from the University of Michigan, Ann Arbor. She's also devoted much of her college life to prepare for an eventual pursuit in the field of medicine. Until the time of pursuit arrives, the year will find her either in a hematology/oncology lab, researching, or in an MPH program—but no doubt writing all the while.

MARIE-CLAIRE SAVRIAMA originated from the Tamil Nadu (Madras). She was born in Réunion Island (French Department in the Indian Ocean) in 1961. After studying at University, she has been teaching the French and English Languages in the French Public Colleges for ten years. As a visiting student at U.C. Berkeley, she is presently making a study on the cultural adaptation of the Tamil Diaspora in California.

TESHA SENGUPTA, born in 1976 in Bihar, India, lives in Honolulu, Hawai'i where she is currently a senior at Punahou School. As both an editor for the school newspaper, *Ka Punahou,* and a captain of the Speech and Debate Team, she is an experienced writer and speaker. Tesha is also highly involved in Amnesty International as the President of the Punahou Chapter and Student Area coordinator for the state of Hawai'i.

KHADINE S. SHAH was born in Trinidad, West Indies. She is currently attending Apopka High School in Florida with future plans of medical school. She enjoys many sports, including martial arts.

NEERA KUCKREJA SOHONI was born in New Delhi, India, and has lived in United States, off and on, for several years as a student, worker, and homemaker, and now resides in California. She is currently an Affiliated Scholar at Stanford University's Institute for Research on Women and Gender. Ms. Sohoni has authored/edited three books dealing with women prisoners, the status of children, and the work of a leading tribal development agency in India. These are her first published poetry pieces for adult readers.

GITA SRINIWASAN, of Indian and German descent, is a doctoral candidate in Cultural Anthropology at Stanford University. She is researching popular Hindi cinema and identity among the diasporic Indian population of Trinidad. She is also a poet and performer. She currently resides in San Francisco.

NEEMA VACHANI is second-generation South Asian and lives in California. She hopes to continue writing. Having finished her undergraduate work, she hopes to spend the next year traveling and exploring.

AMITA VASUDEVA describes herself and others like her as ABCDs. She once told her parents that making her grow up in the U.S. "is a fate worse than death." She is the youngest in her family and the only girl.

SUNITA VATUK is the daughter of an Indian poet and a North American anthropologist. She grew up in the United States with long stays in the Delhi area. She spent over seven years working against U.S. policy in El Salvador and Nicaragua and is now a graduate student in mathematics at Princeton University.

VASANTHI VICTOR was born and raised in Bombay, India, of South Indian parents. She received her education from Bombay University (B.A. in English Literature and M.A. in

Journalism) and was trained as a journalist at the Indian Express in Bombay. She has worked as a free lance writer. She has been a Bay Area resident since 1981, with two children born in Berkeley and Santa Cruz. She is married to an Indian engineer since 1979, which was arranged by parents. She has published a few poems in anthologies and is currently working on a novel from which this excerpt has been taken.

KAMALA VISWESWARAN is Assistant Professor of Anthropology on the Graduate Faculty of the New School for Social Research. She is also an active member of Sakhi for South Asian Women in New York City. She has written extensively on issues of feminism and nationalism. Her book, *Fictions of Feminist Ethnography*, is forthcoming from the University of Minnesota Press in 1994.

aunt lute books

is a multicultural women's press that has been committed to publishing high quality, culturally diverse literature since 1982. In 1990, the Aunt Lute Foundation was formed as a non-profit corporation to publish and distribute books that reflect the complex truths of women's lives and the possibilities for personal and social change. We seek work that explores the specificities of the very different histories from which we come, and that examines the intersections between the borders we all inhabit.

Please write or phone for a free catalogue of our other books or if you wish to be on our mailing list for future titles. You may buy books directly from us by phoning in a credit card order or mailing a check with the catalogue order form.

Aunt Lute Books
P.O. Box 410687
San Francisco, CA 94141
(415) 558-8116